Mr. & Mrs. American Pie

JULIET McDANIEL

Copyright © 2018 Juliet McDaniel

Published by Inkshares, Inc., Oakland, California
www.inkshares.com

Edited by Adam Gomolin, Matt Harry, and Kaitlin Severini
Cover design by Lauren Harms
Interior design by Kevin G. Summers

ISBN: 9781942645863
e-ISBN: 9781942645870
LCCN: 2017955467

First edition

Printed in Canada

For my secret weirdo, Jonathan,
and my unabashed weirdo, Dylan.

And to gin, in all her perfect forms.

Mrs. Maxine Hortence Simmons

Palm Springs

November 1969

ALL I CAN THINK ABOUT IS ESCAPE.

First come the opening volley of mimosas and some light chitchat about the weather. Then our wedge salads arrive, signaling the commencement of mild gossip about people we all hate. Suddenly, as I bite into a crisp piece of iceberg lettuce, I cease being Mrs. Maxine Hortence Simmons, the elegant thirty-six-year-old wife of noted airline executive Douglas Simmons. I am still physically at this table in the sunroom of the Palm Springs Thunderbird Country Club, and yet my body and soul have undergone a total upheaval. It's as if I've been transported from a charming enchanted forest to some dreadful real-life forest, filled with danger and violence. I am no longer a woman, but a woodland creature. I am a darling, defenseless bunny who has found her paw clamped in a trap. My predators are circling, and it's growing dark. My only option now is to bite into my own wrist, chew myself free, and limp off on my bloody stump.

I look to the Cartier watch Douglas gave me on our seventh anniversary and realize that unlike what I've been told about the last moments of one's life flying by in an instant, the last five minutes of my life—and I do hope they are the last—have been an eternity. Not to sound overly dramatic, but I would rather bleed to death than listen to one more second of goddamn Mrs. Joyce Wittenburg Tully. As if it isn't bad enough that she's wearing head-to-toe orange yet again—a hue that by no means works with that pile of tightly coiled copper curls atop her head—she's also droning on about goddamn azaleas. She brought a dozen of them all the way back from Myrtle Beach, through two plane changes, and has dumped them on my lap at lunch with that triumphant, thin-lipped smile of hers. It's the same smile I saw when her husband finally made partner down at the bank. She tells me the azaleas are from her mother-in-law's prize-winning garden, the "pride of Myrtle Beach since 1952!" And then she continues on about how these fragrant-as-a-whorehouse azaleas would look "simply divine" as the centerpiece on my Thanksgiving table.

"You know, to complement your dining room's new tropical theme," she helpfully adds, as though I have not personally toiled over that redesign for five months.

I smile so hard, it makes my derriere muscles clench. If there were suddenly a fire, I would be unable to run from the restaurant and would perish with nothing but thoughts of these prize azaleas running through my head. I look to the brass light fixture hanging over the table and wonder if it could hold my weight, should I choose to hang myself by my Hermès scarf.

"But, Joyce," I say brightly, "azaleas aren't *quite* tropical, are they?" Joyce stares at me blankly. I wonder how many mimosas it would take to drink myself to death. Yet, for some reason, I also feel the pressing need to put Joyce straight when it comes to my home décor.

"The dining room is Palm Springs *moderne* with tropical *touches*," I continue. "Which means we won't exactly be eating stuffing and mashed potatoes while wearing coconut brassieres. It is still Thanksgiving, after all. There are traditions. Right, girls?"

My luncheon companions are useless. Mrs. Mary Jones is as unremarkable as her own name. Say what you will about

Joyce's penchant for orange; at least she has color in her palette. Everything about Mary screams—no, *murmurs*—mousy. From her limp, graying brunette head to her clad-in-beige-pumps feet to her flat-as-a-table figure, Mary looks like a blank slate. I mean, yes, her skin is flawless, but she wears no makeup, has no signature scent, and I once heard her complain that her vanilla ice cream was too strongly flavored. Always the first of us to finish a meal, Mary now sits in front of her empty salad plate, her hands folded politely in her lap and her head slightly bowed, as if she's praying. Assumedly, she is saying a prayer of thanks that the Social Registry accepts people based on birthright and not personality. Meanwhile, Joyce starts up some lecture on the importance of petal count when it comes to judging azaleas. Maybe God will smile upon us and bring the Big One to Palm Springs, opening a tear in the earth that devours us all.

"Joyce, dear, I need you to stop with the azaleas."

This glorious change of subject comes from Mrs. Evelyn Rollins, the grande dame of Palm Springs, albeit a grande dame in waiting given that she's barely a day over forty. Per usual, she's hogging all the attention from onlookers thanks to her pitch-perfect mix of sex and class that all the boys want and all the girls envy. Dressed to the nines, Evelyn also knows how to show off just the right amount of her ample breasts and shapely legs, though never both at the same time. No, that would cross the line from "desirable" to "doable," and Evelyn would sooner die than be obtainable. She refuses to tell us who does her hair (rumor has it, a stylist in LA), where she buys her evening wear (my guess is Bergdorf's in New York), or the name of the red lipstick she's always sporting (probably a custom shade made in Paris).

We all want to be Evelyn, but she'll be goddamned if she's going to make that easy for us. A big reason why Evelyn is such a commanding presence has nothing to do with her movie-star beauty or considerable net worth—at least not directly. It's because even mild approval from Evelyn can mean everything in this town. Just as an appearance on *The Ed Sullivan Show* can turn goofy little British boys into gods, any form of praise from Evelyn can elevate one to new heights of social prestige. If you're golden with Evelyn, doors magically fling wide: ski chalets in Aspen, private beaches in the South of France, even parties at the Governor's Mansion. When Nancy Reagan comes to town, who do you think she's having brunch with?

Inversely, if you are not granted Evelyn's esteem, she will make goddamn sure you are treated as kindly as a thrice-married barmaid in a push-up bra. Two years ago, Evelyn was friendly with one Mrs. Bernice Duke, who had the audacity to show up at the symphony's annual gala in a mink coat that looked just a tad longer and fuller and more expensive than Evelyn's. Within weeks, Mrs. Bernice Duke found herself shunned at the club, her doctor husband lost most of his patients, and their son was denied admittance into the Palm Springs Country Day School. Bernice learned the hard way that it's one thing to imitate Evelyn, but to outshine her is suicide. In fact, if it weren't for Mrs. Bernice Duke and her mink coat, I wouldn't be sitting here today. With Bernice out of the picture, Evelyn needed someone new to kiss her three-carat Tiffany diamond ring, and I was more than happy to genuflect and do so. But I'm no dummy like Bernice. I know that if I'm a bunny caught in a trap, Evelyn's the wolf who will gobble me up. Why, I've yet to attend a dinner party with Evelyn in attendance that didn't feature at least one poor soul sobbing in the bathroom due to a poisonous jab from the grande dame.

What's truly exciting is that exactly three days from today, it will be my well-appointed guest bath in which some poor soul is sobbing! After years of my inching my way closer to Evelyn's vast and powerful social circle, she and her husband, Foster Rollins III, will be sitting in my brand-new dining room. Evelyn's never accepted an invitation to my home. Admittedly, this was the first time I came right out and invited her, but there were numerous hints and much testing of the waters beforehand to see if she was open to the idea. If there's one thing I've learned from years of social climbing, it's that there are unspoken, ironclad rules governing all aspects of womanly interaction. Someday, when Evelyn's moved on to bigger and better things (London? Monaco?), my goal is to take her place as Queen of Palm Springs. And I will rule much the way she does.

"I'm over the moon to have you girls for Thanksgiving," I chirp. "As I was telling Douglas just this morning—"

"Douglas is actually in town?" Evelyn asks, her voice dipped in pure, judgmental gold.

"Yes, he took a few days off for the holiday. He came home last night, and right in the nick of time, I should add. The pool man refuses to listen to me when I give the simplest of directions!" I punctuate that last sentence with a laugh, and I'm happy to see Joyce nodding along in agreement. I've found that nothing rallies the girls of Palm Springs quite like a shared claim of "the help nowadays!" But Evelyn doesn't seem to want to play along.

"Oh," she replies flatly.

Now understand that everyone knows that my husband works for Western Airlines, which is based out of LA and therefore where he spends the workweek, coming home to me and our well-appointed home in Palm Springs every Friday afternoon. Yet there's something about the tone of Evelyn's "oh" that unsettles me. I try to ignore it, but then she lets out another "oh" and this time looks to Mary, who purses her lips as if to hold back her own "oh."

The table is suddenly still and silent, devoid of eye contact. There's clearly something of importance I am unaware of. Being the last person to know something is not a feeling I care for.

"Well . . . ," Evelyn begins, taking the most delicate sip of her iced lemon water. "Last week, on Tuesday, I believe . . . Mary, was it Tuesday?"

"Yes, because bridge is Monday and Women's Club is Wednesday."

"That's right, so it was Tuesday. Anyway, Mary and I were dress shopping, and we happened to run into Jane Allistar. She's learned something, shall we say, *juicy* about someone we all know."

Jane Allistar has this almost creepy gift for life-ruining gossip. I don't know if she has a crystal ball or a sixth sense for personal calamity, but she's predicted with eerie accuracy the ends of several marriages, businesses, and, in one case, a botched nose job. Personally, I steer clear of her. Plus, her husband, Howard, once gave my fanny a pinch at Easter brunch.

"And how is Jane? Is that daughter of hers staying out of trouble at Berkeley?" I'm proud of myself for this delicate jab of my furry paw. It suggests I know something, namely that Jane's daughter is a dirty hippie war protestor, and yet it also gives me some wiggle room to insist that I'm merely being polite by inquiring on the health and happiness of Jane's only daughter. Good conversations are all about balance.

"I haven't a clue," Evelyn responds curtly. "But as I was saying, Jane and Howard were in LA and they ran into someone we all know." For the sake of suspense—she has Hitchcock's feel for timing—Evelyn takes another delicate sip of her water. "Let's just say that Daniel Crouch was with someone Jane described as a 'little blond number.'"

Joyce lets out a tiny gasp as I realize I was holding my breath waiting for Evelyn to reveal the latest man to have gone astray. It wouldn't entirely shock me if Douglas has had a dalliance or three, but it's something of an unspoken rule that once the men flaunt it, divorce is imminent.

"That will be the fourth divorce this year," Mary reminds us. "Whatever will Anita do?"

"She has family money," says Evelyn dismissively. "Anyway, we're all in our thirties now, girls. It's simply good common sense for us all to stash a little something away in a Just in Case Fund. Isn't that right, Maxine?"

I don't like that I didn't see that blow coming. My reflexes are slipping, and Evelyn's been more testy than usual with me. But I don't take Evelyn's bait, and she's emotionless for what seems like half an eon before finally allowing a smile to creep back across her face. "Will your mother be making it to dinner, Maxine?" asks Evelyn.

"I'm afraid not. She's staying in Europe. Her husband has an important speaking engagement at the Louvre that they cannot miss."

"A speaking engagement over Thanksgiving! How awful!" Mary exclaims.

"Mary, dear," says Evelyn, as if speaking to a three-year-old, "Paris is in Europe. They don't celebrate Thanksgiving."

Mary's cheeks aren't smart enough to turn red with embarrassment. "Well, I should think that with all we've done for them, they would find it only proper to give thanks," she says.

While none of us can exactly argue that point, we also can't dignify anything Mary says with a response. Coffee is served, and we all shift our attention to adding cream and sugar to our cups. Three years ago, when Douglas and I were only guests here at Thunderbird Country Club—as opposed to the full-fledged members we are today—Evelyn told me in front of a table of well-heeled acquaintances that my penchant for black coffee was the reason behind my less-than-white teeth. This brought me straight into the dentist's chair, or rather *dentists' chairs*. The American Dental Association has silly rules about how many bleach treatments one can receive per month, requiring me to see two dentists to ensure my teeth were brought to an acceptable level of whiteness in record time. I can feel Evelyn's eyes on me as I now pour a splash of coffee into my cup before dumping in plenty of cream and sugar. While I don't care for the taste of cream, my now-sensitive teeth appreciate how it cools the coffee.

"Maxine, I assume your Thanksgiving dinner preparations are in full swing?" Evelyn asks.

"Oh, of course. I finalized the menu yesterday. You girls are never going to believe this turkey!" Mary and Joyce smile and nod, but Evelyn gets a look in her eye—a sort of gleam that tells me she's brought up the subject for a reason. It's probably to inform me that she's on an all-grapefruit-and-cottage-cheese-diet again or some other inane request that will send me scrambling back to the caterers.

"I know we accepted your Thanksgiving dinner invitation already, Maxine," Evelyn says, pausing to finish off her coffee. "But I'm afraid Foster and I are unable to attend after all."

She drops this on me like an atom bomb, and goes back to sipping her coffee as if she's announced she's unable to join us for squash later in the afternoon.

"You're kidding," I reply in entirely the wrong tone. I go with "Wait just a goddamned minute" when I should choose "Oh, you don't say." This is devastating news, and I have spoken before I thought. I need Evelyn at my Thanksgiving and I need her to love my new dining room. Otherwise, what is the point of it all?

"Of course not," she snaps back at me. "I would never kid about turning down a dinner invitation."

"One that you accepted four weeks prior," I add, once more in entirely the wrong tone. Then again, what tone should I take? I sent out invitations that were quite literally engraved and delivered personally by our housekeeper—who I insisted wear white gloves, for chrissakes—and yet Evelyn still sat on that invitation for two whole weeks before calling with her acceptance. And now, *three days* before Thanksgiving, she gets around to telling me she won't be attending? Something is afoot. My predators are circling, their visages peeking through the low fauna.

"I know you're disappointed, Maxine, but it's simply out of my hands." Mary and Joyce share a look. Is Evelyn merely toying with me to show she's still top wolf? Or am I good and dead?

"Are you and Foster going on vacation?" Joyce helpfully asks.

"The French Riviera, but not until after Christmas. No, our change of plans is in fact due to my cousin coming to town unexpectedly, so we'll be hosting dinner now. I think I've mentioned my cousin before. Joan Ferndell Hearst?" Evelyn says that last sentence a bit louder, because this is a woman who knows what she's doing. I see every head at the tables around us snap to attention at the mention of that most perfect and glorious word of them all:

Hearst.

I now realize how dire my situation is. Never mind the Astors, Rockefellers, Cabots, or even the Kennedys; few names hold as much power here in Palm Springs than California's own Hearsts. What they lack in Old Money they more than make up for in bravado, beauty, and the tiniest touch of scandal, which, if you think about it, is about as California as it gets. They own a castle! An actual castle built right along the Pacific Ocean, which they undoubtedly also own, probably after driving down the price in clever negotiations with God. To know a Hearst, or, better yet, to be even tangentially related to one, is like having a pocket of fairy dust. Sprinkle a little in a conversation at the Club or leave a trail behind you while out shopping and opportunities fall at your feet like cult members.

The Hearst connection has been employed by Evelyn before. Years ago, Evelyn and Foster were wait-listed for membership at the Palm Springs Bath and Tennis Club until a phone call came in from Joan Ferndell Hearst mentioning how she'd love to visit her cousin in Palm Springs, but not if she had to dine somewhere as déclassé as the less formal Thunderbird, where we all sit today. At least, that's what I heard. Who knows how close it is to the truth? I've always found it odd that Joan Ferndell Hearst would call the Bath and Tennis Club rather than send a letter on her personal stationery. Then again, I've also heard that Joan is only a Hearst in a round-about way; her husband, Yates Bixby Hearst, is a second cousin twice removed or something. Regardless, Evelyn is much closer to the Hearsts than any of us, and that's all that matters.

"I'm sure you understand my little predicament, Maxine?" Evelyn says.

Everything is moving in slow motion now, like that final shoot-out in *Bonnie and Clyde*. And indeed, there is a chance that Evelyn's pulling out of my dinner could end in murder. But I shove aside my bunny-in-a-trap thoughts and clench my derriere so tightly, my eyes water. I know exactly how to play this one—the opposite of how Bernice Duke played it: with grace, humility, and maybe a touch of groveling. If I know Evelyn, she's testing me to see if I'll behave. To see if I'm willing to expose myself to this level of her public rejection.

"Of course, Evelyn. You're so remarkably polite. But I simply hate the thought of you rushing about to find the right caterer, bring in your cleaning people, attend to your hair and wardrobe—and on such short notice before the holidays!"

"That's kind of you, Maxine, but you know every caterer in town would do *anything* for me, short notice or not."

I tell myself to stay calm. "Evelyn, I took your advice and got the table that seats fourteen instead of just ten. You know, the Danish teak with the glass mosaic inlay?" I pause to let them all visualize it. "So there's plenty of room around my brand-new table for you to bring the Hearsts."

"Oh, I just couldn't!"

"Oh, but you could! Joan and Yates will feel right at home. I'm telling you, Evelyn, the dining room remodel is remarkable!"

Mary and Joyce share another look before turning to Evelyn, whose gaze has gone from polite to pure steel. There's something I'm missing here.

"I'm sure the room is practically perfection. You did use my decorator, after all." Her coffee finished, Evelyn snaps open her Kelly handbag, pulls out a Tiffany mirror, and applies a fresh coat of her custom red lipstick to her lips. I'm beginning to wonder why, since I'm clearly what she's about to eat for dessert. "I was planning on remodeling the pool house, but alas, *my* decorator was too tied up on *your* dining room."

And there it is. My transgression. Not a mink coat, but a decorator. Evelyn's decorator.

I've crossed that dreaded, barely visible line between idolizing Evelyn and attempting to outshine Evelyn. In less than three meal courses, I have gone from being the grande dame's heir apparent to a nobody.

I am a leper.

An outcast.

Evelyn triumphantly snaps her purse shut.

"Have a lovely Thanksgiving, girls. Maybe next year, Maxine?"

I smile and nod, but Evelyn Rollins has already flounced away, picking my bunny meat from her sharp wolf teeth.

Maxine Hortence Simmons

Palm Springs

Week before Thanksgiving 1969

I'M STILL FUMING over the snub as Douglas and I get ready for bed that evening. He's brushing his teeth in the master bath with the door open again.

"Douglas, you know how I feel about seeing you brush your teeth," I say from my bed. "It's unbecoming to see you frothing at the mouth like some rabid beast. I'm trying to tell you—"

I stop speaking midsentence as he gargles and spits. It's as if he's in some Wild West saloon rather than my cream bathroom with the imported gold-foiled wallpaper that cost more than the bathtub, toilet, and vanity combined.

"I can brush and listen to you at the same time, Maxine," he tells me before turning on the faucet. At least he's rinsing the sink.

My husband of nearly seventeen years, Douglas Rohm Simmons, is of the Sacramento Simmons, known throughout that region for their chain of gas and service stations, which made the family a bundle since you can't exist in California without a car. As the only son, Douglas had an opportunity to run the family business, but after graduating from Wharton, he came back to California and joined a prominent accounting firm. Douglas claimed he wanted more practical experience before taking on the family business, but his father saw it as a clear slap in the face. While we've never discussed it, I've always believed that Douglas hated the idea that his whole life was planned for him.

I've found that most men fall into one of two categories: Fathers or Cowboys. Fathers are firm, resolute, and have all the answers. They make great leaders and everyone holds them in high esteem. However, Douglas was born something of a Cowboy. He needs to be his own man, carve his own path, always be on the lookout for the next great thing to conquer. Fathers may make great husbands, but Cowboys bring a little more, shall we say, "excitement" to the homestead. Of course, a woman must approach a Father differently than a Cowboy. With Douglas, this means constantly adjusting my expectations as he moves from one path to the next without warning.

Case in point: after a few years at the accounting firm, Douglas was poached by Western Airlines, and it became obvious he was never going to return to gas stations. Seven years ago, Douglas's father died without retiring first, leaving Douglas everything. Rather than grow the business or hire someone to run it, Cowboy Douglas immediately sold off the gas stations. That sudden influx of capital, along with my shrewd knowledge of how the upper crust functions, put us in a fantastic position to make quite the splash on the Palm Springs social scene. I spent months hunting down the right house in the right neighborhood while ensuring we attended all the right parties, even driving in on weekends from our then home in LA.

While he might not seem it right now as he sits on the bed in his frumpy pajamas, drying toothpaste clinging to the corner of his mouth, my Cowboy is still something of a catch. I mean, look at that head of lustrous brown hair! Sure, his shoulders are a bit narrow and he's only five foot nine, but I make sure to always put him in the right shoes to add that all-important extra inch. He's a fine earner, and while I'm sure we have plenty of savings in the bank and in investments, he's not stingy. Our home might not be the most expensive in Palm Springs, but it's certainly the finest on the block.

"Why are you upset about her canceling, anyway?" Douglas asks. "You don't even like Evelyn Rollins."

"Douglas! How can you say that!"

"Because you've told me you don't like her a thousand times. It's always 'You won't believe what Evelyn said' or 'Evelyn did the most awful thing at brunch.' I spent a considerable sum on that fur for your birthday, and do you remember what you said? 'Take it back; Evelyn says fox is for cheap starlets.'"

"That's actually a very true statement, Douglas. Mink is what ladies wear."

"My point is, what do you care if Evelyn Rollins and her cousin don't come to Thanksgiving?"

"That cousin's a Hearst!"

Douglas scrunches up his face like I just squeezed a lemon into his toothpaste-caked mouth. It might be the most infuriating thing he's ever done to me.

"A Hearst, Douglas. Sitting at *my* Danish teak dining room table. How can you refuse to see the significance in that?"

My dear husband more than understands how things work around here. Why, no more than two weeks ago he mentioned how many "decision makers" he regularly meets while golfing at the Club. He knows damn well that membership was granted to us thanks to our friendship—*my* friendship—with Evelyn and Foster Rollins.

Douglas lets out a heavy sigh. "It's probably for the best."

"How could it possibly be 'for the best,' Douglas? Are you mocking me? Are you—"

"I think we should cancel Thanksgiving, which, if you'll recall, I never wanted in the first place."

This is the most insane utterance in the history of language. One does not "cancel" a Thanksgiving dinner that has been planned for upward of five months. I'm positively speechless in this moment.

"You really don't understand anything, do you, Maxine?"

"Enlighten me, Douglas."

As he gets out of bed and starts pacing, rambling about the stresses of his job and his long commute, I'm distracted by thoughts of how to fix everything and make my Thanksgiving a night to remember. Evelyn is dead set on not stepping foot in my home that evening; that much is clear. I stole her decorator—I thought I was merely borrowing him—and now I must take my punishment. She said nothing about anyone else she was inviting for Thanksgiving dinner, which leads me to wonder if her Hearst cousin really is coming out to Palm Springs, or if Evelyn and Foster will be stealing away that weekend. If she truly wanted to put the screws to me, she would have stolen all my guests. Then again, the Tullys and Joneses aren't exactly phenomenal catches, especially when a Hearst is involved. Foster owns an oil concern that stretches from here to the coast, so surely his address book is filled with enough big names to scrounge up a few quality dinner guests on short notice. For all I know, Evelyn has been planning this little coup for weeks.

"Do you remember who catered the Rollinses' Fourth of July party this year?" I blurt out to Douglas.

"What?"

"The caterers? Do you recall—"

Douglas stops pacing. He puts his hands on his hips and slouches forward, his body aimed toward me, which does nothing to improve his height problem. "You haven't heard a word I've said, have you?"

"You have toothpaste on the corner of your mouth."

"Do you have any idea how frustrating it is to try to have a serious conversation with you, Maxine?"

"Probably about as frustrating as it is to get you to brush your teeth with the bathroom door closed."

He stares at me. No, it's more of a glare. "You're exhausting," he tells me. "I'm exhausted. The parties and events and galas. All your *planning*. It never stops."

"It's life, Douglas! Our lives!"

"I don't recall you once asking me what life I wanted," he snaps back.

"And you haven't benefited at all from my efforts? Tell me again how it was you just happened to end up filling out a foursome at Bel-Air Country Club with the president of Western Airlines? My *planning* didn't bother you too much then!"

"Do you have any idea what it's like to have to work for a living, Maxine?" he yells.

I want to scream at him that maintaining a home and life that others only dream of is work. But what good would it do?

Without making eye contact, Douglas sulks over and grabs the pillows off his bed. I know this means he'll be sleeping in the guest room again, which is fine by me, on account of his snoring. I thought having separate beds in the same room might solve that problem, but any night he's home, I toss and turn due to the freight train in his upper sinuses.

"We're doing Thanksgiving, Douglas," I say firmly as he walks out the door. "All you need to do is show up. I know you know how to do that."

Now I need to get out of bed to turn off the goddamned bathroom light.

"I certainly hope you don't display this level of rudeness for our guests!" I yell down the empty hallway. I get silence in return.

Our sweet housekeeper, Gina, wakes me promptly at 8:30 a.m. with her usual gentle knock on the door. Ten minutes later she's back with breakfast: a piece of Wonder bread toast lightly buttered, half a grapefruit lightly sugared, and black coffee because Evelyn isn't watching.

When she first started three years ago, Gina always made me oatmeal, which I loathe because it's prison food. I'd never eat it, yet she kept making it. Then one day I went downstairs and found Gina eating my untouched oatmeal. I said nothing, until the next day, when I didn't receive any oatmeal with my breakfast. I asked her to please make sure I was always served oatmeal—which I again never touched. And I now specify that I want the more expensive cinnamon-flavored brand. It's not like Douglas pays attention to that sort of thing. Speaking of my husband, where is he?

"He left as I got here, Maxine," Gina tells me. Her family is from Italy, and though raised in nearby Hemet, Gina still has a touch of a Sicilian accent. I think part of why I like her so much is that no one else can say my name and make it sound as lovely as when Gina says it.

"Did he say where he was going?" I ask, enjoying my black coffee.

"No, but I heard him putting his golf clubs in the car."

I'm relieved he won't be around all day, because this gal has some serious work to do, and I don't have time to keep him entertained.

"Tell me, Gina, does your cousin still work for the Rollins family? Do you think you could ever so discreetly ask her something for me?"

Gina smiles big and broad, because, like I said, I really like this woman.

Gina's cousin Sophia is quick to supply me with the name of the catering company Evelyn hired for her spur-of-the-moment Thanksgiving. The moment they open at 10 a.m., I am on the phone with Mr. Pierre Saint DuPree of Pierre's Fantastic Events.

"Yes, this is Mrs. Evelyn Rollins," I say, doing my best to speak in Evelyn's nasally born-in-California-but-wants-to-sound-like-East-Coast-Old-Money voice. "Great, thank you. Look, I need to cancel Thanksgiving dinner. . . ." I really do sound like Audrey Hepburn in *Charade*.

There is instant panic on the other end of the line. "Of course, it's no problem, Mrs. Rollins." "We hope you are well, Mrs. Rollins." "We trust we haven't done anything to upset you, Mrs. Rollins?"

This puts me in a bit of a pickle. I must ensure that Evelyn never learns that someone pretending to be her called and canceled Thanksgiving. Yet Evelyn will surely call Pierre in a blind rage when none of his people show up on Thanksgiving morning. This requires me to make certain that "Evelyn" cancels on Pierre in a way that will ensure they never speak again. "Look, Pierre, I'm going to be very honest with you. When my guests found out you were catering my Thanksgiving, several mentioned how the beef Wellington you served at the Jaycees' summer dinner made them, let's just say, less than well."

"*Ce n'est pas!* Madame Rollins!" Pierre says, his faux French accent slipping. "I assure you, our *boeuf*—"

"And don't get me started on the stories I've heard about your bacon-wrapped shrimp!"

"Zee are of the freshest quality!"

I raise my pitch for added effect. "Quality? I think not, given the amount of gastronomic distress I heard of!"

"I 'ave never 'eard such complaints, Mees-ez Rollins!" he screeches at me in his faltering accent. "Who ees telling you zees things?"

"I'm afraid I can't bear to hear it anymore, Pierre!" I fume into the phone. "To have my invitees tell me these dreadful stories about your food! It was an embarrassment I shall require some time to overcome! I would sooner serve my guests Alpo than pay for your services!"

"Mees-ez Rollins!"

"Alpo, Mr. DuPree!" I respond. "Better that than chunks of your deviled eggs and goose pâté clogging the most esteemed toilets in all of Palm Springs!"

If I know Frenchmen—even fake Frenchmen—this is a bridge too far for Mr. Pierre Saint DuPree.

"Madame! You can no longer cancel your dinn-air because I 'ave canceled it for you! Consider yourself persona non grata!"

He hangs up on me, giving me no chance to tell him that *persona non grata* is Latin, not French.

This is called salting the earth.

The next few days are excruciating. I'm out every day for brunch or lunch, followed by tennis or shopping or both. I'm in such a state, I start Christmas shopping early. I have my ear to the ground to pick up even the slightest whisper about Evelyn, the Hearsts, or a failed Thanksgiving dinner, and yet there's nothing. I've seen this happen countless times between the notable women of Palm Springs. Tensions escalate into a cold war of sorts, with neither party saying a word to each other, acting instead through their proxies—mutual friends with ever-shifting allegiances. I worry profusely since, while it's a challenge to keep Evelyn as a friend, having her as a mortal enemy is far more horrifying. Unlike Kennedy, Evelyn wouldn't hesitate to push the button and plunge my whole world into a nuclear winter.

Just as I begin to wonder if everyone is purposely keeping me out of the loop, I hear something about a possibly bounced check involving Mrs. Francine Lieberman, who's the slightly older, slightly wealthier Jewish version of Evelyn. I file that tidbit away for potential use later. I'm smart enough to know I need to conquer the upper echelons of WASP life before moving into the Jewish enclave of the Palm Springs Country Club, which believe you me is a tougher nut to crack. Now, I hold a tremendous amount in common with the Jews: after all, we've both had to claw out our own little space in a desert filled with hostiles. Why, I even enjoy kugel, provided the cinnamon isn't too strong! But I shall scale Mount Sinai another day. First, I must conquer Mount Evelyn.

My chance comes on Tuesday night, with Thanksgiving dinner less than forty hours away. The phone rings, and I pick it up to hear Evelyn's voice. She skips the pleasantries and gets straight to brass tacks:

"Maxine, darling, I know this is highly inappropriate and unbearably last-minute, but does your Thanksgiving invite still stand?"

You bet your slowly sagging ass it does, I think triumphantly.

"You and yours are always welcome at Casa Simmons!" I say with genuine joy. "Whatever happened to your Thanksgiving?"

I know I'm taking a huge risk, but I've also spent the last week weighing the pros and cons of saying nothing versus not saying enough. I settled on the only logical response being one of mild curiosity with a smidge of disinterest.

"I called those monsters at Pierre's to confirm and they said my business was no longer wanted! Can you believe it?"

"That's ghastly, Evelyn, but then again, what do you expect from someone pretending to be French?"

We share a hearty laugh, then briefly discuss Mrs. Lieberman. And with that, I have saved my Thanksgiving.

Mrs. Maxine Hortence Simmons

Palm Springs

Thanksgiving 1969

DOUGLAS IS BUSY all week, first with golf and tennis, and then—again according to Gina—he's called away to LA on a pressing business matter. I leave a message Wednesday morning with Douglas's secretary that I expect him back in Palm Springs by no later than 8 a.m. on Thanksgiving Day or I will hold her personally accountable. I remind her that I know all about her having access to petty cash and question if it's accurate to the penny. She sounds appropriately terrified, which I welcome. I don't think this is the same girl I met at the company Christmas party. This one sounds younger and thinner, although that might be because she said her name is Jennifer.

Jennifer.

If there's a more perky and youthful name than that, I haven't heard it. It gives me pause to realize I am old enough to live in a world where Jennifers aren't adorable children, but rather grown women answering my husband's phone and lying—rather poorly, I should say—about him being in a meeting.

I miss the secretary Douglas had last year. Her name was Mildred Klingschmidt, and I was delighted by that. No one finds a Mildred

Klingschmidt even remotely sexually appealing, or at least not in a way that's inherent to a dewy, probably sun-kissed "Jennifer." Men—be they Fathers or Cowboys—are prone to wandering the range. The good news is that most come home to their wives. Every woman knows that a happy, smug man is a million times easier to deal with than one who is grumpy or feeling unimportant. Plus, no man is going to ride off into the sunset with a Mildred. I was so disappointed when Douglas's Mildred retired, leaving me at the mercy of whomever was next in line at the secretarial pool.

On Thanksgiving Day, I wake around eleven with a touch of a hangover thanks to the blanc de blanc I drank for dinner the night before. I can hear Douglas puttering around in the hall and speaking in hushed, businesslike tones. He's gone again when I make my way to the kitchen for a Bloody Mary. I see someone, probably Gina, has placed a large vase of azaleas next to my bed. I'm sure Gina meant no harm, but the azaleas insult my sinuses *and* my sense of style. There's no card, but obviously they are from Joyce. I toss them right in the trash.

It's nearly 3 p.m. when Douglas walks into the master bedroom, not bothering to knock on the door. I'm at my vanity putting on my face when he suddenly materializes in the mirror, holding a drink for me—my signature pink squirrel—in one hand and his suitcase in another. The drink is no surprise, since it's not uncommon for me to sip them all day before a social event.

The suitcase, however, makes little sense.

"I need your attention, Maxine," he says. He's staring at his feet, but his voice is the same one he uses when the office calls after hours.

I sigh. "We have eight guests due in thirty minutes and I have four caterers to supervise." I get back to putting on my eyelashes. "And you're in my light."

Douglas moves slightly, allowing the midafternoon sun to shine in enough for me to get one eye's lashes in place. Through the drying eyelash glue in the corner of my eye, I see him grip that suitcase handle. Whatever the hell he's talking about, he's nervous, meaning this conversation could go in circles for hours.

"There's no need for drama, Douglas. Just spill it." I knock back half the pink squirrel. It coats my mouth and warms the back of my throat. It could stand to be a little pinker.

"I don't know how to best put this. . . ."

I polish off the pink squirrel. Then it's back to the eyelashes.

I hear him take a deep breath. In the mirror I see his knees buckle a bit. Bet he's glad I insisted on that extra-thick padding for the bedroom carpets.

"I'll be staying in LA for the time being," he blurts out in one breath.

"Well, I'll still need you home on weekends," I tell him. "It's holiday party season, and we have a packed calendar."

"We're not going to any parties, Maxine."

I laugh. I think. Or maybe that Valium didn't settle right with the heavy cream from my drink. The thought of Mr. and Mrs. Douglas Simmons not attending any holiday parties is absurd! We're doing Christmas three times this year! Jesus, is Douglas ill?

"I mean it. This isn't continuing."

"So, what, Douglas, you're moving to LA? Going to live in that pied-à-terre all alone?" I'm sort of laughing, but I know he's not joking. He has no sense of humor. Panic rises within me.

He pauses. It's clearly for effect.

"I'm leaving you."

And there it is. The three little words every wife fears.

What follows from me now is definitely a laugh. Or a chortle maybe? A guffaw? Which is the one where you vomit ever so slightly in your mouth?

"I've filed for divorce," he affirms.

"Why in God's name would you do that?" I ask him. "Divorce! Don't be ridiculous."

"I'm leaving as a courtesy, to give you time alone to make other arrangements for yourself."

What a notion of courtesy. He's a fire alarm blaring in the middle of the night as the building burns down.

"Other arrangements? This is my home, Douglas. There are no 'other arrangements'! I live here," I tell him without any waver in my voice. This is exactly the problem with Cowboys. They're prone to veering off the trail until someone yanks them back to the ranch. Well, I know exactly how to get this man back in my saddle.

I give him my coy smile and reach out a hand toward him. "Why don't I come with you to LA? We can hide away in some hotel room for a few days," I say huskily. "I bet that could fix this little problem of ours right up."

He doesn't take my hand and startles me by looking me straight in the eye. "I'm staying, and you will be leaving. There's no seducing or bullying me out of this. This is what's happening. I'm calling the shots."

"Well, good for you, Mr. Shot Caller! Do you feel like a big man? Throwing your wife—your *wife*, Douglas—out of the home she created for you? Dumping me at the curb for Tuesday trash pickup? What a gentleman!"

He has zero reaction to my belittling tone, which instantly drains the blood from my face. If there's one attitude of mine that Douglas will not tolerate, it's belittling. It sets him off like a ten-ton bomb, and yet today: nothing. He's riding his horse right off into the sunset.

"You may want to leave Palm Springs altogether, Maxine." His eyes are back down to the floor. He shifts the suitcase from one hand to the other.

"Leave Palm Springs?" I shriek. "After all the work I've done? Ego-killing, pride-swallowing work just to take us from nobodies to people who have Hearsts at our Thanksgiving table?"

My mind skitters from one divorced couple to another. Marcia Grant, Rose (or was it Violet?) Finkel, and Whatshername Everett all left, and we've never heard from or thought of them again.

But I know the wives who too quickly took their places.

"Who is she?" I demand. "Tell me now before someone else does." The fucking thought of all the whispers behind my back!

"There's no one else, Maxine. Don't be ridiculous."

"I am not the one being ridiculous, Douglas!" I insist. I don't believe him for one red-hot second. "You're the one making bold proclamations and running away from your marriage of nearly seventeen years. If it's not another woman, what is it then?"

"There's no one. It's *my* decision."

He stares at his feet again, his jaw clenched, nodding gently. My head runs from one woman I know to another. He's not rich enough for Evelyn. Too much of a scandal even for that lush Jane Allistar. I know of a few gals who might be looking to move up in the world, but they are mostly cocktail waitresses and shopgirls. No one a man like Douglas would have more than a passing fling with. He golfs only with men. Has drinks at his all-male club. He works with—yes, yes, that must be it.

I stare at his face, scanning it for any emotion, any tell. "It's that Jennifer, isn't it?" I ask.

He flinches.

I throw my pink squirrel glass across the room. Even though it hits the wall several feet away from Douglas, he still cowers.

"This is exactly the problem, Maxine! You're a goddamn spoiled child!"

"Be a man and say it!!"

He looks me right in the eye again, and now I'm the one who flinches. "Yes, it's Jennifer."

I have to laugh. Because of course it's her. As an added bonus, my laughing only makes Douglas cower more.

"You're fucking your secretary." I'm not exactly yelling, I don't think. Because I can still hear the caterers moving around in the kitchen down the hall. "What a cliché, Douglas."

"Maxine, you need to calm down."

"No man leaves his wife for a *secretary*!" I can't believe I have to explain all this to him, and yet here we are. "So you've carried on with this little Jennifer." I wave off her name as I say it. "Fine. I'll overlook it this one time. She goes back into the secretarial pool. You and I move forward. All is forgiven and fine."

I wait for him to agree with me, and he doesn't.

"Douglas, we move forward!" I say with more force. I know he can hear me, but he doesn't seem to be listening. I need a "yes, dear" or even a nod. "Douglas?"

"This is a sensitive matter that needs to be kept private," he says in that angry loud-ish whisper he uses on the neighbor's dachshund when it defecates in our yard. "We still have to get through this dinner you refused to cancel."

"Then why are you telling me this now, Douglas? When I'm doing my face while in my robe on Thanksgiving?"

He can't answer this, of course. Our whole marriage has been him going off in mad bursts. When I first met him, he was going to be the "Gas Station King of California." No lie, those are exactly the words he used on me on our first date. Did he consult with me before suddenly taking a job with that big accounting firm days after our wedding? Of course not. Then when he quit that job to start at Western Airlines, I didn't know until the night before. Yet when I want to move to Palm Springs, he hemmed and hawed for nearly a year before announcing he'd rented a house. All my research into the area's real estate meant nothing. He simply told me I was moving in five days and into a house that looked as though it had been thrown together with parts from the 1943 Sears catalog. Everyone thinks we arrived in Palm Springs in the summer of '62, when in truth we spent all of 1961 languishing in the shittiest-of-shitty part of town.

"Nothing, Douglas? No thoughts on why now was a good time to tell me I've been replaced by a Jennifer?"

"Because I can't take it any longer," he says with a strength in his voice I've never heard before. "It's time for me to tear the Band-Aid off and for both of us to shove on."

His stare is a glare now, and I hate myself for being the first one to look away.

"I'm surprised you packed the suitcase yourself," I finally respond.

Douglas pauses in my bedroom doorway. "Pull it together for dinner, Maxine."

He walks away, suitcase in hand. He doesn't shut the door all the way behind him. I have to get up and do it myself.

I sit at my vanity for I don't know how long. Everything around me feels cold and foreign. I can't remember where I bought the bedside aqua-blue Murano lamps. Or were they a gift? No, they match the bedspread perfectly, so I must have picked them out myself. Was that suitcase Douglas toted out of here new? I don't think I've seen that before either.

I stare at myself in the mirror. I can recognize that it's me. I am still blue-eyed and blond. My eyeliner is still Julie Newmar Catwoman perfect. My hair is curled and full and pulled back in a French twist, just like that picture of Lee Grant I took to my hairdresser months ago. I should stop using setting powder on top of my foundation because it's settling in those fine lines around my eyes. I also ought to tan more. I don't know why I never think of that until it's too late.

I hear Gina's gentle knock and her voice coming through the closed door. "Your guests are here, Miss Maxine."

"Get them drinks and seated," I say in an everything-is-perfectly-fine voice. "I'll make my entrance in just a moment." Douglas's insipid *Man of La Mancha* record suddenly blares through the house. If only *that* were in his suitcase.

I find a barely touched Bloody Mary in the master bath and instantly feel grateful for having made it hours ago and then forgetting all about it. I decide on another Valium, and of course my diet pill, and finally one of those elegant mint-colored tablets that Evelyn brought back from France that she swears by. The fact that the pill is the same color as the dresses my bridesmaids wore is not lost on me, I suppose. I'm behind schedule now and need to hurry. Douglas always under-ices everyone's drinks, meaning I need to get some food in these people or the whole night will crumble.

Oh dear, what does one wear after learning her husband can't bear the sight of her? Can I quickly fashion a funeral shroud out of bedsheets? No, I need to show this husband of mine that this little bunny is going to hippity-hoppity her way through the forest—that this is Thanksgiving dinner, and I'm as happy as can be. I'm still Mrs. Douglas Simmons, and I need to act like it. If I play this right, this night will be remembered as the First Wonderful Dinner with the Hearsts and not the Last Dinner of My Marriage. The tasteful navy chiffon I have laid out doesn't seem right anymore. Aside from not being "Fuck you, Jennifer!" enough, it will only draw attention to my lack of a tan. I pass on the emerald satin cocktail dress—the neckline belongs on a Puritan schoolmarm. I flick through my other dresses. It's not yet 5 p.m., but the patterns are practically screaming at me. Then again, the whole room is a bit screamy. I'm getting that sluggish, walking knee-deep in water feeling that usually means it's time for a little lie-down.

But no! I must soldier through. I have guests and I simply cannot miss the look on everyone's faces when the turkey is brought out garnished with pineapple rings. It's a nod to the style of the new dining room without openly flirting with it! Or at least that's what I thought when I saw the recipe in *Sunset* magazine a few months ago. Christ, I hope I didn't leave that issue in the guest bath.

The Pucci print shift! I slip it on over my head, careful not to ruin my hair. It's perfect. Never mind that I can't get it zipped up all the way. I throw a bright pink scarf around my neck to hide the open zipper. Where are those pink sandals I got for our weekend in Santa Barbara? The ones with the kitten heel, not the flats. I know they're somewhere in this closet.

I'm down on my knees digging toward the back of the walk-in. I glance up to scowl at the low-wattage bulbs Douglas insists I use. And that's when I see it. The tidy little silver box, wrapped up in a crisp black velvet ribbon. Exactly the way it was handed to me in the spring of 1952, when I was barely nineteen and my reign as Miss San Bernardino tearfully ended.

My crown.

Okay, yes, fine, it's really more of a tiara than a crown, but you cannot deny the way it gleams in my hands. Even in this horrendous lighting, it's shimmering like a pile of stars. *My* pile of stars. For *my* head. Jesus, I bet this will catch the lights of the tapers on the dinner table. And with the new mirrored wall? I'll be sensational!

I'm nearly halfway to the living room before I realize I forgot about the sandals. I've come too far to walk back now. Again, thank goodness for the extra-thick carpet padding! My feet feel like two stumps I'm dragging behind me.

"Do bunnies grow their missing feet back?" I ask a caterer in the kitchen, which—hooray—is humming along nicely with everything ready for presentation. The shrimp cocktail is chilled for the first course. All plated for the turkey course are the bacon-wrapped Brussels sprouts, the appropriately candied yams, and the wild rice stuffing. And of course, the finishing touches are still being added to my absolutely divine turkey.

A quick peek out the kitchen door shows me that everyone's obeyed the place cards and is sitting right where I want them. Couples positioned across the table from each other, alternating boy-girl. I'll sit at the head of the table nearest the kitchen and next to Evelyn and Foster. Next to them of course are the Hearsts. I seated Joan Ferndell Hearst with the mirrored wall behind her so she'll have the best-lit seat in the house. Though risky, I settled on Mary and her husband, John, next to the Hearsts, with Joyce and her husband at the end of the table with Douglas. I figure Mary is far less likely to say anything stupid or interesting to the Hearsts, meaning their attention can be squarely on me.

The only thing not perfect is Don Quixote's warbling. I drag my stump legs to the turntable console and yank Douglas's record off with a harsh scratch of the needle. This is *my* entrance, and we're going to listen to *my* song. Besides, I've long believed that Dusty Springfield and I are somehow related.

I take a deep breath. It's time. The triumphant trumpets of Dusty's "You Don't Have to Say You Love Me" roar at great volume, like heaven's angels announcing my presence.

As I push the dinner cart out into the dining room, to the gasps of my guests, I realize two things in rapid succession.

Thing One: this turkey is a goddamned work of art. Like Norman Rockwell painted it and decided it was too perfect for the cover of the *Saturday Evening Post* so he gave it to me. Thing Two: the shoulders on my dress have slid down a good inch, meaning all the scarves in the world can't hide that partially zipped zipper.

I also seem to have forgotten to put on a bra.

So, I suppose there are three things I suddenly realize. Oh well! My nethers are still covered and that's all that matters, right?

And I still have my crown! With the candles and the mirrored wall, it lights up the room like a Hollywood premiere. No one can take their eyes off me. I hear at least three more gasps, and don't think I don't notice that one of them sprung from Mary's husband, Mr. John Jones.

"Why, John Jones," I say. "You gasp like a girl!" I want to tell him that compared to his drab forever-in-beige wife, he looks downright flamboyant in gray. But I keep my mouth shut, because decorum!

I turn my attention to the center of the table. I expect to see Helen of Troy or at the very least, Princess Grace. What I don't expect—and isn't this becoming some sort of theme for my evening—is to be supremely disappointed. The elusive Joan Ferndell Hearst is tall, like tall enough that Douglas is probably jealous of her. She also has next to nothing for a figure, unless being a titless Popsicle stick is what passes as the feminine ideal nowadays, thanks to that Twiggy. Joan is draped in a moss-green crepe dress that might be the third or fourth worst thing presently in existence. Worse still is that she's staring not at me, but across the table at her cousin Evelyn. Can she not hear the music? Does she not smell this magnificent be-pineappled turkey? I'm in a fucking crown!

I choose to make the best of it, but Jesus Christ on a Ritz Cracker is this broad a letdown.

"Hello, Hearsts! Dinner is served!" Am I yelling? I might be yelling.

I see Olive Oyl Hearst arch an eyebrow at Evelyn, and best I can tell, Evelyn is displeased. Her signature red lips are tightly puckered and her eyes are wide enough that I'm sure the thick black eyeliner she wears will crack any second now.

"Maxine," she says as if I were the help, "why are we skipping the first course and moving right to the turkey?" Good Christ, this woman is pissing all over my parade.

"Silly me!" I say, pretending to smack myself on the forehead. A timid Gina pushes the cart with the first course halfway out of the kitchen before disappearing. I yank it the rest of the way into the room, then scurry around the table, setting the martini glasses of shrimp cocktail in front of each guest. Douglas is at the far end of the table, and I can't make out his expression, mainly because that water I've been wading through is now well over my head and somewhat complicating my vision. Joyce's recently overdyed fire-engine-red curls also aren't helping any. I'm nearly blinded by the glare coming off her beehive.

What I can see clearly, sitting in the middle of my otherwise perfect table, shoved into any old vase, is a cluster of azaleas.

"What the shit, Joyce!"

Okay, now I'm definitely yelling. I am louder than the record. I am louder than their polite shock. I am louder than the sound of all the blood rushing to my head.

Before I can continue, Douglas leaps to his feet. The napkin from his lap is stuck in his waistband. I want to laugh, but there are ratty azaleas on my Thanksgiving table. Now is not the time.

"You need to sit down, Maxine. Get some food in you. And cover up." He uses the tone he always uses with me when I'm being ridiculous about wanting a new sofa, or sex on a weeknight, or children.

"I need to carve the turkey," I answer, chipper as a lady selling toothpaste on TV. There's that derriere clinch again.

"Allow me," Douglas insists. He takes the knife from my hand.

"Fine. I'll get the second course going." I shove the empty serving cart through the double doors. The handle gets away from me and the cart soars into the kitchen with maybe a touch too much gusto. I hear it slam into something, and a caterer yelps. I ignore it, and I'm sure everyone else does too.

Evelyn's got the forty-dollars-a-square-foot wallpapered wall behind her and I try not to giggle, but it looks like a massive flowering palm is growing out the top of her head. "Maxine," Evelyn says in that rich-bitch way of hers, "are you feeling all right tonight, dear?"

"Peachy," I tell her. At least I think I'm telling her. Everything is swirling now, so I'm more or less just speaking in the general direction of her flowering palm head.

I take my seat at the head of the table, far away from Douglas. It feels nice to get off my feet. I'm not in the mood for shrimp cocktail, so I finish my wine instead. Dusty's still singing, which is simply beyond lovely, but why am I hearing her and not sparkling dinner conversation?

"There needs to be sparkling dinner conversation!" I say, once again out loud and not in my head, which is positively buzzing. Judging from Mary's startled jump, I think I might have slammed my fist on the table.

Joan's eyes go wide at Evelyn, who is clearly to blame for this fiasco on account of her appointing herself head of the Palm Springs Turkey Police.

"The shrimp cocktail is lovely, Maxine," Joyce mutters from the far end of the table.

"Thank you, Joyce. Did you hear that, Douglas? I did someone something liked!" I may have inverted the words, but he takes my meaning well enough.

"Not the time or place, Maxine," Douglas hisses at me. I can sense it's not the turkey he wishes he was carving. "Why don't you relax, Maxine?"

"'Relax, Maxine. Pull it together, Maxine'!" I mimic. My smile is about to shatter my entire face. He goes back to ignoring me, which I figure is for the best. How awkward he's making things for our guests!

"Miss Maxine?"

It's Gina with that damned serving cart again, this time with all the dinner plates loaded with sides. Once more I circle the table, grabbing shrimp cocktail glasses and setting down plates. My fingers and arms feel heavy, so I'm not as precise as I could be. I polish off someone's drink. A Manhattan, I think.

I suddenly realize my manners. I've barely said two words to our esteemed guests. I rest my arm on Joan Ferndell Hearst's puny shoulder. "I would so love to hear about your castle! Do you two ever dress up and play Rapunzel?"

"I'm sure we don't," she tells me, rudely shoving my arm off her.

"Oh come on, Joan! We're all friends here." I point at Yates, who's wearing a velvet jacket like he's goddamned Hugh Hefner. "Yates, you never do the whole 'Rapunzel, let down your hair' and then climb on up into Joan's tower?" I give Joan a sassy little nudge, and she responds with a glare. My charms aren't working. What nasty bit of gossip did Evelyn poison her with?

"Maxine, dear," Joyce warbles, "maybe we should have a chat in the kitchen?"

"Can it, Joyce!"

Defiant, I circle the table yet again. As I'd hoped when I designed the room, the light rippling off the pool reflects in the mirrored wall. Dusty still swells in the background, promising her man that she'll keep her expectations as low as dirt. Yes, I know it's not subtle, but Douglas can't comprehend what isn't slapping him about the head.

I grab a glass of someone's red wine and swig it. It is my booze, after all. I can feel everyone's nervous eyes on me, like when I was a child and would play Duck, Duck, Goose with my classmates. I bet they're wondering who I'll tap next.

"Isn't this music divine?" I ask the room. Joyce nods like I'm pointing a gun at her. "Not like Douglas's *Man of La Mancha* crap. All that white-knight-on-a-horse, saving-the-world shit. Dreaming impossible dreams is right. Dusty here, she speaks the truth." I hold up a hand to my mouth, stage-whispering to Olive Oyl

Hearst: "Secret fact about my husband: he's as chivalrous as Charles Manson!"

"Maxine, enough!" Douglas booms so loudly, he nearly startles the beige off Mary.

Everything feels slow and blurred at the edges. The candlelight bounces off the mirrored wall behind me, hits my crown, and shines back down onto the table and the faces of my wide-eyed guests like tiny flickering flames. It's beautiful and dangerous all at once, and I can't turn away from it.

I look to Douglas, daring him to look back at me. The first night we met, his look of lust sent a surge of electricity through me. Now he looks up at me from across our Thanksgiving table, and I see only loathing. He wants to ride into the sunset, and I'm the villain in black standing in his way.

But I am not the villain in black. I am Maxine, the righteous gunslinger. And in this moment I know my only chance now is to beat him to the draw.

I pick up my knife and ding-ding-ding it against my glass. "I have an announcement." I take a deep breath and let it out. "You should all know that the role of Mrs. Douglas Simmons will next week be played by some little girl named Jennifer."

There's a chain reaction of stunned stares, punctuated by Mary choking on her wine. The husbands barely move, but I see their eyes dart to one another like they're tossing a hot potato. Joyce reaches across the table to grab her husband's hand. She bows her head down as if praying for this whole moment to go away. Joan Ferndell Hearst mouths something I can't make out to Evelyn, who I swear to Christ looks like she's fighting back a laugh. Yates Bixby Hearst couldn't give two shits about anything, focusing on cutting his Brussels sprouts into bite-sized pieces. Douglas sits with his arms folded tightly across his chest, unblinking in his contempt for me.

There are no sour looks shot in Douglas's direction. Worse still, no one looks at me. Except for Joyce. She looks up timidly as fat tears fall down her cheeks.

"I'm so sorry, Maxine," she whispers guiltily.

She knew. Joyce already knew my husband is a cheat. And if Joyce knows, well then, the whole damn town knows. There's no denying that.

Everything is crashing down.

"This is old news to all of you, isn't it?" My voice is steady. I will not cry in front of these monsters.

Joyce doesn't look at me. None of them look at me.

"All of you sitting here with your 'manners.'" I make air quotes, spilling the last of someone's wine down my arm and onto my dress. It stains immediately, leaving a bright red splotch over my heart. How perfect. "We're all friends, right? So don't hold back. Ask me all about the Jennifer my husband's fucking." There's more gasping. I gasp back, bigger and better. A gasp for the ages. Goddamned Yates Bixby Hearst shovels a mound of candied yams into his mouth, dropping some on his ascot. "Come on! Anyone else here getting slipped the old Dougie on the side?" I think I mean it as a hypothetical question, but by the time the sentence flies out of my mouth, I realize that any number of these people might also be fucking him.

Douglas bangs his hands on the table because I'm too far away from him to hit. Mary flinches and Joyce bursts into loud, body-shaking tears.

There's a sudden silence as everyone looks to Evelyn. There's no way she regrets accepting my Thanksgiving invitation now. This is better than any revenge she could have concocted. She glances to Douglas, who gives her the tiniest of pleading looks before letting his head fall into his hands.

A smile grows across Evelyn's face. Her teeth shine like white, wet fangs. I might be blotto, but I know what that means. She's about to finish me off.

I lock eyes with Evelyn. Daring her to do her worst.

"Well," she says, dabbing at the corners of her mouth with my napkin, "at least Douglas is doing the right thing. You know, marrying the girl he impregnated."

The sound drops out of the room. "Oh Christ, Evelyn," I hear Douglas groan.

No one else says anything. I don't move. I can't move.

"She's pregnant?" I whisper.

I'm saying the words, but they have not sunk in.

"She gets . . . a baby?" I'm whimpering, but the words are like sharp icicles stabbing my brain.

I look to Douglas. His face is cold and brittle. I'll find no sympathy there.

That's when it happens.

I always thought it would be a literal snapping sensation. Like a rubber band, only on a larger-than-the-universe scale. Otherwise, why would they say things like "She just snapped?" Yet there was no snap or break or even a pop. Instead this churning, almost burning, achy sensation eases slowly up from deep within my gut. It builds and gets heavy—and quickly, at that. I'm not strong enough to fight it. It's like trying to hold back an echo.

They want humiliation, I'll give them my humiliation.

I start screaming, and I don't stop. I reach over Joyce to grab the vase of azaleas off the table and hurl them into the mirrored wall, which cracks into a spider's web. Someone begins openly weeping; it might be Mary or it might be Joyce or both. It doesn't matter, because I'm screaming louder than they're sobbing. Douglas grabs me around my waist and I feel I'm no longer on solid ground. I kick and kick and my legs feel thick and heavy like I'm treading water. I bite down on his hand like a starving rabbit on a carrot, and he releases me with a yelp. I shove my hands in someone's plate of candied yams and fling it in Douglas's direction. I slip on something—or maybe I'm pulled down? I feel my knees scrape along the carpeted floor as my hands grapple for the table. It hurts, but everything hurts. My chest constricts with every scream, and my face burns hot despite all the wet tears. Evelyn and Joan cower behind their husbands, and this time when Douglas tries to grab me, I slap him in the face with a plate of Brussels sprouts.

I stagger to my turkey, gently taking it into my arms. Just the bird cradled in my arms like a newborn spilling its sweet-'n'-savory pineapple-and-turkey afterbirth all down my dress, which is, in turn, managing to stick to me in places while falling off in others.

My tongue is thick, and I can barely catch a breath to get my words out. "I've got you. It's all right," I say to the turkey. Then to the room: "None of you fuckers are touching this beautiful bird!"

I don't stop screaming. I don't think I could if I wanted to, and I really don't want to. Screaming is the only thing I know how to do. I'm cornered and it's instinct. I stomp barefoot right through the sliding screen door, stumble out across the patio, and I'm poolside before I take a breath.

I hurtle that turkey over my head toward the pool, but I just can't let go. I feel myself stumble again, and next comes the splash of my body hitting the water. Me and my newly delivered pineapple-ringed baby are going down together. I toss my head back underwater and scream and scream and scream. Then I lie motionless on the bottom of my pool, staring up at the dark, starless sky until all I see and feel and know is blackness.

Maxine Hortence Simmons

Palm Springs

The Morning after Snapping

I'M ON A BRILLIANTLY LIT STAGE in my cotton-candy-pink empire-waist princess gown. I smile out at a clapping audience I can barely see. There's a woman—a girl, really—standing to one side of me, our hands clenched together. Her palm is wet, or maybe it's mine. Both of us tremble, and my feet hurt from being in heels half a size too small. A drumroll silences the audience. I hold my breath so deeply, my chest aches.

Douglas says my name, as if it were the two greatest words ever uttered by man. The crowd cheers and confetti rains down on me like silver and gold snowflakes. I breathe again but feel lightheaded. Am I floating above my body, hovering over this stage? Someone hands me a bouquet of red roses as I'm gently led to Douglas. He holds out the crown—my crown, my thousands of shimmering stars—and I kneel slightly to let him place it snugly on my mound of blond curls. It's heavier than I expected, and digs into my scalp.

The audience fades away as Douglas gives me a kiss on my cheek and whispers in my ear.

"You stupid little girl."

I wake with a start in a bathtub, which I don't immediately recognize as my own. I'm clad only in my underwear and I'm damp all
over despite the fact that there's no water in the tub. As soon as I can
wonder what the ever-living shit happened, I have this hazy memory of being in the pool with my turkey. I can't breathe, because I'm
surrounded by water. But my eyes are open and I see the wavy aqua
image of Douglas looking down on me. My head pops up, gasping
for air as my feet kick violently beneath me, struggling to find solid
ground to stand on, but there's just more water. The turkey is falling
apart, its various parts bobbing up to the surface around me. I hear
people screaming my name. I take heavy steps to the shallow end
and emerge from the pool. I feel my hair, heavy and wet, clinging
to my face and blocking my vision. I'm freezing, so I reach to the
person closest to me for a warm embrace. It's John Jones, and he
steps on my bare toes while dodging my outstretched arms. I crawl
toward the open patio door. There are so many more screams, and
they stare at me like I'm the creature from the Black Lagoon.

How the fuck did I end up a swamp monster in the pool with
my gorgeous turkey? How much did I drink? What pills did I take?

This fuzzed-out memory is interrupted by the movement of a
figure to my right. The figure comes into focus: it's an extremely
pale man in an ill-fitting suit. He looks like a grub on two legs. He
stares at the wall, probably because I'm topless, though if propriety
was of any true concern to him, he wouldn't be in my bathroom.

"Excuse me, sir," I croak out, and dear Christ, it is a croak. My
throat feels like it was diced up by a chef at Benihana. The grub
thrusts something at me, causing me to recoil. It's a thick wad of
papers. Instinct tells me not to take what's being shoved at me.

"Ma'am, under California law, I need to inform you that you're
being formally served legal documents that require your attention,"
he tells me. "I need you to take the papers and sign them."

His words thump into my head. My memories are hazy, but one
fact is in Technicolor: Douglas is really and truly leaving me. Scratch
that; Douglas expects me to leave. Out with the old Maxine. In with
the new Jennifer.

The pregnant Jennifer.

I've been kicked to the curb, which explains why my ribs ache. My kamikaze run at Douglas failed. Now come the terms of my surrender.

"No," I say softly. "I'm not interested in being sued for divorce. Not right now, anyway."

I grab the towel rack to help me to my feet. Mr. Ill-Fitting Suit fights to not see my nearly naked body. "Don't feel bad," I tell him. "My husband also doesn't want to see me naked." I am wobbly, but at least upright. "We've been doing it in the dark for years now."

The light over the vanity is far too glaring. I turn it off before looking in the mirror, seeing that my appearance matches how wrecked I am. My hair resembles a blond bird's nest. I see Ill-Fitting Suit still behind me, but more relaxed, probably because my bare breasts—which look much better than I feel, I might add—are no longer facing him.

"Ma'am, I'm sure you've had one heck of a night—"

"Why would you say that? What have you heard?"

I mean this. I need to know what happened to me. I grab a few bobby pins and start pinning everything back into place, pulling out the azalea petals that are somehow matted to my hair. My eye makeup has smeared and smudged its way into two near-black circles around my eyes. What I initially think is a spider on my cheek turns out to be my left eyelashes.

"Well, I mean . . . you look like . . ."

I turn sharply to him. "I look like what? Finish your sentence."

He again averts his eyes, holding papers I'm supposed to sign for in front of his face like a shield. I slap them out of his hands and onto the bathroom floor.

"You know what I think I look like?"

"No, ma'am," he warbles.

"I think I look like what happens when a man says 'fuck you' to his wedding vows and decides to stick it in someone who is most definitely *not* his wife." I grab Ill-Fitting Suit's face roughly with both of my hands. "You see this? You see this?"

He lets out a frightened little squeak.

"Well, this"—I point his eyes to my trashed hair, naked torso, still wet and grimy panties—"this is what a woman ruined looks like."

I let him go and he breathes with relief. While he struggles to pick his papers back up off the floor, I turn again to the mirror. What the hell is this crusty brown stuff in my side-swept bangs?

"Mrs. Simmons," he says, this time with a little more confidence, "just sign and I'll leave."

I suddenly recall a flash of a moment from last night. I'm in the dining room, atop the table, stomping through the side dishes like some bellowing creature from a Japanese monster movie. I step barefoot in the stuffing, lose my balance, and fall to my knees before the mushroom-filled bell peppers, which I included on the menu as a nod to our Southwestern lifestyle. The candied yams smell delicious, so I grab a handful and bring it to my mouth right as someone—probably Douglas—pulls at me from behind.

"Ma'am?" Ill-Fitting Suit holds out his clipboard and a pen, directing me where to sign.

I snap out of my memory. Since it doesn't seem like I have a choice—or at least not if I want this clod out of my bathroom—I scribble my signature down. He hands me my share of the papers.

"What am I supposed to do now?"

"Your husband set up a meeting for you this morning with an attorney to represent you in this manner."

He hands me a business card for someone named George Scott, Attorney-at-Law. He's all the way out in Indian Wells. My head is throbbing, but my senses are returning—my sense of vengeance among them.

Ill-Fitting Suit stares at my signature on his clipboard, then looks back to me. "Are you waiting for a tip?" I ask him. "Get the fuck out of my bathroom!"

Ill-Fitting Suit gives me a polite nod and exits stage left.

I toss on a robe, but hesitate before walking down the hall. The house sounds empty, but then again, that's how it always sounds. The door to his office is closed and locked. I give it a quick knock before remembering he said something yesterday about staying in LA. I bet that Jennifer has a cute little hippie hole in Laurel Canyon, or worse yet, she's made the pied-à-terre her own. I call for Gina before recalling that she's got the day off. I consider beseeching her to please come in anyway, but I can't bring myself to do it.

Everything in the living room looks in order. The silk drapes are drawn, and I leave them that way, since more than enough blinding sunlight is peeking through. The copies of *Architectural Digest* are stacked neat as ever on the coffee table, and the plush carpeting still holds the shoe prints of where my guests stood the night before. From the cluster of prints near the door, it looks like something of a stampede, as if a herd of zebra fled from an attacking panther. Though the record isn't playing, no one's switched the turntable off, so the Dusty record spins and spins, making me dizzier. I turn it off and close the lid.

I get a vague flash of guests running out the front door, leaving it wide open behind them. I can feel Gina's arm gently pulling me toward the hallway, to the bedroom. Is she saying that I need a bath or am I saying it? The words are garbled in my head. I close my eyes tightly and open them again, now seeing Yates Bixby Hearst's soiled ascot tangled up in the spindly branches of the ficus in the entryway. I leave it there.

The kitchen is spotless. I grab the first glass I can find and get myself a drink of tap water. Nothing is in the sink. The fridge holds ten ramekins of crème brûlée, their tops sugared and ready for broiling, a Thanksgiving dessert I guess was never served. Their heavy vanilla smell makes me retch, but I make it to the garbage can before the bile spills out of me.

Underneath a discarded mound of turkey stuffing, I see a glint of something silver.

My crown. Tossed into the trash along with the other unwanted leftovers.

I remember climbing out of the pool with the crown clutched tightly in my hands, its scalloped edges digging into my palm as Douglas tries to take it from me. I swing the crown at him, cutting him on his chin as he shoves me away.

I pull my crown out of the garbage and wipe it off on my robe. Thank God it's still intact and bile-free. I wash it under the sink, scrubbing with my chipped fingernails to get out the caked-on stuffing from in between the still-shimmering stones. I try not to sob, but it's that or throw up more. I slide down the countertop to a fetal heap on the cool linoleum floor. I force the air out of my lungs, then back in slowly, then out again slower still. If I can breathe, then I can think. I don't want some lawyer in Indian Wells. I want the lawyer Dottie Ross used when she learned her husband, Roy, was screwing some "actress." I reach to grab the countertop, pulling myself up to the sink for more water. Dottie had a plan. She began her ordeal with a broken heart and ended up with the house and two cars, including a little blue convertible that we all thought her driver looked bananas tooling around town in. That's the lawyer I want.

I put the crown on, pushing it down onto my scalp until it hurts. In the phone stand, I find the Yellow Pages and let my fingers do the walking to some lawyers. There are nearly five pages of ads in the book, and even if I ignore the husbands of friends or good friends of friends, there's still plenty to choose from. Surely someone will take my case?

At Neal, Michaels & Kaplan, the receptionist asks my name twice and then hangs up on me. Perkins & Arnold puts me on hold for five minutes before the secretary rushes through something about there being a "conflict of interest" and then hanging up on me. Thomas, Thomas & Tomás tells me the same thing, helpfully adding that I should call someone in Indian Wells or—God help me—La Quinta.

I pace through the kitchen and out to the dining room while on hold at Schultz, O'Leary, Budd & Phillips. Just as in the kitchen, there isn't a trace of the disaster left from last night. The thrown food's been cleared and the table scrubbed down. The linens are all probably in the wash, leaving only the burned-to-a-nub candles and those goddamned azaleas. The patio door is closed, but the torn screen flutters slightly in the wind.

I get another flash of the night before: this time I'm poolside telling everyone how Douglas's dick is like the seventeenth hole at Thunderbird, in that it, too, is something of a dogleg left. Evelyn slaps me, so I shove her into the pool while screaming that if she doesn't float, then she's a witch and we should burn her.

I see my mirrored wall has a crack in it, sprawling out like rivers on a map. I step on a shard of glass and let out an "ouch!" right as Mr. Schultz, Attorney-at-Law, gets on the line.

"Yes, Mr. Schultz," I say, turning away from the mirrors. "How are you—"

"I know who you are, Mrs. Simmons," he tells me. His voice echoes across the line, the way Douglas's does when he has me on speakerphone in his office. "I need you to understand that your husband already consulted with me about the divorce. In fact, I think you'll find he's talked to nearly every lawyer in town."

My stomach churns at the thought of how many people knew this was coming for me. For how many weeks were they whispering behind my back?

"I don't understand—"

He cuts me off. "None of the lawyers Douglas spoke to can represent you now, Mrs. Simmons. You need to find one who doesn't know him. Maybe in Indian Wells?"

"I don't want—"

"I have to ask you, Mrs. Simmons," he says before pausing. "Did you really smear cranberry sauce all over a Hearst and call her a 'Commie red'?"

I hear stifled laughter from more than one person and hang up immediately. I am hit with a flash of me scooping cranberry sauce into my bare hands and rubbing it onto my face, sticky and warm. Joan Ferndell Hearst cowers in the corner. I leap off the table, landing next to her. With my cranberry hands, I push the hair away from her face and see how frightened she is. I smear the cranberries across her face so she'll match me. "Take me to your castle, comrade!" I hiss at her as she shoves me away.

I rub my eyes until I see spots, and it hurts enough to pull me out of the memory. I can still taste the cranberry.

I run back upstairs to the master bath and turn the shower on, making the water hot enough to instantly steam up the bathroom mirror. My hands shake and my chest constricts. I barely get the toilet lid up before vomiting into the bowl. I crawl my way under the water. I let it pound my face until I don't think I can take it anymore, but at least I don't feel the tears pouring from my stinging eyes.

There's another memory, and I'm grateful it's from a long time ago and not last night. Through the ringing in my head, I can hear my mother, plain as day, telling me what she said every time I cried in disappointment as a child.

"Get yourself a plan, you stupid little girl!"

Maxine Hortence Simmons

Palm Springs

The Afternoon after Snapping

THIS IS HAPPENING.

And it's clear I am on my own here.

It's a gorgeous day, so I pace around the pool in a robe and sunglasses while collecting my thoughts. Club soda tastes odd without any vodka in it, but my stomach tells me to sip on it anyway. I nearly retch, seeing bits of my turkey still floating in the pool. I fish out some thigh meat with the pool net, but the reaching and bending and stretching leaves me dizzy. I leave a lone pineapple ring to float in the deep end.

I have a plan to hatch.

There are a few things I know to be true. First, Douglas destroyed this marriage by impregnating someone else. Secondly, gleaning what I can remember from watching an episode or three of *Divorce Court* and the gossip from the girls around town, this means that Douglas is at fault. The party at fault is guilty, and guilty people have to pay. Douglas will need to pay me to no longer be his wife.

I need to come up with a number. Where to even start? I grab a pad of paper and do some more walking around the pool.

On the top of the pad of paper I write:

SHIT I WANT.

Item Number One: the house. But not this one. The Jennifer can have this house because I know it will sting her to receive my leftovers. I want the pied-à-terre in LA, which we purchased last year. I've only been once, but it's a charming storybook-style cottage on a lovely orange-tree-lined street. It's clear to me that I need to think much bigger than Palm Springs, and what could be bigger than Hollywood? Beverly Hills? Plenty of eligible men lying about as well. Maybe old Maxine could land herself a movie star. I wonder what Tab Hunter is up to?

Item Number Two: alimony. Lots and lots of alimony. A woman's got to eat. And vacation. And look good. I have zero intention of staying single for long, and catching a man's eye takes heaps of effort and loads of money. It would help if I knew how much everything cost. I could kick myself for not paying attention to financial matters, but then again, it's not like my philandering husband would want me to know too much, now would he?

I also need a car. Mine is fine, but I'd rather have his since it will sting him more. I put a little star next to *his car* to remind me to use it as a bargaining chip.

On to the lawyer, then. I can believe that Douglas would have met with a plethora of lawyers. If not in their offices than certainly on the damn golf course. What if I went to LA and found a by-the-hour attack dog there? Maybe someone who looks harmless but then can get Douglas on the stand and when he least expects it, goes for the jugular. Or maybe some mongrel who will start by gently nipping at Douglas's ankles before ripping him apart. I have a feeling that most lawyers like to decorate their offices with the mounted heads of those they've killed. But maybe if I pay extra, I can end this whole nasty divorce business with Douglas's head on a stick. Wouldn't *that* enliven my new home?

To hell with the whole lot of them.

I draw a line under the list of items and write in a number. But not just any number. I write down what I know I'm worth:

$2,500,000.

I throw on my most businesslike pencil skirt and a blouse that isn't too frilly. I barely recognize myself. These are my clothes and my hair is in my usual French twist with side-swept bangs, but Jesus, when did I get so old? I tell myself that my puffy eyes are merely the result of too much drinking. The lipstick settling in my lip lines is entirely the fault of the too-dry desert air. To bring a little natural color to my face, I give myself two good slaps, bringing a rosy glow to my sallow cheeks. Then I head right out the door to the law offices of one Mr. Allen Moore, Esquire. If Douglas wants to be a prick about this, well then, I'll just be a bigger prick right back. Isn't that how men play with one another? I must admit it's a touch more honest than the mind games we women deploy, though it does lack creativity.

I take Douglas's car, because it's fancier and its bright blue finish goes better with my outfit. Plus, my car is far too understated for a grand entrance. I can barely drive a stick on a good day and well, blame it on the hangover, I scrape the entire passenger side along a planter on Civic Drive. Upsy-daisy! Silly women drivers! I'm sure Douglas can get that painted right over, good as new. Like I never drove it in the first place. Or ever existed.

The scrape of the car along the planter rattles my stomach. I turn off the car and sit a minute, hoping my heart will stop racing. All I want for today is to hide in my shower or lie dead in bed. Yet thanks to Douglas's litigious nature, that's not an option for me. A caged animal doesn't have time to grieve for her situation. Even if she wishes she could curl up and die, she needs to bare her teeth and claws and fight back.

I eschew an appointment or any of the other social graces and barge right into the law office, steamrolling past the secretary. I can't help but notice the placard on her desk identifies her as a Miss Jennifer Hill. Good fuck, they are everywhere, aren't they? As I storm past her desk, the placard is "accidentally" knocked into the trash by my purse, which I might be swinging a bit like a scythe clearing a field of wheat.

"You can't go in there!" little Miss Jennifer Hill tries telling me as I do in fact go in there, throwing wide open the double doors to the office of Allen Moore, Esquire.

"Coffee. Black with three sugars," I inform her, hoping she'll get the hint that the polite thing to do would have been to offer me coffee, as opposed to her focusing on where I can and cannot go.

"Mrs. Simmons," says Moore, "you can't waltz in here as if my office were the ladies' lounge at Walker-Scott!" He's a stout, completely bald man with a too-short tie. I've been in his office all of five seconds, and I can already see the sweat forming around his ears, making its way down his considerable jowls. He has marks on his nose and at his temples from wearing too-tight eyeglasses. When I slam one of the doors shut behind me, he jumps.

I slap the divorce papers onto his desk and plop myself down in one of his leather wingback chairs. I swiped a pack of smokes from Gina, since I've decided I smoke again. I light up a menthol Virginia Slim for added effect, because you know what? I *have* come a long way, baby! I forgot how fantastic tobacco makes one feel, and knowing that Douglas thinks smoking makes a woman look "cheap" only adds to the allure. Judging from his "Well, I never" scowl, I determine this doesn't meet with Moore's approval.

"This is highly irregular, Mrs. Simmons," is all he can muster. "Where's your attorney?"

I blow some smoke in his general direction. Of course, the first time in nearly sixteen years I need an ashtray, there's isn't one. "I'm confident that we can settle this today, Mr. Moore." I pull my notes from my bra. It didn't occur to me that it's unseasonably warm out today and the—let's call it *warmth*—of my décolletage has caused the ink to run somewhat. Thankfully, I can still make out my writing.

"My understanding is that Douglas wants the house?" I say, as though I'm placing a dinner order. "Why don't we start there?"

"You don't know what you're doing, Mrs. Simmons. I must insist you leave now and have your lawyer contact me so this can be handled properly."

He waves me off in the direction of the door, although his cause isn't helped much by the arrival of Miss Hill with my coffee. I dunk my Virginia Slim in it without taking it from her. With shaky hands, she sets the cup and saucer down on the desk and sits in a chair next to Moore, holding her steno pad so she can take notes on our meeting.

"I've told you, Mr. Moore, we can settle this today, provided you'll stop talking to me like some dumb little wife. My marriage and my time in Palm Springs is over. Fine. I'm ready to move on. Douglas can have the house in Palm Springs. I'll take the cottage in LA." I say this more to Miss Hill than to Moore, to assure she writes down what I'm saying with the utmost accuracy.

"Will you now?" he says to me in a near growl.

"Yes, I will. In addition, I'll require monthly alimony—beginning immediately—the Jaguar, and all my personal effects. Then I'll be on my way." It pains me to say this, but what other option do I have to preserve what little dignity I'm still clutching?

Mr. Moore stares at me. Actually, it's more like he stares through me. It's unnerving, and while I'm sure it's some tactic he learned in law school or from watching *Perry Mason*, I don't care for it.

"This is all cut-and-dry, Mr. Moore. Douglas broke our marriage vows. He's married to me and yet another woman is gestating his offspring." *I can do Perry Mason, too, you jowly little man!* "I am the wronged party. So, let's talk turkey, Mr. Moore!"

He chuckles. It's a wet, raspy laugh, like he's got something festering in his lungs. "Yes, let's talk turkey, Mrs. Simmons. Let's start with the turkey you threw into my client's pool last night in full view of his peers?"

Touché. I walked in here thinking this Moore fellow was someone at least moderately reasonable. I guess I shouldn't be surprised that one of Douglas's lackeys would make me work for it.

"You humiliated your husband, Mrs. Simmons. Most reasonable people would regard what you did last night as an act of malice. You do know what *malice* means?"

I laugh sharply, and it startles Moore, but not as much as I would like. "I want two and a half million and not a penny less," I tell him.

Moore has no reaction. He jots down something on a legal pad. "I'm writing down a number for you, Mrs. Simmons, of what you are legally entitled to from my client."

He tears the paper off the pad, folds it, and slides it dramatically across the desk. I open it with a flourish.

$0.00.

My chest tightens and I feel my left eyelid twitch. I try to keep my voice steady and calm, but I know my tone wavers a bit. I can't lose control here. "This is ludicrous. Douglas is worth millions."

Moore stares at me, unmoving and unblinking, like he's lying in wait to pounce. Everything about this guy feels like a trap. "Mrs. Simmons, since you've made the foolish decision to forego legal counsel, I'll indulge you in a bit of pro bono legal education. Am I correct in assuming you are unaware of something called the Family Law Act of 1969?" He doesn't wait for my answer, and now I know this is a trap. "It's a bill signed this past June by Governor Reagan that designates California as a 'no-fault' divorce state. Do you understand what that means?"

I don't have an answer. But considering most of the men in Palm Springs refer to the governor as "our pal Ronnie," I figure this isn't good news for me. I light up another cigarette, not for effect, but because I suddenly need one.

Moore keeps explaining. "'No-fault' means there's no more 'wronged party,' as you put it. Meaning that this, shall we say, *slight* that you feel Mr. Simmons committed against you has no bearing on the divorce judgment."

I put my cigarette out by grinding it into Moore's desk. "That," I say, pointing to the burn mark in the desk, "is a slight. Knocking up a secretary when you have a wife at home is far more than a slight!"

"The law doesn't care what you think, Mrs. Simmons."

"Well, the law can kiss my ass!" I feel my tough-as-nails facade beginning to crack. "The facts are hardly up for interpretation!"

Moore remains stoic. Not even his jowls move as he continues to stare through me.

"Do you know what a prenuptial agreement is, Mrs. Simmons?" he asks me as he pulls a stack of papers out of the folder in front of him. "You ought to, since you signed one two days before your wedding." He flips through at least ten sheets, finally stopping at a page to point to my former signature—Maxine Hortence. I cringe at the curly, girly handwriting of that someone I used to be. "You—and any judge that reviews it—will clearly see that you agreed that should the marriage end, you would receive a reasonable number of your personal effects. However, anything beyond that—which would include alimony or a cash settlement—you waived all rights to."

He's talking too quickly for me to keep up. I understand him in bits and pieces, but I know better than to tell him this. I have a gauzy memory of a day right before my wedding when Douglas's father—a man I always called Mr. Simmons—whisked me off to his office in Sacramento. There were lawyers then, too, and I remember one of them telling me where to sign. I balked slightly and was told that there could be no wedding without my signature.

Just a little business to attend to and then you can get right back to the romance, dear, Mr. Simmons told me. He was an imposing man, so I did as told.

Stupid little girl!

Moore puts on his glasses and starts reading, "Furthermore, you'll see this document clearly states that Douglas's inheritance is maintained in a separate trust exempt from these proceedings.

"And I quote, Mrs. Simmons," he continues, chuckling the last part under his breath, "'In the event of a dissolution of the marital community, all assets held in the Simmons Trusts prior to the community, or added thereto during the life of the community, shall remain and be the sole and separate property of Simmons.'" Moore gives me a satisfied glare. "In layman's terms, Mrs. Simmons, this means that the bulk of Douglas's wealth is not considered community property, of what you and he own and would be entitled to divide between you. As far as this divorce is concerned, it doesn't exist. Your request for two and a half million dollars far exceeds what this marriage is actually worth."

The thumping in my head roars. This isn't possible.

"Alimony is nonnegotiable," I tell him as firmly as I can muster. "It's what a spurned wife deserves when her husband of sixteen years runs off with something named Jennifer!" I say the Jennifer part loudly enough that Miss Hill startles, dropping her pen. Flustered, she reaches down to pick it up and Moore glances down her shirt.

"Mrs. Simmons, the bottom line is that your husband does not need to stay married to you, and any alleged infidelity is meaningless in the eyes of the law. Regardless, you agreed that you would have no claim to Douglas's trusts, which are his exclusive property, and you also waived any claim to alimony. So you're entitled to exactly what we offered. Nothing."

He points to the paper with the big fat zero written on it. My shoulders tighten and the back of my mouth goes numb. I have no one on my side, little chance of walking away from this unscathed. I'm defenseless again—just like I was last night.

"I am the wronged party," I say maybe a little too softly. "The wronged party deserves justice."

The fuzziness from last night is building, and I need to keep it contained for now. Moore is maddeningly calm. He and Douglas have had months to think all this through.

"Mrs. Simmons, I understand that you're upset," he says in the tone one uses when speaking to a dull-witted child, "but you need to understand that in this case, any judge would find that the law is clearly on your husband's side."

I hear a sniffle from Miss Hill and notice that her eyes are moist. I don't know why the hell she's the one fighting back tears here. I'm the one worth nothing.

I'm getting nowhere with Moore, and since Miss Hill seems to be the only sympathetic ear in all of Palm Springs, I speak to her instead. "It's not like I had a choice in signing that agreement, you know. Douglas's father insisted on it." I lurch forward and tap my finger on her steno pad. "Write that down! And while you're at it,

Miss Hill, write down that I want to know how I am expected to live a single day without any money!"

"Mrs. Simmons," Moore interrupts wearily, "this conversation is moot."

"According to you, Mr. Moore, the last sixteen years of my life are moot!" I bleat out at him. I lurch my whole chair now to Miss Hill's side. From the tremble in her hand, it's clear that she's at least hearing what I'm saying. "I want it on the official record that the only reason I signed my life away was because I was barely twenty, had less than two years of college, and was pregnant with Douglas's child!" A tear makes its way out of my brittle eye. It's matched by several more tears from Miss Hill. She can be won over. I reach for her chin, tilting it up so that our wet eyes meet. "What would you have done if you were me, Miss Hill?"

Moore snorts. "I hardly think that Miss Hill could ever find herself in such a position! She's a woman of honor and morals!"

Miss Hill gasps. I'm not at all shocked. I've heard it all before. From my husband.

"Besides, Mrs. Simmons," he continues, "you should know that my client does not for one second believe you actually were with child."

"Allen!" Miss Hill gasps again. "What a dreadful thing to say! A woman would never lie about such a thing!"

That snapping sensation comes rushing back to me, like it's coursing hot through my veins. I want to lash out in every direction. I want to send every object in this room swirling like a tornado around me. But that's exactly what Douglas and this Moore asshole want me to do. I won't give them that satisfaction.

I walk over to Moore and get in his face. "This is exactly why I snapped!" I say to him, letting those goddamned tears fall wherever they want. "Sixteen years of disrespect. Sixteen years of him cheating on me! Impregnating his secretary! Lying about our dead baby! And he gets to leave me with nothing? Penniless and homeless? Am I just supposed to keep swallowing all that until I choke to death?"

Miss Hill openly weeps. She rushes out of the room, leaving her steno pad behind. I don't take my eyes off Moore.

Moore removes his glasses and rubs the bridge of his nose. "I don't know what you're trying to accomplish here, Mrs. Simmons, apart from making my secretary cry. You can stare at that number all you want. It's not going to magically change. The law is on our side."

"Tell me, Mr. Moore," I almost whisper, "what about the court of public opinion?"

Moore leans toward me. "If you're suggesting some sort of smear campaign—"

"All I am saying is that if I have no money, no home, then all I'll have left is the kindness of strangers. I'll have no other option but to find a lawyer and battle this out in court. Meanwhile, I'll still be here in Palm Springs, living off charity, and everyone will know it." He squints and writes something down on his legal pad. "The cold, hard fact of the matter is, Mr. Moore, that if I went that nuts thinking I was entitled to half of Douglas's wealth, what do you think learning I get nothing will lead me to do?"

This brand of logic seems to hook Moore. I stay as calm and still as I can, hopefully hiding the rage bubbling inside me. If this doesn't work, I don't know what I'll do. From the corner of my eye I see a crystal phallus-shaped Attorney of the Year award and wonder what it would feel like to bash him over the head with it. Would his head crack open like an egg or would he simply slump over onto his desk?

I'm saved by Miss Hill, who returns to her chair and steno pad. "I'm sorry, Mr. Moore," she says, all businesslike. "I know that was unprofessional, but some things are just too ugly." She poses her pen over the pad, ready to write.

This is my last chance.

"Miss Hill," I say, "would you say that your reaction to my plight was unusual?"

Miss Hill looks to Moore, who nods his permission for her to answer. "I don't understand?" she whispers.

"Do you think you're the only woman in Palm Springs who finds my situation heartbreaking?" I say it while looking at Moore, whose brow is downright furrowed.

"No, ma'am. I imagine nearly every woman would be saddened, or angry even, to hear that. Especially the married ones, I suppose." She turns to Moore. "I'm sorry, Allen. But that's the truth."

"All I am asking for, Mr. Moore, is the means to start my life over again and I'll go away quietly." I smile at Miss Hill. "Doesn't that sound fair and reasonable?"

She shoots a tiny nod to Moore. He looks like he's chewing the insides of his cheeks. He picks up the telephone handset. "I'll need an hour to confer with my client. Alone," he adds for my benefit. "Miss Hill, please show Mrs. Simmons to the waiting area."

I follow Miss Hill out to the reception area and take my seat on a sofa. She offers me coffee, which I could probably use, but my stomach feels bitter enough. She closes the door to Moore's office and takes her seat behind her desk.

Miss Hill puts on her headphones and focuses on typing out the dictation. With every *tip-tap-tap* of the typewriter keys, I feel a tiny part of my bruised brain chip off inside my skull. Every so often, Miss Hill looks up from her machine to stare at me, like I'm one of those abstract contemporary paintings hanging in the new wing at the Palm Springs Art Museum.

I try picturing myself sitting all day behind a typewriter or answering phones. It wouldn't be the end of the world. I mean, look how it worked out for Miss Hill, or that other Jennifer.

I always suspected Douglas thought I was lying about the baby. All those years ago, when I told him I was pregnant, I wasn't sure what his reaction would be. I was prepared for sadness or even anger. We'd only been dating for a few months, after all. And while I knew he was the man I wanted to marry, men have a way of needing a little extra push toward the altar. I could tell he was unsure about the whole thing, but three days after our honeymoon, when he went to work and I went to the hospital, bleeding, I thought for certain he'd finally come to believe the pregnancy was genuine. And to hear it from that dreadful Moore. That wasn't so much a slap in the face as it was a shotgun blast to my head.

When Miss Hill finally tells me that Mr. Moore will see me now, I'm steady in my resolve. Moore knows now how I can convince others to view Douglas, so with a little added pressure, I'm sure I can turn this all around for myself.

I saunter in like I own the place. Moore straightens his tie and motions for me to sit. I choose to stand.

"My client has graciously agreed to offer you the Buick and a one-time cash settlement of two hundred and fifty thousand dollars," he says, rushing to get the words out. "And he's willing to give you the condominium in Scottsdale."

"What the hell is Scottsdale?" I blurt out.

Moore rubs his temples like a weary heroine on a soap opera. "Scottsdale is the Palm Springs of Arizona. You'll love it. Or not. Frankly, I don't care. The condo is barely a year old, fully furnished, and comes with the stipulation that you stay in Scottsdale for no less than three years."

"I'm being banished to some place called Scottsdale?" I say out loud, still trying to wrap my head around the notion.

"Call it whatever you like, Mrs. Simmons." Moore sighs. "The main provision here is that you must leave my client alone and stay out of Palm Springs for three years. If you can manage to behave yourself for that long, then the condominium in Scottsdale will be entirely yours. You can sell it, burn it to the ground for the insurance money, or anything else that addled mind of yours concocts!"

Addled mind! At least they are recognizing my capabilities. And with two hundred and fifty thousand, I'm guessing I could make living in a fallout shelter luxurious. Surely Scottsdale has the right people and places to help me start Maxine Part Two.

I nod to Moore and grab my purse. "I assume there will be paperwork? And a check?"

"There's also the matter of your name," he says too casually.

"What of it?"

"Douglas wants it back."

"I have to change my name?"

"Revert to your maiden name, or call yourself Rumpelstiltskin for all we care."

I roll my eyes. Like I would want to keep a name that in all likelihood is about to have a "Jennifer" put in front of it! "Fine," I say flatly. I shove my hand out and he stares at it blankly. "The check?"

"You'll have it by the end of the day. A courier will bring it to Mr. Simmons's home, which you will vacate tonight. Is that clear?"

"Pleasure playing lawyer with you, Mr. Moore."

Robert Hogarth

Scottsdale

November 1969

I WAKE UP knowing it's going to be a slow day, mainly because everyone is still hungover from Thanksgiving or eating leftovers. Sometimes slow days fill me with a type of loneliness I have trouble shaking off. My alarm blares at 7 a.m., as it has nearly every day of my adult life. I know that I don't really need to roll out of bed until 8 a.m., so I lie here on my uncomfortable twin mattress wondering why I don't start setting the clock for eight. Unlike most in Arizona, my commute is measured in feet rather than miles.

I and everything I own reside in two small rooms attached to my tavern, La Dulcinea. When I bought the place five months ago, these rooms were filled with dust and leftover odds and ends from the previous owner, Mr. Owen Benson, who built the restaurant with his bare hands. Like me, Mr. Benson came to Arizona from someplace else, looking to start a new life in a sunny, warm spot. Unlike me, Mr. Benson was looking for a place where his family could worship freely as Mormons without being persecuted. I don't have a family. Or much of a faith. But I do know how to run a tavern.

Once I'm up and showered and dressed, I put on a pot of coffee and read the paper. Usually by the time I get to the editorials, the silence starts to trouble me, so I'll put on the jukebox, just to have noise in the background. On Tuesdays and Fridays, the grocery delivery guy shows up at 8:30 a.m. Every other day, it's common for me to not speak to another living soul until the first customer comes in around eleven, sometimes closer to noon. Most people in the neighborhood still think this place is closed, since Mr. Benson shut it down a month before I bought it. Others pop their heads in and see that I've put in a bar—a big no-no for Mormons—and walk right out. I don't take it personally.

I've been a bachelor all my life and—according to my mother—I've always been "the restless sort." First there was a few years spent as a busboy and later a waiter at a quiet lakeside restaurant in Lake Geneva, Wisconsin. The place was only open during the tourist months, so during the off-season, I eked out a living shoveling snow for public works. Then the restlessness kicked in and I headed south. An old friend from high school got me a job in a Kansas City restaurant run by his uncle. Mr. Babcock taught me how to plan menus, negotiate with vendors, even do the books. Every day of my six years there, I learned something new. Heck, I learned how to cook every dish on that menu, from potpies to chicken à la king. Kansas City was an okay enough place to live—especially since I wasn't shoveling snow—and for a while there it felt like Mr. Babcock might even turn the place over to me when he retired.

Except that didn't happen. Mr. Babcock sold to someone else with deeper pockets, so right before I turned thirty, I moved along. This wasn't as awful as it might sound. Again, no wife, no kids. Just me. I found a job as a host at a real high-class, white-tablecloth, two-sommeliers-on-staff kind of place. I moonlighted as a mailman to make extra money. Once I had a nice nest egg tucked away in the savings and loan, I went west, young man. Scottsdale seemed not too big, not too small, and more important, it was growing every week, filling up the desert with one little ranch house after another. And in those ranch homes are families who need to eat.

What I need now is for a whole heck of a lot more of them to start eating at La Dulcinea. Because aside from it getting lonely behind this bar, my nest egg is down to the yolk.

"And that's why I don't care for azaleas." The blond woman holds her whiskey sour up as if giving a toast and downs the last little bit of it. After moving the lemon paring knife a safe distance from her, I immediately prepare her another drink, because to be frank, if she is this entertaining after only one, I can't wait until she's had a few.

Drink in hand, she's silent once more. She walked in nearly an hour ago with a halfheartedly folded map in hand and dumped enough dimes into the jukebox to play Neil Diamond's "Mr. Bojangles" over and over as she hummed it quietly to herself. After play number three, I made a mental note to remove the record from the jukebox and replace it with absolutely anything else. By play number six, I decided a mental note wasn't enough and found some paper to make myself an *actual* note, which I pinned up behind the bar. I lost count of Mr. Bojangles and his worn-out shoes somewhere around play number nine, but I did let out an audible, reflexive sigh of relief when the bar fell silent as her dimes finally ran out. She hummed for a few more minutes while lazily gazing up at all the framed vintage maps of Arizona I have hanging on the walls.

She sat in a booth, picking at the nut dish before I suggested she come keep me company at the bar. She ordered the sour and I asked how her day was going. Normally, I get a "Fine, thanks," which means, "I'm here for the booze and not the small talk, bub." Other times it's a "I'll be much better once I get a drink in me!" which is a good signal someone wants to discuss the weather or how their sports team is doing, or if I'm really unlucky, politics. But with this woman, she blurted out something about azaleas, and while I'm trying to even picture one in my head, she's off and running with her story.

I've heard just about everything in my life behind a bar, but the things she told me, well, I guess *shocking* is the only word that comes to mind? Shocking and sad. That's what I think to myself—and no one else. A good bartender keeps his judgment to himself. Customers can get booze just about anywhere in 1969—even in Conservative-with-a-capital-C Arizona—and bad advice is in even greater abundance worldwide. This lady isn't different from anyone else. I mean, yes, I guess she is different in that most ladies don't get naked with the same frequency she seems to. And they don't go all cuckoo on Thanksgiving dinner. What's that saying about everyone living lives of quiet desperation? This woman's desperation might be screaming from the rooftops, but the basic principle remains. Plus, people won't come back to a bar if the bartender gets fire and brimstone on them. This is why I keep my mouth shut, pour drinks, and listen.

Hers is a true story, I can tell. Bartenders learn quick when someone is full of S-H-I-T, and this one isn't. Although, I can't figure her out much beyond that. She's in jeans—not quite Haight-Ashbury, but definitely like what the kids wear—and her nails and lipstick are the same shade of blaring red as her shoes and handbag. Her hair is a feat of engineering. I'm guessing she just had it done at that ritzy place around the corner (or at NASA, maybe?). It's tall and taut and yet also full and round, and a blond color you never see out in nature. I do sometimes see it on country-western album covers, and each time, I picture that blonde from *The Birds* and think of how if she had this hairstyle, the birds would get caught in it and not peck her to death.

"I'm Robert, by the way," I finally say.

"I'm Maxine Hortence Sim—" She blanches. "Force of habit. Merely Maxine Hortence now. He got to keep the last name."

"Really?" I want to keep her talking. She's by far the most entertaining person I've met in a while.

"Everything is up for grabs in a divorce. But I made him buy it back from me, that's for sure." She plucks the red plastic sword from her drink and pulls off the sour cherry, letting it drop in her drink. Very few people let the cherry soak. Most eat it the moment the drink is served.

"Are you . . ." She points to her ring finger.

"Nope. Never had the pleasure." My standard response, although I'm a little peeved at myself for how quickly it came out.

She looks me up and down, as if counting my antlers to determine I am at least thirty-five, then pauses back on that left hand. I know that look and I don't care for it. It's a look that usually brings about a game of Twenty Questions.

"Got a girl?"

There it is.

"Nope. I am free and easy at the moment." Her eyebrow goes up a little. "Or at least free."

"That sounds like one of those country-western songs that are so popular out here. That's all I can get on the damn radio, anyway. We didn't have much of that in Palm Springs. Do you like country-western music?"

I shrug. "I don't think one way or another about it."

"Me as well. At least it's not as loud as today's popular music. All that screeching and moaning, it's unbecoming."

"I'm not the biggest fan of Neil Diamond," I offer.

"I think he's divine! Those sideburns." She stabs the cherry with the sword and finally pops it into her mouth. She looks like she has more to say but is careful to chew down every bite before opening her mouth again, even using her cocktail napkin to delicately dab at those red lips.

"What about Broadway tunes?" she says, with yet another arched eyebrow.

And we're back at it.

"I'm an Irish bartender in Scottsdale, Arizona. I know sea shanties and all forty verses of 'Danny Boy,' but other than *West Side Story*, I couldn't tell you anything about Broadway."

Put that in your pipe and smoke it, madam.

"Ugh, that goddamned play," she says a little too loudly. "My ex-husband wouldn't quit with that 'I know a girl named Maria' nonsense."

"Well, Natalie Wood . . . He's only human, after all."

"He's a jerk." She laughs hard and very loudly. "And I'm human too. Yet I never once indulged in any number of tennis pros or other women's husbands. I could have if I wanted to, you know."

I'm glad she's back on track and talking about herself. This is a line of conversation I want to encourage.

"So, tell me, Miss Hortence, after one . . ." Oh goodness, how do I put this?

"Sets herself on fire at Thanksgiving dinner in front of the crème de la crème of West Coast society?" she offers, sounding more than a little proud of herself.

"Yes, that," I answer. I'm already making her another drink. Miss Hortence looks like someone who is accustomed to there always being both another drink and someone there to make the drink. "After *that*, what did you get out of it?" I hand her another whiskey sour.

"I got nearly everything I wanted, and I took the rest."

The way she tells it, Miss Hortence bolts out of the lawyer's office and heads straight for home to grab her "personal effects." "I understood this to mean everything in the kitchen, of course, since Douglas never once even poured himself a cup of coffee," she tells me. "But then I thought, *Screw that*, I'm never cooking again. So I took only the essentials—the brand-new percolator and the fondue pot."

All this fit nicely in her luggage and Lane wedding chest. While she desperately wanted to take the light fixture hanging above the dining room table ("it's a Sputnik chandelier!"), she was even more intent on snagging the chair from her built-in bedroom vanity.

She couldn't very well stuff the chair into a suitcase and she didn't have another chest. It would have fit in the Buick, except she decided that's not the right car for her.

"A Buick is hardly the car one wants when starting a new life. And since I hadn't the time to purchase a more appropriate vehicle, the only reasonable thing for me to do was to take one of Douglas's cars," she tells me.

"That's completely against the terms of your divorce," I point out, proving to her that I've been hanging on her every word.

"Is it though? The settlement specifically said that I can take 'items my husband has no obvious use for.' He has three cars sitting in that garage. Even if that Jennifer is old enough to drive, he doesn't need three cars. Therefore, at least one can be considered as having 'no obvious use.' Naturally, I took his favorite." She pauses for a second, clearly for effect. "It's a Jaguar E-Type convertible."

This is the most shocking thing she's said all day.

"You chose wisely, Miss Hortence. Those are magnificent cars. I mean, I've only ever seen them in magazines."

She's off her barstool in a flash, grabbing my arm.

"I'm parked right out front!"

Miss Hortence pulls me outside and I realize we've been talking for so long that every business along this stretch of Thomas Road is closed and dark. A perfect shaft of streetlamp light pours down upon Miss Hortence's stunning ocean-blue Jaguar E-Type. The poor car is parked half on, half off the curb, but that clumsiness isn't enough to detract from its regal beauty. She has the top down, which is completely insane, since any bird flying by could easily drop some mess onto the cream-colored, soft-as-butter leather interior. Her belongings are heaped up like some old-timey gypsy caravan, in trunks, suitcases, a few loosely-taped-shut boxes, and at least two garbage bags. I can overlook the coffee stain covering the better part of the front passenger seat and almost ignore that the trunk is haphazardly held closed by a bright pink hair ribbon. What my eyes cannot get past is the long scratch in the shimmering paint that extends all the way from the driver's side lock to the back taillight, above which there's a considerable dent.

I run my hands along the dent, realizing it's far too deep to knock out. "Who would do this to you?" I whisper.

Miss Hortence doesn't understand that I'm talking to the car and not her. "I should probably learn how to parallel park."

I don't take my eyes off the car. No, make that I *can't* take my eyes off the car.

"Why don't we go back inside and I let you make me another drink?"

"Fine, but first I have to insist you put the top on." I'm pointing to the car, but that's not how cheeky Miss Hortence chooses to see it.

"Kind sir, you are the first man to ever say that to me."

Once I'm back behind the bar, I take Miss Hortence's insistent advice and make myself an old fashioned—a nice stiff one. There isn't much of a dinner crowd. The Rodriguezes—Manuel and Consuela—thankfully don't need my help in the kitchen. I'm worried if they heard any of Miss Hortence's story. They are a lovely Catholic couple, and I would hate to lose them. Then again, I also don't want to lose Miss Hortence. Aside from being a potentially very good customer, she is the rarest of people: a bona fide hoot.

"Miss Hortence," I say.

"Please, I've verbally exposed myself to you all day. Call me Maxine."

"Maxine." I smile. "I would love if you'd stay and have dinner with me. On the house, of course."

"I would be delighted, Mr. . . . ?"

"Hogarth. But you should call me Robert."

We settle back in a booth and enjoy a bottle of something red. Maxine devours a salad with avocado ("I'm a California girl, after all!") and smokes through half a pack of Virginia Slims. For dessert, she has an Amaretto sour and what she claims is a vitamin.

Besides, I like making people drinks and listening to them talk. I think it's because I'm from the Midwest. We don't like to call attention to ourselves on our best and brightest of days. What's there to say about me anyway? Boring old Robert Hogarth, fan of whatever sports team you're rooting for. Top-shelf smiler and nodder for your political candidate of choice. Impartial listener of all your tales—even those that are bonkers. Maybe *especially* those that are bonkers. I don't ask too many questions. And I hope for the same courtesy in return.

Dinner over, I clear the table and she spreads out that crumpled map of the Phoenix metropolitan area. "So, best I can figure, I'm presently somewhere over here?" she says, pointing to a random spot on the map that's a good five miles from where we are.

"No, you're here."

She nods and smiles. Her eyelashes bat at me in a way that tells me she wants me to take command of this situation. "I'm telling you, Robert, I drove half the night all over Scottsdale—or at least what I think was Scottsdale—and I couldn't find this Kachina Palms Condominiums anywhere! It's literally not on the map!"

I point out that the map is from 1964, meaning the map is older than many of Scottsdale's buildings. "Based on that street address, your condo is likely right over here." I point to a spot on the map that is mostly blank and tan in color.

"Oh, great. Exiled to the middle of nowhere!" she wails. "Like all those prisoners who were dumped on Australia. With my luck, the condo will be overrun with kangaroos and wallabies!"

I give Maxine a stack of dimes under the condition that she play all different tunes, which she's happy to do.

Kenny Rogers's "Something's Burning" comes on. It seems to make her happy as she closes her eyes and lets her head sway back in tune to the music. It's a lusty little number, and I'm not surprised it appeals to her. She looks tired, maybe a little sad. Like those candid pictures the press takes of a movie star leaving a party or a courthouse. And yet Maxine also looks completely normal. Not at all like a woman who's done half of what she's told me about tonight. Yet I know enough about people to understand that you can present yourself to the world one way and be an entirely different person on the inside. Any bartender can tell you that.

The song ends and she lights up her last cigarette.

"Tell me, Miss Maxine Hortence. What now?"

She looks confused, fluttering her eyes for effect.

"You've got the condo in Scottsdale, the car, the alimony, the name." That makes her laugh, deep and throaty. "What's next for you?"

She blows a puff of smoke and watches it slowly dissipate under the lights. "I was a beauty queen once, you know. That's how I met Douglas. He was judging the pageant. In fact, he was the one who put the crown on my head." This makes her laugh. It's a soft, winsome laugh I almost expect will lead to crying. And yet it doesn't.

"Maxine, you could beat out Miss America any day of the week," I say—honestly, I might add.

This next laugh is deeper and without a trace of mourning. "Robert," she says, quite purposefully, "would you be opposed to me frequenting your establishment?"

"I'd be insulted if you didn't become a regular."

She shakes my hand, winks, and, though she's somewhat unsteady in her heels, walks out into the night.

Maxine Hortence

Scottsdale

November 1969

I SUPPOSE THAT old movie line about relying on the kindness of strangers has more than a grain of truth to it. But we also can't ignore the role serendipity plays in our lives. If I hadn't stumbled upon that quaint little tavern and met that dashing Mr. Robert Hogarth, I would still be ambling wearily across the desert with all my meager belongings strapped to my back. Thanks to his Boy Scout–like navigation skills, I finally find my elusive new home.

The three buildings that comprise Kachina Palms are mostly dark when I arrive at 10:30 p.m. The key I received from Moore's courier has a note attached, directing me to Building A, Unit 23. This sounds more like directions to a burial plot than a home. Also included on the paperwork is the name of something called a "building manager," whom I've decided is someone who can assist me with my baggage.

Per the brochure, Kachina Palms "offers residents luxury resort living every day!" I'm not sure the exclamation point is entirely warranted. There are three stucco buildings, which along with a tiny clubhouse and pool area comprise something called a "complex."

I've never lived in a complex before, although I suppose those in the psychiatric profession might conclude otherwise.

Another key opens the front gate and I amble in the near-darkness along narrow, winding pathways. I feel like I'm treading along in circles, since everything looks alike and the faint smell of the pool's chlorine is inescapable. The buildings are all putty-colored stucco with drab, dark chocolate-brown trim. The path is lined on both sides with desert landscaping that could stand to be better maintained. Right as I find the door marked MANAGER, I scuff my ankle on the overreaching frond of an agave plant that needs trimming.

After I've banged on the door for nearly a minute, the manager, one Mr. Gary Walsh, finally decides to do his job. If he's an example of the level of amenities I'm going to find at Kachina Palms, then I'm in big trouble. Mr. Walsh—and I'm using the word *Mr.* quite loosely here—is a pimply faced boy who can't be a day over nineteen. He doesn't so much walk as he lumbers to my car, muttering something about not being paid to be a mover.

"You should be grateful you're not fighting in Vietnam," I tell him, pointing to what pieces of my luggage simply cannot stay in the car overnight.

He mumbles something about flat feet and leads the way to Building A, Unit 23. I unlock the door and Walsh dumps my things one step inside the condo.

My mother always told me that first impressions are everything. People will never doubt what they learn about you in the first thirty seconds of meeting you, so you better present yourself deliberately and with much forethought. If you want people to think you're cute as a button and not at all the type of girl who would steal expensive nylons, then make damn sure they see you as Shirley Temple.

Clearly, my new condominium didn't get a similar lesson. I step over the threshold, take in my new abode, and restrain myself from fainting. To borrow a phrase from the divine Bette Davis, "What a dump!"

Yes, it has two bedrooms, one and a half baths, and plush wall-to-wall carpeting. But the condo needs twice as many windows, which I imagine is fixable, and the ceilings are at least a foot too low, which I'm less sure about. There's also allegedly a weekly housekeeping service, and yet there's enough dust on the kitchen countertop for me to spell out *F-U-C-K* with my finger. I recognize that all of Arizona is one giant cat-litter box, but that much dust shouldn't accumulate in a mere seven days' time, right?

Despite the assertions of Mr. Moore, Esquire, that the place was furnished, there is a plastic—plastic!—picnic table in the dining room, which I should add isn't actually its own room but a wide-open space between the kitchen and the living room. The only thing that suggests it's a room intended for dining—aside from the picnic table—is some gaudy stained-glass chandelier. It's three shades of red, orange, awful, and looks like something someone stole from a bar where everyone dumps peanut shells on the floor. I want to light it on fire.

Off in a corner of the living room I find a cheap turntable sitting on a small folding table. There's a stack of records, and while I justifiably assume it's Douglas's usual *Man of La Mancha* bullshit, I'm shocked to find some of the records to be listenable. The Beatles, the Byrds, Cream, the Doors—if they weren't in alphabetical order, I'd never think they'd belonged to Douglas. I put on *Between the Buttons* by the Stones and turn it up loud.

Try as I might, I can't help but compare this new home of mine to the one I left behind. My dining room in Palm Springs was thought out down to the last tiny detail. My teak table was sourced from looking through dozens of catalogs. The terra-cotta floor tiles, the nubbed linen table runner, the perfectly arranged brass candlestick holders—I curated all of that with care. That dining room was *me*, from start to finish. This is, well, not.

The guest bedroom is empty, save for the fourth and hopefully final plastic picnic chair. Truly, though, the worst was saved for the master bedroom. There—where a bed would be if one didn't care about optimal furniture placement—is this big, round, faux-leopard-print, fur-covered *thing*. It's maybe three feet in diameter and resembles a huge ball of dough that some giant has pressed down in the middle with its fist. I give it a kick and it's squishy, yet firm. I crouch down beside it and run my hands gently along the faux fur, finding a tag.

"'Beanbag Chairs Unlimited,'" I read aloud. "'Groovy seating and sleeping for hip boys and girls.'"

It's a hippie chair. I do have to admit I'm curious what it feels like to sit on a bunch of beans, so I carefully place myself upon it. The beans are surprisingly comfortable, hugging my body as I wiggle deeper into the chair. While I get situated, my hand bumps into something metal partially tucked under the bean chair. I grab it and wrench it free, revealing a children's metal lunch box depicting two rodeo clowns whose names I gather are Wallace and Ladmo, although I can't surmise who is who. Inside the lunch box are three books of matches from tawdry so-called gentlemen's clubs, a dirty old ashtray with a scantily clad brunette on it, and a bright orange packet of what look like empty bubble gum wrappers but according to the label are Zig-Zags, used to roll one's own cigarettes. There's also a wooden cigarette case with the logo from the Thunderbird Country Club carved into it. I pop it open and find two already made cigarettes. Or to be more precise, marijuana cigarettes.

Douglas, I hardly knew ye.

I light one up. I mean, why not? This is my damn home now and I'll do as I please. Besides, I'm long overdue for a smoke break and my purse is all the way in the kitchen.

"What the hell were you doing here, Douglas?" I say to absolutely no one, sans Mick Jagger, who's warbling about some girl named Ruby Tuesday. Better Ruby than Jennifer. Was I truly so awful that my husband needed to cross state lines to sit in a bean chair and escape me? The condo is less than a year old, so did he purchase it planning to leave me? Parents often send their knocked-up teenage daughters off to live with "aunts" to keep their town's prying eyes off the growing bellies. Do wealthy businessmen do the same to their impregnated secretaries? Or was this supposed to be Douglas's escape hatch? I take some satisfaction in knowing that my unorthodox-yet-effective negotiations with Mr. Moore fucked all that up for dear, lost little Douglas.

I stub the joint out. I try to get up, but this delightful bean chair doesn't want to let go of me. I'm like a turtle on its back, unable to flip over or gain my footing. How in the hell does one get out of these things? Is this truly a chair designed specifically for getting stoned in and lying around all day?

I surrender to the beans and stare up at the too-low ceiling. So this is where the last thirty-six years of your life has gotten you, Maxine, old girl. Divorced, lying stoned and alone in some shitty little condo your ex-husband used to escape you and hump his secretary. Is this *really* all I have to show for my life? I suppose it's partly my fault for having chosen poorly when it came to a husband.

Eventually I manage to flip over onto my belly in the bean chair and crawl out of it backward. I will never understand why anyone would choose to get stoned over getting drunk. Aside from being far more delicious, booze is easier to control one's consumption of. Plus, alcohol's never driven anyone to eat an entire Sara Lee strawberry cheesecake that she found stuffed in the back of her new freezer.

I consider finding a hotel for the night, but by the time I get this brilliant idea, it's already 1 a.m. Any hotel that would have me at *this* hour is surely not one I want to be in. I cave once more to the Hippie Bean Chair. Sinking right in and, thank Christ for the cheesecake and weed, I'm asleep nearly instantly.

I wake with a start, gasping for breath as if I've just been pulled from the murky depths of some mossy lake.

That Jennifer's baby.

If they made it here, they made it in this bean chair. It needs to go!

Charles "Chuck" Bronski

Scottsdale

November 1969

I WAKE UP at 4:45 a.m., all ready to go learn stuff on account of my body doesn't know that it's Saturday. I do my fifty sit-ups and fifty push-ups, just like I do every morning. I guess maybe it's a good thing that I don't need an alarm clock anymore. Dad says I'm "regimented," and he ought to know since he is Specialist First Class Pete Bronski of the US Army. He's fighting the Commies over in Vietnam right now.

I think it's cool and all that my dad is a soldier, but that's not what I want to be when I'm a grown-up. I plan on being a top-secret spy for the FBI or the CIA. So, aside from regimenting my body, I'm also teaching myself how to lip-read, since all the spies know how to do that. I figure if I learn how to do it now from watching TV with the sound down, it will be one less thing I need to learn later. Only trouble is that there's not much on TV on Saturdays except cartoons, and cartoon characters don't have lips. I can guess what Porky Pig is saying, but Bugs Bunny and that Yosemite Sam fella talk a whole bunch. There's a preacher fella on one of the channels, so I put him on. I'm expected to keep real quiet and not wake up Ma. Her name is Sharla and she's a waitress at the Pink Pony, which is just about the grooviest restaurant in Arizona. It's where all the ballplayers eat when they're in town for spring training. It's also open till real late, and Ma doesn't get off her shift sometimes until the middle of the darned night. If the TV wakes her up after she's only had a couple of hours of sleep, she'll be spitting nails at me all day long and maybe even into Sunday.

I know that some moms get up and make breakfast for everyone, even on a Saturday. Ma says she brings enough people breakfast and that I'm old enough to throw some milk on my Cheerios all by myself. We're all out of milk this morning, and dry Cheerios are no good. Also no good: Cheerios with water, Cheerios with apple juice, and especially Cheerios with Dawn's baby formula. I will never again be so stupid as to think that all milk is the same. Baby milk is not real-people milk. I bet the happiest day of my sister's life came a year ago when she turned two and Ma said she could start having the good milk. Except that now we go through it so gosh darn quick, I don't have any for breakfast.

Mrs. Scherfenberg—my social sciences teacher—says I'm a good problem solver. I think she's right. Because I remember that last night our building manager, Mr. Walsh, had a poker game in the clubhouse. This happens every other week, and there's almost always food left over. More important, Mr. Walsh doesn't clean up after himself right away, so if I sneak out of the apartment all quiet-like, I bet I can find something better to eat than dry Cheerios. It's only 6:05, so I have at least twenty minutes before Dawn starts fussing.

It's no trouble getting out my front door, since I always keep the hinges oiled so they aren't squeaky. That's one of the things I promised my dad I'd do while he's off at war, along with always doing my homework, minding Ma, keeping my room shipshape, and not smoking cigarettes until I'm out of high school. I figure he would also want me to look out for my baby sister, although she wasn't born yet when he went away. Mom wasn't even all big and pregnant yet. Mom said that Dad had more work to do over there in Vietnam, which is why he's been gone going on two years. Or tours, which is what they call them in the army.

It's still dark out except for some lights over people's doors, so I hold on tight to the railing as I walk down the stairs from our apartment. At the bottom, I look up and see the strangest thing ever. Yeah, I know I'm only twelve, but I once saw a guy in a clown suit walking his dog, which might not sound weird, except that he had on the big clown shoes and they were twice the size of his dog. Even *that* wasn't as weird as what I'm seeing right now. Outside Building A, Unit 23, there's a lady with blond hair who looks like she's playing tug-of-war in the apartment's open doorway. I get behind one of those short, stubby palm trees and even though it's dark out, I can see she's barefoot. The door is wide open, and her hands are out in front of her, holding on to something I can't make out.

I dart over to another stubby palm, this one just a few feet from the bottom of the stairs leading to her apartment. There's enough light coming from her apartment that I can see she's wearing a fancy bathrobe that looks like one of those dresses waitresses wear in a Chinese restaurant. I can also see that she's pulling on something that looks like a giant garbage bag, or maybe Santa's sack of presents. Except there is no Santa, and I've never seen a garbage bag that size. The blond lady squats down low and pulls with all her might, letting out a whole bunch of cuss words while she does it. She falls forward onto whatever it is she's yanking. It's quiet enough outside that I hear her land on it with a squish. What in tarnation could she have that makes that noise? Is it the world's biggest water balloon? I move a little closer, but she still can't see me. I should probably be a gentleman and offer to help her, but what if she's doing something, well, *criminal*? I hear more grunting and heaps more swearing, so I peek around the side of stairwell. She's back in her apartment now, trying to push whatever the heck is stuck out. "Gosh darn it!" she grunts, only she doesn't say *gosh* or *darn*. She says God's name and what holds back the Colorado River. She's loud—or at least it sounds loud compared to how quiet everything is in the morning. I see the light over the front door go on in the apartment next to hers.

"Son of a witch!" she yells—only it's more of a piercing scream and she doesn't say *witch*. It works, though. I hear a loud thump, then another, then two, three more even faster after that, and I duck behind the stairs as whatever she was pushing goes tumbling down like a giant Slinky. I'm thinking it's going to make a splat when it hits the bottom of the stairs, but it's more like a thud. From my spot behind the stairs, I can see it lying there, half on the pathway and half in the bushes. I move closer until my head is right up against the steps. It's definitely a bag and it's definitely stuffed with something. But what?

I hear footsteps on the stairs and take a step back, making sure I'm in the shadows. She stops halfway down the staircase and I hear the click of a lighter. Her bare feet are right in front of me and the left one has a streak of dirt on it. I'm starving and should probably just get to the clubhouse, but all my spy instincts tell me I need to see what she does next.

The half-smoked cigarette is thrown over the edge of the staircase, landing on the decorative rocks around the plants. She gets to the bottom of the stairs and it sounds like she's kicking the bag, which now doesn't sound like it's filled with water. Her foot leaves a dent in the side of it, like the way a pillow does when you punch it. Now that it isn't stuck in the doorway, she's able to grab on to it and drag it behind her. It looks heavy.

"Stupid fudging Douglas and your stupid fudging fudge chair!"

I didn't know you could use the *f*-word twice right next to each other in a sentence. I bet this woman got tons of demerits when she was a kid. Margaret Nicholls—this girl I know from school—her dad is a police officer and she said he gives tickets to grown-ups who swear in public. It's called being disorderly.

I don't know who Douglas is, but he must be way worse than a police ticket.

She pulls the bag behind her, still cursing. When she gets to the curve in the path around Building A, I run out from the staircase. First, I stomp out the cigarette she threw on the ground and then I toss it in the trash can next to the pool gate. Then—and I know it's not the smartest thing to do, but it is the bravest—I follow her, keeping out of sight. She drags the bag all the way to the back of the building. I have to crouch behind a car, which is parked in a spot you're not supposed to put cars. I can't see her, but I figure it's probably better that she can't see me.

I can hear her though. Heck, I bet all of Kachina Palms can hear her and most of Scottsdale, too. The blond lady's over by the Dumpster, making such a racket. She's all about fudging up this Douglas fellow and making him wipe the smart-aleck grin off his shoot-eating fudging face. Then she starts in on someone named Jennifer and how Jennifer is a gosh-darn stitch mother-fudging home-wrecker pile of shoot who's a—*cunt?* If that's a word, it's a new one for me. Even with all the cussing, I can hear her trying to get that bag into the Dumpster. I'm positive there's a body in there. Maybe two—this Douglas and Jennifer lady.

All the hairs on my arms are standing up. I saw that once on *Batman*, and Batman told Robin it was his bat instincts warning him the Penguin was near. I think my instincts are telling me that this blond lady is way scarier than the Penguin. He only uses pink gas to make people fall asleep. This lady has dead people in a huge sack. I want to pop my head up over this car and look, but what if she sees me? She's already killed two people. I'm a kid, and most people don't really want to kill kids, but I'm also a witness. I need to get out of here and go to the Feds.

I keep my cool and slowly crab-walk backward away from the car. Holy moly, this car might be the coolest thing I've ever seen in my life. It's like something out of a movie. It's curvy and small and bright blue with creamy-white seats that look like real leather. It's not a car some Ordinary Joe who works in an office drives. This is a rich guy's car. The guy who drives this car wears one of those expensive black suits with a bow tie. He talks like he's from Europe and knows how to eat with chopsticks. Either that or he's a spy. Yeah, I can absolutely see James Bond in this car. But what is it doing at Kachina Palms? And why did it show up the same night this cussing, angry blond lady showed up? Is she a Russian?

I stand up and walk like a person once I reach the corner of the building. I look back and see the blond lady has most of the huge bag in the Dumpster, but some of her Chinese robe is pulled up and stuck under it. She yanks her arm back hard, but that robe sleeve is stuck. She flaps all around like how a fish does when you pull it out of the water, except that a fish isn't also saying "donkey-kissing son-of-a-gun Richard-head and the cunt you rode in on."

I run all the way back to my apartment and up the stairs. As soon as I reach the top stair, I hear Dawn wailing. I rush through the door and go straight to her crib in our room. She's jumping up and down like a monkey at the zoo and her poor little face is all red and wet from tears. I pick her up and bounce her on my hip.

"Sorry, Dawnie! You're fine. We're all fine," I say in that super happy, high voice people always use when talking to babies. I want to ask her how it is that her screaming doesn't wake up Mom when even a whisper out of me sounds like the whole world is ending. Like Ma always says, it's a good thing Dawn's so darn cute. She's got blue eyes like me, but her hair is all blond and curly. Her little fat cheeks get bright red out in the sun or when she's fixin' to start screaming. My hair's stick straight and dark. And when I feel like screaming, well, I guess I just stop myself.

I keep Dawn on my hip and shove her dolly in her face, which seems to make her happy, since she stops her fussing the second it hits her mouth. She might be little, but she's got the grip of King Kong.

I pick up the phone to dial the police, but I stop myself. I learned in school that one of the worst things a kid can do is prank call the police, and what I'm about to tell them sounds like a prank call:

"Oh, hi, police. My name is Charles Thomas Bronski and I want to report a dangerous Russian spy. She's a lady with big messy blond hair and she's wearing a Chinese dress. I just saw her dump a giant bag filled with dead bodies in the Dumpster at the Kachina Palms Condominiums in Scottsdale, Arizona. Gee, thanks."

I hang the phone back up and feel stupid because I'm too scared to make the call. And I guess I feel stupid because what if I imagined the whole thing? I could be sleepwalking or something. I should pinch myself and see if I wake up. Dawn must be able to read my mind or something, because she grabs at my head with her little fingers. I keep my hair in a buzz cut, so when she finds nothing to grab, she sticks her wet baby fingers in my ear.

Nope. I'm awake.

Dawn has that look that tells me she's gonna start screaming if I put her down, so I take her with me to peek out our front door. From here I can see over to Building A, where the blond lady stands outside her closed door, trying to get back in her apartment. The door's locked and she slams it hard with her elbow and screams. It's not some little scream either. It's the loudest, longest scream I've ever heard—and I live with a two-and-a-half-year-old. It's not an angry scream, like when the enemy attacks someone in a war movie. It's a sad, awful scream, like the kind ladies make when the massive radioactive spider comes at them in a monster movie. I duck back in my apartment, and when the screaming stops, I look back out again. She's got her knees pulled up tight against her body and she's sobbing like Dawn in her crib.

I don't know what to do. I know this whole darned morning's been me saying how I've never seen anything like this, but I really, truly never have. I'm only an hour into Saturday morning, and it's been one "I've never seen" after another. Would a spy who dumped two bodies in a Dumpster cry like this afterward? Or lock herself out? I feel all wrong inside for just standing here, so I close the door. I can't believe Ma is sleeping through all this.

I put Dawn in her crib with a bottle and her dolly while I try to figure all this out. I grab my notebook—not one I use for school, but one I use to keep track of what I'm learning about being a spy. Police detectives always write down clues, so I do the same:

Strange blond lady (Strange = loud, cussing, and wearing her nightclothes outside)

Bag with ~~bodies~~ make that MAYBE bodies

That's the furthest I get when I hear the sirens. It sounds like a cop car at first, but then I hear the sound the fire truck makes when it gets to the intersection down the road. Then another fire truck. They sound like they're right outside the building, and when I peek out my back bedroom window, I can't see trucks, but I do see flashing lights reflecting off the cars in the parking lot.

I pop my head back out my front door. There are lots of people slowly coming out of their apartments, and they're all pointing and walking toward the Dumpster. I hear them say "fire" and "Dumpster." I definitely smell smoke.

The blond lady sits on her doorstep. She's not crying anymore, but she still looks scared. It reminds me of that one time I helped Mr. Walsh free a baby jackrabbit from the pool filter. The poor bunny was curled up tight with its big glassy black eyes quivering. It was too scared to move, and that's exactly how this lady looks. My instincts start telling me that she needs help. And unless I want to be a bad person, I should be the one to help her.

"Check on top of the doorframe," I whisper, which is stupid since there's no way she can hear me whisper from all the way over here.

I still have my spy notebook in my hand. I curl up the long sides into the shape of a tube and shove it out the door. I put my lips to the rolled-up notebook and say in the deepest, fakest voice I can make, "Look on top of the doorframe!" The blond lady snaps her head toward me and I pull the notebook inside the front door before she can catch me. This time it works! On her very tippy-tippy-toes, she reaches up and, thanks to her extra-long red fingernails, the spare house key falls down and hits her on the head. She shakes hard like a wet dog, and I hear the key ping onto the concrete doorstep.

"What are you doing?"

Oh, beans. That's Ma.

Except she's not saying it from behind me. She's saying it from right in front of me as she comes up the front steps.

"Tell me you didn't call the fire department, Chuck?" she says. She's got a jug of milk in her hand.

I shake my head and step back into the apartment. She comes in right behind me.

"I thought you were sleeping," I say.

Ma hands me the milk, which I see now is a little less than half-full. She also sees that I see this. "I got thirsty on my way back from the store. You must have woken up after I left."

"You gotta work today, Ma?" I ask her. She's in her waitress uniform.

"No." She looks down at her uniform. "I got home so late, I guess I fell asleep in it. Just left it on when I got up and went to the store."

I bring the milk into the kitchen and when I turn around, Ma is standing right next to me.

"I saw Walsh in the parking lot. He said everybody thinks some new lady in Building A started that fire. You see anything?"

I shake my head again.

She reaches up to get herself a glass from the cabinet. She has on those stockings that ladies always wear that make their legs look like the color of butterscotch pudding. I don't understand why they wear those. It's like putting fake skin on top of your real skin.

"Does the new lady drive a groovy blue car? A convertible?"

"Walsh didn't mention a car. He just said she's a real piece of work." Ma gets some water from the tap and walks away. "I'm gonna take a Valium and get some sleep. You be a good boy and look after your sister."

I sit down in front of the TV with my notebook. I have a lot to write down before I forget it all.

Robert Hogarth

Scottsdale

December 1969

I DON'T LIKE being a worrywart, but after meeting Maxine and spending an entire day learning all about her, it troubles me that she hasn't been in the bar for two weeks. What if she's dead in a ditch somewhere? Or worse still, did something foolish with a bottle of aspirin and a jug of wine?

She's called four times since we met. The first was a day or so after moving to town, and the call was nothing more than her asking what time I usually open and what the soup of the day is.

"Gazpacho," I tell her.

"Oh, Robert!" she purrs. "In December?"

The second and third calls were much longer. One came before the restaurant opened, and while I know it sounds crazy, as soon as the phone rang, I was sure it was her.

"La Dulcinea—"

"Robert, dear, it's me. You wouldn't happen to know of any leftist radical types who know how to rig a golf bag with explosives?"

It's an interesting way to start one's day. By the third call, which came one night after closing, she had me telling her all about the old movie theater I worked at as a kid back in Libertyville, Illinois. She howled through the story of how legend has it that Marlon Brando briefly worked at the theater until the day he put Limburger in the air vents.

"Please tell me he wore his leather jacket over his red usher's coat?" Maxine laughs before instantly becoming deadly serious. "Is Brando single? Do you have his phone number?"

"Maxine, he worked there years before I did."

"Oh." I hear her fidgeting with whatever carton her dinner is coming out of. "Well, do you know anyone else famous? And eligible?"

The truth as I see it is that I enjoy Maxine's company. I don't want to say I'm lonely. I'm honestly not. I've always been plenty happy to be by myself, which makes my chosen profession a good one for me. Talking to customers is not a problem. But making friends? I don't know how to do that. I work all day, six days a week, and live out of the tiny apartment in the back. I should probably find a church to go to on Sundays, but frankly I'm not all that interested in that. Plus, I'm Catholic, so that's an hour of sitting, standing, and kneeling followed by maybe fifteen minutes of socializing, provided I stay for the bad coffee and doughnuts. Chances are, I'm not going to find anyone at church who can make me laugh even half as much as Maxine does. That woman can spin a yarn, as we say back home in Illinois. When Maxine tells me all about some rivalry between a Betty and a Patty over whose maid got her tennis whites the whitest, I'm enthralled. It's like I'm right there, in this other universe with the upper crust of exotic Palm Springs.

And yes, I do worry about her. I've known a lot of sadness, or rather, sad people, in my day. Maxine is that, in addition to angry. She doesn't break anything or beat on people. Well, at least not physically. All of her anger she directs at herself. She stubbed her toe last week while on the phone with me and I heard her muttering under her breath, "Stupid girl. Stupid, stupid girl." And the drinking. Oh my gosh, the drinking. I realize she was in here on a particularly bad day, but that was not novice-level imbibing. That was a quantity of consumption a person takes years building up to. I bet she could toss back a handle of Johnnie Walker and still put her lipstick on straight. Not sure if that's something to be proud of or not.

I flick on the neon OPEN sign at 10 a.m., and seconds later I hear the bell over the door ding. Maxine makes quite the entrance, walking quickly into the room, stopping, looking around as if it's the first time she's seen the joint, and then dramatically rushing to the bar.

"Robert, dear!" she exclaims, whipping off her sunglasses to reveal two bloodshot eyes rimmed with what looks like smeared soot. With a flourish, she sets a fondue pot on the bar. "Please tell me you remembered to buy some Gruyère and Swiss!"

Last time we spoke, she mentioned a fondue pot that she "smuggled out of the divorce" and was shocked to learn that I don't usually have the appropriate cheeses lying around. "I got the cheese and the bread," I tell her. "But don't you want to wait until dinner?"

She flounces behind the bar and gets right to fussing over the fondue, adding a pinch of mustard powder and too much white wine. "I haven't any food in the house and I am in dire need of a drink, so fondue for early lunch it is!"

I get some music playing on the jukebox, because if I don't pick at least three hours' worth of songs, she will, and I cannot handle any more Neil Diamond.

"What have you been up to lately?" I ask her, getting behind the bar to make her a Bloody Mary.

"I've been toying with the idea of joining a country club again," she tells me. "Do you know which one the politicians are members of?"

"Not a clue," I tell her honestly. "You thinking of a run for office?"

"Oh, hell no! I'm thinking about finding a politician to court me," she says matter-of-factly.

"That's a terrible idea," I blurt out before I can stop myself. I see her eyes fall onto her drink as she takes too big a sip. "Politicians are far too stuffy for you," I add, hoping to save myself from my rude comment. "You've been through too much and are far too bright a spirit to settle for a boring man."

She smiles, thank goodness. "That was a very poetic way of saying that I'm too big a nutcase to be a politician's wife."

"Not what I meant, Maxine," I say gently but firmly.

She shrugs and rather than stab me with a fondue stick, hands one to me. We toast by crossing sticks dripping with white gooeyness.

"To the dirty beatniks who gave us fondue!" she proclaims.

"I think this is Swiss?" I say, chewing down a generous bite. "I mean, it's Swiss cheese?"

"They're probably dirty too."

We eat in silence, save for Maxine's occasional humming along to the music. By the time the fondue is mostly gone, so are her two Bloody Marys and half a bottle of Chianti. While she's in the ladies' room, I snatch the bottle and hide it in a cabinet behind the bar, hoping that "out of sight, out of mind" will prevail. It doesn't.

"Are you cutting me off, dear-heart?" she says with a raised eyebrow while tapping a red fingernail on her empty wineglass.

I pour some water in the glass, hoping the humor of it will save the day. Maxine doesn't find it funny.

"Well, look at you!" she says snidely. "You haven't even asked me out on a date yet and here you are, telling me what to do."

She really has a knack for pushing people into corners. I reach under the bar and pull the Chianti back out, filling her glass until it's half-full. Maxine stares at me, waiting for an explanation, the glass held up between us.

I finally break the silence. "I worry about you, Maxine. You seem so . . ." I don't finish the sentence, because I don't want to say the wrong thing again.

She downs the wine in one gulp. "Why?" she asks me, very quietly.

"What?" I say too quickly.

"Why are you worried about me?"

"Because you're my friend and a nice person—"

She interrupts me with a sharp, angry laugh. "You barely know me."

Maxine is right and wrong about this. I want to explain myself, but I also know I want to choose my words carefully.

"Maybe *know* isn't the right word, then, Maxine. Maybe *understand* is better?"

"You understand what it's like to be very suddenly meaningless, Robert?" She's stern and making her way toward indignant. "You comprehend what it is to be irrelevant? You know what it's like to wake up in a place that's utterly unfamiliar? Wearing clothes that you know you bought, but you swear actually belong to someone else?"

That last part makes me flinch. She notices it too. I can tell because she stops talking and puts her hand on mine.

"I'm new to town too," I say slowly and quietly. "I would never forgive myself if anything happened to you on my watch."

An up-tempo song comes on the jukebox. Maxine lets out a sigh and drops her head onto the bar like an overdramatic teenager.

"May I confess something to you, Robert, dear?"

"I'm all ears, Maxine."

She takes a slow, deep breath in and out. "I think I'm stuck."

"Stuck? I don't follow?"

"Well, you asked me the last time I was here what's next for me. It's been two weeks and . . . well . . . I don't have an answer. I think what I've been doing is best called 'wallowing in self-pity.'"

I know this is true, but I also don't know if she's ready for anyone to agree with her on this bit of self-awareness.

"I'm very sorry to hear that, Maxine," I tell her, hoping it doesn't sound condescending.

"No, no, I'm sorry," she says, patting my arm. I don't pull away. "Only pitiful people beg for pity, as my mother would say."

"You deserve some time to regroup." I pour her more wine because, let's face it, I'm not a shrink, I'm a bartender. To my surprise, she sips it this time.

"I'm too unskilled for meaningful work. Too old to be a first wife. Too young to be a widow. I look terrible in black and enjoy relations with men, so being a nun is out of the question. My only accomplishment outside of marrying well is winning Miss San Bernardino, which is impossible now. The only pageants left for a woman of my age are for mothers and wives, and I lack both children and a husband."

Now she downs the wine in one gulp. I pour myself some and do the same.

"What would you do if you were me, Robert?" she asks. Her big blue eyes are wet, but she's doing a good job holding back the tears.

It's a fair question. But it's also fair that I don't have an answer. None of what I say would be advice so much as commiseration. I've bounced all over since I was kicked out of college, and not once did any of those cities feel like home. Heck, "home" doesn't even feel like home. I'm the odd duck no matter where I fly to. But how do I tell Maxine any of that without it also being an open invitation to start a conversation I'm not interested in having?

More customers come in and, to my surprise and disappointment, Maxine decides she's done with me for the day. While taking an order, I look over my shoulder and see her stow the fondue pot behind the bar. I pretend I don't notice when she swipes a nice bottle of gin, leaving cash in its place.

I offer to leave the bar in the hands of the Rodriguezes and drive Maxine home. Surprisingly, she agrees. Kachina Palms is right at an intersection where the suburbs meet the middle of nowhere. Arizona's filled with lots of streets like this, bustling with homes and businesses and then you turn the corner and find nothing but red clay and tumbleweeds.

I help her out of my car and she points in the direction of her building. I've only had one glass of wine and I'm still all turned around. Everything about the three bland stucco buildings and the winding little paths makes the Kachina Palms feel like one big maze. Maxine drops her purse and then kicks it while trying to pick it up. She lets out a scream and I see a scrawny boy with a crew cut, maybe eleven or twelve years old, dart out from the pool to have a look at the commotion. He sees us and runs off.

"I think that boy is a Peeping Tom," Maxine loud-whispers while we walk up a flight of stairs.

"He's just a neighbor kid," I tell her.

"He's always carrying a notebook and a pencil. And he looks at me!"

"He's doing his homework, and of course he looks at you."

We reach Unit 23 and Maxine doesn't bother looking for her keys. The door's unlocked and she walks right in, as could any garden-variety ax murderer.

"Maxine, you didn't lock?"

"Oh, don't worry. All those Manson people are in jail."

I stand in the entryway, uncertain if I should make myself at home. Maxine doesn't flick on any lights, but there's a glow coming from what I guess is the kitchen, keeping the place from being pitch black.

"The maid has the night off," she says drolly. "Otherwise I would invite you in."

"I'm tired anyway, Maxine. And you should get some sleep yourself."

"Yes, well, I have *such* a busy day ahead of me tomorrow."

Before I can turn and walk away, she leans in and kisses me on the forehead. I can smell the wine in the air between us, but for some reason I'm unable to move.

"You should get a library card," I whisper, wondering how the heck my brain just came up with that.

Her uncoordinated hands push my head away roughly.

"That's some goddamned sage advice," she tells me. "I'll hop right on that in the morning."

I leave, closing the door behind me. I let out a sigh of relief when I hear her lock it.

Maxine Hortence

Scottsdale

December 1969–March 1970

THE GODDAMN LIBRARY? Really, Robert? I all but lay myself bare and the best advice he can muster is "get a library card"?

No wonder he's single. I've been racking my little brain over how *that's* possible, especially with that perfect head of thick, wavy hair. He's such a pleasurable man to look at. With the sleeves of his white button-down rolled to the elbow, giving the world a glimpse of his biceps flexing just so while he pierces the lid of the V8 can with a church key. Robert Hogarth might be the rarest of men—one who looks equally at home shingling a roof as he does piloting a yacht.

Alas, after "get a library card," I know that his finger has never met a band of gold simply because he is oblivious to the wants and needs of the opposite sex. He is, as they say in polite circles, "of a different persuasion." It is—as the kids say—"a total bummer." Yet what about my life as of late hasn't been a total bummer?

So, fine, Robert, I'll do it. In the interest of friendship and leaving no stone unturned, I'll get a goddamned library card. At this point, I'd resort to witchcraft and voodoo if I thought that would help.

"Excuse me," I say to the librarian at the Scottsdale Public Library. "Can you please direct me to the books on witchcraft and voodoo?" She greets me with a startled look that reminds me of Joyce Wittenburg Tully, as if puzzled why anyone would bother talking to her. I wonder if Joyce ever thinks of me. I know for a fact that my Thanksgiving was the most excitement she's ever experienced. If Joyce had any brains, she'd see my absence as a way to climb up a ring or two socially. But that girl's just never had any get-up-and-go.

"I'm a new resident," I finally say in my most businesslike voice, "so I'll be needing a library card as well."

The frumpy librarian clutches at her heart. "We don't carry that sort of material here," she whispers harshly at me. "Why don't I get you a new resident packet, courtesy of the Scottsdale Welcome Wagon?"

She hands me a tote bag filled with crap. When her phone rings, I grab the first book I see and run out.

The holidays hit and I'm fa-la-la-la'd deeper into misery. I lie and tell Robert I'm spending the holidays with my mother in San Francisco. In reality, I hide in the condo with a stack of gossip rags and takeout. Christmas comes without a single card, although I don't know why I'm so surprised. Normally, on the first Tuesday of December, we girls would all gather at Evelyn's home and write out our Christmas cards together over tea cakes and coffee. Did everyone send their cards to Mr. and Almost Mrs. Douglas Simmons this year? No, make that Mr. and Whore Douglas Simmons. Or did that Jennifer take my seat at Evelyn's table?

God damn it, I'm so pissed I didn't get that book on voodoo. How I'd love to put a pin right through Evelyn's eye and send blood spurting all over their Christmas cards. Let's add a little gore to all those tasteful Currier and Ives snow scenes, shall we?

There is, I'm happy to say, more to Scottsdale than just quaint churches, expensive dress shops, and taverns run by handsome-yet-unavailable men. Tucked in town is a tiny, narrow road behind a brand-new shopping mall where I find Scottsdale Books and Newsstand. It's a dusty hole-in-the-wall bookshop run by an even dustier little man named Earl who whittles behind the counter. I wonder what Robert would think if I took up whittling? Is that enough of something to do?

"We don't have ladies' periodicals," Earl informs me without looking at me. He has droopy, dentally challenged facial features. "Try the supermarket." He sounds as gruff and parched as the landscape around him.

I pull my list from my pocketbook and silently offer it to him. He lets out a long whistle while reading it before giving me an equally long stare over the top of his crooked glasses.

I stare back while tapping my foot. "The library didn't have them."

"That's cuz they're pornographic. And the one about voodoo is too Satan-y."

More staring. It's off-putting. Someone should tell him that.

"Where did ya get these from?" I don't care for his questioning tone. My former mother-in-law spoke to me that way, and I don't imagine Earl would like to know that he sounds exactly like the seventy-year-old fixture of the Sacramento First Presbyterian Church Ladies' Prayer and Cards Club.

"They were mentioned in an *Arizona Republic* article about a recent President's Commission on Obscenity and Pornography."

He blinks at me as if clearing up his eyesight will somehow aid in his comprehension of what I just said.

"President Richard Nixon has tasked a group of lawmakers, historians, and experts on democratic civilization to determine what is and isn't pornographic for a modern, educated society. They determined none of these books to be illegal, which I take to mean they are also moral. I hardly think that the president and the venerable *Arizona Republic* would be encouraging Americans to read anything truly ghastly. Do you?"

More staring from Earl.

"I'm broadening my horizons!" I say.

"Gonna have to order them in. From Canada."

"Yes, well, do that, please."

"Gonna take four weeks."

"I could drive to Canada, find a bookstore, purchase them, and return home in less time," I inform him.

He nods toward the door while resuming his whittling. I admire his quiet firmness, although I also sort of hate him for it.

"Fine." I smile through my clenched ass. "Order them and add to it an instructional guide on stage acting."

Earl nods, folding up my book list and shoving it into his shirt pocket.

"Anything you can recommend for me to read while I wait?" I ask.

He pulls a paperback out from under the counter and, without comment, bags it and rings me up. I hand him my cash.

"Don't you need my name. For the order?"

"Nah, you're memorable."

On New Year's Eve, I crawl into bed nearly thirty minutes before midnight. I've read everything in the house, so I resort to leafing through the Welcome Wagon bag. I throw away all the flyers for churches and anything having to do with children, leaving me with restaurant menus and a refrigerator magnet with emergency numbers. A glossy brochure catches my eye, probably because I mistake it for a fashion magazine at first. At second glance, I see that the elegant woman with the radiant smile who graces the cover is also wearing a sash and crown. She's Mrs. American Pie, and unlike most beauty queens, she's not only gorgeous and sexy in a wholesome way, she's also the nation's best wife and mother.

Well, shit. I could do that.

If I had a husband and kids. Which I don't.

I toss the brochure straight in the garbage.

While digging for cigarettes, I pull out my stolen library book. It's a massive tome with an elegant white cover entitled *Napoleon in*

Exile. Exile. You and me both, short stuff. I flip through the book, stopping on a sketch of a grand mansion that looks like a Colonial crossed with a Mediterranean. Lots of small square windows next to round archways with a walled-off terrace and lavish garden out back. It's a look that immediately resonates with me. It's imposing and stately, yet unfussy.

I keep reading, and it turns out that Napoleon and I have a lot in common. He also suffered through some unpleasantness that led to his banishment. While I have my dingy, boring Scottsdale, Napoleon was dumped on some shitty rocky island named Elba off the coast of Italy. Rather than wallow or kill himself, Napoleon decided to show France where they could stick it, and built himself a goddamned castle. Granted, he was exiled along with a modest number of household staff, master craftsmen, and a boatload of riches. I have the money and good taste needed to acquire those things as well.

I like this Napoleon fellow's grit. There's a lesson to be learned here. Be Napoleon. Shake your fist at adversity. Look the cruel world in the eye and say, "Fine, I accept the misery you've bestowed upon me. I will take this steaming bag of shit you've placed at my feet and mold it into paradise." Wouldn't that twist the panties of those bitches back in Palm Springs to see little Maxine so triumphant?

As 1969 finally gives way to 1970, firecrackers go off outside. Not one or even five. More like twenty to thirty, like when popcorn hits hot grease. I rush out my front door to see that gangly boy with the crew cut shoot a Roman candle overhead. It whistles up fast like a rocket ten times its size, chased by a plume of smoke and a trail of light. I follow its path into the dark sky, and right when the fuse at the rocket's tail seems to sizzle out and fade, it explodes in bright white and yellow sparks that float down through the air.

I want the boy to light another and another until the whole sky is filled with sparks. But when he sees me, he skitters away like a frightened cat. I stay outside until all of Kachina Palms grows quiet again and the lights of the condos all snap off.

Back inside, I pull the Mrs. American Pie brochure from the trash and tuck it inside the Napoleon book. A girl can dream, right?

The second day of 1970, I wake with a plan to conquer. What I need for myself is a little Napoleon and a whole lot of beauty queen. Both probably often feel like shit on the inside, yet manage to look like winners on the outside.

First visit: Broadway Department Store furniture department.

"I need everything," I tell the salesman, not bothering to take off my sunglasses though I'm indoors. It's a look I'm starting to love.

He quickly sizes me up and, based on what he sees (first impressions!), guides me to the midcentury modern furnishings. But I'm done with those clean Danish lines and space-age chromes.

"None of this will do," I tell him. "I need pieces that say, 'Welcome to my luxurious villa off the coast of Italy and/or Spain.' Find me that."

I leave him fumbling through catalogs of heavy, dark wood and ornate wrought iron and take the escalator up three floors to ladies' fashions. I'm descended upon by a snooty salesclerk who's got Evelyn written all over her.

"No, not you," I say as if commanding my troops. "You." I point to a perky young brunette in a striped minidress. "What's your name?"

"Jenny," she tells me.

"Yeah, that's not happening." A pretty blonde in a Sharon Tate hairdo pops out of the back room in a floral maxi dress, looking every inch a lush hippie dream. "Don't tell me your name. In fact, take off that name tag and come over here and assist me."

I give Sarah—which is what I've chosen to call her—a few pages I tore from *Vogue* of a stunning photo spread about these glamorous jet-set, filthy-rich socialites who've eschewed the traditional staid costuming of the upper crust. These leggy babes are decked out in gypsy-like silk kaftans and beaded peasant blouses, armloads of silver and copper bracelets, and perfectly smudged makeup and artfully tousled hair. It's still beauty queen, but with some genuine sex appeal. Sarah manages to pull a few things together for me and is kind enough to advise I buy the rest elsewhere at a few hipper dress shops. She also proves most helpful when it comes to ringing me up.

"Do you want me to put this on your store credit card?" she asks.

"That would be perfect, dear," I tell her, doing my best to contain my glee. "It's under Simmons. Mrs. Douglas Simmons." If Napoleon could spend France's money, I sure as hell can squeeze a few more coins out of my ex-husband.

There are setbacks, especially when it comes to my condo remodel. In keeping with my shitty luck, the so-called Homeowners Association has a book of rules thicker and more restrictive than the Old Testament. As that greasy little property manager Walsh explains it, I'm not allowed to repaint the entire building or place two large stone lions at any of the entrances.

"Fine, then, Walsh," I tell him. "I'll simply place those lions on either side of my front door."

"You can't do that," he snaps back at me. "They're too big. People will need to walk around them."

"These lions were handcrafted and flown to me from a village outside Naples," I explain to him. "They are art, and I choose to believe my neighbors will take the time to pause and admire them rather than see them as an obstacle."

His blank stare tells me he knows nothing about art.

I toss the HOA manual at his feet. "I defy you to find exactly what part, subsection, paragraph, or line forbids me to have art!" He doesn't bother, which is good for him since, unlike most radicals of our time, I've read the rules and know exactly how to walk between them. Thankfully, this little standoff proves beneficial, because Walsh doesn't bat an eye when I bring in carpenters to throw up two low half walls to separate the living room from the dining room.

"Open flow" my ass. A well-balanced home needs clear-cut spaces for lounging and eating. We're not animals.

Since my new wardrobe is all about copper and velvet, I figure my home should reflect that too. I couldn't find proper window dressings, so I instead found a seamstress to whip up some deep-blue velvet curtains trimmed in bright gold silk cording. Overhead lighting simply won't do, so I've replaced all that ugliness with hammered copper wall sconces. Much to my dismay, there is a very specific HOA rule about using candles so close to one's walls, but modern technology has given us lightbulbs that come close to replicating the warm, skin-flattering glow of candlelight. My dining room table features ornate, heavy legs with vines carefully carved into the rosewood. I round out each room with additional decorative touches of shag sheepskin rugs, turquoise-colored leather floor poufs, brocade black-and-gold velvet-flocked wallpaper, and an assortment of decorative copper vases, bowls, and trays. The Napoleon book goes right in the middle of the coffee table, flanked by matching candelabras.

"Looks like Janis Joplin lives here," Walsh muses while supervising the installation of my new avocado-colored side-by-side refrigerator-freezer combination.

I persevere, my days filled with purpose to make my Elba—and, in turn, myself—the very best it can be. Within two weeks, my condo goes from writing its suicide note to being a masterpiece. While I initially decide I will smoke only on the veranda and twice weekly burn bergamot incense, I forget one morning and light up a Virginia Slims menthol in the hallway. But you know what? Tough shit. This is my castle and I'll make and break any goddamn rule I please.

I decide not to turn my nose up at the community pool. It's awash with children on the weekends, so I avoid the area entirely Friday afternoon through Sunday. During the week, however, the space is all mine, as the children are in school. As I feared, the poolside furniture situation is quite dire, so I buy my own. In keeping with my Elba theme, it's actually more of a formal chaise made of iron and linen and yes, I suppose it isn't entirely intended for outdoor use. It's a bit unwieldy lugging it down the stairs and across the cool decking to my favorite spot at the far end of the pool.

I still need to look good. I buy eyeliner and lashes that look extra mysterious on the second day of wear, after sleeping in them. But my sandals and kaftan always match and my hair and nails are more than presentable.

Everything else I need for the day—my sunglasses, Swedish Tanning Secret oil, cigarettes, magazine or novel—I bring with me in a straw tote. I also carry with me an ice bucket from the Beverly Hills Hotel, which while sleek and stylish, is also large enough to hold ice and a bottle of whatever I'm drinking that day.

I don't know any of the neighbors. Occasionally, someone will make accidental eye contact with me, which is uncomfortable for all involved. I see that scrawny boy with the crew cut everywhere. I asked Walsh if the boy was available to run errands for me. Walsh claimed it would be a violation of child labor laws and added that the boy has enough work to do dealing with his often-absent mother and baby sister. While poolside during the week, I see the boy come home every day at lunchtime, racing in and out of his condo with his school satchel flung over his back. He's in and out too quickly to be eating lunch. So what is he up to?

This is when I realize I've gone from wondering what the wealthy denizens of Palm Springs will be wearing to the annual Valentine's Dance at the Club to pondering the activities of a grubby child. My, how the mighty Maxine has fallen.

When the exile ends, I'll be thirty-nine. I'm sure that between now and then, I can find a way to shave a few years off that tally. Let's say I'm able to pull off being thirty-three when I make my triumphant return to California, this time in Beverly Hills. I've ruled out "wife" and move into contemplating actress. That would be interesting. I might be a bit too "mature" for film, but there are scads of women my fake age on soap operas. If I had that damn library card, I could get some books on the subject. And maybe a trashy novel or six. For research.

Charles "Chuck" Bronski

Scottsdale

April–May 1970

MY DAD IS off at war and I write to him every week. I've seen from watching Walter Cronkite that Vietnam is a place that's real remote. It's like if you live way out past Queen Creek on a cotton farm. The mail doesn't come in or out of the place regularly. Sometimes we get mail from Dad in these thin square envelopes with all sorts of stamps and foreign markings on them. It's been a while since I've gotten one, but Mom says that as long as the army checks keep coming, he's probably still out there in the jungle somewhere.

This morning, there's a knock on the door. It's an army man and he asks to speak to Sharla Bronski.

"She's sleeping, mister."

"Can you please wake her, son? It's important."

Even if he didn't say it was important, I would have figured, since he sounds serious and looks even more serious in his olive-green suit with matching hat. Plus, he called me "son," and grown-ups who aren't my parents only do that when they are bossing me around for a good reason. I'm halfway to Ma's room before I start to worry about what this guy's good reason might be.

Ma doesn't invite the army man in the house. Instead she closes the door behind her and they talk outside for what feels like a long time. I go to the kitchen, but the window isn't open very far and if I open it more, it will make a noise. I can't hear what the army man is saying, but Ma keeps saying that she doesn't understand. Her voice sounds all high and squeaky, and also kinda scared.

Ma finally comes back in the house holding some papers in her hand, and stomps to the bathroom. She slams the door behind her and when I knock on it, she tells me to leave her alone.

"But what's going on with the army man?" I ask. "Is Dad coming home?"

"I don't know. I don't know anything!" she yells. It sounds like maybe she's crying.

"Well, what did he give you, Ma? Can I read it?"

She shoves the papers under the door. I'm so nervous, I can barely make out the words. One of the papers is a Western Union telegram:

> The Secretary of the Army has asked me to inform you that your husband, Specialist First Class Peter M. Bronski, was reported missing in action on the western border of Vietnam on or about March 31, 1970. We will continue to attempt to update his status and will inform you of new developments.

This doesn't make a lick of sense to me. He's in Vietnam with the rest of the army, so how come they don't know where he is? I bet he overslept and missed roll call one morning.

"I'm sure he's fine," I tell Ma through the door. "You know how he's always late to stuff."

She doesn't say anything, but I also don't hear her crying, which is good. There's nothing worse than when a mom cries. I'd rather have her yell at me or toss me in my room with no supper than be around her when she's all sobby.

"You know how when he was home on leave, he told us about that time he and his buddies snuck into an Officers' Club? I bet he did that and is hiding so he doesn't get in trouble." That doesn't sound right to me. But I say it anyway to make Ma feel better.

She comes out of the bathroom and rushes past me.

"I gotta go to work. You mind your sister and stay out of trouble. That means no messing with that crazy blond lady. You got it?"

I nod. Ma caught me snooping around the lady's flashy convertible last week and just about tanned my hide. "Can I call you at work if another army man comes to the door?" I ask.

"No one's coming back today, Chuck."

We got the telegram on Saturday, April 11, 1970, at around eleven thirty in the morning. I've been keeping close track of all the days since, ticking them off on a paper since Ma doesn't have a calendar in the house. We haven't heard anything in twenty-three days. My teacher, Mrs. Gagliardi, said that lots of soldiers go missing and they're found later, maybe just a little banged up and in a hospital. War is super confusing, she tells me. So I shouldn't give up hope. I told her I never would. But just in case, I come home from school at lunchtime each day to see if an army man is waiting. And to give Dawn a diaper change. Ma's gotten real good at sleeping through her crying.

The good news is that I'm old enough to get a job working at the clubhouse after school and on weekends. Mr. Walsh, the Kachina Palms building supervisor, says that it's against the law to pay me, so I'll be doing an apprenticeship. I thought only wizards had apprentices, but I looked it up in the dictionary (we do have one of those in the house—it keeps the couch level after one of the legs busted off), and it's something junior businessmen do to learn how to be not-junior businessmen. Only in my case, I won't be a junior businessman, but the guy who keeps the clubhouse and pool area clean. Mr. Walsh is even going to show me how to fill the vending machines.

I have another job too, although I dunno if it's really a *job* job. Ma's working extra shifts at the Pink Pony, which means I'm in charge of Dawn. She's two and a half now, so that means she's a pro when it comes to getting around on her own. In the time it takes me to bend down and tie my shoe, she'll be out of her crib and climbing up the kitchen counters.

After school, me and Dawn head to the clubhouse for my first day of being an apprentice. I found one of those portable playpens in the Dumpster a few weeks ago. I cleaned it out and it works great for keeping Dawn in one place while I'm cleaning the clubhouse. She has a special shriek that tells me she needs a new diaper. Now, I know diaper changing is something moms are supposed to do, but it's 1970 and she's my little sister and all. I can't leave her sitting in her mess all day. Sometimes a man's gotta do what a man's gotta do. That's something I think I heard my dad say once. But just cuz I'm willing to do what a man's gotta do, that don't mean I'm gonna do it in public.

As Dawn and I hustle toward our apartment, I see the blond lady coming out of her place. She's a real interesting lady in that she's not like most of the ladies at Kachina Palms, who are moms or grandmas. This blond lady has big messy hair, like those rock 'n' roll girls on *Ed Sullivan,* and she's wearing high heels with feathers on them. She sits at the pool in a bathing suit that's in two pieces—a top and a bottom. It kinda makes her look like Honey Ryder in that James Bond movie. She never smiles, and all she does all day is lie around the pool, reading books. (I bet she works nights like Ma does sometimes. Her car is gone a lot after dark.) Mr. Walsh calls her all sorts of mean things, including "crazy old witch." But I also know that she gives him five dollars every time he carries her shopping bags from her car to her condo, which for a while was nearly every day.

The strangest thing about her is that she brings her own chair to the pool. It's huge, like a couch people normally keep in their house.

But here she is, dragging it down the stairs from her apartment. The thing's made of metal, so it makes one heck of a racket as she pulls it to the pool. I'll hear it go back up around dinnertime. I don't know why the chairs already around the pool aren't good enough, or why she doesn't get a bike lock to keep her big metal chair locked up when she isn't sitting in it.

I get Dawn home and all hosed down and diapered, which isn't easy since she's feeling extra wiggly today. I dunno if it's sweat or baby pee, but her clothes are all wet, so those need a change too. I didn't have time to fold the laundry, so I have to dig through the clean clothes hamper to find a dress for Dawn to wear. The phone rings twice, so I waste a bunch of time answering it. The first caller wants us to subscribe to some paper. The second call is to remind Ma that the electric bill is overdue again. I take a message for both calls and pin them up on the fridge where Ma can see them when she gets home. I don't want to be gone from the clubhouse for too long, but Dawn's going to be hungry soon, so I throw together Spam sandwiches. We don't have enough bread for both of us, but that's okay. I can just eat plain Spam. Right as I'm thinking that we better hustle back to the clubhouse, Dawn pops open her sippy cup and spills water all over herself. I figure she can air-dry, but Dawn has other ideas. She's got her wet dress half off herself by the time I find another clean one.

As we're walking by the pool again, I see the Honey Ryder lady isn't in her chair. She's floating on a raft in the middle of the pool. And unlike most people, she's facedown and not moving. As much as I really don't want to be any later than I already am for work, I need to investigate this.

I hush Dawn so we can get closer. The gate on the pool's fence creaks bad and I decide I need to start a to-do list for myself with *oil the pool gate* on it. Honey Ryder doesn't move. She's not snoring, either. Heck, I can't even tell if she's breathing.

I gotta do something. If I call the police and this lady's just sleepin', then she's gonna be hoppin' mad at me, which will get Mr. Walsh all mad at me.

There's a big wooden box off to the side of the pool where they keep life preservers. I take all of them out of the box except for two I leave as cushions on the bottom. Dawn goes in the box to keep her from running off on me. I grab the net on the long pole that I use to get leaves out of the pool. With the net out in front of me, I lurk over toward the lady.

I hold the net pole the opposite of how you're supposed to, so that I can poke the edge of the raft and sorta push it. If I can get the raft to float close enough to the other side of the pool, then I can get a better look at her or maybe pull her onto the decking. But this poking-the-raft thing doesn't work.

I swing the net pole around so I'm holding it the right way. It's a whole lot easier to control and it only takes two tries to get the net on her. Trouble is that while I'm aiming for her feet, I land the net smack-dab on her head, like she's some big blond butterfly. Make that an angry big blond butterfly.

"What the sugar!" She starts screaming all kinds of cuss words and kicks like a donkey. I try pulling the net off her noggin, but that only makes her fight me more. She falls right off the raft and into the water, still screaming. One of her feet pops up out of the water before she does. "Are you trying to kill me!" she screams while splashing around.

I throw a life preserver at her and she grabs it and throws it right back at me, knocking me in the head. I want to tell her that I'm trying to save her life, but none of that comes out of my mouth. "You need a bike lock for your chair," I try to explain. "If you lock the chair up at night, then you don't have to keep luggin' it up and down the stairs."

There's a whole lot more cursing as she climbs up the pool stairs and out of the water. Her big blond hair is stuck to her face and neck and when she rips off her sunglasses, she's got black stuff smeared all over her eyes—makeup, I bet. Even with all this mess, I can see she's a pretty lady. Almost like a movie star. She's got these big blue eyes and long black eyelashes. They're like the kind you see on girl animals in cartoons. You know, so you can tell the girl bunnies apart from the boy bunnies.

I shove my hand out. "I'm Charles Bronski. You can call me Chuck." She shakes my hand and her long red fingernails poke me a little.

"Charles," she says, looking behind me, "why is there a baby in that box?"

Oh shoot. I forgot about Dawn. I run over to her while trying to explain to the lady. "That's my sister, Dawn. I put her in the box so she wouldn't run away. I'm the one who told you where to find the spare key." I right away wish I hadn't said that.

"Maxine Hortence," she tells me, and it takes me a second to realize that's her name. "What's this about a key?"

"You couldn't get in your apartment. The day of the Dumpster fire."

Mrs. Hortence stares at me for what feels like a whole bunch of seconds. Then she puts her sunglasses back on and lies in her chair. "Well, I'm sure I don't know anything about the fire, but thank you for your assistance with the key. And the bike lock suggestion."

She pulls a book out of her bag. It's thick and red and called *The Spy Who Came In from the Cold*.

I've got no idea what to do, so I say, "If you're some kind of a spy, you need to know that I am a loyal citizen of the United States of America!"

I don't think this is at all what I should have said. I'm thinking this mostly cuz she starts laughing. It's not a laugh like she just heard a great joke. It's the laugh grown-ups make when a kid says something dumb. Not a little bit dumb like on that TV show where kids say the darndest things to that Art Linkletter fella. We're talking so dumb that I could get kicked back to kindergarten.

"Aren't you a riot!" she yells while laughing. Then she smiles at me.

"I gotta go," I tell her. I practically run back to the clubhouse.

Dawn and I get back to the clubhouse, and all I can think about is how I sounded stupid while talking to Mrs. Hortence. I've read just about every Hardy Boys book there is and seen a whole bunch of *Dragnet* reruns, and I still don't know how to interrogate someone. Now I'm stuck in this clubhouse, trying to get my baby sister to eat her dang lunch.

"Whatever are you shoving in that precious baby's mouth?"

I'm startled and snap my head around so fast, my neck muscles burn. Mrs. Hortence stands in the doorway. I didn't even hear her sneaking up on me.

"It's only a Spam sandwich," I say to Mrs. Hortence and Dawn. "A Spam sandwich, flying into the airport!" That part I only say to Dawn while flying the sandwich at her mouth, which is hanging open from all her screaming.

"Spam is ghastly and darling Dawn knows it," Mrs. Hortence tells me, like she's angry at me.

"Well, it's all we got at the house, so she's gotta eat it."

Mrs. Maxine takes her hands off her hips, like she's suddenly changed her mind about being all huffy with me. I don't know what the big deal is about me feeding my sister a Spam sandwich, but Mrs. Hortence looks like she wants to start crying. She stares at Dawn before finally reaching over and picking her up. Mrs. Hortence is a stranger and Dawn doesn't like strangers, so she starts hollering. Mrs. Hortence shoves her into my arms. "Come with me. And bring the Spam."

I stand in the doorway to Mrs. Hortence's condo. I know that I shouldn't go into a stranger's home, but people have been going in and out of her house working on it and even from out here I can tell it's not like the other condos at Kachina Palms. I go in and leave the front door open, just in case me and Dawn need to make a quick getaway.

Mrs. Hortence's condo looks the same as ours as far as all the rooms being in the same place. But everything else is different. I don't mean "different" like she's got a couch that's a different color or something. I mean "different," as in the whole place looks like it's from a movie about genies or pirates. For a second I thought she had candles lighting the place, until I see they're lamps that look like candles. There are fancy rugs on top of the already fancy carpet. The whole place smells like perfume and oranges. The only normal thing in the condo is a TV, but even that is the biggest TV I've ever seen. I bet it's in color. That's when I realize that while all of us have condos, Mrs. Hortence has a lair.

"Your condo is super nice, Mrs. Hortence."

"That's because it's much more than a condo. It's my Elba. Do you know what that means?"

I don't, and she tells me an "Elba" is a special place that someone uses to plan their return to power. I still don't get it. I don't tell her that though, since I've already been dumb enough around her today.

"Do you know who Honey Ryder is, Mrs. Hortence?" I ask her.

"You can stop with the Mrs. Hortence business," she tells me. "I'm Miss Maxine."

"Okay, Miss Maxine," I say. It sounds funny to be calling a grown lady by her first name, but I guess if *Miss* is in front of it, it's all right.

"Now come here with your sister so I can teach you something."

I put the Spam sandwiches down on the kitchen counter and take Dawn. Miss Maxine opens her fridge and I guess I'm surprised. I always thought that fancy people would have a fridge filled with food, but hers is almost empty. She pulls out a bunch of jars and brown bags of stuff and puts them all out in a line on the counter.

"Have you ever painted before, Charles?"

"Painted? Like a wall or something?"

"Okay, well, have you ever drawn a picture of anything? On a blank piece of paper?

I nod. I don't know what this has to do with Spam sandwiches, but I sure am ready to eat.

She takes the bread off the sandwiches and puts the Spam on two matching plates, cutting it up into smaller pieces with a knife. "You need to think of Spam as that blank sheet of paper. It's nothing on its own." She squirts some mustard on one of the pieces of Spam. "But if you add something to the paper, then it's art."

Miss Maxine offers the Spam covered in mustard to Dawn. She wiggles hard in my arms and screams.

"And like art, you'll find that not everyone likes it."

"She likes ketchup on her hamburgers," I say.

Miss Maxine digs into one of the brown lunch bags and pulls out a handful of ketchup packets. She tears one open with her teeth and squirts it onto another piece of Spam. This time, Dawn eats it right up while kicking her feet all happy-like.

"Now let's see what you like," she says to me, dumping out more of the brown lunch bags onto the counter.

"How'd you get all these sauces and stuff?" I ask her later, in between bites of my Spam and duck sauce, which Miss Maxine says ain't really made of duck.

"I'm thrifty," she says back to me.

"Nifty," I think I say. I don't know what *thrifty* means, but I suspect it means you're some type of specialist in Spam. Dawn keeps trying to gobble up all of my chow, so Miss Maxine takes her from me. I know I shouldn't let a stranger hold my sister, but Miss Maxine is a grown lady and grown ladies are all like moms anyway. Besides, Dawn doesn't like being held and after she lets out one scream, Miss Maxine hands her right back to me. I'm good at holding Dawn tight in one arm while I eat with the other. I give her a packet of duck sauce to chew on to keep her busy.

"How'd you know so much about Spam sandwiches?" I ask next.

"It's rude to ask too many questions, Charles." This is funny because she starts asking me questions. "Where's your mother all day? I never see her."

I tell Miss Maxine about Ma working at the Pink Pony and about Dad being in Vietnam. I don't want to tell her about the telegram and the whole "missing in action" thing, but I do anyway.

"That's dreadful, Charles. I'm so sorry to hear that." Her voice is all soft, like she really means that she's sorry.

She puts her packets of mustard, ketchup, duck sauce, and something called soy sauce, soup crackers, and regular crackers into a lunch bag. She hands it all to me.

"Take it and use it when you need it." Miss Maxine sounds super serious, like she's giving me directions I need to follow to the T. "Don't keep it in your kitchen at home. Maybe put it in your room. You have a room?"

I nod. A real strong nod.

"Keep it there. Maybe in a hiding spot. That way it will always be there when you need it. No one but you will use it."

I nod again. Of course I have a hiding spot, I want to tell her. All spies do. I bet she already knows that.

Maxine Hortence

Scottsdale

April 1970

LOOK AT ME, meeting the neighbors! At least I don't need to worry more about having a budding Peeping Tom in the neighborhood. Charles is merely a put-upon boy. His childhood and mine are plenty similar, what with being at the mercy of strangers or far-flung relatives while our mothers are off doing what have you. At least Charles and Dawn's mother keeps a roof over their heads.

Charles's thinking that I could pass for some sort of Lady James Bond makes me think that all these spy novels and that acting book I got from Earl are paying off. If I'm to use my time in my Elba constructively, I need to find exactly who I'll be once this whole ordeal is over. I've abandoned the whole "politician's wife" idea as far too staid and conventional. The so-called dirty books Earl ordered more than proved that to me. All those seedy adventures of the young, beautiful, and largely undressed inside those paperbacks make me yearn for a life I could have enjoyed had I not decided to become a wife at age twenty. I've conjured up a new persona to try on for a while. If anyone asks, I'll claim it's training for a potential career in the theater. It's not entirely a lie.

That's when I remember that darling Spanish adobe church on Main Street. I do believe I have found something to do, Robert.

I spend three days planning everything out about the character I intend to play. I purchase a long black wig and a dowdy beige dress on sale. With my E-Type being so flashy, I need to park it a block away from the church. I wait outside until I see Wednesday morning Mass let out, and sneak in when I hope no one is looking.

I dart inside the confessional and can scarcely believe it when I begin to tremble. The little window opens with a swoosh and I realize I am *actually* doing this. I bet this is exactly how Judy Garland felt the first time she took to the stage!

"You may begin," says a gentle baritone.

I panic. What if priests have some divine power?

He sighs. "I'll help you along then. 'Forgive me, Father . . .'"

"What?" I'm honestly not getting the hang of this.

"Repeat after me, and I'm sure it will all come back to you. Can you do that, dear?"

"Yes . . . Father." *Get on the ball, Maxine!*

"Forgive me, Father . . ."

"Forgive me, Father . . ."

"For I have sinned . . ."

"For I am sin."

"Close enough."

"I'm so sorry, Father. I'm quite nervous," I say in a breathy Marilyn Monroe voice. This isn't the voice I initially wanted to use, but I think I need to work up to a British accent. And let's face it, what woman *can't* do a Marilyn voice?

I tell him my name is Sabrina and then he cuts me off to remind me that there are no names used during confession. This throws me, because he's limiting my character choices by keeping this so impersonal. I've meticulously planned this moment, although I am not as they say on Broadway "off book." I pull from my handbag some notes I've prepared on index cards, a sort of loose script for me to follow. I regain my footing, telling him that I'm devastated over my extramarital affair with a painter from Paris named Paul. I have so many glorious details I want to share about this Paul, but I'm also so nervous, I can't see the note cards well in the dim light of the confessional. It's a good thing I went with the Marilyn voice, since I am most certainly barely able to breathe in this moment. The priest clears his throat—twice—and tells me I need to seek forgiveness from not only God but also my husband, who I told him is named Alan.

I burst into fake tears and it feels amazing. I mean, it would feel more amazing if I could get actual tears to flow, but I have the whimpering noises down quite well. I remember seeing this movie when I was a child where the handsome leading man dived off a cliff with his arms widespread, landing with barely a splash into the ocean. That's how I feel as I vow to say the Rosary thrice daily, recommit myself to my husband, and of course end the steaming-hot affair with the painter.

I dash from the confessional and, while I'm certain no one is chasing me, I run the entire distance to my car, my chest heaving, sweat pouring from my underarms. This confession thing is without a doubt the one thing (sorry, Robert) bringing me bundles of joy. Pope Paul VI and a legion of furious nuns couldn't stop me now.

As the weeks drag on, I find myself in a fantastic pattern. I find some practical, technical advice in a book called *A Handbook of the Stanislavski Method* written by some stern-looking New York acting coach. My extensive trashy novel collection and vast imagination help me fill in the blanks of my characters. One week I'm a hippie girl who sinned with my father's best friend, contracting a horrific venereal disease. Another I'm a wretched little girl who sinned with the family gardener, but as I tell the priest, I'm sure God is "groovy" with it, since my husband is too injured to love me in a marital way. My alter egos have lain with all manner of businessmen, bankers, ranch hands, drifters, poets, and sculptors. The week my latest batch of books are late to arrive at Earl's, I decide to wing it and tell a thrilling tale of how I deflowered the bag boy down at the Totem Discount.

With each confession, I hear the eagerness growing in the voice of the priest, who I learn is named Father Simon Lundberg. By confession number four, I sense that Father Lundberg is enjoying this as much as I am. I understand now what that acting book means when it tells me that "the character comes alive if you believe in what you're doing!" I believe, and now so does Father Lundberg.

"Tell me, my child, why do you think you were so easily tempted by this man?"

"Well, Father, he smelled of Old Spice and winked at me down at the soda counter."

"And which soda counter was this?"

"The Sugar Bowl, Father."

"That's on the corner of Scottsdale Road and . . . ?" I can hear his pencil scratching away on his notepad.

"East First Avenue, Father. The southeast corner."

Eventually, I come to see us as creative partners in this endeavor. Like the titans of the Great White Way, Papa Lundberg and I know that give-and-take is essential to all strong performances. I always leave his church feeling loads better than when I entered. And I know I am *this close* to making myself cry on demand. I see serious potential in further developing that skill.

Robert's begged me to tell him why in the hell I do this, but I refuse to answer. Right now all I can say for certain is that I love the thrill of getting by with it. Somewhere along the way, I left feeling not so much flushed or as if I could suddenly run a three-minute mile. I felt somehow lighter. I have control over everything about myself in that confessional. It's as if for a few moments I don't mind that I'm now Maxine Hortence, a nobody from Nowheresville with no husband or babies or even any pressing social engagements. I'm freer and looser. Like I have a "life" rather than a "predicament."

The only more exhilarating thing in my whole life was when I won Miss San Bernardino. When I felt that crown hit my head,

Jesus, it was like the sky opened, the angels sang, and glitter poured down on me for hours. *That* was even better than some whispered lie in a confessional.

Lucky for me, I know exactly how to recapture that feeling. It will come the moment that beauty queen crown is placed on my head again.

Charles "Chuck" Bronski

Scottsdale

May 1970

EVERY DAY FOR the next three weeks, Miss Maxine comes to the clubhouse. She says she's decided it's "appalling" that Dawn and I eat Spam sandwiches every day, so she's going to feed us. All the food she brings is wrapped up all fancy-like in a tinfoil swan. No, really! The tinfoil neck and head is just for decoration. The belly of the swan is where all the food is. I guess that sounds kind of gross, but the food is tasty. Her boyfriend or friend or something owns a restaurant, and now Dawn and I get all the leftovers.

Then one day after school, Dawn and I are in the clubhouse when I hear Miss Maxine's heels clicking fast toward us. She walks in all dressed up and holds out a set of car keys, jingling them in our faces. At first I think she's trying to keep Dawn entertained. But then I realize she's talking to me and saying the best words I've ever heard.

"Tell me something, Charles. Do you know how to drive?"

Miss Maxine tells Mr. Walsh that since she is a paying resident of Kachina Palms and I am his apprentice, he's required by law to loan me out to her. If I learn to drive and take her on errands around town, she'll pay me actual money.

Her car. Oh my gosh, her car. It's even more special on the inside than the outside. When Miss Maxine turns it on and hits the gas, the car roars so loud, it makes my tummy rumble. At night, when I'm almost asleep, I can feel that rumble coming up from my feet. To me, this car is proof that Maxine is a spy.

This is super embarrassing, but my first lesson doesn't go so well. I always thought I was tall, but I guess I'm not since, even with the seat all the way forward, I can't see over the dashboard. I try sitting on a Sears catalog Ma has lying around, but that isn't enough. So, Maxine runs up to her condo and comes back down with a bunch of magazines taped to a Bible to make it thicker. I can't help but see that one of them magazines is a nudie one. I only know what they are because I once accidentally saw some teenagers looking at them in the alley behind the clubhouse. Miss Maxine catches me staring at it and I get extra embarrassed.

"Charles, if you're sitting on the naked people, you can't possibly also look at them."

That makes sense. Plus, I really want to drive this car.

We find another box and put barefoot Dawn in it in the backseat. I know it probably looks weird to see a baby in a box in a spy's sky-blue convertible, and weirder still when Maxine puts sunglasses on Dawn because she's worried about her getting gunk in her eyes. Dawn loves the wind.

Nobody in the movies or on TV ever tells you this, but driving is the scariest thing in the whole world. I don't know why we don't see more people driving down Scottsdale Boulevard screaming their heads off in fear. "Charles, I'm going to reach in front of you very slowly and turn on your hazards."

"What are hazards! What!"

"They are special lights that tell everyone behind us to shut up with the goddamn honking and drive around us."

There is an awful lot of honking. Then she tells me I can push on the gas (right pedal) a little more, only I can't tell what she means by "a little," and by the time she yells stop (left pedal), I've hit this big brick log-like thing in the Wild Stan's Liquor Barn parking lot.

"No worries, Charles. As long as we get to where we need to go, all is well."

It's a good thing I learned how to drive so quick, because Miss Maxine and Dawn and I have a lot of shopping to do. Dawn and I never wait in the car. We always go into whatever shop Miss Maxine's buying stuff at. She tells everyone we're her "wards," and then the person she's talking to will tilt their head a little to the side, make a frowny face, and say something like, "Ohhh, isn't that precious?" I watch *Batman* all the time, so I know what a *ward* is. It means that Miss Maxine is like Bruce Wayne and I'm like Dick Grayson. We're Batman and Robin! How cool is that? We drive around Scottsdale in our E-Type Batmobile and any day now, we're going to solve some crimes before running back to the Batcave at the Kachina Palms Condominiums.

We go to the bookstore every week. Miss Maxine reads a lot of books she says the library doesn't have. She also keeps buying me Hardy Boys books, which is great since they are sorta spies.

Miss Maxine also goes to church. She goes to church a lot, actually. It's the one place where she makes me and Dawn stay in the car. Miss Maxine says it's because what she's doing is personal.

"So it's classified intel?" I ask her one day.

"Precisely," she tells me.

Today, Dawn and I are sitting in the spy car down the street from the church, just like always. Except this time, I hear Miss Maxine yelling from around the corner before I see her. It's a good thing we have the top down, since Miss Maxine races over and doesn't bother opening the door. She hops over it and lands on her side in the front seat, ducking down like she doesn't want anyone seeing her.

"Go, Charles! Right pedal to the floor!"

I pull away fast and see someone—a guy in a dress?—running after us. Thanks to the car's amazing engine, it only takes a few seconds before we're way too far away for him to reach us. But I know that was a close one.

Miss Maxine's all sweaty and shaking in the front seat. Her face is wet and her eye makeup is all over, like she's a messy clown. I think maybe she was crying, except then I see she's smiling.

"Real tears! Real tears!" she says to me, like I'm supposed to know what that means. Is it spy code or something? "I made myself cry! Oh, Charles, I think I can pull this off!"

When we get back to Kachina Palms, she makes a big fuss about us getting out of the car real quick-like and heading back to our condos.

"I'm afraid your days of driving are done with for now, Charles. I need you to swear to me—"

She stops in the middle of her sentence and shoves the Bible wrapped in magazines out at me, putting my hand on top of it.

"I need you to promise me, Charles, that you will tell no one, and I mean no one, of our adventures as of late. Can you do that for me?"

"Yes, ma'am."

"And you swear on this Bible?"

I nod.

She runs back up the steps, taking the Bible with her. I hear the door to her Elba slam shut.

Robert Hogarth

Scottsdale

May 1970

I'VE BEGGED MAXINE to stop with the confessional hijinks, but honestly, that's the very least of it.

She's got kids now. Kids. As in actual human children. She very casually first mentions to me one night over dinner that she's met two neighbor kids who seem far too young to be so much on their own. She asks if it's okay to take any leftover food to them, and of course, I say it's no problem.

The next night, she arrives at her usual time, but completely sober. She isn't at all sober by the time I drive her home and walk her up to her unlocked condo. But I'm thinking to myself that it's a start. As she's kicking off her shoes, she puts all the leftovers in the fridge and mutters something about how much Charles enjoys anything covered in duck sauce.

"Who's Charles?" I ask.

"My ward!" she scolds me. Then she stumbles off to bed and I use the spare key she recently gave me to lock the place up.

The next night, she breezes in and out of the tavern, announcing she's merely passing through to pick up more leftovers. When I hand them over, she gives me another peck on the forehead. I don't smell any booze on her breath. In fact, she smells like floral perfume. But not in a heavy, covering-up-the-whiskey sort of way: in a pulled-together, refined-lady sort of way.

It's Thursday, meaning day four of Maxine not quite being herself. She comes flying into the bar with two kids—an adorable baby and that gangly boy I've seen lurking around Kachina Palms. In a rush of excitement and amid the baby's crying, Maxine demands I let them all into the back room. I oblige her, mainly because she looks on the verge of emotional collapse, and once the four of us are standing in my office, she crumbles further.

"What in the blazes, Maxine!" I say quietly, although I don't know why, since the room is so small that these two big-eyed children are going to hear us no matter how softly we speak.

"We were at the church—"

"You took the kids with you?"

"We waited in the car, sir," the boy tells me.

"Who is this?" I say to Maxine, who is pacing giddily. "Who are you?" I say to the boy.

"Chuck Bronski, sir. This here is my sister, Dawn. I'm Miss Maxine's driver." He puts his hand out for me to shake, so I do.

"Robert Hogarth. Maxine's bartender." *Wait, her what?* "How old are you, Chuck?"

"Twelve."

"Sixteen," Maxine says over him.

This is not good. I know that, as a bartender, my job is to listen and help out when able. But dragging kids into her madness?

"Maxine, a word?"

I pull Maxine into the adjoining room where I keep my bed and belongings. Bringing her in here was clearly a mistake, since she's instantly preoccupied with a photo of my parents and sister.

"What in heaven's name are you doing with two kids? That boy is clearly not of driving age."

"I told you, I've taken on two wards. Who's this?" She points to a photo my sister sent me of her wedding day.

"That's Holly. My sister. Their mother made *you* their guardian?" I might have put too much negative emphasis on the "you."

"Yes, Robert, I've been deemed worthy of helping out two children. So sorry if that shocks you!"

I apologize for my tone and Maxine proceeds to tell me how she's had it up to here with Chuck and Dawn's mother, some "barfly" named Sharla, never being around.

"Charles said that he woke up once not long ago to find a man in the family bathroom whom Sharla claimed was his 'uncle.' I'm telling you, Robert, if you had seen the look on Charles's face when he told me that he has 'lots' of uncles! And how much he wishes that some of the ones he hasn't seen in a while would stop by, and yet they never do. It damn near shattered my heart into a million pieces!"

I don't know how good or bad Maxine had it growing up. In fact, she's never once mentioned anything about her childhood. It's like her entire life started the day she won that beauty pageant and met Douglas. I want to think that Maxine's caring for these kids strictly out of the goodness of her heart. But it doesn't always feel that way. I can't help but worry if this is just Maxine trying on a new role for herself. What happens to the kids if she gets tired of playing mother? I keep this to myself for now.

After Maxine takes the kids home—with promises that she'll do all the driving from now on—I start to think about my own childhood, and I realize who Maxine reminds me so much of.

When I was about Chuck's age, my great-uncle Clyde passed away from a train accident that wasn't accidental in the slightest, unless of course he really did fall asleep on the tracks. My widowed great-aunt Edna moved in with my family. I recall helping my mother prepare the guest room downstairs, promising that I would always bring Great-Aunt Edna fresh flowers from Mrs. Shipley's garden for that vase on the bedside table. My older sister was already helping my father at our family restaurant, leaving me anxious to do my part around the house.

But none of this happened after Edna made that room her own. She never once went to church and rarely emerged. Barring major holidays, she ate all her Sunday suppers in her room, not even looking at me when I'd bring her a plate. The one exception was her Wednesday-morning walk, which she took without fail. I heard my parents whispering often about not having any idea where Edna went. I felt the solitary walk was unsafe and to be honest, I also read my fair share of Hardy Boys books and this was as close to a mystery as I was going to get in Libertyville. I decided to follow her.

Edna walked slowly, but with purpose, from our home on Third Street the several blocks to the main drag, Milwaukee Avenue. I thought at first she would stop in at Lovell's Pharmacy, but she kept walking, past the library and public rose gardens, skirting the edge of Butler Lake, all the way to the cemetery where Great-Uncle Clyde was buried. There, I hid behind a tree and watched in shock as she stomped on Clyde's grave and then spit—spit!—on his tombstone. It was the first time I'd ever seen a lady spit, and she did it with such vigor and precision that I pictured her as a dragon spewing fire over a squadron of knights. Then she cursed a blue streak before slinking off to the side of the mausoleum hidden from the street. I watched from afar as she drank from a small black flask she had tucked in the pocket of her housedress. There was more swearing in between sips, but never any tears. I think that's the part that startled me the most. I'd expected frail crying and got stomping and swearing instead.

I felt terrible for watching this sad ritual. Every time I'd decide to tell my parents about it, something would stop me. I'd tell myself that these weekly fits at the cemetery made Edna feel better. Yet if that was the case, wouldn't she eventually stop doing it? Edna lived with us for years and I followed her three other times. It was always the same, right down to my doing nothing. Not even offering an arm to lean on for the walk home.

When I was fifteen, Edna moved into my cousin's house. My mother was upset, thinking that she hadn't been hospitable enough. I knew it was simply because Edna's legs weren't what they used to be and my cousin's home was much closer to the cemetery. I wanted desperately to share the secret of Edna's Wednesdays with my mother to ease her concern, but I said nothing.

Weeks after the move to my cousin's house, they found Edna dead behind that mausoleum. Everyone assumed she knew she was nearing her end and wanted to be close to her beloved Clyde. I knew differently, but again, kept my mouth firmly shut. What good would it do? Why make everyone feel as guilty as I did? Besides, I had so many other secrets at this point that keeping them all to myself was second nature.

When I met Maxine, I instantly felt that same pain and anger coming off her that I once knew from Edna. If my friendship and those kids keep Maxine from slipping into the same dark space Edna languished in, then how could it be a bad thing? Maybe I'm here to help Maxine grapple with her grief and steer her in the right direction. I can't yet say what she brings to my life—at least not beyond being a fun-loving, always unexpected break from the loneliness of bachelorhood.

A week or so later, I leave the tavern and head over to Maxine's. It's dark out and yet there's Chuck, leaving with his cute baby sister on his hip. Maxine took them all to the movies to see some crazy Western with a bunch of singing cowboys.

"It was kinda hokey," Chuck tells me, "but Dawn loved it!" I give him a pocket notebook so he doesn't need to lug around the full-sized one. Maxine told me he'd been asking for one.

"Cool!" he yelps before composing himself. "I mean, thanks, Mr. Robert."

I'm surprised to find the door to her condo locked. Miracles do happen! I hear Maxine moving around in there, so it doesn't seem right for me to use my key. I ring the bell instead. It startles the hell out of me to not hear a ding-dong, but rather "Ode to Joy."

"Darling!" she yells. "You're just in time for dinner and *Hawaii Five-O*."

This couldn't be more concerning to me. Maxine never feeds me. I feed her. Plus, one look around her condo tells me that she's spent some time since I was last over here (which was days ago?) turning her den of iniquity into something that more closely resembles Beaver Cleaver's home. The ashtrays are emptied and I don't see a single soda can lying out. And my goodness, is that a copy of *Ladies' Home Journal* on her coffee table?

She's in the kitchen cooking me up some breakfast for dinner—scrambled eggs, sausage, and there're two English muffins in the toaster. "The kids said they enjoyed the cowboy movie," I finally say.

"I know you're thinking I had them out too late. Well, I figured since their mother is nowhere to be found, it's better they spend the bulk of their time around adult supervision."

"Nowhere?" I ask. "Did she run off?"

"She might as well have," Maxine scoffs, adding salt and pepper to the eggs. "Charles almost got detention because Sharla can't take three seconds out of her day to sign his report card. So I did it. And there's never any food at that house."

"They're lucky to have you, Maxine," I say hesitantly. "Seems like you've really taken a liking to them as well." I need to gently probe further. "I bet a lot of people wouldn't do for them what you have."

She flips the sausages with a look of pure-as-snow innocence. "Two clearly neglected children have crossed my path and I am doing the right thing by taking them in as much as I can."

I've been wanting to broach this delicate subject with her since I first met the kids. Here's my opening. "Have you considered maybe contacting the authorities?"

She slaps a pat of butter on each of the English muffins. "And have them sent to some awful foster care? Do you think I'm a terrible influence on them or something?"

"Not at all," I say. "In fact, I've never seen you so happy."

"Yes, well, they need looking out for and heaven knows I have the time and money to do so."

She pushes past me with a plate piled high with my dinner and motions for me to follow her to the dining room table. I sit next to her and smile. Because who wouldn't? But it also seems like there's something afoot here I'm not yet aware of.

Maxine lights up a cigarette. "Did you know that they give awards—beauty pageant awards—to women who excel at being a wife and mother? It's true."

I smile and nod while thinking to myself how if there were awards for changing the subject, Maxine would have a gold medal.

Maxine Hortence

Scottsdale

May 1970

I SWEAR TO CHRIST, Robert sometimes acts like seeing me with children is akin to seeing King Kong playing checkers with the pope at the White House. As much as I'd love to say that he's jealous he's not the only person in my life anymore, I know that's not really true. I find myself daydreaming often about throwing every man in the world into a bubbling lava pit, or trapping every last one of them in a room with poisonous snakes, or maybe just instituting a world-wide castration program (the discarded products of which would then be fed to ravenous dogs). Yet each and every time I let my mind wander in that direction, I stop myself. *What about Robert?* I think to myself. He's truly a good man.

And it's high time that he learns to trust me. That Berlin Wall he's thrown up around himself is coming down. And unlike Dick Nixon, I'm willing to resort to force if need be.

Plus, I need to see if we can turn some heads. A sort of two-birds-one-stone situation, if you will.

I arrive at La Dulcinea right around dinnertime, overdressed and looking fabulous. Robert has no idea I called ahead and told Consuela that I was planning a special night out for the two of us. Robert's surprised when Consuela takes his waiter's pad and tells him to fetch a suit coat and tie from his backroom hovel.

"Where are we going?" he asks, nervously retying his tie.

"For a night on the town."

"Is it your birthday or something?"

"Sure," I tell him, furious at myself for not coming up with that in the first place. "And before you say a word, it's my treat. I know how the tavern is struggling and I'm flush."

I let him drive the E-Type, but I don't tell him exactly where we're going. Instead I tell him to turn left or right until we end up at the restaurant at the Biltmore Hotel, at the base of Camelback Mountain. I've read that Marilyn Monroe came here in 1955 to dry out after a disastrous affair. I can see why, what with all the delicate white lights dotting the grounds and perfectly manicured courtyard.

I take Robert's arm and he tries to pull it away. I laugh it off. "I'm not going to bite, dear-heart."

He relents because despite his walls and what he's hiding behind them, Robert is a gentleman. He stiffens as we walk through the crowded dining room to our table. As I hoped, heads turn and couples whisper to each other. There's a big charity auction scheduled in an hour in the Aztec Room, so anyone who's anyone in Phoenix is here.

As we're seated, Robert's nervous leg accidentally bumps into the table, knocking our water goblets. "I don't like being on display like this, Maxine," he whispers, noticing we are sitting right in the center of the restaurant.

"We make for a lovely couple, Robert. There's no shame in that."

"They're staring."

"I'm sure it's at me." I point down to the plunging neckline on my violet silk maxi gown.

He looks wan, so we order Caesar salads quickly and I insist on him having a full glass of wine. This unwinds him a bit, although his eyes keep darting off in all directions.

"Why do you always leave the last bite of food on your plate, Maxine?"

I'm not shocked he's noticed I do this. It's sweet. "I knew this girl in high school who said that if you want to find a husband, be sure to always leave at least one bite left over on your plate," I explain. "I'm beginning to think that girl was full of shit." I feel a tiny twinge of I don't know what for not telling him that I learned that stupid superstition from my mother.

"Robert, I have something important to discuss with you."

"I figured as much," he tells me. "Why don't we leave and discuss it in the car?"

"This won't take but a minute." I pull my notes from my purse and look him dead in his gorgeous blue eyes. "You and I are going to cut the shit tonight, Robert."

"We have shit that needs cutting?" He stifles a fake laugh.

"Buckets of it."

Robert runs his hands through his goddamn fantastic head of hair. I clear my throat with a sip of water (yes, water!) and begin to lay out the shit we need to cut.

"Ever since I met you, Robert, I've been trying to understand why it is that I have no desire for you."

He looks like I just told him I ran over his dog and does he please have a shovel I can borrow to scrape the remains off the road.

"We're friends, Maxine."

"I have had lots of friends in my lifetime, dear, and none are as handsome as you."

He leans back in his chair, desperate to find more distance between us. I stay in my seat, fighting the urge to get closer. With a deep breath, I dive in.

"You're a bit . . . peculiar, aren't you, Robert?"

"I'm terribly normal. Boring, even." He swallows hard. Part of me wants to kiss him on the forehead and run home. I can't do that though. *How to Win Friends and Influence People* says that humor is the key to sticky wickets like this one. I've prepared my remarks with that in mind.

"You wear loafers?" I ask.

Robert quickly points to his shoes, which are indeed loafers. "I bought them at JCPenney—like everyone does."

"Would you say you stand lightly in those loafers?"

"I have no idea. Watch me walk out the door and you tell me." He makes a gesture to get up but stops himself when I reach for his arm. "I really think we need to talk in the car, Maxine," he says quietly, while giving a smile and nod to the young couple finishing dessert at the table next to ours.

I am undaunted.

"You are a man who always rings twice?"

"That would be rude," he retorts. "But I did enjoy that movie." He rubs his neck as if it aches. Or maybe he's looking for the knife I'm slowly shoving in. God damn it, I hate doing this, but he's left me no choice.

"You're in the way of the uncles?" I read from my prepared remarks.

"My sister has two kids. Yes, I am an uncle."

"You throw parties with an open guest list?" I realize I said that too loudly, and bring it down a notch.

"How would I know how much food to make?" He takes a joking tone with this one. That's good, right? If we can laugh about the uncomfortable things in life, then surely we can talk about them openly.

"You're a gentleman of the piers!"

He pauses and looks around the room. A much older couple with precise posture likely due to the sticks up their asses sits one table over from us. Rather than engage in dinner conversation with each other like normal people, they decide to stare accusingly at us. The frizzy-haired wife gives me a quiet tsk-tsk. As if I'm going to take my social cues from a woman who looks like her hair was permed by a dog groomer. Yet Robert's rapid eyes keep falling on them.

"Don't look at them," I tell him sternly. "Look at me. I'm here, trying to talk to you."

His eyes fall on the door to the kitchen behind us. "We live in the desert, Maxine. There are no piers."

I'm at the bottom of my list and, well, out of ideas.

"You're . . . an evening botanist!" I nearly scream, again drawing the eye of the nonspeaking couple, and to be fair, a waiter or two. The poodle-permed wife holds her fork aloft, refusing to shove her chicken Kiev into her terse little mouth until she's certain I've noted her displeasure with me.

Robert laughs. It's a laugh that's pure performance, as if he wants the whole restaurant to know how hilarious I am. I'm merely telling a funny joke over dinner. I'm certainly not attempting to assure my now best friend that his secret is safe with me so he can drop the act.

I abruptly stand up at the table, tossing my napkin down. I grab a wad of cash from my purse and reach over to set it by Robert's plate, to assure no one thinks the lady paid for this meal.

"Fine. Let's talk outside then," I growl softly.

I don't look back, but I can tell he's not behind me as I speed through the restaurant. Once I hit the lobby, I can hear his rushing steps. I stop in the courtyard and light up a cigarette, giving him time to catch up to me.

"Maxine . . ." He puts a patronizing hand on my shoulder. I want to shove it off or break it in two, but I don't.

There's no one around, so I let loose. "I've told you everything, Robert. I hold nothing back from you in our friendship, trusting you implicitly. Things I couldn't imagine telling anyone else on earth about that dreadful marriage and my Elba. Yet you don't recip-rocate any of that trust. I think I've proved myself to be a woman who understands the whole glass-houses-and-stones thing." I look to him for a response.

He gives me nothing.

"That's what hurts, Robert."

"Maxine . . . I don't understand this conversation."

"Oh, Robert!"

I watch him stand up straight. He squares his shoulders and raises his chin, like a man in a beer commercial. Like a man about to climb on a horse and ride off into the sunset.

I'm crying and despite my newfound ability to cry on demand, I find it impossible to make myself stop crying when need be. While I know my tears are real, I understand that Robert might be suspicious.

"I'm not faking being upset, Robert. This is hard for me."

"It's hard for me too, Maxine. I don't know what you want from me."

"You know, Robert, I'm an open book to you. You know the good and the bad, because that's what friendship is. Two people giving a shit about each other."

"When have I not been there for you?" he snaps at me, clearly frustrated and yet unwilling to tell me what I need to hear to make all of this awfulness stop. "I feed you *and* I make you drinks!"

"You are deliberately missing my point, which is that you tell me nothing about yourself despite knowing—which is a form of taking, I might add—everything about me."

"I am your friend. I'll always be your friend."

"Because you can't be anything else?" I whisper. "Or because you truly care for me?"

"Can't it be both?" he mumbles.

I look at him and see his jaw locked tight, his shoulders forward and tense, the tiny lines around his eyes when he squints. It's the way someone looks when they're feeling trapped.

"It can definitely be both, Robert," I tell him softly.

I drive us back to La Dulcinea without a word between us.

Robert Hogarth

Phoenix

May 1970

MAXINE IS A NO-SHOW FOR DAYS. Thursday night after La Dulcinea closes at 11 p.m., I decide against stopping by her condo. Maybe we need the time apart until relations between us normalize again. I can't decide if it's better for us to spend time together in public or in private. In public, she's maybe less likely to bring up the Topic again. But on the other hand, if we're in private, I don't need to worry about anyone overhearing if she does bring it up, and I can walk out her door if need be. Mostly, I don't want to think or worry about anything right now. I'm all keyed up and know that my insomnia is definitely going to defeat me tonight. Rather than go home, I decide to have a beer or two elsewhere.

Normally, when I want to have a beer in a bar I don't own, I drive the two hours south to Tucson to a place called the Graduate. It caters to guys like me, and while I'm always looking over my shoulder when walking into the signless building, I'm fine once inside. Sometimes I'll even talk to someone, provided he comes up to me first. The last time I was at the Graduate, one of the bartenders, a sweet southern boy name Eric, told me about a new place opening in Phoenix that I should check out. Of course, it's all hush-hush, but if I give Eric's name at the door, they'll let me right in. Eric also mentions he'll be there every night opening weekend, which is a heck of a good incentive for me to work up the courage to drink a beer in my own town.

I'm not completely oblivious to my realities, which is why I leave my car at La Dulcinea and walk a little over a mile to the address Eric gave me. It's on a quiet, empty street where all the storefronts are closed for the evening. There's no sign out front and the windows are carefully covered with black paper. I don't bother checking the front door, which is certainly locked, but I know it's the right place. I head to the dark, rocky alley around back and thank my lucky stars that La Dulcinea doesn't need to require its patrons to slink through a hole in a chain-link fence. Eric's name gets me in no problem, although the friendly, incredibly large doorman does helpfully tell me that Eric doesn't usually show up until after midnight. I can wait.

The bar isn't much—some mismatched tables and chairs and a few barstools—but everyone is smiling and a couple of Everyday Joes even dance to the transistor radio sitting by the cashbox. There's nothing on the walls, no fancy bottles on display, and no beer taps, but my bottle of Bud is cold thanks to the coolers filled with ice. It's good and dark and yet with the bar's tiny size, I can still see from one end to the other.

I let myself picture how hilarious it would be to bring Maxine to this unnamed dive. She'd find the hole in the fence exciting and probably say something utterly inappropriate to Mr. Muscles at the door. He wouldn't flinch, since I'm sure he's heard it all. Maxine would demand some ice from the coolers and a napkin to wipe down the barstool before setting her velvet-clad keister down on it. And beer in a bottle? What was she, raised in a barn? She'd tell me to remind her that the next time we pay the place a visit, she needs to at least bring some mixed nuts from La Dulcinea. Knowing Maxine, she'd bring enough to feed the whole bar. I'm embarrassed to admit it, but I'm so deep in Maxine thoughts that I don't notice the gentleman who's suddenly sitting beside me.

"Evening," he says with a polite nod. He's in a well-pressed button-down, chinos, and—yes, Maxine—loafers. His sandy-blond hair is a little too short, revealing a tan line that runs from his ears all the way around his nicely sized noggin. I can't tell in the dim light if his eyes are blue, green, or hazel, but he gives me a little smile and I decide they could be bloodred and I wouldn't care.

"Evening," I finally remember to say back. I will never be good at this.

"Come here often?" he blurts out. Maybe he's no good at this either.

"Nope. First time. Stumbled upon the place." I laugh nervously. He's drinking water. A nice teetotaler. I could certainly do worse. "I own a bar not far from here, in Scottsdale."

He nods and smiles. "Sounds like you're new in town," he says. "Most people from around here use Phoenix and Scottsdale interchangeably."

"The Phoenix Metro Area. Valley of the Sun," I say before realizing how stupid I sound. I take a swig of my beer. "I'm from the Midwest. Chicago. Moved recently." What is it about being around a good-looking guy that makes me incapable of speaking in full sentences? I need to start taking pointers from Maxine.

"I was born and raised out here," Mr. Sandy Blond tells me. He looks at his watch and then around the room. I bet he's waiting for his date to show up.

What would Maxine say to him? I think to myself. "Has the Valley of the Sun changed much since you were a kid?" I ask him. I think his eyes are more hazel than blue.

He pulls his shirt cuff down over his watch. "There's a new building or housing complex every week," he says, looking over his shoulder, but not at me. "And places like this sure as shit weren't here." He chuckles.

I join him in looking around the room. A few more guys have come in since me, and someone's turned the radio up. It's starting to feel more like a real bar and less a top-secret, grimy hideaway.

I'm debating between asking his name or asking what brought him here when the bar's not-in-use front door flies open. By "flies open" I mean that it explodes into the room with a violent crack and before I can duck, Mr. Sandy Blond is waving a badge in my face while slapping handcuffs on me. I instantly recall what a bartender in Chicago told me years ago, and go limp on the floor. I see cops storming the place, yelling and waving their batons. I feel a dull, hard thud on my head and then nothing.

I come to in the paddy wagon, cursing myself. No wonder Mr. Sandy Blond's hair was so short.

There are mug shots and fingerprints and a whole lot of waiting around in a cramped, filthy cell before the Phoenix PD allows me my one phone call. I've dreaded this more than anything all night. I dial up Maxine and shockingly—in a night filled with shocking— she answers on the third ring even though it's barely 8 a.m.

"Maxine— "

"Oh, thank Christ, Robert. I've been worried half to death." I can hear Chuck in the background asking if it's me. "Your car is at the tavern, but you weren't there and then you weren't at home. I was going to start calling hospitals!"

"There was some trouble last night. I'm—"

"At St. Joseph's or Good Samaritan?" She's breathless. And I don't think she's faking.

I don't answer. My throat feels tight and dry as my stomach drops. The hand holding the phone goes pins and needles as I grip it tighter.

"Robert! Robert! Are you there?" She's not yelling. It's a harsh, wavering whisper. "Please talk to me!"

"I'm at the jail downtown." There's a gasp. "I was at a bar. It was raided." There's a horrible pause of at least a minute or two, or so it seems.

"I know exactly what to do. Sit tight, sweetie. Maxine's coming."

The phone goes dead. I let my body slide down the wall to the floor and stay there until they put me back in my cell.

Maybe two hours later, there's a commotion in the room adjacent to the cells, which to me clearly signals Maxine's arrival. I'm led to a small, windowless room by Mr.—no, make that Officer—Sandy Blond. He sits me down in a chair in front of a table. I can hear Maxine's angry hullabaloo, but I can't make out what she's saying.

"What hand are you?" says Officer Sandy Blond.

"Excuse me?" This sounds like a trick question, and my head is pounding.

"Left- or right-handed?"

"Right," I say as he handcuffs just my right hand to the table.

"I would have guessed you were a lefty." He laughs at his own joke and leaves without another word to me. He's not as attractive in this bright light.

I wish I could laugh at my own jokes.

The commotion is right outside the door now. Maxine's voice is like a civil defense siren. Finally the door opens and Maxine shoves right past two cops and she's on me like a golden retriever puppy. She wraps her arms around my torso, clutching me to her bosom. For half a second I don't mind it.

"Oh my heavens, Robert!" She kisses me hard on the cheek, surely leaving some of her coral-red lipstick behind. "I was up all night worried to death!!"

More clutching, which I can't do much about, other than to gently pat her back with my one free hand. She's in a short white rabbit-fur coat, which seems awfully dressed up given the hour. I guess my head has stopped bleeding, since I don't see any blood ruining her coat.

"What is this?" She points an accusing finger at my handcuff. "I demand you unshackle my fiancé!"

Her what?

"Ma'am." One of the exhausted-looking uniformed cops sighs. His name tag reads SGT. JOSEPH. "He's in custody."

"Robert, I've tried explaining to this . . . officer . . . that last night you went to visit a new bar up the street from your tavern. You were merely canvassing the new competition—as any smart business owner would do—when these brutes arrested you!"

Joseph rubs his temples in frustration. "That true, Mr. Hogarth?"

"I—"

"He had no idea what sort of establishment he was accidentally walking into! How could anyone expect that sort of thing! Right, honey?"

I nod, probably too vigorously considering my brain feels loose inside my head. I'm still trying to get over my amazement at the smarts involved in Maxine's brilliant acting performance. The cops, however, aren't convinced. Officer Sandy Blond joins us, because even Bette Davis had her critics.

Officer Sandy Blond raises an eyebrow. "He's your fiancé?"

There's that word again.

"We are due to marry today," Maxine says through choked-back tears. "His children are in the waiting room, for heaven's sakes!"

This is when I realize that under the coat, she's in a white lace minidress complete with shiny white boots. It's also when time ceases to function properly for me. I no longer feel as though I'm within my own body. It's like I'm sitting on a sofa in someone's living room watching a TV show called *The Maxine Comedy Hour*, which costars someone who looks exactly like me but clearly isn't me.

What in God's name did she say about *my* children? I bet I'm still unconscious and all this is a bad dream.

"So I'm supposed to believe that the night before your wedding, your fiancé went out to a bar that he had no idea was an illegal homosexual establishment?"

Oh, Maxine, that's a darn good question.

"And what's so strange about a man wanting to enjoy a beer out on his last night of freedom?"

"At a homosexual—"

Maxine covers her ears with her white gloved hands. "Would you please stop saying that to me! How on earth would he have known that?" She sobs. "He's a red-blooded American man! He made two gorgeous children!"

"Ma'am, I was there. I sat next to him at the bar and said hello."

"You propositioned my fiancé?" she shrieks before turning to Joseph. "What sort of sick police force are you operating here? Officers attempting to seduce an innocent man minding his own business at a local bar—I should write a letter to Dick Nixon!"

Officer Sandy Blond throws his arms up in outrage. "He had to crawl through a hole in the alley fence and give a secret code to the doorman to get in."

Maxine looks toward me. In an instant, her crocodile-tear-soaked eyes plead with me to snap out of it and come to my own defense.

Miraculously, I'm able to speak. "I used the front door, Officers."

"Of course, you did, my love!" She smothers me in her arms once again. This time, I can feel actual tears on my cheek. I only wish I knew if they spring from real emotion or if that confession-booth acting is paying off.

"The front door was locked," Officer Sandy Blond tells Joseph.

I shrug. "The bar didn't look open, but when I turned the door handle, it was unlocked and I walked right in."

"It was locked," Officer Sandy Blond is emphatic.

Joseph, though, is starting to buy what we are peddling. "Did you check the front door first, Detective?"

"Sir, they're always locked. I snuck in the back and Vice used the ram and busted in."

All eyes back on me. "I walked in the front door." My voice is firm and insistent this time.

Maxine has her second wind. She pries her mitts off me and gets in Joseph's face. "Now will you please free my intended? I'll not have my wedding day further sullied by all this awfulness!" She goes so far as to stomp one booted foot.

"What's the rush?" sneers Officer Sandy Blond. Maxine is taken aback. "If you're just going to the courthouse instead of a real church, what's with all the urgency?"

My fiancée rallies, although meekly. "If you must know, Detective, I'm in the family way. Plus, what with his two children being motherless due to a horrible accident back home in Illinois, we don't feel the need to waste any more time."

I choke on the absolute nothingness in my mouth, setting off a string of coughs as I gasp for breath. Maxine is again at my side, thumping on my back as I fight to take in enough air.

"Darling, your asthma!" To the officers: "That's why he moved to the desert, you know." I nod vigorously in agreement.

"I tell ya what," says Joseph as he unlocks my handcuff. "Why don't you let me take the two of you over to the courthouse? I'll personally find you a JP and heck, you're gonna need a witness, aren't you?"

"We appreciate the offer, sir," I warble, "but—"

"Absolutely not! I don't want your name and the constant reminder of this ghastly day forever etched onto my marriage certificate! Not to mention how terrified the children will be. Kids can sense when things are off! They're like dogs before an earthquake."

No one in the room has a clue what to make of that. Maxine seems to recognize this and simply whimpers, "The children!" into her white lace hankie.

"Fine, ma'am. I understand I'm not your favorite person right now—"

"I should say not!"

"But I'm still taking you two over there and making sure you get hitched."

I'll never be able to recall much else about my wedding day beyond a few murky snippets. I guess in that sense I'm like any other groom on his Big Day. Was Father in this sort of daze when he married Mother?

Chuck and Dawn are there in their Sunday best. Little Dawn is in all white with pink ribbons in her hair. Chuck has his unruly cowlick pinned down with Brylcreem. He's in a brand-new suit that fits him perfectly. When did Maxine get him that? We get a few minutes to huddle alone as a family—dear God, what am I saying? We speak in the whispers of all good conspirators.

"Don't worry, Mr. Robert," Chuck says. "Miss Maxine told us all about your cover almost being blown. I think it's real brave of you to do all this for your country, sir. Your secret is safe with Charles Bronski! I mean, Charles Hogarth!"

Dear God, what has she told this boy? How much does he know? Does he think all homosexuals are spies or just this one?

Maxine hands me a gold ring. I try shoving it on one of my fingers.

"No, dear, that's something you're going to give to me during the ceremony."

"Did you steal these?"

"Steal? My sweet betrothed, there was no need. While I was getting dressed, Charles let his fingers do the walking and found an all-hours pawnshop. There were so many rings there to choose from."

With the light coming in the window and hitting her all-white outfit and poofy blond hair, she looks downright angelic. Like she wants me to know that she's the one saving me.

"What?" She catches me staring.

I point to what she's wearing. "You had that in your closet?"

She hesitates for the slightest of moments. "Bought it three years ago after seeing Nancy Sinatra play the Sands in Vegas. Douglas told me the hemline was 'unbecoming' of a woman my age, if you can believe that."

I laugh and it rattles my brain. "I can believe anything right now, Maxine."

There's an elderly, somewhat befuddled justice of the peace, whose hand I can feel myself shaking after Maxine all but extended my sweaty palm for me. There's talk of us needing a blood test,

MR. & MRS. AMERICAN PIE

which Sergeant Joseph was kind enough to insist wasn't needed in this case due to "extenuating circumstances." In one second, Maxine is using a comb from her purse to fix my hair and the next we're holding hands, staring at each other in front of the justice's desk, flanked by two children I have no memory of fathering.

"No guests?" says the justice of the peace.

"Just these fine officers, Your Honor," chirps Maxine. "We wanted an intimate affair, seeing how this is Robert's second marriage." She leans in a little closer to him. "We also must think of the children, you know. They loved their late mother dearly."

The justice of the peace nods and smiles. I look to Sergeant Joseph, who is unmoved, and Sandy Blond, who scowls.

Maxine pulls a ring for me from her dress pocket. She winks and I finally understand this is real.

"I, Maxine Antoinette Hortence, do solemnly swear to love, honor, cherish, and—" She bites her lip and shifts uncomfortably in those boots. "And . . . obey . . . for all the days of my life."

"Antoinette?" I whisper as she shoves the ring onto my finger.

She shushes me. I take a deep breath and get all my business out in one breath. "I, Robert Thomas Hogarth, do solemnly swear to love, honor, cherish, and care for you for all the days of my life." I get that ring on her finger lickety-split, the finish line in my sights. Oh my sweet Lord, my head is throbbing to the beat of my heart.

We kiss perfunctorily on the lips and I'm proud I remember to close my eyes while doing so. Chuck bursts out in a round of applause, which is quickly followed by Dawn's happy squeaks. Maxine gives Chuck a kiss on the cheek and takes Dawn into her arms, smothering the little girl's chubby cheeks in lipstick kisses. There's a clap or two of congratulations out of Sergeant Joseph before my wife whisks us into an elevator. As the doors close, we're finally alone. Man and wife, like figurines atop a cake. Plus, two kids I apparently had with my imaginary dead wife.

Maxine's cackle signals we are back in reality. "I told you, Robert. You can trust me. I'd never in a million years let anything dreadful happen to you." She leans in and whispers in my ear, "Arresting you for the company you keep! It's barbaric!"

Having the real Maxine back with all her immoral outrage is oddly comforting. I take her hand and give it a quick squeeze. "Thank you, friend."

Then it hits me.

"Maxine?"

"Yes, Robert."

"Are you really pregnant?"

"Of course not, dear." She laughs as the elevator doors open. "But we really are married."

"Oh."

I throw up in the courthouse parking lot. While I'm certain it's a case of the nerves, Maxine sees the sizeable lump on my head and decides I need a doctor immediately.

"And how will I tell them I got it?"

"Oh, Robert, lots of men get stumble-drunk the night before their wedding. A doctor won't think twice."

She's got a firm grasp on my arm and I let her lead me through the parking lot to her E-Type. The kids scramble in the back and from my slumped view in the passenger seat, I see the two cops standing outside the courthouse, staring daggers at us. We aren't out of the woods yet.

"We need to honeymoon, Robert. They're watching us," she tells me.

I can't think of anything beyond getting out of their crosshairs. But I'm starting to think that doctor is a good idea.

"Old Tucson!" Chuck yells after Maxine explains what a honeymoon is. "That's where I'd want to go, anyway. And they have doctors there."

Charles "Chuck" Bronski

Old Tucson

May 1970

WEDDINGS IN REAL LIFE sure are a lot different than the ones I see in the movies. Those weddings never start at a jail. They never have that many cops standing around, watching. I didn't even know that Miss Maxine and Mr. Robert were engaged. I guess I should've known, though, since she bought that wedding dress last week and all. It still felt more like those surprise parties I see on TV than a wedding.

That's all I can think as we speed away from the courthouse and toward Old Tucson. Miss Maxine's driving on account of Mr. Robert's not looking too swell. He's got his head partway out the window of the front seat like a dog, while me and Dawn sit in the back. We're still in our fancy wedding duds, and I realize how weird we're gonna look at Old Tucson dressed like this. I won't say anything to Miss Maxine, though. She's already real worried about the car that's been behind us since we left Phoenix.

"Is it still there, Charles?" she asks me again.

I turn around and look out the back window. I don't know who they think we're running from, but we're the only ones on the road now.

"We need to pull over," Mr. Robert moans. "Right now!"

Miss Maxine skids the car off onto the gravel shoulder. Mr. Robert leans his head way, way out the window and I can hear him puking his guts up. It's real loud and kinda gross. Miss Maxine rubs his back.

"Get it all out, sweetie. You'll feel better."

"I got it on the car," Mr. Robert says, and it almost sounds like crying.

"No worries, dear. It's the Arizona desert. It's bound to rain at some point."

Now understand that I've wanted to go to Old Tucson since about forever, or at least since I was five years old and saw a commercial for it on TV. It was just about the coolest thing I'd ever seen in my whole dang life. My dad told me that someday we could go and I'd learn how to lasso a bull and ride a horse. But we never did, cuz it's expensive and then Dad had to go to Vietnam and Ma had Dawn. So I guess it's kinda funny that I'm finally going to what might be my favorite place ever, but with two people who are just pretending to be my mom and dad.

I don't want to sound ungrateful, but Old Tucson's a lot smaller than it looks on TV. And it's not just cuz all the horses are ponies. What kind of a cowboy rides around on a busted-down old pony? Nothing's real here. The old-timey buildings are just fake fronts, like billboards with nothing behind them. There's a bunch of cowboys and old-fashioned ladies walking around, but there's also a bunch of regular-looking folks. And it's pretty dang hard for me to imagine I'm in the Old West when the teenager standing next to me is wearing a Three Dog Night T-shirt. Dawn looks even more out of place cuz she's a baby, and I ain't never seen a baby in an Old West movie. I think they were always at home with the womenfolk or something. Then again, I don't look right here either. My shoes are real shiny since Miss Maxine paid a guy at the courthouse a quarter to make 'em that way.

We walk along Main Street—which is funny since it's the *only* street—looking at all the fake buildings until Mr. Robert says he's gonna puke again.

I was right that Old Tucson has a doctor, but he's not named Doc and he doesn't work in the building that says HOSPITAL, which is another fake sign. His name is Dr. Sawyer, and he works in a trailer next to the pony pen. Miss Maxine tells Doc Sawyer that we were on a hayride and Mr. Robert took a tumble. She looks at me and winks, so I go along with it and sneeze twice.

"Sorry," I say, trying to make my voice sound like a cowboy. "All that doggone hay surely makes me sneezy."

Doc Sawyer shines a penlight in Mr. Robert's eyes and gives the lump a good eyeballing.

"Mr. Hogarth, I haven't seen a lump like that since the last time one of the actors got kicked by a horse," says Doc Sawyer.

"It was a substantial tumble," Miss Maxine tells him.

"You're going to need to wake him up every hour tonight to make sure he makes it through the worst of this concussion," Doc says as Miss Maxine gasps. "It's merely a precaution. He'll live. You kids want lollipops?"

After the doctor's visit, Miss Maxine watches the ladies' room door while I sneak in to change Dawn's diaper. I do not one little bit like being in the ladies' room, but Miss Maxine has never changed a diaper before. I don't know how this could be true since she's a grown-up lady, but she swears she's never done it. Something about her having a "delicate constitution," which makes no sense to me. We're all Americans and we only got one Constitution.

Or is Miss Maxine telling me she's not American? I tell myself to think about that later—when I'm not a boy diapering my sister in the sink of the Old Tucson ladies' room.

Miss Maxine decides we need to get pictures, seeing how we're already all dressed up. Part of me is wishing for a pony ride, shiny shoes and all, rather than having to smile for a camera. I know it's weird, but I can't smile when I don't mean to be smiling. I see something nice or funny and it's an automatic thing to smile. But when someone tells me to smile, I can't. I don't get it. If I'm thinking really hard about something, shouldn't I be able to do it?

First, Miss Maxine decides we all need cowboy hats from the souvenir shop. She gets girly red ones for her and Dawn, tying Dawn's on under her chin so she can't pull it off. Mr. Robert and I get manly brown cowboy hats, and I am not trying to be boastful here, but all the kid-sized hats are too small for me.

"You have a brain twice the size of most boys your age," Miss Maxine tells me.

I get real excited when she says I can take my tie off, but then get un-excited when she puts a bolo tie on me with a big turquoise stone in the shape of Arizona. I'm feeling guilty for not liking her gift to me when I see that Mr. Robert doesn't look too dang thrilled about wearing one either. What I really want are some cowboy boots, but instead she pays the man at the cash register and we head off to get our pictures taken.

We stand outside in the shade while Miss Maxine tells the photographer, Mr. Johns, where to set up the camera. Once all that's in place, we need to wait some more while she goes to the ladies' room to freshen up.

"Miss Maxine sure is a feisty lady," I say to Mr. Robert.

"That she is, Chuck. That she is."

"She probably shouldn't take the Lord's name in vain so much though."

"You want to be the one to tell her that, Chuck?"

"Oh no, sir."

"You're a smart kid, Chuck."

"Thank you, sir."

"You can call me Robert."

We all take our places behind a huge old wagon wheel with the cactus-covered mountains behind us. Miss Maxine holds Dawn, who's given up on trying to get her hat off, but now can barely stay awake. I stand between Robert and Miss Maxine and when the photographer tells Robert to put his hand on my shoulder, he does it. I look up at him and see he's having trouble smiling normal-like too. I've never posed for a family picture, so I try to imagine that the people standing behind me are my honest and true mom and dad. I can't all the way remember what my dad looks like, but Ma says I have his nose. That gets me thinking too much about my nostrils, and I realize I'm making them twitch all funny-like.

Cheese! Flash! Click! Cheese! Flash! Click! We stop to wipe the drool off Dawn's chin. *Cheese! Flash! Click!* The photographer says we'll have the photos in seven to ten business days and Miss Maxine says he better make it more like five to seven. Dawn falls asleep on my shoulder while we walk back to the car, leaving my dress shirt all wet from sweat and baby spit.

On the drive home, Miss Maxine keeps looking at me in the rear-view mirror, so I close my eyes and get still. She and Robert talk quietly, so I know she thinks I'm sleeping.

"We're not going to be in trouble for having the kids out so late?" Robert asks.

"They're staying with us for a while," Miss Maxine says, which surprises me enough I open my eyes for a second before closing them again.

"What?"

"That mother of theirs is a real piece of work, Robert. You know how she's a barfly at the Pink Pony? Apparently, she met some ball-player and took off to travel around with him. After not so much as a word to me for weeks, she shows up at my door, suitcase in hand, and asks me to 'watch them' for a few weeks. Watch them! Like they're plants that need watering? I wanted to tell her that even Marilyn Monroe wouldn't ditch her kids for Joe DiMaggio, but she's not one to give two shits about criticism."

I don't know why Miss Maxine is saying this to Robert since Mom told me she was going away for work. I didn't know there was such a thing as a traveling waitress, but she said it's 1970 and there are all sorts of new things out there in the world I don't know about. It's okay though, since I have a job working for Miss Maxine now and I can't be away all summer.

"You're kidding?" says Robert. "She left them?"

"She mumbled something about sending for them at some point, and I felt compelled to let her know that life on the road with some shortstop probably isn't an ideal environment for growing children."

A shortstop? I bet Miss Maxine didn't understand what Mom said to her. Short Stop is probably the name of the restaurant she's working at, the one that feeds all the ballplayers when they're on the road.

"What if they need a doctor or something?" Robert asks her. "Is this legal?"

"It's fine, Robert. I had the good sense to get a letter from her, making me their caretaker. And we've got the spare bedroom. If Charles isn't comfortable in there, he can sleep on the divan in the living room."

"We don't have a spare bedroom. *You* have a spare bedroom. *I* live in the apartment attached to the tavern." I don't want to open my eyes to look, but Robert says this like a stern dad on TV.

"You can't be living in some dingy bachelor pad now that we're married, Robert."

"We're not really—"

"Yes, we are really. Keeping up appearances is important now if this is going to work for us. For you."

"This is never going to work for me!" Robert says loudly.

I don't want them arguing, so I fake mumble in my fake sleep. They stop talking until I'm quiet and still again.

Robert mutters so quietly, I can barely hear him. "I can't believe this is happening."

I hear him rolling down his window and smell the dusty, warm air blowing over my face. It feels good, but it's making me sleepy—for real.

"I know this is far from ideal, Robert. But the four of us are going to be just fine. Better than fine, even. Those kids will have a safe home and an adult to look after them. You won't have to worry about anything but keeping that tavern on track." She sounds like someone who is telling the truth. And I've heard Miss Maxine say all kinds of stuff today that isn't true, so I know the difference. "You can always have faith in me having a plan."

"You have a plan, Maxine? What the heck does that mean?"

"All it means is that I hope what you take away from this day is that I'm a trusted, close friend you can rely on."

"I do, Maxine." Robert sighs and rubs his head. "It's just that sometimes it feels you're, you know, plotting."

Miss Maxine doesn't answer. Instead she clicks on the radio and hums along softly.

Robert yawns, which makes me yawn, but I keep my eyes closed and I don't think they notice. I fall asleep wondering if the shortstop is why Ma hasn't called to check on us.

Robert Hogarth

Scottsdale

June 1970

THE MORNING OF my first day as a married man starts with me waking up in the recliner in Maxine's bedroom with what feels like a hangover and features a whole lot of screaming—make that shrieking—from little Dawn. I follow the clamor down the hall and find Maxine in the master bedroom. She's got a plastic tablecloth—one of those red-and-white checked ones you put on a picnic table—spread out on the bed and has little Dawn lying on top of it. Dawn's naked as the day she was born and probably about as pink thanks to all her shrieking and sobbing. Maxine has one hand, which is sheathed in a dishwashing glove, resting on Dawn's tummy, which is why the little pink shrieker is flailing around like a turtle on her back. I make a few funny faces at her, because isn't that what you do when a baby is making a racket? Her scream instantly turns to a giggle.

"Are you making faces at me, Robert? That's hardly helpful!"

The bottle of baby powder slips out of Maxine's plastic fingers and hits the floor. Mercifully, it's not open, but when Maxine moves to pick it up, Dawn flips right over and, fast as a little Olympian, is off that tablecloth and rubbing her bare bottom on Maxine's pillows. We both scramble to grab her—and I swear to God, I'm not making this up—we smack right into each other like the Stooges. My vision goes double again for a second, but I can still make out a blurry, naked Dawn leaping full speed off the bed and running with her hands up in the air, laughing as she flies out of the bedroom with Maxine chasing after. I pick a white towel off the bed and rub it on the back of my head, surprised to find there's no bleeding.

"Not the divan!" I hear Maxine beg from the living room.

I stumble out into the living room right as Maxine grabs Dawn off the pristine cream-colored couch, which, judging from all the "water" dripping down little Dawn's frantically kicking legs, probably isn't so pristine anymore. Maxine holds the baby out at arm's length to me.

"Would you please take her? I think I'm going to faint."

For some reason I can't move. Maxine might as well be holding out a wild, snarling wolf.

Chuck comes through the front door carrying an overstuffed garbage bag in each hand. He drops them with a thud and snatches his sister away from Maxine's still outstretched arms. Dawn settles down instantly and fidgets with the rim of his baseball cap.

"You didn't get all the diaper stuff laid out first?" he asks Maxine. She shakes her head. "Yeah, that's real important to remember, Miss Maxine. Can I have that diaper you got there?" he says, pointing to the thing I'm just now realizing I'm holding in my hand.

Still holding Dawn on his hip, Chuck crouches down on the floor and puts the diaper down, the shape of which, when spread out like that, I finally recognize. Holding the diaper down with his knee, Chuck uses his one free hand to rip off the plastic tabs on each side of the diaper. He sets Dawn upon it and, while blowing raspberries at her to keep her preoccupied, swiftly pulls each side of the diaper around her chubby legs and hips, sealing it shut in a flash with one hand. Firmly diapered, Dawn wiggles free and takes off down the hall, laughing to herself.

In awe, Maxine holds out the bottle of baby powder.

"Naw." Chuck waves it off. "When she's hungry or all kicky and bite-y, it's best to skip the fancy stuff and stick to getting the diaper on. It's safer that way."

Still dazed, Maxine murmurs to herself, "Bite-y . . . ?"

"I don't wanna talk out of turn," Chuck says with the seriousness of a person thirty years his senior, "but if you're gonna convince the contest people you're a mom and dad, you gotta act like you know what you're doing with a baby."

The kid has a point, I think.

Wait. What?

"Contest people, Maxine?"

Suddenly snapped from her trance, Maxine darts off toward the kitchen. "Breakfast on the veranda first, Robert!"

"What veranda?" I mutter as she walks away.

I splash some water on my face and join Maxine and the kids for breakfast on the veranda, which is Maxine's patio that overlooks the pool. Chuck carefully sets Dawn into a high chair. This explains to me why one has been missing from La Dulcinea.

Maxine swans onto the veranda and drops two doughnuts of differing varieties onto our plates. We also each have a glass filled with a beverage that might be named after Agent Orange, and coffee for the grown-ups. It occurs to me that I have never seen Maxine this pulled together this early in the morning. Or, for that matter, sober. With us all served, she sits down and, with a big, toothy smile that announces I'm about to receive a sales pitch, slides a brochure across the table.

"I've had a revelation," she announces, leading me to think this won't be a sales pitch so much as an attempt to save my soul. She taps on the brochure with one manicured nail. "This right here is that plan I mentioned yesterday."

I look at the glossy full-color brochure in my hand. The first thing that catches my eye is the photograph of five very pretty women in fancy dresses wearing crowns and sashes. The headline above them reads *MRS. AMERICAN PIE 1970*. And below that, in smaller type: *The most exceptional from among us!*

"A beauty pageant?" I flip open the brochure. There are more smiling women pulling cakes out of ovens, reading to well-scrubbed children, and straightening a broad-shouldered man's tie.

"Well, yes, a beauty pageant, but there's more to it than that, Robert. See?" She takes the brochure from me and reads aloud from it. "'The Mrs. American Pie Pageant is a beauty and talent competition exclusive to housewives. The annual event seeks to find the one lady who best exemplifies the ideals of American wife, mother, and citizen.'"

"You want to do this?" I fear I already know the answer.

"No, Robert, I want to *win* this." I can hear the fire in her belly being stoked. She keeps reading. "'The panel of judges gives marks for beauty, poise, manners, gentleness, and womanly skill.' That's me. That's what I do!" She gestures to the table and, oddly, both of the kids.

"But you're not a housewife," I point out. "Or a mother."

She tosses her head back and laughs. "Of course I am." She dangles her left hand in front of my face, wiggling the finger with the gold band on it. "I got married yesterday to the most charming man in the world, who just happens to have two beautiful children I am now the mother to!"

I choke on my last sip of coffee. Maxine is kind enough to pat me on the back, as if burping a baby.

I catch my breath. "Chuck, why don't you and your sister go watch TV? I need a word with Maxine."

Chuck does as he's told, and once I hear *Rocky and Bullwinkle* coming from the living room, I slide the patio door shut and turn my attention back to Maxine. She's still got that damn smile on.

"There's no way we can do this," I tell her.

"I don't see why not," she says, as if I'm the crazy person. "It solves all our problems."

"Solves? No, Maxine, this creates problems. Namely, drawing attention to ourselves when—need I remind you—attention is a very bad thing for us."

She opens the brochure and points to a photo of a smiling square-jawed man flipping burgers at a backyard barbecue while his wife, in her Mrs. American Pie sash, stands at the ready with an empty platter. "Do you think," asks Maxine, "anyone questions the 'nighttime gardening' of this fine man?"

Maxine stares at me and says nothing as those words sink in. Still, I'm not convinced.

"What could be straighter than having a wife deemed the best in all the land? Plus," she adds, "think how good it will be for business. Scottsdale's La Dulcinea Family Tavern—home of Mr. and Mrs. Arizona Pie! The papers will give you free press, and you need more patrons."

I hate that this is true. Business is slower than I projected—no, make that "hoped"—it would be. If it doesn't pick up considerably in the next six weeks, I'm going to need to let the Rodriguezes go. That means doing all the cooking, serving, and bartending myself.

I'm not going down without a fight here. This is insanity. So I ask, "And what about the kids? You expect them to lie?"

"It's a tiny little lie and besides, Charles is all on board. You know, he's the one who came up with the idea of being your son with me as the stepmother. Or rather, new mother, since your wife died tragically last year a few months before you and the kids moved to Arizona."

I'm almost certain that's child abuse, but I don't say anything. I can't take my eyes off the brochure and all the unquestionably straight men in it.

"You aren't bothered that all the neighbors know these kids aren't yours? Or mine?"

She shrugs that right off. "The neighbors didn't say shit when these kids were running around barefoot, starving, and clearly neglected. I think we're good."

Maxine pauses for dramatic effect and, I think, to let me consider how she might look dressed as Mary Poppins.

"Robert," Maxine coos, putting her arm on my shoulder. "This is good for all of us. You can save your tavern. The only thing in this whole world I've ever been halfway competent at is being a wife. The kids will finally be part of a real family."

"There's nothing 'real' about us, Maxine. We're as fake as they come." I point to a brochure photo of a family standing arm in arm at Mount Rushmore. "That's real."

"Oh bullshit, Robert. You think these people always look this perfect while picnicking in the park?" She points to a photo of a family of five sitting up straight on a red-and-white checkered blanket with a banquet of mouthwatering food laid out. "They're eating hot dogs off fine china. Our fake will at least be realistic." She grabs the brochure from me and tosses it over the balcony. "And I tell you another thing. I'm pissed as hell that this cruel world has conspired against us to keep us from having a family. Aren't you mad? Don't you deserve to be a father and a husband? Trust me, you do."

I've never let myself even consider it. There's just no point to it.

"Look, Robert," she says to me as if she's at her wit's end. "I know all this isn't real. You're not actually my husband. The kids' mother will one day return and want them back. But this"—she points to the pageant brochure—"entering this let's me pretend that I have a real husband and real kids. And that makes me happy. So can't I just be happy a little while longer? Can we do that?"

This plea I recognize as sincerity. It's also impossible for me to deny. I guess I feel safe in knowing that she's got her head on straight. Or at least as straight as Maxine can make her head.

"What's this entail? Some photos and an entry form or something?" I ask gingerly.

"It's nothing really," she says, beaming. "There's next to no chance we can win this year. The whole thing will be over and done with in no time."

I finally let myself smile at her. "I can probably handle that."

She pulls me into a hug and squeals in my ear, reminding me that concussions take a while to recover from.

"Let's pretend to be a nice, normal family, okay?" I suggest.

"Oh, Robert," she whispers into my ear, "we're gonna be goddamn normal, it will make everyone else feel like shit!"

And with that, I start my life as an all-American husband and father. Nothing to hide here. No, siree! Just good old heterosexual fun. Boobs, blondes, and baseball are all *this* guy dreams about! I can't sleep that night, and it's not all because the recliner in Maxine's bedroom is uncomfortable.

"What will the children think if you're on the divan?" she tells me at bedtime while making a big show of fluffing a pillow for me on the empty side of her bed.

"I've never shared a bed, Maxine," I say with enough terseness to hopefully shut down any further questioning.

She lets out a dramatic long sigh. "I want you to know that if I could, let's say 'give you what you need . . .'"

"Please don't say that, Maxine."

"Maybe just grow a male member for a night or two . . ."

"Maxine, don't call it that—"

"You know, for sex."

I flop down in the recliner. "I'm fine, Maxine. No need for us to discuss this."

She throws a pillow at me. "I'm merely stating that it's perfectly normal for a person to have certain physical needs. Lord knows I have them."

Great. Now I feel guilty for not only thinking that Maxine was purposely making me uncomfortable, but also for ignoring that this might not be an ideal situation for her either.

"Well, we're only married in a legal sense," I tell her, not even sure where I'm going with this. "You could go do things . . . to keep from lacking . . . ?"

"Robert Hogarth. Whatever are you saying?" she taunts, pretending to clutch some invisible pearls.

"I'm saying that there's no real reason why you can't, you know . . ."

She laughs openly at my struggle to speak about the carnal details. "Christ, I can't even tell you how many times I've dreamed of straying from my last marital bed. Here's hubby number two all but giving me permission."

I grab a blanket from the edge of her bed and settle into the recliner.

"You can come into bed with me anytime you want, Robert. The right side is always yours," she tells me before clicking off the bedside light.

"I'm fine where I am," I assure her.

But I'm not fine. My mind is restless, moving too quickly over one crazy moment of these last few days to another, slamming around my head like a pinball in a machine. When my thoughts do stop, they settle on one memory from my youth.

It started in college, when I moved a whopping thirty miles south of my hometown to attend Loyola University on the far north side of Chicago. It was a forty-five-minute train ride, but it might as well have taken me to a different planet. Everyone back home knew me. I don't mean only the people who frequented our family restaurant or the fellow parishioners at St. Joe's, but everyone in the whole town. It was suffocating. But at Loyola, I was just another nineteen-year-old guy in a white shirt and navy-blue tie, my hair neatly parted to one side and my backbone as straight as Dwight D. Eisenhower himself.

Everything instantly felt different. There were books I'd never heard of and art—real art! Heavy oil paintings of Jesuit fathers and frescoes of Bible stories hung in the hallways of the stately all-brick buildings. My first week living on campus, I saw an honest-to-goodness opera, met a girl from Brazil who spoke three languages, and drank a warm beer on the rooftop of de Nobili Hall while looking at Mars through a telescope. I never wanted to leave campus, but I did, every weekend, to stay with my folks back in Libertyville. Mom insisted on it, saying I still needed a strong family to keep me out of trouble. Never mind the fact I had been a straight-A student all through high school and the most trouble I'd ever gotten into was a tardy or two when the snow was high in the winter.

One Monday, I was in a bathroom at Loyola. From my stall, I overheard two boys speaking in hushed tones about the men's department at the Marshall Field's down on State Street. If you went into a specific changing room, they said, and stood with your legs just so and your feet aimed in a particular way, it would signal the guy in the room next to yours to come in and "be with you." There was something about the way my classmate said it, *be with you,* that instantly told me everything I needed to hear. I spent all week thinking about those words. *Be with you.* Even today, it makes my heart race and my palms get clammy. As the week dragged on, the thought of having to go home to Libertyville for the weekend weighed heavier on my mind. I don't know what scared me more: going home or going to Marshall Field's.

On Friday I sat in Father Neidermann's class as he gave a monotone reading of Wordsworth's poem about happy warriors. It teaches that "good boys" are steadfast and true to their God and nation. We are selfless, strong, and ready to plunge into any battle with smiles on our faces since we know we are on the side of morality. I'd heard the poem a million times before. It's a staple of boys' English lit courses, since it fulfills a poetry requirement while still being the manliest of the poems. The language might be flowery, but the hands holding those flowers are muscular, battle-scarred—and most important, unafraid. It's that "unafraid" part that suddenly got to me, along with the line "More brave for this, that he hath much to love."

Now, looking back, I realize I took that line out of context. Wordsworth was speaking about going into battle. He wasn't offering euphemisms for trysts in a department store changing room. But still.

More brave for this.

Be with you.

I called my mom with some excuse about needing to spend the weekend in the Loyola library and, for extra measure, added it was for my religions course. Lie accomplished, I took the Howard-Englewood-Jackson Park L train into Chicago's downtown—the Loop, as the locals call it. Before my brain could stop me, I was standing in that men's changing room, trying to wrangle my feet into doing something suggestive. I had only heard about how to do this and never seen specifically how it was done. Twice, I left the changing room to exchange the clothes I was supposedly trying on. I didn't make eye contact with anyone, yet I could feel all eyes on me as I grabbed the first three pairs of trousers I could see and rushed back into the changing room. I realized nearly forty minutes had gone by, but I didn't care. I didn't think about leaving. I just thought about those words.

Be with you.

Finally, someone tugged at the locked changing room door. My first thought was that I'd been caught. My second thought was how stupid I was for locking the door. I scrambled to unlock it but didn't dare open it, which brought back my first thought about being caught. I grabbed the trousers and held them up to myself as if to say to any Marshall Field's employee who might enter that I was still contemplating my pants options. Better to look like the world's pickiest shopper than, well, you know.

All was quiet outside the changing room door until this wisp of a boy, maybe all of nineteen, with too-long blond hair let himself in. He said nothing as he pressed himself up against me, pushing me with just enough force against the changing room wall. I could feel his lip stubble on my neck as his fingers dug in slightly to my flank, setting off a wave of vibration, rolling through me like I always imagined an earthquake ripples across the land. My mind emptied of all thought, but it didn't matter, because my body took over and knew exactly what to do.

It was everything I needed and everything I feared needing.

When we were done, he left without a word. I didn't know if this was normal or just his way. I was grateful, though, since I didn't know what to do with myself and didn't want anyone to witness me in such an awkward state. I pulled my pants back up, getting angrier at myself for not paying attention to what color eyes he had. My legs didn't want to work, so I sat down with my shirt still unbuttoned.

This was my mistake: lingering too long. Store security didn't knock. He barged in and grabbed me by the collar, making me instantly wonder if I was wearing my own shirt or one of the store's. I played dumb, telling them I was a nice boy from the suburbs attending a college filled with nice Catholic boys and they could call over there and speak to my dorm head if they didn't believe me. That backfired in a big way. A day later I was expelled and back on that train to Libertyville, not sure what to say to the disappointed, heartbroken parents who were waiting for me with Bibles in one hand and rosaries in the other.

My mom sobbing through a Hail Mary is the last thought I have as I drift to sleep in Maxine's recliner. I wake the next morning with my hands balled up in fists and my neck absolutely furious with me. My penitence, I guess.

Maxine insists on keeping the kids with her most days, but occasionally on a day when Dawn is content to take all her naps, I get to spend some time with Chuck at the tavern. He's good company and an excellent helper. Even when I suggest he go find something fun to do outside, he tells me he'd rather learn how to clean the tap lines or tighten the screws on the barstools.

The kid sure does have a lot of questions, though. And not of the "Why is the sky blue?" variety. Every time I feel like we're a normal mentor and mentee, or maybe even an uncle and nephew, out comes his ever-present notebook and a litany of oddball requests.

"So, back in Libertybell, Illinois—" he asks me over patty melts at the bar.

"Libertyville. Liberty-ville, Illinois," I correct him.

He jots it down in the notebook and underlines it.

"So, in Liberty*ville*, Illinois, what hospital would I have been born in? I mean, if I were a real boy."

"You *are* a real boy," I insist.

"Yeah, but you know." He waves his pencil around. "What hospital?"

I come back from behind the bar and sit down next to him. "Why don't you tell me about this notebook?"

"It's what Miss Maxine calls my *doh-see-aye*. There are sections all about you and Miss Maxine, and even me and Dawn—or the me and Dawn we're supposed to be for the pageant people."

He hands me the notebook, which is filled with tidy childlike writing. I see under the heading for my name a list of details like *prefers brown shoes* and *keeps to himself*. Maxine's section is pages longer than mine, with notes that include *lime green = bad, grass green = good, regular green = ??* and *Virginia Slims*, which is underlined three times. His own page tells me he's a *clean kid* who enjoys football, reading the Hardy Boys, and being helpful.

"I know that real spies wouldn't keep any evidence lying around that tells the world, 'Hey, I'm a spy!' But Miss Maxine says that writing stuff down helps a fella remember it. And I'll keep the dossier in a hiding place when we're around the judges."

I feel that fluttering stomach of mine and swallow hard. Is all this a terrible thing to do to this sweet kid? His dad's dead or missing in the jungles of Southeast Asia, and his mom is doing the devil knows what, and the only two adults in his life are a nervous Nellie closet case and a possibly deranged, certainly loony drama queen.

"Are you okay with all this, Chuck?"

He stares at me blankly before scrunching up his nose. "I dunno what ya mean?"

"Okay with pretending that I'm your dad and Maxine's your mom so she can win a silly contest."

He perks up. "Oh yeah! It's fun. I mean, most kids spend their summer going camping or staying with some grandparents or something. I get to practice being a spy. By the time I get to college, I'm going to know way more than the other guys and graduate at the top of my class."

That's a tough thing to argue against.

"Will you promise me that if you don't want to do this anymore, you'll tell me?"

"Sure," he says, picking up his pencil. "You gotta promise me you won't call the contest silly around Miss Maxine. That will make her hoppin' mad."

Unlike most fathers—there, I said it—I don't have a nine-to-five job, which Maxine calls "less than ideal," but also says she'll frame it more as me being a "dedicated and diligent breadwinner." I don't get home until nearly ten each night, and while Dawn is down for the count, Chuck is awake and always hungry. I've moved my meager belongings in, and I say "meager" because Maxine wouldn't let me bring any furniture from my rooms at the tavern. It's a strange feeling to be driving home every night rather than just wandering out from behind the bar and into a room marked PRIVATE. This morning, I promised I'd knock off early and be home for dinner at the right time. I also remember I have keys to the condo and don't need to knock.

"Honey! I'm home!" I holler out in my best Ricky Ricardo voice, which, to be fair, probably makes me sound more like Carmen Miranda.

I find Chuck watching TV while Maxine bangs around in the kitchen, yelping out to me that dinner's nearly ready.

The framed "family" photo from our "honeymoon" sits prominently on the dining room table, looking better than I expected. Maxine's downright maternal with bubbly Dawn in her arms. I look natural enough, although my grin is a little wider than something I'd imagine a father figurehead like Ward Cleaver or Ozzie Nelson might sport. That Mr. Johns was really onto something when he told me to put a firm fatherly hand on Chuck. I look like the sort of father a boy might turn to. I picture myself sitting in my favorite chair in my book-lined den, wearing a nice cardigan I always change into after coming home from a long day at the office.

I catch Chuck staring at me as I stare at the photo. "This turned out very nice," I finally say.

"Yes, sir." He lowers his voice and leans in closer: "But I still don't like the bolo ties."

"I don't either, Chuck."

From the kitchen, I hear the refrigerator slam shut and dishes clank. Maxine yells out, "Dinner will be ready in just a moment, you two!"

"Why do I smell bananas?" I ponder out loud.

Chuck shrugs.

"What did you do today?" I ask in my *Father Knows Best* voice.

"I watched *The Brady Bunch* and took lotsa notes. Do you know how to build a really big house out of cards?"

"Build a house of cards? No."

"Get to the table, you two!" Maxine cheerily beckons. She emerges from the kitchen with bowls in each hand and a cigarette dangling from her lips. With a proud smile, she sets plates in front of us. Normally, when you receive a plate of food, a quick glance should tell you what you're eating. That is not the case tonight.

"It's something new I found called ham and bananas hollandaise!"

I gingerly poke at the food on my plate with my fork and sure enough, under a layer of zit-yellow hollandaise sauce and wrapped around a whole peeled warm banana is a thin slice of pineapple-glazed ham.

"Maybe we should get a Lassie," I mutter. "A good hungry Lassie who can't see or smell."

I can't take my eyes off the atrocity on my plate. The sound of Maxine opening a soda can startles me, and then I realize she's having a Tab and several Virginia Slims for dinner. Chuck dives right in as Maxine smiles at him. She sees I'm not eating, and that just won't do.

"Eat up, Robert. There's whole milk in your glass, as you prefer. You see, Chuck, Robert is from the Midwest, which is dairy country. I myself only drink skim milk since it's less fattening."

Chuck puts down his fork and picks up his pencil to scribble all the intel down in his dossier. I find dinner is manageable if I eat the ham and hollandaise minus the warm banana. We eat in uncomfortable silence broken up only by Maxine's occasional contented sigh as she flicks her cigarette delicately into the elegant crystal ashtray.

His plate clean, Chuck gently dabs at the corners of his mouth with his napkin, which he then carefully folds and places to the left, then the right of his plate.

"Thank you for this lovely and creative dinner, Miss Maxine," he says in an overly practiced manner. "May I please be excused?"

Maxine bolts from her chair and walks to the kitchen. I don't know why I didn't notice before, but she's dressed in all black, like a lady cat burglar. "That was excellent, Charles. But you may not be excused because I have dessert for you."

"I love dessert!"

"Me too, Chuck," is all I can think to add. He immediately makes note of it in his book.

Maxine plops a dish of red Jell-O in front of him and scoops up the dinner dishes. I join her in the kitchen out of young J. Edgar's earshot.

"I'm a little worried we're getting ahead of ourselves here," I tell her.

"Whatever do you mean, Robert?"

"The boy's all . . . indoctrinated, and our whole week has been nothing but pageant prep. Isn't this all overkill for a contest we're never going to win?"

Maxine doesn't look up from rinsing the dishes. "About that, dear-heart, they actually held the contest a few weeks before I told you about it. There's already a winner for this year."

"Then what the hell are we doing all this for?" I hiss. There are empty booze bottles lined up all over the counter and on instinct, I gently place each one in the trash.

"Because I've read the bylaws. If Mrs. Arizona Pie, as well as her first and second runners-up are deemed unsuitable to wear the crown, the state committee can give the crown to anyone they choose. And that anyone will be me."

"You lied to me about this being no big deal?" I ask.

"No," she tells me with a straight face. "I simply found a way to make it a very big deal. A very big *good* deal for all of us."

Maxine pulls all the bottles I just put in the trash back out and places them gently in an empty second garbage bag. Before I can ask what the bejesus is going on, Chuck materializes out of thin air beside me, holding out his licked-clean Jell-O bowl. I see now that he, too, is in head-to-toe black.

"That was some mighty fine Jell-O, Miss Maxine. I really liked that there was nothing in it except Jell-O."

"Thank you, Charles. Why don't you finish packing your kit and wait for me in the living room?"

He does as he's told, taking his place on the couch. I can see the back of his head as he stares straight forward with perfect posture, like a sentinel waiting to attack. Maxine goes about loading up that garbage bag with more bottles.

"Maxine, what are you and the boy up to?"

"Nothing you need worry about, Robert."

"Maxine . . ."

Exasperated with me, she sets the garbage bag down with a clank. "Look here, Robert. You know damn well I am grateful to you for doing this with me."

I nod in agreement.

"And you also know that there are some aspects as to how I handle certain things that both of us strongly prefer I keep to myself."

"Yes, but the boy—"

"The boy is fine. I would never let anything happen to that little charmer."

"From where I'm standing, it looks like the two of you are about to commit a major crime."

I see Chuck's head spin around and look toward us. I smile reassuringly. He resumes his post.

"You are being overdramatic, dear-heart. I'm merely taking my darling stepson out for some nighttime owl watching, which I recently read in the *Phoenix Gazette* is something that people actually do around here for kicks. I mean, can you believe it!"

"Maxine, the bigger question is whether the cops will believe it."

"There aren't going to be any cops, and please work on not underestimating me."

"Sure. Should I write that down in my *doh-see-aye*?"

"Oh, Robert. Don't tease me." She walks off in a huff. In her all-black getup with that garbage bag slung over her shoulder, she looks like Audrey Hepburn by way of Santa Claus from hell.

"Come along now, Charles. We have matters to attend to!"

Maxine Hogarth

Scottsdale

June 1970

I WILL SAY THIS for those bra burners, they're onto something when it comes to men underestimating us females. If there was one part of this fake—no, let's make that *arranged* marriage—I was hoping to avoid, it's some guy thinking he knows how to wife and mother more than me. Are you the one chasing a toddler around the house for fifteen minutes, five times a day in a futile attempt to get her to wear pants? Did you spend three hours at the library and then on the phone calling former pageant contestants? Because I did. Now I have a lengthy list of potential cooking, sewing, cleaning, and mothering competitions for the state and national level. Who in this family spent four hours perfecting—perfecting, Robert!—that divine-looking Simple Supper Mold? It was anything but simple! And let's not forget that while you are sleeping soundly every night on my recliner, I'm up late reading all the latest child-rearing books along with *The Art of War.* But sure, Robert, second-guess my ability to win a beauty pageant. Guess I'm the only one in this relationship who knows to "appear weak when you are strong."

I push all of this out of my mind and focus on the now.

Operation Night Owl is under way as young Charles and I drive ourselves out to middle-of-nowhere Mesa. Halfway through the trek, the roads narrow down to one and the streetlamps become fewer as the number of trailer homes increases. It's dark as all get-out and while the windows are rolled down, that merely lets in more dust than cool breeze. At one point I swerve to avoid a reckless (or suicidal?) jackrabbit sitting in the middle of the road. The streetlamps gradually return as we wind our way past one golf course then another, followed by several planned communities offering something called "quality adult living." I know that my idea of "quality" certainly doesn't include the shuffleboard and bus trips to a shopping center that the billboard totes as selling points. Eventually we reach the turnoff for our final destination.

"What's a *chat-ee-u*?" Charles asks, pointing to the billboard announcing the neighborhood.

"It's *sha-toe*," I tell him. "It's French for 'home.'"

He looks around at the scrubby ranch homes all in tan and sand. Each one looks like the one next to it, the only difference being some have a carport on the right and others on the left. Most front yards are still rustic desert, while others have lawns, albeit that scratchy Bermuda grass that most days feels as hot as the concrete.

"I thought French houses would be fancier?" Charles says, practically reading my mind.

"They are *much* fancier in France."

When I reach the golf course, I turn left into an unpaved alley with rows of homes running along either side. I'm slow and careful to count the low-slung rooftops, which I can barely see peeking out over the top of the tall cinder-block fences. Once I reach the fourth house on the left, I cut the lights and drive a bit farther, stopping at the fifth house on the right.

"Are you ready for your mission?" I ask Charles with all the seriousness of a military general.

"I stand in the middle of the alley with my binoculars. But I'm not looking up high at the trees. I'm looking at both ends of the alley. If I see a car coming or anyone takin' out the trash, I blow my bird whistle and aim my binoculars up at the trees."

"Excellent, Charles!"

"But, Miss Maxine, I don't see any trees?"

I decide to ignore this minor wrinkle because as Sun Tzu says in *The Art of War*, "All warfare is based on deception."

"Charles, I'm going to teach you a little trick that has always served me well. It's called 'playing dumb.' Have you heard of it?"

He nods. "You aren't dumb, Miss Maxine."

"No, I'm not. And neither are you. But in my experience, the people who are the very best at playing dumb are usually the smartest people in the room. Right now that's you and me, Charles. So, if need be, play as dumb as you possibly can."

He nods and for some reason shoves his hand out for us to shake on it. For half a second I see Robert in his grin. Which makes no sense, but it soothes me. Then Charles hops right into position in the middle of the alley with his binoculars raised and the bird whistle pursed between his lips. I quickly dump the bag of empty liquor bottles into the fifth house on the right's trash can and snap three photos with my new Instamatic camera—with a handy wrist cord and fast-locking disposable flashbulbs. It doesn't occur to me that those bulbs are quite hot post-use, and I singe my fingertips popping the used one off to put a new one on.

With my camera loaded and around my wrist, I grab another garbage bag filled with some of my used reading material. Then I limber up my arms with exercises I learned in my high school calisthenics class. I have a cinder-block fence to climb over!

Easier said than done, Maxine! The garbage cans along the fence aren't stable enough for me to stand on. The one full can is extremely clanky thanks to all the glass bottles inside it. I want to jump to reach the top of the fence, but I also don't want to scrape my entire face along the rough surface. I try climbing the wooden gate in the fence, but I fail at that, too, since I don't want slivers in my hands.

"Charles, dear," I whisper, "could I trouble you for a boost?"

Charles hustles right over, stopping just short of touching me. I realize the easiest spot to boost me from involves giving my derrière a good hoisting, and yet that hardly seems gentlemanly, or for that matter, ladylike. Charles moves in the direction of my backside before immediately recoiling. He does this three times in rapid succession and I'm sure if it weren't so dark in this alley, I would see his cheeks flaming bright red. He finally gets down on one knee and puts his hands together.

"I seen it in Westerns. This is how ladies get on horses. Put your foot in my hands and I'll lift ya."

That seems like a plan, except that I lose my balance and damn near fall tits over ass into the alley dirt. Charles helps me to my feet and even dusts off my pant leg. Thankfully, my camera is fine. I'm debating pulling the car closer to the wall and climbing over from the roof when I see Charles yank on the top of the wooden gate. It swings open with nary a creak.

"The one 'round the pool is never locked either," Charles offers.

"Well, you might have suggested that beforehand!" I point to the alley. "Get back in position."

Keeping close to the fence, I slip into the backyard, thankful none of the lights are on around the tiny kidney-shaped pool. To my left, I see a tall shadow against the fence. It moves and I flatten myself up against the wall behind me. Is that a big shaggy dog? Oh God, what if it's a coyote? I immediately see the women of the Palm Springs Bridge Club tittering over how I was found in the backyard of a three-bedroom tract home with my face torn off. I don't breathe. I stare at the shadow, which is now unmoving. My body is paralyzed, my head unable to turn, as I slowly pan my eyes across the yard. I could kick myself for wearing false lashes today! It makes squinting all the more difficult. I must discover the source of that menacing shadow!

Landscaping, as it turns out. A sprawling, supposedly decorative hunk of pampa grass, which to me in daylight always resembles a hula skirt big enough to fit the Jolly Green Giant. In truth, there's nothing "grassy" about it, since it's a good five feet tall with an especially unappealing top third that resembles an old feather duster. But fine, if I must, I'll hide behind it. Here's hoping nothing is living inside that thing.

I whisper to myself, "Move swift as the wind. Swift as the wind."

I steal across the yard and crouch low to the ground. *Be as still as the mountain,* I think, wondering why the fortune cookie people don't get that Sun Tzu to write for them. He seems to really know his shit. With the gently swaying pampa grass to shield me, I get a good look inside the house.

At the dining room table sits my target—Mrs. Bridgette Rose McBain—the current Mrs. Arizona Pie. She's bathed in the soft golden glow of the dining room's overhead lighting. I don't know what the hell type of bulbs she's using, but they are incredible—like candlelight. Her long chestnut hair is down and loose, falling in effortless waves against her baby-blue blouse. I bet she uses hot rollers, but still, the end result is heavenly. Even from here I can see how shiny that hair is. I notice her dewy, wrinkle-free skin, even her bright Irish eyes. She's toiling away at a sewing machine, although from the satisfied smile on her face, *toiling* isn't the right word. I can't tell what she's making other than to notice it's white. Probably some lovely, virginal summer dress for her next official appearance at a store's grand opening. Or maybe a slinky yet still virginal nightie to wear for Mr. Donald McBain, who's in middle management at a firm in Tempe. Whatever it is, I'm sure it's being sewn with tenderness and with her family's well-being first and foremost in her mind. Every stitch she runs through that machine has her love woven into it. I can see that much from halfway across her dark backyard.

Donald enters and I dart out of view behind the pampa grass bush monstrosity. *Let your plans be dark and impenetrable as night,* says Sun Tzu. I take a few slow, deep breaths. I peek my head back around and catch Donald with his rugged man-hands on Bridgette's shoulders. He and his thick blond hair are admiring her handiwork. He's so appreciative of all she does that he gives her the sweetest little kiss on the top of her impeccable head. One of their two gorgeous children—the girl about nine who looks like a Tammy or a

Sally—walks in the room, and Dad is quick to call her attention to what Mom's working on. Tammy—I decided—beams with pride and points to the fabric, undoubtedly noticing the tidy, perfectly rowed stitches and crisp seams.

That racing heart of mine! I duck out of view again. Can I really go through with this? I mean, yes, physically I can get the dirty magazines set up on the poolside table, although using the Instamatic flash will almost certainly draw the attention of the McBains. Donald has strong, broad shoulders, so his bottom half is likely equally athletic. Bridgette's body is simply divine, despite going through the rigors of childbirth twice in three years. She has the legs of a gazelle, so I can only assume that she can run like one.

Oh, but it's more than that, Maxine, I think. I steal another look and see the younger child—a boy of seven who is certainly Donald Junior—has joined the rest of his family in admiring mother's sewing. They are breathtaking. My plan is to plant booze and pornography around the patio and photograph it. But would anyone believe that story? Bridgette practically has a halo hanging over her. It would crush the little ones, who maybe right now won't understand why Mommy is in bed all day sobbing or why the big trophy and shining crown are no longer displayed in the living room. There will be whispers all over town about Bridgette's morality—at the grocery, the couple's favorite restaurant, even the church and school. Eventually the kids will understand their mother's downfall. That's when they'll stop looking up at her the way I see them staring right now. All that wonder and admiration will dim from their eyes. Can I honestly do that to them? No, I can't.

Bridgette stops sewing and I linger, because at this point I simply must see what she's making. Junior is practically bursting with excitement. Whatever it is, Bridgette hands it to Donald. I can't make it out except that it's white with red piping. Pajamas maybe? He runs into the next room to change and I see Bridgette take this opportunity to get a few measurements from the boy. I bet he's growing fast and in need of new pajamas to match his father. Adorable!

Donald reenters and gives his family a little ta-da spin in the garment, which looks more like a long-sleeved, old-fashioned nightgown? How quaint. I would have guessed he was more modern than that. Reminds me of a story I read once about an Irish farmhand in the 1800s who did all sorts of things in a barn with the mayor's daughter. I file that thought away for later. Bridgette hands Donald one more piece of white cloth and as he pulls it over his head, the children begin to clap.

I damn near fall over. My heart stops racing because it stops beating entirely. I cannot believe my incredible luck. Those aren't pajamas Donald is wearing. As sure as I'm standing here, that's a white hood and robe. I'm hiding in the backyard of Donald and Bridgette McBain, of the Chateau Homes McBains. Of the Mr. and Mrs. Arizona Pie McBains. Of the Ku Klux Klan McBains. Oh yes, I can do this.

"Attack like the fire. Fall like a thunderbolt," I tell myself.

I sprint from my hiding spot with the Instamatic raised to my eyes. Thanks again to the false lashes, I can't entirely tell if I'm getting a good shot of the KKK Family of the Year. I snap and wind to the next shot, clicking off two before it dawns on me my flash isn't going off. Then again, the McBain Klan—every damn pun intended!—hasn't noticed me yet either. I push that flashbulb tightly in place, dart right up to the window, and with all the courage I can muster, I take my shot. Donald and Tammy notice instantly and rush to the window to look out. I run like hell.

"Bird noises! Bird noises! Tweet! Tweet!" I yell loudly enough for Charles to hopefully hear. The backyard lights all pop on as I nearly yank the gate off the hinges barreling through it. My bag of magazines gets caught as the gate flies back at me, so I drop it and run to the car, where, thank Maker's Mark, Charles is already sitting, his eyes wide with fear.

I jump in the car and fire her up, not bothering to close the door. I can hear *der Führer* McBain's shouting getting louder as he reaches the alley. I floor it and peel away.

Charles's head spins back as far as it can go. "Was that a ghost?" he yells.

"No, but it was dead meat!" I'm laughing so hard, I feel a crying jag coming on. I take a right turn hard enough that my car door slams itself shut.

"Did we accomplish our mission?"

"That we did, young Charles. That we did!"

"Do you have the goods for me?" I mutter quietly to the scrawny, pimply faced kid working the Fotomat in the Sears parking lot. He's not wearing his MY NAME IS JASON name tag today, but I think he's the same dull-eyed boy I dropped my KKK beauty queen photos off with a few days earlier.

Jason nods. He slides a thick envelope across the counter to me. Charles looks at me expectantly and I nod, giving him permission to snatch up the photos and immediately start flipping through them. From the way his face lights up, I'm guessing they turned out well.

"I need a few minutes to finish up the"—Jason leans over the counter and gets his torso and face uncomfortably close to me—"the photo retouching you wanted."

I push Jason away, safely back behind the counter where he belongs. "We'll wait outside, but be quick about it."

Charles and I step outside. He's right to be excited by the photos. In my favorite of the bunch, you can clearly see Bridgette's flaring, unladylike nostrils as she pulls the hood off her hateful husband while pointing right at me. I get a tingle just recalling it all.

"What did that guy mean by 'retouching'?" Charles asks. I should have known Jason's slip of the tongue wouldn't get past Charles.

"I had a few photos that weren't crystal clear," I say.

"Like what?" he asks.

"That's classified information, Charles." His eyes go wide and he's instantly silent. I'm speaking the boy's language now, and know there will be no further questions. As much fun as it's been including

Charles in all my pageant preparations, there are some things a twelve-year-old doesn't need to know. Like that for twenty bucks, a Fotomat employee will doctor a beauty queen's medical reports or falsify a voter registration card. I'm banking on the pageant committee being extremely gun-shy after the whole KKK thing, so it shouldn't take much to cast the first and second runners-up in a disparaging light. Just a few small tweaks to a couple of documents should do the trick.

"Can I ask you something real important?" he says in barely a whisper. "Is my mom ever coming back?"

"She assured me she was, Charles," I tell him in what I hope is a soothing, motherly voice. Although, I'm not so sure Charles—or frankly, myself—can recognize motherly. I mostly know it from all those television shows I've had Charles watch recently. "Are you unhappy staying with me and Robert?"

"Not at all, ma'am. I'm having a lot of fun with all this pageant spy stuff." He fidgets with his ball cap. "It's just, she's never been gone this long before."

"If it helps any, I think she's gone longer now because she trusts that you are in good hands." That doesn't seem to appease him. It hurts my heart to see the boy in such a state. "You know . . . ," I begin, "I spent much of my childhood being looked after by others and I turned out no worse for wear."

"You did?"

"My mother . . . traveled often, as fate necessitated. And children—as you know—need stability, so while she was . . . elsewhere dealing with . . . some hard times that befell us, I was left in the care of an aunt and uncle." Most of this is quite true and all of it sounds believable. I've told some variation of this to many people over the years, although always substituting *hard times* with *critical family business* and adding in a father, of course. I've found the key is to always keep any reveal of personal information vague and nonchalant. Charles's questions come tumbling out in rapid fire. "What kind of hard times? Where did she go? Why couldn't you go with?"

"Now, Charles, it's never polite to pry, dear," I say firmly. "My mother's personal matters are exactly that—personal."

I make a mental note to be extra brusque with Mrs. Sharla Bronski, should I ever see her again. I haven't told Robert that prior to riding off into the sunset with that two-bit, minor-league short-stop, Sharla gave me the birth certificates for both of her cast-off children. Dawn's father is listed as a Mr. Pete Bronski while Charles's father is represented as nothing more than an X.

"I sure don't mean to sound ungrateful, Miss Maxine," Charles says.

"You are anything but ungrateful, dear," I tell him, gently mussing his hair. "Why don't we check in with Jason the Fotomat boy?"

I am going to win this damned pageant by hook or crook. Charles, that diaper-phobic baby sister of his, and everyone else on the planet is going to see—no, make that *feel*—the maternal instinct and love I have within me. It will knock them off their goddamned high-and-mighty feet.

Robert Hogarth

Scottsdale

June 1970

"I'M NOT THRILLED about the cowboy hat, Maxine," I try telling her as she puts it on my head. "It feels too"—I lower my voice since the kids are around—"too camp."

She dismisses this concern as she does all others she disagrees with: with a Queen of England wave and a megawatt smile. "You look perfect. Manly and virile." She stands on her tiptoes to adjust the brim. "Besides, we have a theme to maintain, Robert."

I know all about "keeping up appearances," but Maxine and her gosh-danged "themes" take everything too far. It makes me nervous and then some. We stand at the front door of her condo as she sees me off to work in the morning. Perfectly on theme as a fashionable Southwestern American couple, with Maxine in her ornate turquoise necklace and Indian beaded sandals and me in my brand-new tobacco-brown cowboy hat. We look like a couple who's never been to a ranch or seen a horse a day in their lives. And yet here we are, Mr. and Mrs. Marlboro Man. Never mind that I'm from Illinois, while Maxine is from—where is Maxine from? San Bernardino, California? She mentioned once not being from there originally, though. Her mother is French? Or married to a Frenchman? Either way, neither of us is remotely "on theme," anywhere outside of a Halloween contest at a Milwaukee YMCA.

I take the cowboy hat off the moment I'm in the car. I do have the sense to bring it into the tavern with me, though. A gentleman never wears it indoors, but he sure as heck better have it sitting behind the bar lest he get in Dutch with the missus. This is a good call, since Maxine and the kids do indeed pop in for a late lunch. They stumble in, with Chuck charging ahead to dunk dimes in the jukebox. Maxine struggles to balance a fussy Dawn in one arm while carrying a bright pink diaper bag and grown-up lady handbag on the other arm, all while teetering in heels. She makes it to the corner booth, but Dawn's sticky little baby fingers reach out and grab at Maxine's pearl necklace.

"Charles!" she warbles, sending the boy running over with a booster seat. Chuck slides into the booth, blocking Dawn in on one end while Maxine piles up the diaper bag and handbag on the other end. Dawn's happy to slap the tabletop with both hands, but we all know that won't last. Thankfully, Chuck's a seasoned pro at tying down his sister. In less than three seconds, he's got the chair's straps secured around all four of Dawn's limbs. We all breathe a silent sigh of relief when we hear the strap click. Of course, this also signals to Dawn that she's trapped, which prompts a good long minute of her bucking and hollering.

Maxine collapses with all intended drama, letting her forehead rest on the table.

"And how's motherhood treating you today, Maxine?" I inquire.

Maxine's hand shoots up. "Mrphnnee," she moans.

"What's that, Maxine?"

She lifts her head, revealing that her hair resembles the tumbleweeds that get caught in the fence out back after a dust storm. Normally, she's a big blonde, but now she looks like one of those girls in *Valley of the Dolls* who wakes up on the beach after a bad night. I whisper, "You haven't been drinking too much, have you? You don't look . . . great."

She stares up at me with her smudged, probably slept-in eye-liner, and I realize this is the first time I've seen her without her false lashes on. "Robert, darling, let me ask you something." Her voice is stone cold. "Do you have any idea how mind-numbingly boring it is to be around a two-year-old all day? It's far worse than a hangover. It's the nuclear bomb of hangovers."

"I'm sorry," I whisper back while giving her hand a pat.

Maxine bites her lip and swallows hard. "I think our daughter might be feral," she whimpers.

"You're the one who insisted we have children, Maxine."

Friday comes around and I arrive at the condo at 4:04 p.m., instead of the requested—make that demanded—four o'clock sharp. Chuck is in his Sunday best with enough cream in his hair to make it stiff and shiny. He sits in front of the TV, watching yet another report from Vietnam.

I hear the piercing scream that can only mean one thing: Maxine is attempting to change Dawn's diaper again. Chuck stops himself from getting off the divan and with sympathetic eyes tells me that Maxine made him vow not to help her this time. "Even if she begs me for it," he adds.

There's more screaming—this time maybe from Maxine—and I decide to heck with all that and charge off toward the kids' room. We're not going to win any crowns if the neighbors think we're child murderers. But I don't take more than two steps before a bare naked Dawn runs by in a blur, followed by Maxine, who appears to be wearing a black garbage bag like a poncho.

"Catch her!"

Dawn runs right to me and I carry her off to the bedroom where Maxine's already got all the diapering equipment laid out.

"We can't have you running around like Lady Godiva. No, no, no!" I say in my best, most high-pitched I-suppose-this-is-how-you-talk-to-a-baby voice. She squeals back, so I figure I'm doing some-thing right. I take a deep breath, think manly thoughts, and change that darned diaper. I even manage to distract her with my keys for long enough to get a dress on her.

"How the shit did you do that?" Maxine yells at me from the doorway.

I lose my grip and Dawn takes off running before I can get her shoes on.

"The book said—"

"The book?" she snaps back.

"Yeah, the Spock book. I've been reading it and it says that a battle of the wills won't work with most kids. You've got to turn stuff like getting diapered and dressed into a game."

"You've been reading the baby book?" She's missing my point altogether.

"I'm also wearing the hat," I point out, tipping my John Wayne ever so slightly.

This softens her instantly. "Manly *and* on theme." She takes off her garbage bag poncho to reveal a dress that's very demure-yet-sexy-housewife. I have no idea if that's an actual fashion term, but it should be. "Do I look all right?" she asks, knowing the answer. "It's always a challenge to find something that doesn't show too much leg or too much boob or is too tight all over. You can do boob *or* leg and still get by with being a lady, but never both. Such a fine line between wholesome and harlot!"

"Please tell me Chuck doesn't have that written somewhere in his notebook."

"Har, har, Robert!" She checks her lipstick in the mirrored closet doors. "I've hung your suit in the bathroom along with some new Brut cologne."

I close the bathroom door and I can still hear her standing—or rather, pacing—right outside the door. I'm expecting to find the suit is some wide-lapelled suede Davy Crockett getup that's straight out of *Hee Haw*. Instead it's a nicely tailored, boring dark suit.

I put it on and come out to the bedroom, where she's waiting with a lint brush.

She takes the lint brush across my shoulders. "My last husband would never wear anything I bought him."

I catch our reflection in the mirrored closet doors. She's got me in a tie that matches the red in her dress. Even with Maxine in ridiculously high heels, I still look tall—and, I guess, strong—next to her. The suit does wonders for my shoulders. I don't know if we scream "husband and wife," but I bet if no one looks too closely, we could pass for dating.

"Remember: tonight, look at me, not them. We'll be fine," she assures me.

She sweeps the lint brush across my behind, startling the bejesus out of me. I pull away and stagger to regain my balance.

So, okay, maybe it is our first date. Our first awkward and awful date.

Maxine Hogarth

Phoenix

June 19, 1970

WE WALK INTO a stuffy, wood-paneled conference room at the Phoenix Convention Center at exactly 5 p.m.. I know Robert was annoyed that I made us wait in the lobby for six whole minutes, but pageants are all about following the rules. If the rules stipulate that an emergency meeting of the Mrs. Arizona Pie pageant committee begins at precisely 5 p.m., then I'm not going to make an entrance at 4:54 p.m. Does this man listen to *anything* I say about first impressions? At least he's wearing the suit I picked out for him. Thank heaven for small miracles, right?

Charles has this thing called a Pez dispenser that gives children their candy one piece at a time so they don't eat it all in one gulp. That's exactly the approach I've taken with Robert and this pageant. He gets the truth one piece at a time. If all goes according to plan, the Hogarths will walk out of here tonight with tickets to the national pageant. Unless that happens, Robert doesn't need to know a thing about it.

At the front of the room sit five semi-imposing-looking judges, each with a small stack of manila folders in front of them and pens in their hands. The sixty-ish man with a tragic comb-over sitting one chair left of center—the gruff, all-business fellow named Mr. Glick—calls the meeting to order. Sitting next to Glick is a tense-looking woman who pageant materials tell me is Mrs. Marjorie Holmes. She's well known to all of Scottsdale and Phoenix for being the woman who complains about comic books and rock 'n' roll music corrupting the minds of the youth. There's a smattering of people—mostly well-dressed women—in attendance, and we all rise and say the Pledge of Allegiance. Charles snaps his hand to his heart like a dutiful soldier and enunciates every word. I certainly hope the judging panel makes note of this, along with little Dawn, who attempts to mimic her patriotic brother, holding her dolly across her chest. It's the sort of perfect moment all the planning in the world can't create. Like Sun Tzu tells me, "If you know the enemy and know yourself, you need not fear the result of a hundred battles." Robert catches my eye and I give him the quickest of winks.

With our undying devotion to Uncle Sam out of the way, we all take our seats. As we practiced at home, once I'm comfortably seated with my skirt arranged properly, Charles places Dawn on my left knee. Unfortunately, Dawn isn't interested in cooperating. As she did roughly 75 percent of the time we rehearsed this scene, she's all squirms and is about to squeal when Charles reaches out to her. She crawls happily—a little *too* happily—into his lap. I give the judges a glance and thank heavens none of them have noticed. I have a Plan B, of course, which is to keep a rattle in my hands at all times. Whenever someone from the panel looks over, I can rattle the toy in Dawn's face. This should make it clear that though she might prefer her butt in her brother's lap, her attention is always on me.

Mr. Glick gets right down to business by introducing the pinched-looking woman seated to his right. Not that I need an introduction to Mrs. Alice Depwelt, the first ever Mrs. American Pie from way back in 1939. Alice is the gold standard among us pageant girls. Everyone thinks that brushed-out, bangs-to-the-side look was created by Jackie Kennedy's hairstylist, but in truth, Alice Depwelt wore it first and Jackie copied her. According to Glick, Alice was sent over all the way from the national office in San Francisco to help with the selection of the new Mrs. Arizona Pie, 1970.

"Excuse me, Mr. Glick," says Alice, interrupting. She's got a throaty, thick-syrup voice that all good socialites cultivate through years of elocution lessons at their all-girls schools. "I think everyone in this room will agree with me that we need to proceed quickly. I am here to assure those wrongs are quickly righted. Preferably in the next"—she looks at her watch—"twenty-two minutes, as I have a plane to catch."

Mr. Glick nods and mutters something as the other members of the panel purse their lips or tightly nod in what Alice takes as agreement. She snaps open her folder and clicks her pen. "Let's get this boat on the water!" She consults with the paperwork in front of her. "Where's this first runner-up? Bellows?"

Oh, Bellows! That name feels tragically appropriate given it's the sound a tugboat makes, which is exactly what Mrs. Bellows resembles in her frumpy orange dress. She timidly stands on her swollen ankles and hurriedly walks to the podium positioned in front of the panel. "I'm Elizabeth Bellows," she all but whispers.

"There's a microphone in front of you, dear," Alice says. "Use it." Oh my! That woman does have snippiness for days!

"Sorry," Mrs. Bellows whispers, and then discovers her microphone. "I'm Elizabeth Bellows."

Mr. Glick pipes up, "Mrs. Bellows, you are ready to assume your duties—"

"No, she isn't, Mr. Glick," interrupts Alice. "How far along are you, Elizabeth?"

"Excuse me?" she responds. And then into the microphone: "Pardon?"

"You're pregnant."

Mrs. Bellows's eyes grow wide. Puzzled, she looks down at her midsection as the rest of the panel murmurs to one another.

Alice holds up a mailing envelope I anonymously sent the state pageant board, waving it slightly. "Someone who goes by the unhelpful moniker of 'Concerned Arizonan' sent me paperwork that appears to show that you are at least five months along, Mrs. Bellows."

Mrs. Bellows starts to say something—again not into her microphone—prompting judge Mrs. Holmes to jump in. "This is *hardly* the year for the pageant to be such a stickler for the rules!" she says with a shocking amount of sarcasm.

"Do you care to elaborate, Mrs. Holmes?" Alice shoots back.

"Well, I mean, what with all that's happening in Illinois. Clearly, the pageant is abandoning all sorts of long-standing rules. Why not allow for a contestant who is with child?"

"I'm not . . . ," Mrs. Bellows mumbles, as everyone ignores her.

"Mrs. Holmes," says Alice, "I sincerely hope you are not comparing this pageant making the brave, and frankly timely, decision to accept black contestants to Mrs. Bellows here, who is pregnant despite her husband being overseas for nearly two years?"

"I'm not pregnant!" Mrs. Bellows screams straight into her microphone. "Someone is lying about me!" She pulls the frumpy dress close to her body, revealing no belly. There are gasps from the audience, which is certainly what I was hoping for at this moment. I was worried that sort of thing only happened in old movies.

Mr. Glick pounds his gavel and everyone settles quickly, although I'm a little worried poor Mrs. Bellows is confused. Why she's still at the podium is anyone's guess.

"Mrs. Bellows!" Alice speaks up over Mr. Glick's gavel banging. Alice reaches over and yanks the gavel from his hand. She sets it on the table and out of his reach. "Mrs. Bellows, we cannot have any additional black marks on this pageant!"

Mrs. Holmes snickers openly and Mrs. Depwelt shoots her a look that could curdle milk. It shuts Mrs. Holmes right up.

Mrs. Depwelt continues, "So, I'm sorry, dear. But this is not your year. Take care now."

Mrs. Bellows is obviously relieved to be dismissed and scurries right out of the room.

I'm certain Alice Depwelt understands this is all pageant trickery, which is a time-honored tradition in beauty pageants, right up there with fraternities hazing freshmen or the Masons requiring a blood sacrifice. Provided you aren't caught red-handed pleasuring a judge or putting rat poison in another girl's blueberry pie, pageant trickery is considered part of the game. Alice shuffles through some papers and photographs. "Let's move on to the second and—heaven help us—third runners-up." A blonde in a red-and-white polka-dot dress hesitantly stands. I know this woman to be second runner-up, Mrs. Thompson.

Everyone in the audience, as well as on the panel, sits at rapt attention. My ouster of Bellows gave them enough of a taste to know something *really* good should be coming next. Alice glances down at her watch and then back to the papers. She nods as if to say, *Can you believe the lighting on this clandestine shot of Mrs. Thompson exiting a filthy adult movie theater?* Yes, yes, I can believe it.

Finally Alice speaks. "Mrs. Thompson? You are free to go. Thank you for your interest in the pageant. And on your way out, perhaps you should check the bushes for photographers. You're being followed, dear."

Thompson quickly rises and sprints away, like a deer fleeing a hunter's crosshairs.

"Mrs. Kolchek?" asks Mrs. Depwelt.

A tall, broad-shouldered woman in a brown dress tentatively raises her hand and then stands.

"Nice to see you wearing clothes, dear. You, too, may go, with my apologies."

I see the flash and hear the click of a photographer's camera go off. The audience gasps again as *dressed* settles in. In fairness, the woman whose body I had the Fotomat boy place Mrs. Kolchek's head upon in the photos was merely topless and not fully nude. It was more "arty" than "filth."

"I think I'll stay and watch," Mrs. Kolchek counters in the deadest of deadpan.

I look to Robert and smile. His eyes grow wide.

He whispers in my ear, "Why do you look like a cartoon villain who has a lady tied to the tracks?"

"This is how pageants work, dear," I whisper back. "And get that look off your face. I'm about to have a moment."

The unflappable Alice lets out a sigh. "This brings us to . . . Mrs. Maxine Hogarth?"

All right, Maxine, this is it, I think. *This is what all your hard work has led to.*

I snap to my feet in a move I believe exemplifies grace and determination. With brisk, purposeful strides, I walk to the podium, an easy smile on my face. Not too toothy; not too cat-who-just-ate-several-birds. Once at the podium, I expand that smile to something that says "gracious hostess" and look each judge in the eye.

"Mrs. Hogarth," says Alice, "Our 'Concerned Arizonan' doesn't seem to have sent us any 'helpful' information about you."

I laugh gently, as if the sound coming out of my mouth is more than enough to blow away whatever silly accusations Alice is suggesting. "When I read in the paper last week that the pageant unfortunately needed a new queen for this year, I sent my application right in. You know, just on the off chance the pageant needed more viable contestants."

Alice doesn't bat an eye at that last comment. Nor does she budge to call me out on my trickery. So I continue. "As you'll see from the enclosed contestant materials, I was a Miss San Bernardino, so I understand how some poor dears can be overtaken by competitiveness."

This seems to satisfy Mr. Glick and two other panel members, although Mrs. Holmes's lips are turned down in a schoolmarm frown. Ever the pro, Alice is pure poker face.

"Why don't you tell us a bit about yourself, Mrs. Hogarth?" says Mr. Glick.

"I'm Maxine Hortence Hogarth, formerly of Southern California," I say in a tone of voice I've dubbed "the Rose Petal." This tone is subdued and even. It says that I'm never the loudest in the room, yet still a voice worth listening to. "I'm recently wed to Mr.

Robert Hogarth, whom many of you may know as the proprietor of the charming family restaurant La Dulcinea, over in Scottsdale."

This sends all eyes over to Robert. I fear the worst, but thankfully he keeps those cheeks of his well within acceptable levels of red. When he gives the audience a friendly nod, I notice that most of the women sit up a little straighter in their chairs and nod back. I give him an adoring stare.

"If I could be so blunt," says Mrs. Holmes, holding up our Old Tucson "family" photo, "if you are only recently married, how do you explain the children?"

"I'm so glad you asked, Mrs. Holmes. While Robert and I have not yet been blessed with a child, I am twice blessed to be the new mother to his beautiful children, Charles and Dawn," I gush. This tone I call "the New Mother," since it requires me to sound a touch overcome with warm emotion. I put my arms out to call attention to Dawn and Charles, who, exactly as we practiced, smiles and waves—first to the judges, and then to the audience.

"And their mother?" quizzes Alice.

I take my tone down to "Horrible News." It's nearly a whisper, but deeper to suggest the seriousness of it all. "I'm afraid the poor woman has passed on."

The audience and panel offer their condolences in the form of sighs and headshakes. I don't dare look at Robert. I take it on faith that he's smiling and nodding his way through this. In all the scenarios I've run through my mind, so long as Robert doesn't vomit or scream at me, we'll get through this fine.

It's time for me to finish them off.

I take a deep breath and dive in. "From the second my dear Robert put this band of gold on my finger, I promised him, the children, and God that I would pour everything within me—everything I am—into raising these darling babies. Though they are not of my body, I can swear to you all today that Charles and Dawn are part of my heart."

I hear sniffles coming at me in all directions as I look over to my family. Charles is practically vibrating in his seat. He gives me a smile that more than makes up for the fact that Robert's eyes are darting around the room like a trapped animal's.

I think of Thanksgiving and coming out of that pool to the screams of my guests. Cue the tears.

Charles smiles widely and gives me an enthusiastic wave. "That's my mom!" he shouts. That boy has earned himself a new pocketknife.

Mrs. Holmes bursts into tears. Mr. Glick grapples for his gavel. He bangs it harshly on the tabletop, as if he has no other outlet for all the emotion welling inside him. The other two women on the panel embrace.

Alice is silent and steely, so much so, my toes curl. From over the top of her glasses, her eyes bore holes into me. I can't show any weakness. I can't give her a nanosecond of fear or even uncertainty. I hold her gaze, not pleadingly, but as if to assure her that I am a worthy adversary. The room grows silent and I feel stillness all around me.

Mrs. Alice Depwelt breaks the stare. I allow myself to blink, but otherwise don't move a muscle. Without a word, Alice rises from the table and collects her things, stuffing all the papers and photos into a Hermès briefcase and snapping it shut.

"You'll do," Alice announces. "See Glick for your crown."

I squeal with schoolgirl delight and rush to thank each judge. Ancient Mr. Glick puts the crown in my hands, while Mrs. Holmes takes the bobby pins I "happened" to have in my purse to affix it to my head. I get some more tears to well up in my eyes just in time for a newspaper photograph. I smile my whitest, brightest toothpaste-ad smile for the camera. As the flash goes off, my derrière stays unclenched. Goddamn, I forgot how good it feels to win! I look to Robert, who smiles broadly and shakes his head as if to promise me he'll never doubt me again.

"We did it!" Charles gushes while grabbing my arm and pulling me out into the aisle. I feel people patting me on the back and shaking my hand, but I can't make out faces or hear most of what they're saying. Robert approaches with Dawn in his arms. I take her in and give her a kiss, leaving a coral-red lip print on her darling cheek.

I lean into Robert for what better look like a tender hug. This is the only moment I couldn't practice for. He accepts me warmly.

"I can't believe you did all this," he says in awe.

"I told you to have faith in me," I whisper back. "We need to let that Kolchek woman leave first," I insist. "It's safer that way."

Robert "Mr. Arizona Pie" Hogarth

Phoenix

June 19, 1970

WELL, THIS EVENING sure as heck explains what Maxine's been up to. Crazy as it sounds—and bear in mind that I'm without question now an expert on the art of crazy—I'm glad Maxine didn't tell me everything. It's one thing to know your new wife has pulled the hood off a family of racists. But all this other cloak-and-dagger stuff? Maybe Chuck is right about her being a spy. I'll never look at a socialite the same way again—nor will I ever make an enemy of one.

I sit with the kids in the lobby for what feels like hours while Maxine spends forever and a day first in the bathroom getting her crown properly placed on her head, and then glad-handing and posing for photos with all the judges, audience members, and some guy who wandered into the convention center in need of directions. Maxine was spot-on about Mrs. Kolchek. She sulks in the shadows of the coat check before finally giving up and going home.

As the crowd thins out, I get a chance to look through the bright pink "contestant packet" Maxine handed me earlier. It's a full itinerary for the five days we'll be spending competing in the national pageant, where all families are put up in cabins at a resort. In this setting, the women are judged at all things related to keeping house. I'm laughing on the inside at the thought of Maxine and the other contestants being studied in their natural habitat, like an episode of *Mutual of Omaha's Wild Kingdom*. I can hear Marlin Perkins telling us in hushed tones how the North American housewife is known for her ironing skills and predatory instincts over a hot stove. Wait. Where is this resort?

I flip back to the folder's bright pink cover.

Palm Springs?

The Palm Springs?

Did Maxine know this? Who am I kidding? Of course she knew. This woman knew the names, addresses, blood types, and God knows what else about the judges and competition tonight. She had a fresh pack of bobby pins in her purse on the assumption she'd be putting on a crown tonight. A lack of attention to detail is hardly one of Maxine's flaws.

"Maxine," I say in a voice so deep and firm that even I'm surprised, "I think it's time for us to get the kids home."

She gives the photographer a final smile and pries herself away. I not so gently grab her by the arm and steer her out the doors. Chuck walks quickly to keep up, singing that awful "Arizona" pop song I wish I had never put in the jukebox. He's got Dawn dead asleep on his shoulder.

"Robert!" she yelps as I half drag her across the empty parking lot. "What has gotten into you?"

I stop at the Jaguar and feel my face growing red. I wave the pink contestant packet in front of Maxine's startled face. "When were you going to tell me about Palm Springs?"

"Oh, is that what you're in such a tizzy over?" she says.

"I'm not 'in a tizzy,' Maxine! This is me trying to understand why you would enter a contest under completely false pretenses, with two kids who aren't ours, when you know—you darn tootin' well know—we're all going to land on your ex-husband's doorstep?"

My carrying on only makes Chuck sing louder. He walks fast in circles around the car, belting out something about taking off your rainbow. That tune is not leaving my head anytime soon, and that makes me all the madder.

"For starters, Robert," Maxine finally says, "I had no idea when *we* entered the pageant that the contest was in Palm Springs. Moreover, I only learned three days ago that Western Airlines is a sponsor."

"Are you trying to kill me?" I am literally hopping mad and pacing about the parking lot in wide, angry steps.

"Car! Now!" She flings the door open on the E-Type.

I get in the driver's seat and sincerely hope that Mrs. Kolchek is lying in wait in the backseat. No such luck.

"What the dickens are you thinking!" I quasi-yell, my finger right in her face.

"Get that finger out of my face!" she full-on yells back at me. Her head snaps to the left and she waves and smiles big as one of the judges walks across the parking lot. The second the judge is out of sight, Maxine gets back to screaming at me. "For someone who won't shut the fuck up about not 'really' being my husband, you sure as shit are acting like you are!"

I grip the steering wheel with both hands, and that wedding ring digs into my flesh. Maxine leans back against the door, the tip of her crown gently tapping against the window. "Western Airlines is a sizable company. Judges from these things are always from the marketing department, and Douglas is in accounting. They never let those math weirdos be out in public, and besides, no one knows that Maxine Simmons is now Maxine Hogarth. I'm telling you, we're fine."

"But, Maxine—"

"Robert, look at me," she pleads.

I don't want to see her. I don't want to be here. I can't breathe. This is like getting bounced out of college all over again.

"Robert," she whimpers, putting her hand on top of my shaking one. "Think about why we're doing this. It's for the kids, for me, for your business."

"There's too much that can go wrong, Maxine." I want to pull my hand away, but I can't move.

"Look at me," she insists.

I tilt my head up just enough to meet her gaze. She puts her hand on my heaving chest and pushes gently, as if to show me at what speed my heart should be beating. "I was wrong not to tell you everything," she admits. "Remember what I promised you on our wedding day? I swore I would never let anything bad happen to us."

"I can't do this."

"Yes, you can."

The car windows are fogged up from our breathing. I can't see anything but what's in front of me. Like all that exists right now is inside this car.

"Please believe in me, Robert. Believe in us." Even with her crown askew and her lipstick wearing thin, she still has more confidence than I ever will. It's maybe a little too infectious.

"I need honesty, Maxine. Can you please aim for that?"

Maxine nods and I nod back. She lunges forward and gives me a warm, reassuring hug that lasts long enough for my heart to begin beating normally again.

I start up the car. There's a loud tap on the window, followed by Maxine's startled scream. It's Chuck, with Dawn still on his shoulder, looking like a rejected puppy. Maxine gets out of the car and flips her seat forward, giving him and Dawn room to climb in and get seated. Then Maxine gets back in the car and shuts the door. She and I stare at each other, wordlessly sharing in our shame at nearly forgetting our fake children.

"Y'all might not want to ditch us in front of the contest people," Chuck says flatly. It might be my imagination, but he sounds genuinely terse.

Chuck gets Dawn in her car seat and himself seated next to her. I put the car in gear and drive us home. Maxine sits hunched over slightly in her seat to give the crown atop her head enough room.

Charles "Chuck" Bronski

Scottsdale to Palm Springs

July 1970

I DON'T WANT to sound ungrateful, but Miss Maxine is driving me nuts. And not only me. I think Mr. Robert is feeling it too. He and I spent nearly an hour getting his car all packed up with Miss Maxine's essentials. My Boy Scout handbook says essentials are stuff like a pocketknife and a poncho. For Miss Maxine, "essentials" are things like seven pairs of white shoes that all look the same and fifty million tubes of lipstick and a whole suitcase of something called "unmentionables." Somehow me and Mr. Robert manage to fit five leopard-spotted suitcases and four pink suitcases piled into the trunk and tied to the roof. We're pretty happy with ourselves when she tells us we need to unpack everything and repack it all in her teeny-tiny, itty-bitty James Bond car.

"I need to make an entrance, Robert. That pinewood derby bucket of yours won't do."

Robert rubs his temples. "But, Maxine, my car is a family sedan. It's got *family* right in its name for a reason."

"Exactly. Everyone will be driving in one of those. If we arrive in the E-Type, we'll look endlessly more sophisticated!"

"It's not going to fit, Maxine."

"Of course it is! I got it all out here in that car."

"You didn't move to Scottsdale with a husband and two kids!" Mr. Robert points at me. I'm glad he did this, because to be totally honest, I'm getting sick of always having to remind them about me and Dawn. I know we've only been a sorta-kinda family for three weeks, but come on. Robert pulls Maxine aside. Grown-ups always do this. They think walking four steps from a kid means we can't hear them. I can hear them.

Robert puts his hands on his hips like he's about to give her a good talking-to. "Maxine, do I need to remind you how you acquired this car?"

"I *earned* it," she snaps, whipping off her sunglasses.

"You don't worry that the car's former owner might not see things that way?"

She stares at him like she's thinking it through. I want to know who had the car before she did. Miss Maxine doesn't look like a car thief, but then again, I probably couldn't tell you what a car thief really looks like. On TV they are all grubby and have mustaches.

Mr. Robert continues. "Can't you see how flaunting the car might be considered antagonistic?"

I don't know what that word means, but I write it in my notebook to look up later.

"Maxine?" Mr. Robert says all impatient-like.

"For the last goddamned time, he isn't going to be there."

"It's at a golf course, Maxine. That's his natural habitat."

She turns on her heels and walks back toward the condo.

"Where the heck is she going?" Mr. Robert says to me. Like I know.

Miss Maxine calls out over her shoulder, "I'm getting some goddamned hair ties to hold the trunk closed!"

We get on the road to Palm Springs at 4:35 a.m. This is thirty-five minutes late, according to according to Mr. Robert, although Miss Maxine says we'll make that time up when she takes over driving once we get to Blythe. Mr. Robert said he needs to drive under the speed limit since one bump and all of Miss Maxine's unmentionables will be littering Highway 10. Boy, I wish I knew what *unmentionables* were, especially since everybody keeps *mentioning* them. Mr. Robert looks at Miss Maxine like he's hoping she'll say something about how we're packed like sardines in the tiny E-Type. There's a suitcase where my feet are supposed to be, and Dawn's car seat has a hatbox underneath it. Miss Maxine rolls her eyes at Mr. Robert and turns up the radio to that song where the lady sings "Oooh, child" and says that everything's going to get brighter. I sure hope so. Sometimes these two are like Mr. and Mrs. Brady and sometimes they are more like Lucy and Ricky. Today is a Lucy and Ricky day. Except there's no one laughing.

Once we clear Phoenix, it's all desert. It's too hot and dusty to put the top down. I'm bored looking out the window and honestly, I just want to get this contest started. I've done all this practicing stuff and now I'm itchin' to go do it all. I'm not talkin' about the which-fork-to-use-at-dinner stuff or all the rules about which side of Miss Maxine I'm supposed to walk on, or the three different tie knots I need to wear depending on the event, or how to hide that Dawn still likes me best. No, I'm all excited about putting my new spy skills to work. Miss Maxine also had me make up a few cover stories about meeting my grandma, some lady named Lula.

Grandma Lula lives in France, but she came home to America to meet her new grandkids. She gave me this big book of children's adventure stories. They were all in French, but every night she'd read me one, saying the page in French and then in English. I don't know the rest and Miss Maxine says it won't matter since people don't want to listen to kids tell stories.

"The whole point of the exercise, Charles, is to assure people understand that you've met my mother and that she lives in France," Miss Maxine told me. Then she laughed out loud at something in her head. "As if Lula wouldn't kill you where you stand before letting you call her Grandma."

Dawn's being a good baby. She must like sitting up higher in her seat since she's clapping her hands and making her funny little squeal-y noises. Miss Maxine turns around in the front seat and dangles a toy out in front of Dawn, who dives forward to grab it only to have the straps on her seat hold her back.

Miss Maxine tickles her in the face with a stuffed rattle bear. "Who's the prettiest little girl in the world?" Dawn squeaks and squirms. "Who's going to help me win the crown?"

This goes on for miles until no one finds it fun anymore and Dawn does something God-awful in her diaper. Mr. Robert pulls the car over and I grab the diapering supplies just figurin' I'm gonna be called in for the big cleanup. Miss Maxine takes the supplies from me.

"You boys go for a walk up the road a bit." She sounds nervous. Maybe even kinda scared. "I think Dawn and I are ready to do this ourselves."

Mr. Robert and I unload some luggage to give Miss Maxine room to do what she's got to do. Then we do what we're told and I count out a good fifty paces from the car. All we can see is Miss Maxine's hind end sticking out the passenger side. Everything is quiet and still, which trust me, knowing my sister, doesn't mean much. She's got a hair trigger and can blow at any second.

"Can I ask you something, Mr. Robert?"

"Only if you promise to drop the 'Mr.' and just call me Robert."

"Okay, Robert, sir. What was all that about it being a bad idea to bring Miss Maxine's car?"

"Well, for one, we have to unpack half the car before we can get your sister out."

I look at him and try real hard to raise only one eyebrow so he knows that I know he's trying to change the subject. I dunno if I can raise only one eyebrow, but it works anyway.

Robert lets out a sigh. "Fine, it's not like you aren't going to figure it out. This car once belonged to Maxine's ex-husband."

"Miss Maxine has an ex-husband?" I try picturing this, and all I can figure is that he was a master enemy spy or maybe a cat burglar in Europe like in those Pink Panther movies. "Is he dangerous?"

"Not really. He's a jerk, though. . . ."

"So, he's gonna be all mad that you're with his girl now?"

"If the 'girl' you're talking about is Maxine, then no. If you mean the car, though, then oh yes."

"So she honest to goodness *did* steal the car?"

"Yup."

"Wow."

We get back to staring at the car. Dawn's countdown hits zero and her internal nuke bomb goes off. We hear her loud, sharp scream, and Miss Maxine pops out of the car. She waves at us like she's flagging down a police officer.

Robert turns to me. "I'll rock-paper-scissors you for it."

"On three," I say.

One. Two. Three. My rock beats his scissors.

He walks toward the car and Miss Maxine meets him halfway to hand him a crumpled diaper.

We get across the Arizona border to Blythe, California, and stop for gas. I've never been anywhere but Arizona, so I'm curious. It looks just like Arizona, which is pretty disappointing, but Miss Maxine promises me the rest of California is much better.

"Did you know that in California you can go surfing and skiing on the same day?" she tells me.

"Are we gonna see the ocean?" I ask. "Groovy!"

"No, no ocean this trip. But we will be seeing Palm Springs. With beautiful red desert and lush golf courses."

"Sounds like Scottsdale to me." I right away feel bad for sounding bummed out.

I see her watch Mr.—I mean, Robert—walk into the station to pay for the gas. When she knows he can't hear her, she leans in close to me. "Listen, I need you to be my eyes and ears at this pageant, okay?"

"Yes, ma'am," I say, "like always."

"Do reconnaissance, or whatever you call it. Crawl behind enemy lines and gather intelligence. Like in those books and movies you love. The James Bond stuff."

I hate it when I start to feel too much like a dumb kid, but that's where I'm at again. A dumb kid with expensive, grown-up equipment. "Who's the enemy, Miss Maxine?"

"The other contestants. We need to keep a close eye on them and make sure there's no sabotage or general tomfoolery. That sort of thing."

"Gotcha!" I say, pretending I'm not surprised that there's sabotage at a beauty pageant. I've seen those on TV and everyone looks so pretty and nice. "Do you want me to also keep an eye on your ex-husband?"

Miss Maxine rolls her eyes and slumps a little. "You know about *that*, do you?"

I nod. I hope she doesn't ask me how I know it.

"His name is Douglas Simmons and I hate to disappoint you, but he won't be there."

I nod again. Harder this time.

"Now don't tell Robert anything about the mission. Got it?"

Robert gets back in the car and he and Miss Maxine decide to stop being Lucy and Ricky and give Mr. and Mrs. Brady a try.

"Your nose is as red as a Kennedy's," Miss Maxine tells Robert while smearing white sunscreen all over his face.

"I hate wearing this stuff, Maxine. I'm all goopy."

"You'll thank me when you aren't burned to a crisp."

He stops fussin' and lets her rub it around until his face looks normal again.

True to her word, Miss Maxine decides it's time for her to drive and we are back on schedule quickly. It's a good thing the roads are all flat desert cuz Miss Maxine has what Robert calls "a lead foot." I have to lean over and close Dawn's window most of the way to make sure nothing blows in and hurts her soft little face. With her diaper changed, she conks right out.

"Charles, dear, while we're driving, why don't you quiz me?" Miss Maxine says. "I put the contestant biographies in your knapsack."

Normally, I wouldn't open any book that's this shade of bright pink, mainly cuz there are some things that, like Robert says, "just aren't proper for a boy to see." He says that's doubly true of any book owned by Miss Maxine. But she says these are study materials, so I open it up.

"How come this looks like a yearbook, Miss Maxine?"

"It's the pageant yearbook, Charles, which for our purposes also serves as competition research."

Each page has a big picture of a pretty lady wearing a crown and then a couple other pictures of her with her husband and kids. The ladies all have something called a "personal statement" where they talk about themselves. The first page is for Mrs. Arizona Pie, except that someone has used a pen to put big black *X*s over her eyes. I flip through a few more pages and see that Miss Maxine's written on a bunch of the pages.

"Start from the top, please, Charles. You can skip Arizona, obviously. Give me the state and I'll recite back the contestant. From there we can discuss strategy."

I see Robert shake his head, but he doesn't say anything.

"Mrs. Arkansas Pie," I say, looking at a dark-haired lady in a fancy dress sitting on top of a big horse.

"Nanette Barker. She's not *really* competition. We can move on."

"But she's in the book, Miss Maxine."

She ignores what she always told me about keeping your eyes on the road and turns her head to look at me in the backseat. She squints the way she always does when she's about to explain something to me. "Read aloud the portion of her personal statement that I've underlined."

"'I love my husband, my children, and my country.' Isn't that what you're supposed to say?"

"Everyone loves their husband, kids, and country. That's like saying 'I breathe air.' To win a pageant, dear Charles, one needs to bring something more to the table. You need to love all those things in a way that is unique." Miss Maxine reaches back and taps on the photo in the book. "Forward to Mrs. Idaho."

Mrs. Idaho Pie's picture is bigger than all the other ladies' pictures. She's a super-duper fancy-looking lady with blond hair that makes her look like a movie star. Or maybe she looks like a star because of the fluffy white fur coat she's wearing wrapped around her bare shoulders.

"First impressions, Charles? Be sure to read her statement."

I firmly believe in the mission of our former First Lady Mrs. Johnson and her desire to "Make America more beautiful." I believe that beauty should start with every woman's personal appearance, and that of her home and family. Elegance is patriotic! That's her whole statement. Most ladies have one that's much longer, but I guess Mrs. Idaho kept hers short to make room for her big picture.

"I think Mrs. Idaho wants to be famous," I tell Miss Maxine, whose big smile tells me it's the right answer.

"Excellent, Charles. This is why I will make sure that Mrs. Idaho never feels special in my presence. If you flip forward to Mrs. Rhode Island, you'll see that she has an obvious need to please people. I will be polite—but vocal—in my disapproval of everything she does."

"But why will she care?" I ask.

"Oh, she'll say she doesn't care. She'll even tell me she doesn't care. Mark my words, it will eat away at her psyche." Miss Maxine points to her brain when saying *psyche*, which is super helpful since I didn't know what that word meant.

"Give me another, Charles."

"Wisconsin."

"Too easy. She has a whole brood of children, so I'll mention how I admire how selfless she is to do that to her body."

That sounds like a nice thing to say to me, but Robert breathes in loud through his nose while shaking his head.

"Texas."

"Even easier. I'll mention how *my* hairdresser never lets me *near* that shade of blond and ask for her advice on how to convince him that I can pull off that much brass."

"Maxine, do you think these are appropriate things to be teaching the boy?" says Robert.

"The boy needs to learn how to deal with other people. If he chooses a career in business or politics, he needs to be prepared for shark-infested waters."

"It's a beauty pageant, Maxine. For housewives."

Miss Maxine puts her hands to her mouth like people in horror movies do. "Robert Thomas Hogarth! That is the most sexist and appalling thing I've ever heard you say!"

"How is me saying that women aren't as awful as men sexist?"

"Because women *are* every bit as horrible as men!"

Robert snorts. "Untrue. I don't see women out there starting wars."

"That is pure ignorance, Robert. We women might not have bayonets and nuclear bombs, but we battle."

"What do you know about violence, Maxine?"

"I'm a woman, Robert. A *W-O-M-A-N*. The fact that you're a man makes me far more of an expert on this subject than you'll ever be."

She pulls the car off to the side of the road and we come to a stop with a hard jerk.

"Furthermore!" she says loudly enough to wake up Dawn. "I know what beauty pageants are truly all about. You are a stranger in a strange land here, Robert. You are about to tread onto enemy territory you know nothing about. You would be wise to stick close to me lest you get your head shot off!"

Robert looks angry and sick and unhappy all rolled up together. "This is *exactly* why I didn't want to do this, Maxine."

"Yeah, well. Too late now, dear-heart."

Miss Maxine gets back on the road. Dawn falls asleep again. I don't want them to keep arguing, so I change the subject.

"Hey, Miss Maxine, why does this yearbook start at Arizona? Where's Alaska and Alabama?" I flip through and see that a few other states are missing.

"There's never been a Mrs. Alaska Pie because the poor women up there are too busy trying to stay alive as opposed to entering beauty pageants. There's no Alabama, Mississippi, or, strangely, Utah, for reasons I can only assume are related to Mrs. Illinois."

This gets Robert's attention. He turns back in his seat as I flip to the right page. Mrs. Illinois Pie is a lady named Maisey Walker. I don't want to be rude, but the first thing I notice is that she's a black lady. The second thing I notice is that she's a very beautiful black lady. I've heard that expression before, about a woman who "lights up a room." I always thought that meant some teenage lady dancing on a beach in a surf movie or something. Now that I've seen the picture of Mrs. Illinois, I know that expression is about her. I know a lot of kids, and none of them have moms who look like this.

"Can I see that?" Robert takes the book from me and I feel funny about it, but I didn't want to let it go. I want to read more about Mrs. Walker.

"It's 1970 and they are finally getting around to integrating?" Robert says to Miss Maxine.

"I'm not thrilled about Mrs. Illinois," says Miss Maxine. Robert gives her a shocked look. "Not because of *that*! Goodness, Robert."

"Well, what is it then?"

"Read her statement. Charles, pay attention."

Robert reads it out loud, "'I think Mrs. American Pie is first and foremost about setting a positive example, not only in her home, but in the community. She may be beautiful and gracious, but also real. Women should not so much look up to her but see her as the type of person they could easily be if they keep their crucial roles of wife, mother, and citizen in mind.'"

We all sit quietly and think on that, which I bet is exactly what Mrs. Illinois wants us to do.

"Chuck, do you have your flag handy? We might need to pull over and let you hold it up so we can salute it," Robert says in that tone grown-ups use when they want to be funny without sounding like they want to be funny.

"Robert, stop playing around. This Maisey Walker is the only woman in that book I can't figure out how to beat. I mean, look at those children! That husband!"

I lean over Robert's seat to get a good look at the other photos. They look like an ordinary family, I suppose. Nothing special. I mean, in our photo we all have the cowboy stuff on. This family is just kinda sitting there with a girl a little older than Dawn on Mrs. Illinois's lap and a boy about eight standing next to Mr. Illinois.

"I've never met a black person before," I blurt out, unable to hold it in any longer. I don't think it's wrong of me to say it, but it still feels weird coming out of my mouth. I don't want to be prejudiced. I want to like all Americans all equally and stuff. But it's true. I've only seen black people on TV.

"Well, you will soon, dear."

"You don't think the pageant will eliminate her right away?" Robert asks.

"She sang at a church service attended by President Nixon, Robert. Black or not, she's not getting knocked out of this thing early. It's too obviously racist. If bigotry gets in the way for her, it will happen later."

I want to say something about how Miss Maxine doesn't have any notes written on the page for Mrs. Illinois.

"Hey, Miss Maxine, do you think the other pageant ladies write notes in the book like you do?"

"If they're worth their salt they do, Charles."

"Because you aren't in the book, they still have that KKK lady in there."

"That's right," she says, laughing. "They have no idea what's coming."

We stop once more when we reach the WELCOME TO PALM SPRINGS! sign so that Miss Maxine and Robert can change seats. Miss Maxine says it won't look right if she's the one driving.

"If there's one thing I hope to impart upon you children it's that appearances matter," she tells me and Dawn.

"Criminy, Maxine," says Robert. "That's *really* what you want to teach them?"

"Yes, really," she says while putting on more lipstick. "They know that all that 'be a good person' stuff is included in my teaching of 'appearances matter.' Right, Charles?"

"Appearing to be a good person matters," I tell them. It takes a couple seconds for me and them to realize how that sounds. It ain't great.

Thankfully, Robert laughs and repeats it to himself, then laughs some more. "We should put that on the Hogarth family crest."

"I considered a family crest," says Miss Maxine, "but decided it was too stuffy. We need to be ordinary, but in a better-than-ordinary sort of way."

We reach what looks like downtown Palm Springs and Miss Maxine gets real quiet all of a sudden. She puts on her big sunglasses and has her head turned to look out the window. When Robert asks if he needs to turn right or left, she doesn't say anything, just points to the right.

Palm Springs does look a lot like Scottsdale, but with nicer cars and fancier people. We stop at a light and I see this group of women standing around talking outside a Spanish mansion. Each one is in a bright dress and I want to tell Miss Maxine how they look like all the varieties of ice cream behind the glass case at Thrifty Drug. But when she sees the ladies, she turns her head away from the window and sinks a little lower in her seat. The lady wearing the pistachio-ice-cream-colored dress stares at the E-Type and says something to the other ladies, who all turn their heads and look. Another lady, this one in a bubble-gum-pink-ice-cream dress, leans over to get a good look in the car. She's staring right at us with this worried look on her face and I don't know if I should wave or smile or what.

"Miss Maxine, some ladies are lookin' at us all funny-like!"

"Robert, go!" She stomps her foot while ducking down in her seat.

The light turns green and Robert guns it so hard, we squeal going around the corner. Miss Maxine sits up and gets back to staring out the window. Robert looks like he wants to say something, but knows she'll get ticked off if he does. I'm too curious to keep my mouth shut.

"Do those ladies know you or something?" I say, like me asking is no big deal.

Miss Maxine snort laughs. "They thought they did!"

I don't get it. You either know somebody or you don't. Or maybe they knew Miss Maxine by some other name? I know ladies take their husband's last names, so maybe Miss Maxine had a different first name when she was married to that other guy? We turn down another street and Robert pulls over next to a sign for the Whitewater Country Club. He puts the car in park and kills the engine. Then we just sit there. Robert and Miss Maxine don't say or do anything. It's dead silent in the car except for the *tisk-tisk-tisk* of the sprinklers on the golf course.

"You ready for this?" Robert says to Miss Maxine. He reaches over to pat her arm and she grabs his hand. With her other hand, she flips down the car visor and looks at herself in the mirror.

"Do I look ready?" she asks him.

"You look gorgeous . . . as always."

"Like a winner?"

"You bet," he says. "Right, Chuck?"

"Yup. You're gonna win this thing, Miss Maxine! Right, Dawn?"

Dawn hears her name and wakes up with a start. She yawns and falls back to sleep again without saying nothin'.

Miss Maxine takes her hand away from Robert's and fluffs her hair. "Let's go win this bastard. And, Charles, start calling me Mom."

"Yes, ma'am." Oops. "Mom."

Maxine Hogarth

Pageant Day One

PALM SPRINGS HAS GONE TO SHIT.

At least that's my main takeaway. I recently read somewhere that Frank Sinatra now spends most of his time in Beverly Hills and—let me tell you—without the chairman of the board tooling around the links in his custom cart, Palm Springs doesn't have much going for it. The stucco buildings all need a good hosing down to scrub away the red-dust grime. I think it's entirely possible the city has lost its caché altogether. It's like there's hardly anywhere fabulous left anywhere anymore. Except for Monaco, of course. But I've never been.

Was I thrilled to see Mrs. Martha Becker and her usual cadre of snippy broads standing at the Howard Manor valet? No, I was not. And the way they were gawking at me while I sat helpless at the red light? I can't even believe it. Didn't they get enough to eat at their breakfast, staring at me like I was prime rib? That one in the gaudy pistachio dress—I think she calls herself Tricia—bent down and peered over the top of her sunglasses to get a better look inside the car. Like she was standing in judgment of Elizabeth Taylor fresh from stealing away Eddie Fisher. Listen here, Tricia, I'm no Elizabeth Taylor: I'm Debbie Reynolds. I'm the lovely, charming, innocent wife who was wronged by some tawdry little vixen named

Jennifer. So goddamn you, Tricia, for putting a damper on my triumphant return.

Per usual, Robert is an absolute dear-heart and stops the car outside the club to give me a moment to compose myself. I would chop off a finger for a cigarette right now, but since smoking is for some godforsaken reason falling out of favor for the ladies, the pageant has insisted we "refrain from smoking during the course of the pageant." Bastards! I reach for the next best thing—my trusty tube of lipstick. Robert keeps his eyes on the road, not so much as blinking, as we pull up the long and winding drive to the Whitewater Country Club. There's a line of cars as we approach the main clubhouse and I am quite proud of the way the E-Type stands out among all the drab family sedans. I very much wish to point out to Robert how right I was in bringing the car, but I know my Robert. He's a typical man. And when dealing with a typical man, a woman needs to use subtlety when pointing out how dead wrong he can be.

Will this line ever move? It's nearly noon, meaning two things are about to happen: my hot-rollered hair will wilt and Dawn will do something ungodly in her pants. Neither is ideal.

"Only two more ahead of us," Robert says, as if reading my mind. "What happens after they take the car?"

I read from the information sheet I earlier removed from the pageant binder. "It says that we check in at the pageant concierge desk."

"I need to use the bathroom," Charles announces.

"No, you need to 'excuse yourself,'" I remind him. "But you won't be doing that until after we've shaken hands and smiled politely with all the pageant officials."

I see Robert's eye twitch at the mention of "pageant officials." Unfortunately, those words came out of my mouth at the exact moment we're stopped in front of a large banner proclaiming Western Airlines to be proud sponsors.

"It's a big company," I say just loudly enough for Robert to hear, but not Charles. "And remember, I have a new last name."

"But he lives here, *remember?*" Robert says through clenched teeth. "And you're not supposed to be here, *remember?*"

I swear Charles has a gift for knowing when to change the subject. "I've never seen so many flags in one place in my life!" he bleats, pointing out the window.

There are indeed countless flags. There are small ones on sticks in the grass along the driveway, each no more than a few inches from the next. Up above, there's stars-'n'-stripes bunting strung between the palm trees that line this stretch of Whitewater Club Drive. As we inch closer to the main clubhouse, the quantity of flags thickens, with Old Glory fluttering from lampposts, flowerpots . . . The fountain at the end of the drive is circled by shiny tin pinwheels I know I've seen at the five-and-dime. The main clubhouse was refurbished just a month before my exodus by an architect who studied at Frank Lloyd Wright's academy. Yet you'd never know of its cultured upbringing by looking at the building today. I cringe upon seeing its long, clean lines and high, rectangular windows utterly ruined by the liberal application of red, white, and blue tinsel.

"Hey! There's Mrs. Rhode Island Pie!" Charles yelps, as if he's seen a real celebrity and not some two-bit Jackie Kennedy impersonator.

Climbing out of a beige sedan is Mrs. Betsey Biddle, a brunette in a boxy navy-blue suit and formal hat—yes, a hat on a one-hundred-degree day. She darts past our car with some gangly teen boy and two mousy identical twin girls. Her pear-shaped husband is so laden down with bags that he can't pull the mostly ash cigarette from his lips.

"Oh, to hell with this," I think out loud. "Charles, grab your sister and the diaper bag. We'll walk the rest of the way."

Robert is confused. "I just leave the car here?"

"In park, engine off, leave the keys. Have you never used a valet before?"

"Never while parked two blocks from the valet stand!"

Thank goodness Charles knows how to do what he's told—and without all the theatrics.

"What about all the luggage, Maxine?"

"Valet, Robert! You are Mr. Arizona Pie and not Mr. Arizona Pack Mule!" I hand him his hat, which he puts on his head without so much as a grumble. It's a shame to cover up that great head of hair, but first impressions. . . .

Some people have faux furs; I happen to have a faux-mily, I tell myself, quickly looking them all over for errors. Charles is looking neat 'n' tidy in his button-down. With any luck, Dawn will keep the ties on her sunbonnet out of her mouth. I'm ready for my entrance. Shoulders back, chin up, calm, confident strides as if all the world is watching. If only my husband weren't walking three steps behind me.

"Robert!" I hiss at him. "Next to me, please?"

He catches up, nearly tripping over his own feet, but recovers nicely and offers his arm. Since this is not a sophomore homecoming dance we are strolling into and we are supposed to be newlyweds, I try to take his hand, but he recoils and, sweet baby Jesus, I hope no one is watching, because I just accidentally slapped my husband's tush in broad daylight.

Robert freezes and turns redder than the stripes on the flags engulfing us. "What the holy heck are you doing?" he whispers.

"I'm trying to walk into this pageant like I've already won it. And to do that effectively, I need to be holding my handsome husband's hand," I whisper back.

He wipes his hand down the front of his chinos then thrusts it out in my general direction.

"What *are* you doing?" I'm beginning to wish we had stayed in the goddamned car.

"My hand was sweaty." He rubs it up and down on his pants once more. Again I try to take his hand, but rather than take mine, he skitters behind me and then to my opposite side.

"Take. My. Damn. Hand. Now."

Robert takes my left hand into his right hand. His palm is a little damp, but his grip is . . . not bad. Not too tight, yet also not limp. He gives me a nod, takes a deep breath, and just like that, we're walking hand in hand, smiling. And we're not at arm's length. With every step, we stand a little closer to each other. You'd never know I'd forced him into this. Well, maybe *forced* is too strong a word. *Conned*? *Cajoled*? Let's go with *cajoled*. Makes me sound mysterious.

Robert leans in closer. "You should at least tell me what your ex-husband looks like. Just in case."

My hubby sure does know how to kill a mood.

"He's not going to be here. But to humor you, picture a shorter Fred MacMurray crossed with Andy Griffith . . . only more Satan-y."

Robert's unable to chastise me for that little quip thanks to our arrival at the clubhouse, where all the contestants are gathering for a meet and greet. Without even being told, that brilliant Charles hands me Dawn, who's luckily in that most adorable but rare of baby moods—sleepy without being grumpy. Her little cheeks are slightly flushed, the curls around her forehead a bit damp, but it's nothing I can't quickly brush into place with my fingers.

We barely have one foot in the clubhouse reception room before some perky little thing with a clipboard comes bounding over like a beagle. Her name tag reads MISSY, and I swear I've never seen a ponytail pulled quite that tight or bouncing with that much energy. "Arizona Pies!" she whoops as every head in the place snaps toward us. "Don't you look handsome in your cowboy hat!" She giggles.

Robert blushes and flashes a nervous little smile that is undeniably sexy. It's not handsome. It's not dashing. It's *S-E-X-Y* with the emphasis on the *S-E-X* part. Missy coos like a melting dove, and Mrs. Idaho Pie's constantly batting eyes go for a long stroll up and down that husband of mine. That sexy-sex husband of mine. I can't wait to remind him of this perfect moment the next time he frets about getting caught in our ruse.

"So, do you rustle up cattle for living?" Missy squeaks out.

"Only thing I rustle up are drinks for people at my tavern," he says, still smiling.

Charles—bless his soul—stifles a laugh with a sudden cough. Robert flashes me a look that's somewhere between "Rescue me" and "Too late, I'm already dead."

"Missy, I see your clipboard there. Do you need to check us in? Introduce us to the judges? Orient us in some way?"

She looks at me like I just peed on her lawn, which is fine, and she points to the open double doors behind her. "Meet and greet is about to start. Go knock 'em dead."

As I turn to usher my faux-mily into the dining room, I see her. Breezing up the path to the clubhouse is one Mrs. Maisey Walker. Her strides are so graceful and gliding, I wouldn't be surprised if she were on roller skates. Her simple pink-and-white gingham shirtdress shimmers in the desert sun, and her whole flawless face looks to be lit from within. Her hair is swooped up in a gentle chignon complete with a not-too-gaudy gold hairpin. I can tell from here those lush lashes are real and her petal-pink lipstick perfectly matches the pink in her dress. Mrs. Maisey Walker couldn't be a more natural, perfect beauty. Watching her is like seeing a bright butterfly blissfully float down an otherwise unremarkable street. She sees me basking in awe of her and gives me a wide smile and nod. I smile back, probably looking like a fawning royal subject or perhaps a drunk monkey.

Robert leans in and whispers to me, "Maxine, you're gawking."

"She looks like a Disney princess," I whisper back. "Bluebirds are about to land on her shoulders."

"Let's get you kids something to eat," he exclaims, as if a full buffet is going to be enough to take my mind off the positively perfect-looking Mrs. Maisey Walker.

Robert pulls me into the dining room before I can get another good look at Mr. Walker, whom I sincerely wish had two heads.

Robert Hogarth

Pageant Day One

FIRST IMPRESSIONS OF the meet and greet is that it's not a whole heck of a lot different than all those Sundays after Mass when we'd head down to the basement of St. Joe's for coffee, juice, and doughnuts. It was called "fellowship," and it gave my parents a chance to catch up on town happenings (or gossip, more likely) while we kids got to run around and eat sugar after fifty-five minutes of standing, kneeling, sitting, and more kneeling—all in Latin. Except here, with the pageant, I don't know anyone, the kids are forced to sit still with smiles on their faces, and the pastries are much fancier. It's all of the silent judgment with none of the familiarity.

Chuck sets off to find a high chair while Maxine keeps Dawn on her hip and hits the buffet. All the contestants, along with their husbands and kids, mill about in the country club's restaurant. Despite being in a huge building called the clubhouse, the restaurant has its own name: the Penthouse. Not to sound like a yokel, but I always thought a penthouse was a lavish apartment in a skyscraper and not some ground-level banquet room. As entertaining as it would be to hear Maxine's thoughts on this, she's too busy giving me color commentary about everyone in attendance.

"Good Lord, would you look at the ass on Mrs. Vermont," Maxine whispers. I look in the direction where her eyes are pointing and see an otherwise slender woman with very large hips. It's funny, but since I met Maxine, I find myself looking at far more women than I ever did before.

Chuck waves at us from a table he's pulled a high chair up to. Maxine heads over to get Dawn settled while I make them both plates of fresh fruit. I turn from the buffet line and bump right into the rotund man I recall seeing with Mrs. Idaho in the parking lot. He's already downed a glass of Clamato juice and there's still a little foamy bit of red gathered at the corners of his mouth. He's in a black Western-style suit with a white dress shirt and a black bolo tie. I'm grateful Maxine didn't put up a fight this morning when I refused to put my bolo tie on.

"Virgil Gail!" he announces boldly, shoving his meaty paw at me. His grip is surprisingly weak. I see Maxine rush past, trying to catch Dawn, who somehow managed to wiggle out of her chair.

"Robert Hogarth," I tell Virgil. "The woman pulling the small child out of the plant over there is my wife, Maxine. She's Mrs. Arizona Pie."

"Sure, sure," he says in a gruff voice. "You folks own a ranch or something?"

I hate this cowboy hat.

Thankfully, Maxine has captured Dawn and interrupts on my behalf. "Robert owns a tavern, actually. La Dulcinea—it's one of Scottsdale's better-known spots."

"In Idaho, only cowboys wear cowboy hats."

"Yes, well, Scottsdale is a totally different animal, now isn't it, Mr. Gail?" Maxine says in that clenched voice of hers.

Mrs. Idaho Pie comes prancing over in head-to-toe red, white, and blue. "The Arizona Pies!" she breathlessly coos, reading my name tag. I don't know if she's the world's biggest Marilyn Monroe fan or unable to breathe in her tight blouse. "I'm Muffy Gail. I see you met my Virgil." She wraps her arm around Virgil's tree-trunk-like arm and cuddles up to him, like a cat who wants her dinner. Maxine also notices this and slips the arm that isn't holding Dawn around my back.

"And those are our boys, Lou and Stu." Muffy nods in the direction of two round identical twin boys in suits that match Virgil's. They're maybe ten years old and stand perfectly still and very close together nearly in the center of the room.

"Who's this little cutie-pie?" Muffy asks of Dawn in a baby voice that is barely any different than her usual voice.

"This is our daughter, Dawn," Maxine says, beaming with pride.

"Just Dawn?" Muffy asks.

"Dawn Hogarth," Maxine repeats.

"But not Dawn Marie Hogarth or Dawn Anne Hogarth or Dawn—"

"Dawn Lorraine Hogarth!" I blurt out. Lorraine is my mother's name and, oh my God, I can't believe how easy it was for me to lie like that. Maxine smiles proudly at me, while Dawn squeals and laughs, reaching for me to take her from Maxine.

"Aw, you're a little daddy's girl, aren't you, Dawn Lorraine?" Muffy squeaks. "I just think all girls should have two names. If Heavenly Father ever blesses us with a sweet little girl, I'll name her Daisy Rae or Susie Bea. Why, you could have named your little angel April Dawn!"

Thankfully, the room is filling up, and with the excuse of needing to mingle, Maxine pries us away from the Gails.

"April Dawn?" Maxine whispers. "Why would she give our little girl a name that sounds like a feminine hygiene product?"

I stifle a laugh but probably blush. We sit down next to Chuck, who's eating all alone and nearly done with half a pineapple stuffed with cottage cheese. His eyes never stop moving around the room.

"Are you ready to go scouting, Charles?" Maxine asks him, quietly enough that she clearly doesn't intend for me to hear her. He nods while chewing his food, motioning down to the notebook sitting on the table. "You're my eyes and ears. Remember that."

Chuck gives her a small salute, grabs his notebook, and slips away.

"Is that a good idea, Maxine?" I am about 85 percent certain it is not.

"It's harmless. Gives the boy something fun to do while the grown-ups talk," she tells me.

The Walkers take a seat a table over from us. Aside from Mr. and Mrs. Walker, there are two small children—a girl maybe a year older than Dawn and a big-eyed boy who might be seven or eight. I understand why Maxine was staring at Mrs. Walker. She's not so much beautiful as she is stunning. Mr. Walker—Daniel, if I'm remembering right from the yearbook—is equally good-looking. As he helps her cut her fruit salad into child-sized bites, his little girl stares up at him as if he hung the moon, which is entirely possible considering he's at least six foot four. The Walkers are what my mother would have called "a handsome couple."

Maxine pokes my leg under the table. "You're the one gawking now, Robert," she says in a low voice.

Then a fake smile snaps to her face, warning me that we have strangers approaching.

"Can you believe that?" says a twangy Mrs. South Carolina Pie as she suddenly drops into the seat next to Maxine's. I see a flash of annoyance over the sudden intrusion streak across Maxine's face before her fake smile takes over again. Thanks to Mrs. South Carolina's staring at the Walkers' table, we all have a good idea the "that" she refers to.

Maxine asks in her overly sweet voice, "What do you mean?"

"Looks like Colorado doesn't want to sit with Illinois," she says. "I'm Wanda Clarke, by the way." Wanda has bright orange hair that I'm sure Maxine will have plenty to say about. She also has freckles and big blue eyes. I ask for IDs all the time, so I know this woman is barely twenty-one. She has a blond boy, maybe all of two, sitting in her lap. He busies himself with a coloring book. We all exchange names and shake hands.

"I bet they're racist as the day is long," Wanda says, getting back to the Colorados.

"We haven't met them yet," Maxine tells Wanda, "but I'm sure they're lovely or they wouldn't be here."

"You can say that again," Wanda continues, just a little too loud. "I met Maisey on the way in. She smells like roses. I don't mean fake perfume roses. No, ma'am, I mean freshly cut, right-off-the-bush roses. Makes me think she's got flower petals stashed somewhere on her."

Oh, Wanda, if there's a way to make that happen, Maxine will figure it out.

A tall, thin man in a beige suit and avocado-green tie joins us with two plates piled high with eggs and bacon. He still moves like a man who's entirely unaware of how long his limbs are. When he sits down next to Wanda, he smacks his knee into the edge of the table.

"This here's my husband, Roy."

Roy and I shake hands and I notice he has three zits on his chin and a nick on his upper lip from shaving. He's practically still a boy.

Someone comes by with another high chair and Wanda sets her boy, Scotty, next to Dawn. She starts babbling away at him and, like a good boy, Scotty listens and occasionally throws in an incomprehensible word or two.

Roy Clarke explains to me that he's a short-haul truck driver, mostly going between his and Wanda's hometown of Columbia, South Carolina, into Tennessee and North Carolina with hauls of refrigerated meat. I slip into bartender mode, listening and nodding, occasionally offering an "Oh boy!" or "What's that like?" as Roy tells me all about the differences between "truckin' cow" in the summer versus in the winter (it smells a whole lot worse in the summer). In between Roy's conversation, I can pick up bits of what Wanda and Maxine are discussing. Wanda is convinced that Mrs. New Jersey "isn't fooling anyone" with the big cocktail ring she wears and that Mrs. Wisconsin is in fact fooling *everyone* by hiding that she's "at least" twelve weeks pregnant.

"Alls I'm sayin'," Wanda tells us in between big bites of waffles, "is that there's a dead rabbit somewhere in Sheboygan and it's all her fault. Just look at her!"

I can't help but look. Mrs. Wisconsin sits with five kids, all dark haired like she is and all eating from plates stacked with sausages. Maxine says she's "positively glowing," but she looks normal to me. She catches Maxine and Wanda staring at her and smiles. We all smile and wave back with Wanda adding, "Hey there, Ingrid."

The women get back to chatting and Roy gives me a nudge. "Why doesn't anyone warn us about the way girls talk *before* we get married?" he jokes. "I can't believe how much I know about lady things now. You know what I mean?"

I laugh and nod, because that's what I always do when someone brings up something I know nothing about. A loud bell chimes and everyone turns in their chairs to face the podium. A woman I recognize from the Arizona pageant as Alice Depwelt taps on the podium microphone, sending a high-pitched ripple through the dining room.

"Now that I have your attention," says Mrs. Depwelt in a voice that sounds part librarian, part nun, "I'd like to welcome you all to beautiful Palm Springs, the Whitewater Country Club, and of course, the 1970 Mr. and Mrs. American Pie pageant." Mrs. Depwelt pauses, waiting for the smattering of applause to gradually build to outright applause.

"While I'm sure you've all read your information packets, *ladies*, I'm going to take a few moments to go over some basics, *gentlemen*." This we all recognize as a joke, and one that's probably true since I know I didn't read the information packet beyond seeing that Western Airlines is a sponsor.

Mrs. Depwelt goes on to tell us how every minute of our three days here is planned out for us with activities for either just the moms, the moms and the kids, the dads and sons, the moms and the dads, or the whole darn family. All of these activities will be monitored by the judges and pageant officials, and then scored from one to five. If three judges are watching Maxine bake cookies, their scores will be added up and averaged out for her final score in cookie baking. While Mrs. Depwelt doesn't come right out and say it, it sounds entirely possible that someone with a clipboard will creep into our cabin and score us on our sleeping.

"And to keep everyone on their toes," Mrs. Depwelt explains, "no one will learn their scores until the following day." There are murmurs (mostly from the women) that tell me this is somehow a big deal. "Every morning on your cabin's front door you'll find an itinerary for the day, along with the previous day's scores and your current ranking."

I get it now. Keep us in a constant heightened state of panic. Sounds great.

"We'll all gather here every morning for the day's orientation. You should also note that not every event is acceptable for young children. We do have a nursery in one of the rooms here at the clubhouse with trained nannies on staff."

As if on cue, Dawn throws her sippy cup to the ground. Maxine is quick to pick it up, but rather than give it back to Dawn to throw again, I see Maxine pull a biscuit or something out of her purse and offer it to Dawn. Quick as a flash, Dawn grabs it and shoves it in her mouth without even looking at it.

Mrs. Depwelt continues. "When you leave here today, you'll all be escorted to your cabins. There you will find your itinerary for the day's activities, as well as any materials you may need to successfully complete your tasks. Tonight will bring a series of live competitions I think you will all find great fun." Something about the way Depwelt cackles a little while saying "fun" tells me that this evening will be rough. "Of course, by the end of this evening, we'll have whittled down the contest to ten remaining contestants. Those of you who don't make the cut will be welcomed to stay overnight, but you will need to depart before breakfast."

Maxine pats my hand and smiles in a way that she intends as reassuring, but I always take as meaning that trouble is waiting around the corner.

Everyone mills around outside the clubhouse as golf carts slowly arrive to take each family to its cabin. Maxine has Dawn sound asleep on her shoulder, which I'm sure Maxine loves, since it looks so darn cute.

"Hi there!" Chuck says loudly and suddenly. I turn around and see him talking to the Walkers. "The info packet says we're gonna be neighbors. We're the Hogarths from Arizona."

Hearing him announce my last name as if it were really his is like something out of *The Twilight Zone*. I rebound quickly and shove my hand out, which Daniel Walker takes and shakes, reminding me that I'm the only one who sees all of this as unreal.

"Robert Hogarth," I tell him.

"Daniel Walker," he tells me. His voice is deep and friendly, with a faint, nasally Chicago accent. "This is my wife, Maisey."

"Nice to meet you, Mrs. Walker," I say, taking her hand.

"Please, call me Maisey," she says with a bright smile.

Maxine and Maisey introduce themselves to each other and to the kids, Ruthie and Danny Jr. Maxine talks a mile a minute, veering from asking Maisey how long their flight from Chicago was, to sounding a little too surprised at learning Daniel is a high school science teacher, to marveling about the therapeutic properties of the dry desert air. Maisey and Daniel laugh politely when Maxine makes a terrible joke about how the town should have been named "Palm Dustbowl."

Someone in the small crowd behind us murmurs something about "photos," and that quickly snaps Maxine out of her rapid-fire small talk. Maisey grabs up Ruthie in her arms and I guess Daniel and I don't look like we know what to do since both our wives frantically wave us closer to them.

"Gather 'round, Hogarths!" Maxine says through clenched teeth. "Smile and wave for the camera."

Maisey looks to Daniel, silently telling him to follow our lead. Daniel and I rush to our wives' sides as a photographer pops up in front of us. He says nothing, but motions for us to get in closer to one another, which we do. He snaps the photo and rushes off to another clump of contestants. Daniel and I relax our poses, but Maxine and Maisey stay stiff and smiling.

"Judges," Maisey says in a loud whisper.

A much older man wearing Coke-bottle glasses walks slowly past the contestants outside the clubhouse. He's got a clipboard in one hand, and there's a too-large-for-his-body blue ribbon pinned to his beige suit that reads JUDGE. Maxine gives him a smile and a wave, and Maisey does the same. I look to Daniel, who shrugs at me and gets right to waving, and before I can think about how ridiculous we must all look, I'm waving too.

Here we are, two families smiling and waving at an old man as he wanders by, as if it were the most normal thing in the world. Except I can't think of a single situation where a total stranger would stand fifteen feet away, scribbling down notes and assessing points. What are they looking for in a competitive family smile and wave? Do we need to be in sync? There's no way he can tell from this distance if any of us has anything in our teeth. Is he going to deduct half a point because Maxine and I aren't standing as close to each other as the Walkers? I put my non-waving hand gently around Maxine's waist.

"Good idea," she whispers through her unrelenting smile.

The old man shuffles into the clubhouse. We all—Hogarths, Walkers, and the rest of the contestants—let our arms drop and faces relax. Chuck shakes out his limbs and little Danny Walker copies him. It's sweet relief when Missy bounces over to announce the next golf cart will ferry us away.

Maxine Hogarth

Pageant Day One

WE ALL PILE into a golf cart, which is of course festooned with more flags. With Robert riding up front with Missy, I take a seat in the back with Charles, balancing Dawn on my lap. Missy guns it and I damn near tumble out. Missy sees this in her rearview mirror, and I swear to God the look of sheer terror on my face only prompts her to drive faster, kicking up pebbles into my mouth and pinging them off my red cat-eye sunglasses. I see up ahead that the path veers to the left, which Missy chooses to respond to as if it were a hairpin turn at a dead man's curve. Dawn squeals with joy and digs her sharp little fingernails deep into my arm, apparently not realizing that my firm grip around her waist is all that's keeping her from being airborne.

Missy finally finds the brake pedal, slamming us to a halt in front of a teeny-tiny, stout log cabin with a little path leading up to it. There are two pine-green front doors in the middle of the cabin, both of which are more than half-open. On either side of each door is a window with matching pine-green shutters and a window box with some red and white geraniums. I brought along a cowhide rug to lay in front of the fireplace, although a quick disappointing look at the roof reveals there's no chimney. Missy is already out of the golf cart and skipping up the path alongside Robert when it occurs to me that most homes don't have two front doors.

"It's a duplex!" Missy squeaks with far more enthusiasm than warranted, given the bad news. "You get the cabin on the right and Mrs. Illinois Pie will be on the left!"

I want to make some clever quip about how as Mrs. Arizona Pie I'm always to the right (at least politically), but I can't muster it. I'm hot and tired and thoroughly exhausted from all the smiling, and on top of all that, I'm not even granted my own cabin. It's like getting an Amtrak ticket for coach when you were expecting Pan Am first class. Worse still is our proximity to the Walkers. While it might be true that every contestant is my competition, any judge who pops by the house will be seeing me in direct comparison with Maisey.

"You better let me go in first," says a mildly less chipper Missy as we all reach the door of the dumpy duplex. "Mrs. New Hampshire Pie had the scare of her life today when they found a critter in their cabin."

Forget Amtrak. This cabin has officially been downgraded to Greyhound.

We huddle in the doorway while Missy gingerly walks into the cabin. It's dark in there and my eyes haven't adjusted, so I can't see much. I can hear Missy clapping and stomping through the place. I don't hear any hisses, growls, or whatever the hell noise Gila monsters make, so I assume all is well.

"I'm going to turn the lights on now," Missy says. "So you should clear out of the doorway in case a bat flies out."

Holding Dawn tightly, I run back to the golf cart. She fusses and tries wiggling free, but it's nothing the animal crackers in my purse can't handle. "Dawn, sweetie, you don't want rabies now, do you?" I ask her in my singsongy voice as she gnaws the head off a lion. "No, you don't! No, you don't!" Her happy squeals assure me that she understands the risks.

Robert and Charles disappear inside the cabin and I hold my breath. After an eon or two, Charles reappears in the doorway and gives the all clear. He's grinning like the Cheshire cat, which concerns me. If there's one thing boys like, it's wild beasts. But I have faith that he's not putting me or his sister in harm's way and decide to give the cabin a second chance.

It's worse than I thought. The entire cabin—or should I say the Hogarth side of the cabin—is one room with exactly two windows. There's one along the back wall, where two folded-up twin beds are unmade and haphazardly shoved next to a small crib, which itself is touching a frumpy couch that is bumped up against a thrift-store dining set. It's like all the furniture was arranged by a crossword puzzle fanatic. The other window is above the tiny sink in the kitchen area, which is nothing more than a counter the size of a sheet of paper, a mini-fridge, and a stove pulled out a good foot from the wall and clearly not level. The entire room smells faintly of mothballs, dust, and sadness, although at this point the sadness may be emanating from me. I spy a narrow door along the wall shared with the other half of the duplex and, though overcome by uncertainty, I manage to open it and take a peek inside. It's dark, but I can make out a light dangling from the ceiling from a pull switch.

"Wait!" yelps Missy as she firmly pushes me out of the way. "I forgot to check that room."

She tugs the light on and a scream involuntarily leaps from my body.

"Is it a bat?" asks Charles.

"No bat," Missy happily answers. "Just a bathroom."

All of the blood rushes from my head into my toes. I want to grab on to something to steady myself, but there's nothing in this room that looks sturdy enough to bear my 115ish pounds. This monstrosity is hardly a "bathroom." For starters, there is no bath—just a white vinyl curtain hanging in front of a two-foot-square area with a shower nozzle jutting out of the wall and, below it, a concrete floor with a drain. There *is* a toilet, thank Christ. Although just the mere fact that I'm thrilled to see an actual toilet in an alleged bathroom speaks volumes. Why is there a mirror above the toilet?

"Where's the sink?" I manage to ask. My eyes are pulled back to that floor drain, certain I'll be seeing a roach eke out of it.

"Oh, you gotta use the one in the kitchen. I think they figured since that sink's only a couple of feet away, there's no reason to put another one in here. But look!" Missy reaches past me and flushes the toilet. Its resulting gurgle reminds me of a dying fish. "The potty is real!"

The gurgle fades to a tuberculosis-like choke, and Missy gives the toilet's handle a firm jiggle. We all stand still as the tank hisses loudly while refilling before belching out a clunk felt through the floorboards, before finally bringing us back to a blissful silence.

"Well, I'll be on my way then! If you need anything, just head up to the clubhouse. Otherwise, I'll see you Arizona Pies at tonight's event!"

Missy darts out like a demon being called back to hell. I can't take my eyes off the "bathroom."

"Maxine?" says Robert. "This isn't what you were expecting?"

Is he goddamned kidding me?

I fight to maintain my composure, but I might faint. "Saying that this cabin is a far cry from the world-class amenities one expects from Palm Springs is like saying there's a difference between a pig wearing a dress and Sophia Loren. So, no, Robert, this isn't what I was expecting! And *that*," I say, pointing toward the so-called bathroom, "is like something out of a mental institution . . . or women's prison!"

Charles covers his mouth with his hand, as if I can't tell from his red face and shaking body that he's laughing at me.

"You've been to a women's prison?" Robert asks, biting his lip.

"Or a mental institution?" Charles snickers. That oh-so-clever quip is enough to get Robert laughing.

"Laugh it up, chuckleheads!" I tell them. "I won't be the one staring at myself in the mirror while urinating."

That only makes the laughter worse. What is it about men and repulsive bodily functions?

We hear the honking of another golf cart as it approaches.

"That damn well better not be the judges," I grumble.

Charles peers out the window. "It's the Walkers." He gives a wave out the window.

"Maisey Walker," I mutter out loud. Then again, louder, "Maisey Walker. Good Lord, even saying her name causes a smile. Maisey. Do you see that?" I point to my mouth. "Maisey. I just involuntarily smiled. It is physically impossible to say her name without a smile. Maisey!"

"Nothing you're saying or doing makes any sense, Maxine."

"You just said my name and you know what? No smile!"

"Maxine!" Robert says too loudly, giving me the openmouthed grin of a crazy person. "Should I say it like that?"

I cross my arms in front of my chest and glare. It's going to be a long three days.

Robert Hogarth

Pageant Day One

WHEN MAXINE SEES the Walkers standing in the front yard, looking down the path, she makes all of us head out for more smiling and waving. Three carts go by so quickly, I can't tell if the people on them are competing families or judges or both.

After what feels like hours but is only a few minutes, Maisey asks the question on all our minds. "Do you think we really have to stand out here and do nothing? I haven't unpacked yet."

"The itinerary says we can't start unpacking until eleven and it's still ten till," Maxine tells her. "You definitely don't want to be the only gal not outside right now." As I look down the path, I see that Maxine is right. All the other families stand outside, smiling and waving. "Plus, Maisey, rules are rules."

Maisey nods. "Oh, I know all about crazy pageant rules. In the Mrs. Black Chicago pageant, they made you wear the sash around town. If word got back to the pageant officials that you weren't a perfect lady all the time, the pageant could take your prize package away."

"You've been in pageants before?" Maxine says, sounding far too surprised.

"A handful," Maisey muses.

Daniel pulls Maisey closer to him and quickly kisses her temple. "Maisey is being too modest. Truth is, we have a whole wall at home for all her sashes and crowns. She's been Miss Uptown, Miss Black Cook County, Miss Juneteeth—"

"Come on now, Daniel," Maisey says through her smile. "It's not polite to brag."

"In college she was Miss Alpha Kappa Alpha *and* Miss Maroon and White," he says.

Maisey gazes up at Daniel. "And then I met you my sophomore year and became Mrs. Daniel Walker."

"I was Miss San Bernardino," Maxine blurts out too loudly.

Maisey and Daniel nod as if appropriately impressed.

"Maisey, are those all pageants for . . ." Maxine lets her sentence trail off and looks to me, as if I'm going to finish it.

"For black women?" Maisey answers. "Sure are. But after I won Mrs. Black Chicago, Mrs. Depwelt asked me to be Mrs. Illinois."

I can see Maxine's face light up. It's worrisome, but I remind myself she's been relatively nice to Maisey up to now.

"Didn't you win your local pageant?" Maxine asks her.

Maisey shakes her head and lowers her voice. "I'm not supposed to bring this up to anyone, but there wasn't a Mrs. Illinois Pie pageant."

"Really! What happened?"

"Nothing happened. No one entered, and Mrs. Depwelt asked me to just take the Mrs. Illinois Pie title. She says that's common for Hawaii and Alaska. But this year, Illinois, Washington State, both Dakotas, and a few other states didn't have anyone who wanted to be in the pageant."

"I bet it was bra burners." Where other people blame Communism or hippies, Maxine always goes straight to braless women, which is funny since she often complains about having to wear one. "Everyone's so terrified of feminists. Of course, these are the same people who think that we women are harmless little flies," Maxine says and Maisey "mmm-hmms" in agreement. "I personally have no problem with feminists. I just don't care for such rigid thinking. I simply don't understand why I can't be drop-dead gorgeous and the smartest person in the room."

This makes Maisey laugh. It's a lyrical lilt, like Audrey Hepburn's.

We're all saved from more of Maxine's probing questions by another golf cart full of judges. Like soldiers at revelry, we snap to it and wave and smile. I can faintly hear the gears in Maxine's mind working overtime.

Maxine Hogarth

Pageant Day One

IT'S TIME TO make this shit-house a shit-home!

Experienced Pageant Queen Maisey and I go our separate ways into our hovels to get cracking on the decorating. We have exactly forty-five minutes to complete this task. It's enough to make a girl think that the judges are hoping some of us drop dead from exhaustion rather than be eliminated later.

I start by employing Charles as my furniture mover. Not that there are many options in this space. This isn't a matter of thinking like Jackie Kennedy, wondering where best to put the ottoman in the Lincoln Bedroom. It's more like *How in the hell do we keep these glorified cots out of the kitchen?* I fully realize that we are a nation of immigrants, but if we've learned anything from the Irish, it's that no one should have to live as though in a subpar, lice-infested tenement in New York's worst neighborhood.

Robert's job—apparently—is to stand next to me and subject me to an annoying line of questioning about our new neighbors.

"Did you know there were pageants for black women?" he asks me as I'm trying to envision the vaguely peach-colored divan moved against a wall.

"No, but if black women aren't allowed to compete in pageants, it makes sense they'd start their own, right?" I tell him. "Charles, let's move this divan to the center of the room. Let it break up the space a little." This allows for the bedroom area to be somewhat separate from the rest of the dining area. Miss Maroon and White? That has to be made up.

I also have Charles put Dawn's crib in between the two twin beds. I'll admit to feeling smug about this choice since, while it shows the judges I never want to be too far from my baby girl, it also puts some space between parents and oldest child. Robert and I will have much plotting to do each night and undoubtedly most of it won't be "Charles appropriate."

Of course, there's a chance I won't want to hear what Robert has to say.

"Is it normal," he asks me, "for a woman to have won that many pageants?" He helpfully points a thumb to the wall we share with the Walkers, as if I didn't know whom he was speaking of.

"Robert, dear-heart, if you'd been paying attention, you'd have heard they were all from when Maisey was a Miss and not a Mrs. This pageant is about more than merely being the prettiest girl in the room."

"I heard her say something about Mrs. Black Chicago," Charles not so helpfully adds. I have him arranging his collection of Hardy Boys books in alphabetical order by title.

"And she's got two kids," Robert mutters.

I want to argue back that I also have two kids, except I know this isn't exactly true, or at least not in the way that Robert means. Instead I ignore it and get my attention to repurposing the cowhide rug I brought to lay in front of the fireplace I was certain we'd have. I instead cut it in two and drape it over the curtain rods in both our postage-stamp-sized windows. Neither "curtain" wants to obey me and stay in place, but thank heavens I brought plenty of double-sided tape. I bet Maisey doesn't know how to use double-sided tape in lieu of a sewing machine. Hell, I bet she didn't even bring double-sided tape with her, since—unlike me—she doesn't need anything to help hold *her* bosoms in place inside her evening gowns. I guess women's measurements aren't a factor in the Miss Alpha Kappa Alpha pageant.

With the living room conquered, I move to the kitchen and dining areas. I don't like that we only have the one family photo and I could smack my own fanny for not thinking to take more pictures of the kids. I bet Maisey's practically wallpapered her cabin with photos of the kids at all stages of their lives. Well, I see your two adorable, well-scrubbed children and raise you one toddler with blond Gerber Baby curls and a preteen boy with impeccable manners.

"These are cute. Are they Dawn's?" Robert asks, pointing to crayon drawings I've pinned on the fridge.

"Yes. She's aggressively modern in her style, which doesn't go with the room's overall mood one iota. Then again, the theme of the day does seem to be Let's Make Do."

On our way out of Scottsdale, I had the foresight to stop at a gift shop off the highway, and purchased a number of Arizona-related items. There are the tea towels with needlepoint saguaro cacti, which match the place mats I bought. I was so hoping the gift shop would have a framed photo of Barry Goldwater, but alas, I settled for a wall clock in the shape of Arizona. Unsurprisingly, the clock hands are cacti. Ever prepared, Charles brought his pennant from Old Tucson, which I let him hang near his bed. How is Maisey going to pepper her home with all things Chicago? I've got Robert's manly cowboy hat resting atop the fridge and she has, what? Al Capone's derby?

"Where's the third bag from the gift shop?" I yell, not so much out of frustration, but because Dawn is screeching like a wild animal to be let out of her crib. "It has all my figurines in it," I moan.

I tear through the kitchen with no luck. I make Charles and Robert lift up the divan and drag out all the suitcases they grumbled about having to put under the bed in the first place. When I still don't find the goddamned bag, they grumble even more about having to put all the suitcases back.

"Oh shit," I unfortunately say out loud, finally checking my handbag, where indeed, the figurines sit in their plastic shopping bag.

Robert lets his side of the divan fall with a stern thud. "You didn't think to check your purse?"

I bet that's not how Daniel Walker ever talks to Maisey when she's misplaced her Chicago-themed figurines (snow globes, I'm guessing).

Dawn lets rip a banshee wail that makes us all cringe. Charles frees her from the crib and she celebrates by running from one end of the puny cabin to the other. Time's running short, so I make quick work of tearing the price tags off my items and throwing together an artful centerpiece. I've got three pieces of petrified wood along with small figurines representing a cowboy, a roadrunner, and yet another cactus. The cowboy and roadrunner are the same size, which doesn't look right at all, so I put the cactus between them. Dawn apparently thinks the whole table is crap since she grabs a cactus and a cowboy and shoves them straight into her mouth. I swap her a small candy cane for the cactus and swipe the cowboy when she's got her guard down. Both are covered in baby spittle, which I quickly wipe off on my skirt, because that's how low toddlers make one sink.

With the judges due in fifteen minutes, I snap on my trusty Playtex Living gloves and grab the scrub brush to Pine-Sol the ever-living shit out of that "bathroom."

"I can help with that," Robert says while trying to take the bucket from my hands.

"Not a chance in hell, mister."

"Maxine, I've lived alone for years. No housekeeper. I think I know how to make a toilet Ty-D-Bol fresh."

I shudder at the thought of those dreadful commercials. While on one level I understand the sailing captain in the boat is meta-phorical, on another, deeper level, I cringe at the thought of him not only being in my toilet but looking north while I use it.

"I can't risk anyone finding out that I let my husband clean. I mean, when we're at home, you damn well better chip in, but here? Not a chance." I'm sure Maisey isn't having this problem. I bet Daniel is sitting on a couch right now, smoking a pipe and reading some tome on Winston Churchill, utterly oblivious to the fact that Maisey's on hands and knees in a life-and-death battle with bathroom tile scum.

Robert comprehends nothing. He waves his arms around the room. "There's no one here, Maxine. I'll do the bathroom. You do the kitchen."

My husband literally pulls the mop bucket from my hands, and I feel a physical twinge of pain from my ovaries when I yank the bucket back.

"Robert," I say with all the calmness I can muster. "I simply cannot allow it. For the duration of this pageant, my job is to cook, clean, mother, and make it appear as though I'm not wearing a padded bra under my dress. Your job is to stand around handsomely and watch me do all those things with a big shit-eating grin on your face. If the judges see any deviation from that, they will run me out of here faster than Gloria Steinem at the Playboy Club."

Charles "Chuck" Bronski

Pageant Day One

I'VE LEARNED THAT going to a beauty pageant isn't the same as going to summer camp. I mean, I've never actually gone to summer camp, but I've seen them on TV and they aren't anything like what's happening right now. We're sleeping in a cabin, except we're not roughin' it like in the Hardy Boys, since the cabins are decorated all fancy. We're not even in the woods. I mean, there are trees out back, but there's a golf course too. I was hoping there'd be a swimming hole or boats to take out on a lake. No luck. A map at the clubhouse says there's a pond by the ninth hole. I'm guessing I'd get in big trouble if I tried swimming in it. I've never swum in anything other than a swimming pool. I bet it's groovy to swim with fishes and seaweed and stuff.

Also, when you're camping, there isn't something called an itinerary that tells you what stuff you're supposed to do and when you are supposed to do it. Right now it's noon, and that means the pageant people expect us to be having a cookout with the Walkers. I was hoping this meant we'd go fishing and eat whatever we caught. Or maybe roast weenies on sticks over a campfire. What it actually means is that someone in a golf cart brings over a grill and a box of food.

"Can I help with the grill?" I ask Robert.

"Sorry, kiddo," he says, "this is a dads-only grill." He nods over to two golf carts on the path where four people with big blue judges' ribbons pinned to their shirts write stuff down on clipboards. "Why don't you see if the ladies need some help?"

Miss Maxine and Mrs. Walker are busy making the picnic table look pretty for us to eat at. All the other pageant ladies are outside their cabins with their picnic tables. It looks kinda weird to me to see all these little houses with two families each outside, everybody doing the same thing. I've always lived in an apartment, so I guess that's what people in neighborhoods do? The same judges watching Robert and Mr. Walker are staring at Miss Maxine. How do you give a score for putting the dishes on a picnic table? It's not like baseball, where if you cross home plate, you get a point. I suppose if the food is tasty, that's a point. But setting a cup down on a table? How does one lady do that better than another?

"Do you need any help?" I ask Miss Maxine. Dawn doesn't seem super happy to be here either. She's fussing a lot, probably because she's in an itchy dress with all these ruffles. Miss Maxine is trying to hold her while putting plastic silverware down on the table. Every time Miss Maxine gets a fork where she wants it, Dawn reaches over and grabs a paper plate or pulls on the tablecloth.

"We're fine here, Charles," Miss Maxine says to me while not taking her eyes off those judges. "Maybe you could help the men with the grill?"

"I tried that. They said it was dads-only on account of the judges."

Dawn hollers and knocks over a stack of plastic cups. I catch them before they can hit the grass, and I put them back on the table far enough away from her that she can't just go and knock them over again. Dawn kicks her feet all mad-like as Miss Maxine tries to keep a grip on her. The judges roll away in their golf carts and the second they're gone, Miss Maxine holds Dawn out to me.

"Be my hero, Charles, and get her cleaned up before the next batch of judges comes by?"

For some reason, Dawn is really sticky today. Actually, I think I know why. I've seen Miss Maxine shoving those little-baby-sized candy canes in Dawn's mouth. I don't know where Miss Maxine found candy canes in July, but it takes Dawn maybe five seconds to end up all pepperminty and sticky. She wiggles out of my hand on the path and by the time I catch her, she's got tiny red pebbles stuck to her face. I brush 'em off with my shirtsleeve, and that gets rid of the rocks but leaves her face all fuzzy.

I plop her in the kitchen sink, which contains her long enough for me to grab a towel. I put her on my hip—trying real hard to keep her sticky fingers from getting me all sticky too—and wet the towel with water that isn't too hot and isn't too cold, just how Dawn likes it. I should call her Goldilocks.

"I'm gonna rub your face clean now, Dawnie. It's just water, so be a good girl and don't freak out on me."

She freaks out on me. Her gooey baby claws grab at my hair while her chubby legs kick me all over, smacking into my . . . well . . . my um, you know . . . pork and beans. I don't like that babies can kick and punch and yet the non-baby holding 'em still has to be all careful not to squish or break the angry baby. It's just not a fair fight.

"Maybe your next diaper will smell like Christmas," I tell her.

I remembered to stick Dawn's teething rings in the fridge when we got here, so I give her one of those to keep her little mouth busy before going back outside for the cookout that's not really a cookout.

"Thank you, Charles," Miss Maxine says to me while also smoothing down my messed-up hair. "Why don't you and Dawn go play with the Walker kids?" She says it in that way grown-ups do when they say it like it's a suggestion, but they mean it as an order.

Ruthie and Danny sit on a blanket over by the cactus. They look all nervous when I walk over. I don't take it personally. Ruthie's only four and Danny's eight and when you're that age and a bigger kid walks over, it's kinda nerve-racking.

"Can Dawn play with you, Ruthie? She's got a dolly too."

Dawn knows the word *dolly* and holds it out to Ruthie. Compared to Ruthie's cute little dolly in a pink dress, Dawn's dolly looks like it's been run over by a truck. I also notice that Ruthie's doll is black. I don't think I've ever seen a toy—like a dolly or a G.I. Joe—that isn't white. Guess it makes sense that if there are black kids, there'd be black dolls.

Ruthie makes her dolly talk to Dawn's dolly, which seems to make Dawn happy enough. I'm glad I don't have to keep holding her. My arm's numb.

"I like your airplane," I say to Danny.

"I made it with my dad!" he tells me, holding it out. "I painted it all by myself and then he helped me put it together."

It's a World War II US bomber and while I want to tell Danny that they weren't ever painted bright orange and yellow, I don't. I spin the propeller with my finger. He runs around making bomb-dropping noises. I sit and watch, wishing I could go do something more fun.

Miss Maxine and Mrs. Walker have done a fine job on the table, I suppose, but Robert and Mr. Walker's hot dogs and burgers are amazing. Mr. Walker explains how if you put the buns on the grill for a minute, they get all toasty. I'm ready to dive in. Except the ladies aren't sure who should sit where. At first, we all sit clumped together with our families. Then a lady judge—the one who won last year and always wears her crown—and a guy with a big fancy camera pull up in a cart. Miss Maxine and Mrs. Walker give each other a weird look and before I can put a dog on my plate, everybody's getting moved around.

"Should we alternate? A Walker then a Hogarth then a Walker?" Miss Maxine says to Mrs. Walker.

"That's a little too obvious, I think," says Mrs. Walker. "Maybe put all the kids together at one end?" She looks over her shoulder and sees the photographer coming over. "Maxine, you and I should sit opposite each other at the end. It'll make serving easier."

They plop Ruthie and Dawn in their booster seats, with me and Danny sitting next to our sisters. Mr. Walker and Robert sit by us, and even though the food is already in the center of the table, Mrs. Walker and Miss Maxine each take a platter and pose for the photographer.

Finally it's time to eat, except we gotta say grace. Now, Miss Maxine had us practice this a whole bunch at home. Robert learned at least three different prayers that Miss Maxine said were good, and even Dawn usually manages to be quiet, although she doesn't bow her head. The problem is that Miss Maxine taught us to fold our hands in front of us while Robert says grace. So, when the Walkers all take each other's hands, I don't know what to do. Robert grabs my hand for me, but when I try taking Dawn's, she screeches. I figure it's the touching part that matters to God more, so I put my hand on her back. She doesn't hate that. Although I am a little ticked off to see she lets Ruthie take her other hand.

Even once we've figured out where everybody's gonna sit and who's gonna be touching who and where, we still need to figure out which dad is gonna say grace.

"Robert, do you want to?" asks Mr. Walker.

"Unless you, of course—" says Robert.

"I don't have a problem—" Mr. Walker says back.

"I mean, we're Catholic—" Robert goes on.

I slam my eyes shut so tight, I see specks of red.

"Dear Heavenly Father!" I blurt out. I know right away that it came out too loud because Robert gives my hand a hard squeeze. I say the rest in my normal voice. "Thanks for the food we're gonna eat. Thanks for the Walker family eating it with us. You're a great God. Amen!"

Robert lets go of my hand, but I kinda don't want to open my eyes.

"That was a lovely prayer," Mrs. Walker tells me in a super sweet voice.

"Thank you, ma'am."

Robert pats me on the back and when I look at Miss Maxine—sorry, Mom—she smiles and nods. So, I guess I didn't completely biff it.

The photographer and lady judge leave and we all get to eating. This is the greatest hot dog in the history of the world. Robert told me once how in Chicago—where he's from and I'm lying about being from—no one ever in a million years would be caught dead putting ketchup on their hot dogs. I remember this and since my cover story has me being born out there, I only use mustard.

"You cook a mean hot dog, Mr. Walker!" That part I'm not faking.

"Thanks, Chuck. Too bad they didn't give us any relish or celery salt for these dogs, though."

"I haven't had a good Chicago dog in forever," Robert says.

"By 'forever' Robert means a little over a year," adds Miss Maxine. "Robert and the children moved from Libertyville right around the first of last year," she finishes.

"January the sixth, 1969!" I tell them. I memorized everything Miss Maxine made up for us.

"A cross-country move with kids in the dead of winter," says Mr. Walker. "I do not envy you."

"Goodness, how old was little Dawn?" It's a good thing Mrs. Walker is busy pouring more iced tea while she says this, or she'd notice Robert and Miss Maxine looking at each other all terrified-like.

I swallow my food without chewing it. "She's three next month!"

"We've had her hearing tested," Miss Maxine says quickly. "She checks out fine and all the latest books on childhood development say the same thing, that she'll talk when she's ready."

Mrs. Walker waves and makes baby faces at Dawn, who loves it and squeals. "I think she's great at expressing herself."

"She's not a great little eater, though," I say. I don't think Dawn has kept a single bite of food I've fed her in her piehole all day. I put a little piece of hamburger on a fork and try to airplane it to her. She screams and bucks in her seat.

"Lemme try," Ruthie says. She loads up a fork with way too much potato salad. "Here comes the train. Into Union Station. . . . Chooo-chooo!"

Dawn laughs, but still won't eat.

"Is she feeling all right?" Robert asks me.

"Heavens no," Miss Maxine almost shouts. She runs over and puts her hands all over Dawn's head, which only makes Dawn fussier.

"She only ate a little fruit at the meet and greet," I say.

"Or she's overtired from the long drive out here." Miss Maxine tries offering Dawn an itty-bitty piece of hamburger. Dawn refuses. Her tiny baby brain is probably trying to figure out what all these giant humans are doing.

"Kids can be such picky eaters, Maxine," says Mrs. Walker.

Miss Maxine's right eye gets squinty, but she doesn't say anything mean.

After the cookout, I'm stuck watching the kids again while Mr. Walker and Robert put the grill away. I see Miss Maxine carry some dirty dishes into Mrs. Walker's house and, seconds later, there's a scream from inside. Like a loud, terrified lady scream from one of them horror movies.

"Bat!" I say to Robert and Mr. Walker as they run past me.

We get inside the cabin and it takes a few seconds for my eyes to adjust. The Walkers have their furniture set all different than ours, with their couch—I mean, divan—pushed against a wall. Miss Maxine points at that wall with a shocked look on her face.

It's not a bat. It's not even a mouse. It's Miss Maxine seeing the Walker family photo.

"Is that President Nixon?" I say real loud. I can see better now and yup, that's a photo of Mr. and Mrs. Walker holding Ruthie and Danny Jr. next to President Nixon. The Walkers are all dressed up. President Nixon looks like he always does, only smiling.

Mrs. Walker makes that laugh grown-ups make when they think something is funny, but don't want to sound like they are coming right out and laughing in someone's face. "President Nixon came to our church last year," she tells Miss Maxine, who doesn't take her eyes off the photo. "He took photos with lots of people. I was too nervous to say much to him."

This seems to make Miss Maxine happy to hear. She takes her hand away from her mouth and makes that big fake smile for Mrs. Walker.

"But you did sing for him," Mr. Walker says. "Maisey is a soloist in the choir."

"That's lovely," says Robert, also with a fake smile. His isn't so big, though. "Isn't that lovely, Maxine?"

Miss Maxine nods. She looks at the photo and then back to the Walkers, and then back to the photo. "You voted for him?" she asks. She says it like she's asking the Walkers if they killed someone.

The Walkers look at each other and Mr. Walker shrugs.

"Sure, we did," says Mrs. Walker.

Miss Maxine laughs very loud and short. It startles Mrs. Walker. Robert looks at me like he expects me to do or say something.

"Our family photo is at Old Tucson," I say, all proud. "It's a cool place. I mean, it looks cool on TV." I don't see any point of lying to the Walkers. They seem like nice people, and I wouldn't want them to waste their time and money going to Old Tucson.

Without saying anything, Miss Maxine turns around and walks out.

A little while later, we're in our cabin getting ready to go to some big event back at the clubhouse. Dawn won't stop fussing, although Miss Maxine isn't much better. She rushes back and forth across the cabin, grabbing a dress and running to the bathroom to put it on. Then she'll come back out of the bathroom, put on some shoes, grab a different dress and go back in the bathroom.

Every time she comes out of the bathroom, she seems madder. "I mean really, Robert, Richard Nixon." She makes her voice really high and squeaky: "'Sure, we voted for him!' Does she really think the judges are going to buy that?"

"Voting is secret, Maxine," Robert says, sighing.

Maxine's back in the bathroom with another dress.

"Are you ready to go?" Robert asks me.

I look over to my knapsack, all packed up. "I've been ready for almost a half hour," I tell him.

Miss Maxine can't stop talking. "I think that Maisey Walker is trying to get in my head." She puts on different shoes and right when I think she's going to turn around and go back in the bathroom, she picks up her purse and stares at us. "Why are you all standing there? We can't be late."

Robert Hogarth

Pageant Night One

HONESTLY, I DON'T know what exactly I was expecting when entering a contest where my every word and movement is judged day and night. My only excuse is that the last few weeks with Maxine and the kids have started feeling normal to me. I mean, in the back of my mind I know my marriage is a sham and the kids are on loan from a woman currently following around some two-bit shortstop. But then again, isn't 1970 a little weird for everyone? I saw a grown man at the bank the other day wearing lace-up paisley-print bell-bottoms and sporting mutton chops. There are nuns protesting at the Pentagon, and a movie star is the governor of California. Every rock song on the radio is about *S-E-X*, and every news broadcast is blood and guts. I live with a woman who could at any moment light herself on fire just to assure all eyes are on her.

The world is weird for everyone, so it's probably not *that strange* that I'm sitting in my tan suit at the Whitewater Country Club dinner theater waiting to watch my bride prove there's no wife better than her. Then again, I bet I'm also the only man in here who doesn't give a fig about the bathing suit competition. But I might steal a glance at Daniel Walker and that Mr. Wisconsin Pie. Provided no judges are in the room. Or my wife.

Chuck's a live wire, twitching with excitement over every new experience. "Is this going to be on TV?" he asks me, noticing the bank of bright lights aimed at the stage.

"Nope. This is a preliminary round, so small potatoes, kiddo."

He deflates instantly, slumping in his seat. I don't think he's having much fun today, but the kid sure keeps looking for that silver lining. He's even able to find something of interest during an intense reading of the night's program.

"Good," he says, pointing to the section on the program called *Let's Meet Our Judges*. "I need to figure out what these folks're all about," he says in a serious tone. Poor kid's going to be disappointed to find the judges are all old beauty queens, corporate sponsor executives, and some local weatherman, the ridiculously named Dale Thunders.

Chuck points to the program's photo of Thunders. "Do you think that's really his name?" he asks me.

I squint at the black-and-white photo. "I don't even think that's his real hair," I say, pointing to Thunders's toupee.

Chuck looks closer at the photo and chuckles a little. I'm glad he's found something entertaining in all this. At the pageant's request, all children under the age of three were to be dropped off in the babysitting room. So, in a lot of ways, this is like a guys' night out for me and Chuck. Except that we're in suits Maxine picked out for us and about to watch her and a bunch of other ladies competitively pose in skimpy swimsuits.

The mood in the theater is low-key, although that's probably from everyone being exhausted. The poor Minnesota Pies—a quiet family of seven with ghost-white blond hair and the last name of Gundersson—are sunburned to a crisp. Mr. Nebraska Pie is glad-handing left and right, pressing a business card for his accounting firm into everyone's palms.

Finally the lights dim and with a prerecorded drumroll booming through the speakers, the pageant officially begins. We're only two rows back from the stage, giving us a great view of the action. "America the Beautiful" blares, and the women take the stage one at a time in alphabetical order by state. It's a lot like all the pageants on TV, with one pretty lady after another coming out in the same bathing suit. There's less glitz than in most pageants, and the whole thing feels a little like a small-town community theater in that nearly everyone looks nervous. Well, not Maxine. She walks across the stage as if she were born to do this, giving a graceful wave to the audience. Mrs. Idaho Muffy Gail blows kisses to the crowd, while Maisey walks out there and smiles as though all one hundred people in the audience are her close personal friends. With all the women in position, the music comes to an abrupt end. Dale Thunders isn't only a judge, but he's also the host, taking the stage in a loud red plaid suit, holding note cards. His bald head already sweats under that toupee.

"Who's ready to be entertained!" Thunders yells into the microphone with such force, it squeals and fuzzes with feedback. "Let's meet—"

Thunders is cut off by the music, which also startles some of the less polished contestants. The music cuts out again and Thunders gets right back to his hosting duties. "As I was saying . . . let's meet our contest—"

More blaring music. This time, a clearly flustered Thunders drops the note cards. As he fumbles to pick them up and put them in the right order, the music keeps stopping and starting again. Chuck looks to be holding back his laughter, which can't be said of most of the audience. Finally Thunders has himself pulled together and the music stops.

"Let's meet . . . ," he says hesitantly into his microphone, "our . . . contestants . . . !"

This would be a logical time for the music to start, but there's dead silence. Thunders consults his cards and calls out, "Maxine Hobarth," a mistake I'm proud to say my "wife" ignores. Thunders isn't so lucky as he stumbles through Maxine's favorite pastimes, telling the audience she enjoys "cooking and coquetting" rather than "cooking and crocheting." "Coquetting" is more than accurate, I think. I doubt if anyone noticed Thunders's mistake, though, with

Maxine's blond hair shining like a big, bold beacon under the lights. When posing at each end of the stage, she lets her backbone slip just a bit, resulting in the most ladylike of butt wiggles. I can't imagine how many hours she spent practicing that move.

As the women are paraded out from Arizona to Wyoming, I recall being eight or nine years old and sitting at the kitchen table with my dad. My sister left her paper doll collection piled high on the table and like the good annoying brother I was, I found the most ridiculous top to go with the most outlandish bottoms. Everything about it was hilarious to me, and my dad joined in, putting a brown turtleneck sweater with a long, fancy feathered skirt—that sort of thing. Dad grabbed a copy of *Life* magazine and tore a photo of a dog out of it, placing an elegant wedding gown over the pup and sending me into a fit of hysterics.

When we were done, Dad made a big deal about telling me that while this was fun, he didn't ever want to catch me playing with my sister's "girl things" ever again. I don't know if it was then that Dad looked at me and realized who I was, or if something I did or said earlier had tipped him off. Either way, I felt like I'd been caught doing something awful and unforgivable. From that day on, I made sure that everything I said or did around anyone was on the up and up. Next time Dad and I talked, it was me asking him to show me how to change the oil on the Ford. I bet I'd have a tough time explaining to him what I'm doing at a beauty pageant—ring on my finger or not.

But there is a ring on my finger. I bet I could come home with my beautiful new wife. This time, Mom might cry happy tears when she and Dad pick us up at the train station. Of course, we'd have to say that the kids are Maxine's and come up with a story about how she's a widow, but it could work. I know from the Christmas card my sister sent last year that Dad's thinking about retiring from the restaurant. Maybe with a family of my own, he'd see me as fit to take over the Hogarth Family Diner. Maxine and the kids could erase all that mess from my time at Loyola. Mom will think all those hours spent saying the Rosary really did the trick when it came to setting her only son straight to the ways of God.

The gasps from the audience snap me out of my ridiculous fantasy land. Maisey Walker is onstage in her bathing suit. She walks across, flowing gracefully, her smile growing brighter when Thunders reads aloud her many musical accomplishments. Aside from singing, Maisey Walker is a much-awarded pianist and occasional contributor to the *Chicago Defender* newspaper. Thunders puts the emphasis on *occasional*, which I know from reading the rule book is because working women aren't allowed in the pageant. Way to meet the feminists in the middle, Mrs. American Pie.

As her name is read, Mrs. Michigan Pie throws herself from the wings onto the stage like a ball shot from a cannon. She recovers and finds a less awkward stride for a few steps. Yet as she reaches her first pose, at the exact moment Dale Thunders is telling everyone how her pie crust won "most flaky" three years running at the Washtenaw County Fair, Mrs. Michigan Pie gets cocky. She tries a little chorus-line-styled kick and goes flying backward as her high heel flies up into a stage light with enough force to blow it out. As she lies moaning on the stage, a torrent of sparks rains down around her.

Maisey and Mrs. Idaho Pie rush onstage to help the flailing Mrs. Michigan—whom everyone can plainly hear is cursing her little heart out, blaming everyone from God to the lighting crew. Chuck doesn't take his eyes off the stage and I'm thinking he's getting quite the education tonight. Maxine keeps that smile on, but I know she's cherishing every second of this. As someone helps Mrs. Michigan to her feet, there's a rip of fabric, a scream, and the whole room goes dark thanks to a quick-thinking stagehand.

Dale Thunders's microphone is dead and yet his voice doesn't know it, shouting out what's on all our minds, "Holy damn! Did this place just turn into a titty bar?"

Chuck's eyes are wide in shock, but he covers his mouth to hide his laughing. I'm thankful I told him to leave his notebook in the cabin. I'm also figuring he's going to remember all this without writing it down.

The lights come back up on the dripping-with-sweat Dale Thunders. "Well, folks, I sure hope you'll accept my profoundest apology for my little slip of the tongue. Looks like Mrs. Michigan Pie will be fine. No permanent damage done, thank you, Lord Jesus."

There's a smattering of applause. Although, can it be called "applause" if only six people clap? Anyway, it doesn't matter, because when the contestants are narrowed down to twenty, Mrs. Michigan Pie doesn't make the cut. She hobbles offstage, still in only one shoe.

Oh, and Maxine makes it to the top twenty. I should probably have been more nervous about that, but I wasn't. After all her gamesmanship and—let's be honest—conniving and mild evildoing, it never occurred to me that she could be eliminated right away. That's simply not the woman I fake married.

There are more surprised murmurs when Mrs. Illinois Pie advances, but also some loud and vigorous clapping to drown out those murmurs. My goodness, that Daniel's smile is hot enough to start a fire.

Once again, the lights dim and the *tip-tap* sounds of twenty women quickly exiting the stage fill the room.

"Is it over?" Chuck asks.

"I don't think so. The program says they end the night with ten contestants."

"It's so hard to decide which ladies are losers. They all seem real nice, except maybe for that swearing lady. But if I hurt myself like that in front of all these people, I would be barking mad too."

"You know what, Chuck? You might be the most decent person I know."

Chuck gives me a proud smile. "Thanks, Mr. Robert," he says. "I mean, Dad."

Dad.

Maxine Hogarth

Pageant Night One

I WISH I could say I feel a sense of accomplishment making it past the first cut, but I don't. My so-called competition is simply too underwhelming. Of the contestants we bid adieu to, most of them could barely walk across the stage while waving, let alone be crowned the nation's best wife and mother. That someone ended up mostly topless onstage is likewise no surprise. That sort of thing happens at nearly every pageant—and often on purpose. Frankly, I'm mildly shocked it was Mrs. Michigan. My money would have been on Mrs. Idaho Muffy Gail, who's giant shall we say "Yukon Gold potatoes" would have made for a better show.

All of us "winners" quickly head backstage to throw on matching circle skirts and button-up blouses over our bathing suits. Seconds later, Missy calls "Places!" and we all get in a line like a gaggle of Rockettes—just as we practiced earlier in the evening, for a whole ten minutes. Most pageants stress the importance of practice before a public performance, but since this is an early round and it's not televised, I guess Depwelt and the other pageant people decided "Why bother?" Hence the kazoo that is presently clenched tightly betwixt my lips.

The opening bars of "You're a Grand Old Flag" ring out and the curtain rises. Here we are, twenty of America's most beautiful and perfect housewives, dressed in matching day outfits, arms linked, buzzing along to the song with our kazoos. And to think I once thought wearing white shoes after Labor Day was the most mortifying thing a girl could do. Thank Christ the lights are too bright for me to see the audience. I can't imagine that Robert is watching any of this with a straight face.

I keep hum-buzzing (hummzing?) along to the tune of the music, which is nearly impossible to hear. It's as if a hive of bees has taken up residence inside my brain, leaving me unable to hear anything but the damn hummzing. There's also a phenomenal amount of spittle building up in this damned kazoo. It's nearly enough to make me choke.

Big finish, ladies! We each raise our hands high in the air, and it takes all the strength I have left in my trembling lips to hold the kazoo in place. As the lights go down and the audience politely applauds—most likely because they are so goddamned glad the buzzing has stopped—we Pies throw our kazoos behind us and offstage. I see some of my rivals wipe their spitty hands on their skirts. I choose to delicately blot my mouth with the palm of my hand. To my abject horror, there's a small river of spit running from my bottom lip down my chin.

The curtain comes up once more, and we twenty Pies all step forward in a line to the front of the stage. Another curtain falls behind us, allowing Missy and the stagehands to prep for the next event while we Pies and the audience meet the judges.

That moron Dale Thunders takes the stage with his best Lawrence Welk impression. "How 'bout that musical number? These gals really gave that their all, didn't they?"

Being from Palm Springs and seeing Thunders do the weather report on TV, I know what the rest of the audience is beginning to suspect, namely that Dale Thunders is a drunken fool. The man reeks of Aqua Velva and Wild Turkey, and while I'd like nothing more than to straighten his garish toupee, that would require me to touch him, which is almost as vomit-inducing as those disgusting kazoos.

"Before we get going on our next competition, let's lend an ear to the president of the Mr. and Mrs. American Pie pageant, Mrs. Alice Depwelt!"

Mrs. Depwelt glares at Thunders as he hands over the microphone to her. She directs our attention to the judges, seated at a long table in the front row. I'm only half listening as Depwelt introduces the first two judges—Mrs. American Pie 1950 and Mrs. American Pie 1969—a mother-daughter duo. The spotlight shines down on them, revealing a pair of pinched smiles and matching orange dresses. It's clear the mother is calling the shots since she looks lovely in that color while her daughter looks downright sickly, like she's just stepped off a rocky plane ride and could spew.

Dale Thunders is also a judge, which I'm considering a good thing since he's too repugnant for most of the contestants to consider screwing, although I suppose hand jobs are still a possibility. It's doubtful any amount of cajoling would rouse the loins of the next judge, the very elderly gentleman I recognize from the golf cart earlier today. He's Mr. Tipply, the owner of the company that provided the cabins' ovens and refrigerators, and if he's a day under ninety, I'll eat my hat. The spotlight shines directly on his face and he doesn't squint in the slightest, probably because he hasn't seen anything since the early 1920s.

The spotlight flies back on Alice Depwelt. "We also have a late-addition judge from our fine sponsor at Western Airlines."

My heart beats a tiny bit faster. Nothing to worry about, I assure myself.

Alice keeps reading from her little pink note card. "Some of you in the audience who live in Palm Springs may already know him, since rumor has it he's infamous on this town's many golf courses."

No. I look out for Robert, knowing he'll be far more level-headed and calm. But I can't see anything beyond the glare of the lights.

"Please give a warm welcome to Mr. Douglas Simmons."

My knees give. I don't fall, although I wish I could fall through a trapdoor on the stage, perhaps into a pool of starved sharks. As the spotlight careens off Depwelt and onto the judge's table, there's Douglas. While all the other judges smiled and waved to the audience, Douglas instead glares pure murder at me. The first time I saw him this furious was our first Easter together at his parents' home. His sister's husband kept plying me with tiny glasses of sambuca, and by the time the glazed ham was on the table, I was throwing up herbed carrots in his mother's guest bathroom. Douglas had to carry me to the car to bring me home. He didn't say a word to me for three days. Instead he would glower at me. When he did finally speak to me, it was to tell me his mother found my apology letter "adequate." Something tells me no amount of apologizing will calm his rage tonight.

Just past Douglas at the judges' table and off to the left, I see Robert. He isn't clapping. His head snaps from left to right, as if he's looking for an exit. Charles stares up at me, his eyes wide and his hand covering his mouth. He tugs on Robert's sleeve to get his attention, directing Robert to look at me.

When Robert catches my stare, I do the only thing I can do. I mouth *I'm sorry* over and over and over. I half expect him to get up and run out, but he stays in his seat, staring right through me. The spotlight pulls off Douglas, and all I can think to do is pretend that he never saw me. Maybe I'm imagining his glare? Maybe he still has no idea that Mrs. Arizona Pie once was Mrs. Douglas Simmons? Either way, there's a blindfold going over my eyes and a hot iron is placed in my hand, so there's no time for me to run now.

Charles "Chuck" Bronski

Pageant Night One

ONE DAY I was home sick from school and there was nothing on TV except these shows for ladies, so I watched one. It was mostly really boring, with grown-ups talking to each other about stuff, but then at the end, a lady was kissing this one guy when another guy walked in the room. I know that doesn't sound like a big deal, but the guy who walked in was supposed to be dead and the lady was his wife. Then there was some punching and the lady screamed and the show ended.

That's how Miss Maxine and Robert act when the last judge—Douglas Simmons—is introduced. Except I don't think this Simmons fella was dead.

"Is that Miss Maxine's ex-husband?" I ask Robert once all the clapping stops.

"Not now, Chuck," he tells me, sounding almost mad. He takes the program out of my hands and flips to the back. "Douglas Simmons" isn't anywhere on the judges list. From where we're sitting, I can see the side of Simmons's face. Miss Maxine is right about him looking a little "Satan-y."

The spotlight goes to Mr. Thunders. He sounds like that guy Andy Griffith always keeps in the drunk tank down at the Mayberry police station.

"Who in the audience likes a well-pressed shirt?" Mr. Thunders yells.

All the ladies turn and look behind them as another curtain goes up. Miss Maxine and all the other ladies have blindfolds on and irons in their hands. In front of each of them is an ironing board with a pile of men's wrinkled shirts. Each lady has another lady standing next to her who isn't wearing a blindfold. I want to ask Robert what the heck is going on, but he's tapping his foot all nervous-like, so I leave him alone.

"Let's get this game going!" yells Mr. Thunders. "First ten women to iron five shirts all nice and proper get to continue on toward being . . . Mrs. . . . American . . . Piiiiiieeeee!"

None of the ladies move.

"Oh," Thunders says. "I forgot to say that you can go. GO!"

The women go nuts, throwing their irons down on the first shirt all lickety-split. Mrs. Kansas Pie knocks her iron to the floor and her helper lady walks her offstage. I never saw Miss Maxine practice for this, but she irons that shirt like she's mighty furious at it. She slaps the iron down and pushes fast and hard, like she's real quick mopping up something Dawn spilled. With one shirt done, she shoves it in the direction of her helper. That lady looks it over and raises her fist high for the judges to see. A bell goes off, telling everyone that Miss Maxine finished a shirt. Before it even goes ding, Miss Maxine is angrily ironing another shirt.

At the end of the line, Mrs. Oregon's shirt catches on fire! She rips off her blindfold and runs off screaming. Miss Missy has to put the fire out with an extinguisher. Even with all the ruckus, Mrs. Walker finishes ironing all five of her shirts way ahead of the other ladies. Now I've read a lot of comic books, so I know a superpower when I see one. I guess I thought those were all make-believe, but now I'm thinking Mrs. Walker might be Captain Ironer.

"Come on, Mrs. Arizona!" I yell as loud as I can. "You can do it, Mom!"

All the people in the audience are on their feet like they're watching a boxing match and not a beauty pageant. Four more ladies finish their shirts. That movie-star-looking lady from Idaho finishes and the lady from Rhode Island burns her hand but still gets her last shirt done. This means Miss Maxine needs to finish her last shirt before anyone else can win the tenth spot.

Robert finally gets off his rump and stands next to me, helping me cheer on Miss Maxine. It works, and she throws her last shirt behind her maybe half a second before the lady next to her can finish. My fake mom's a winner!

"My mom's a winner!" I yell while jumping up and down.

Miss Maxine blows us kisses from the stage. Then I see her eyes turn to that Simmons fellow. She watches him go out the back door, then smiles and nods to Robert.

Maxine Hogarth

Pageant Night One

NORMALLY WINNING SOMETHING as shitty as tenth place would curdle my blood, but knowing that my goddamned ex-husband is now my judge, jury, and executioner is more than I can handle. The second that curtain hits the stage, I kick off my heels and get my head ready for what comes next. The way I see it, I've got two options: fight or flight. Since Robert didn't choose flight—as I first feared—I'm going with fight.

No big surprise, Douglas is loitering outside the backstage dressing room. I barely notice the hostile glare at first, because he's wearing a ridiculous shirt with wide lapels and the top two buttons undone. He was always downright militant about how inappropriate other men looked when displaying anything more than a half inch of chest below the collarbone.

He grabs me by my arm and pulls me into a secluded stairwell. I wasn't expecting that.

"What the hell part of 'Stay out of Palm Springs' do you not understand?" he snaps at me.

The sound of his voice is like a slap across the face. But I've assumed this would be his first question for me, so the whole time I was ironing, I thought through exactly what to say. "I was invited here. And last I checked, it's a free goddamned country, Douglas. I don't think President Nixon or Governor Reagan have issued any decrees barring the former Mrs. Douglas Simmons from roaming freely across this great land."

"You need to march your ass right to Depwelt and quit or I'll do it for you." He points in the general direction of where he wants me to go, which I don't find at all helpful since it's the bottom of the stairs.

"No," I tell him. I clasp my hands behind my back so he can't see that they're shaking.

"What?" he cries.

"I'm not leaving."

"Then I'll make you." He takes a quick step toward me and I don't flinch. I don't think I could move right now if I wanted to. He takes another step toward me. He has a healthy tan. "I'm a sponsor and a judge. I'll get your ass bounced right out of here. And then I'll have my lawyer sue your ass to get back your alimony."

Is he wearing cologne? Douglas thinks cologne is for pretentious Europeans and homosexuals. Yet I'm getting a definite whiff of something musky and overtly manly coming off him. I bet the Jennifer wants him to wear it so she can pretend he's not almost as old as her father.

I stick to my guns. "You're not going to do any of those things, Douglas. Would you like to know why?"

"Enlighten me, Maxine."

"Because you want everyone in Palm Springs to forget about me. And should you decide to force me to leave, I'll do something they will never forget." I wish I could slap him. Let him explain a black eye to his new wifey. "Think back on our years together, and I think you'll recall exactly how determined I can be."

Ponder he does. Maybe he's thinking back to '66 when I told that infamously hot-tempered Vera Miller that I saw her husband buying drinks for some coltish brunette at the Palm Springs Hilton at 2 p.m. on a Tuesday. Suddenly Mr. Miller couldn't make that weekend's golf outing with Governor Reagan, and Douglas got to take his spot.

"You know what I'm capable of, Douglas," I remind him. He might also recall what happened when our next-door neighbor decided to paint his garage trim a shade of green Douglas called "garish." Who does he think wrote all those letters to the town zoning commission, the mayor's office, and the newspaper editorial board? My poison pen changed laws and got that garage painted a solid white.

Douglas paces a little and rubs his face with his hand. His gold wedding band catches the light and shimmers in my face. It's wider than the one he wore with me and the band is newer and unscuffed. He catches me staring at it and I fear I've nearly lost my well-earned upper hand.

"Mutually assured destruction," I tell him.

"What?"

"It's a term used by military strategists to explain why there will never be a nuclear war. If the Commies bomb us, we'll bomb them right back. Since we'll all be destroyed, no one drops a bomb. Mutually. Assured. Destruction."

I lunge toward him with some vigor. He recoils, but he's also got his back to a wall. "To be blunt, Douglas, you fuck this up for me and I will fuck up your entire world. Mrs. South Carolina, Mrs. Kansas, and at least half a dozen members of the audience saw me walk back here with you right now. I could let out a scream, throw myself down that flight of stairs, and tell everyone you pushed me." I walk closer to the stairs and cling to the hand railing, as if I were staring over the precipice of the goddamned Grand Canyon.

"You're batshit," Douglas whispers to me, unmoving. Has he lost weight? His shirts fit him better across his shoulders and chest. I hope Robert isn't melting down in the cabin, or worse yet, in public. I need to find him.

"What's it going to be, Douglas? Mutually assured destruction? Or a quick tumble down the stairs for me and an arrest record for you?"

"I stay away from you and you stay away from me?" Douglas asks, clearly realizing he has no option but to cave.

"You give me the same average score as all the other judges."

Douglas laughs and puts his sunglasses on. They're aviators like Steve McQueen wears. Douglas is no Steve McQueen. "Those judges will see through you in a heartbeat."

I leave him laughing to himself.

Charles "Chuck" Bronski

Pageant Night One

IF SOMEONE HAD told me two days ago that I would have the best time ever at a mom pageant, I'd figure that person was pulling my leg real hard. Sure, there's lots of boring lady stuff like fancy dresses and so much perfume that my eyes burn. But there's also ironing contests with fire and danger. It's like a demolition derby or a bunch of dress-wearing Evel Knievels!

I don't think I need to learn how to iron blindfolded (actually, why does anyone need to know how to do that?). But I think there is a whole bunch of other good stuff I might need to do without looking, in case I'm taken captive behind enemy lines. Or locked in a car trunk by a Commie or diamond smugglers. I start a list:

* Shower (including hair washing)
* Tie and untie at least five different knots (hard ones)
* Use pocketknife to cut through ropes
* Put a Band-Aid on a cut
* Throw a knife or ax and hit a target
* Take a Daisy pump-action BB gun apart, clean it, put it back together ★

I can't do that last one yet, which is why I put a star by it. It's on the list for me to do later, once I convince Miss Maxine to let me have a BB gun.

Robert and Miss Maxine say nothing to each other the whole way back to the cabin, and even once we're all inside and getting Dawn settled. I think it's because of Miss Maxine's ex-husband. I didn't like the look of the guy. Last summer I had a paper route in a nice part of town. Guys who looked like that Simmons fella never tip and they're always angry if the paper isn't folded up and left right against the door.

Dawn's super fussy. She's moaning in her crib, so Miss Maxine picks her up and puts her cheek against Dawn's cheek. "Does she feel warm to you, Robert?"

Robert puts his hands on her head and Dawn can't hold back anymore. She screams, and with the scream comes some bright pink baby barf.

"Is that blood?" shrieks Miss Maxine.

Robert looks closer at the barf. "I bet it's something she ate," he says, trying to be all calm. "You kids didn't give her anything, did you?"

"I bet it was the candy cane." I tried whispering this to Miss Maxine, but we're all in a huddle around Dawn, so Robert heard.

"Where'd she'd get a candy cane?" Robert asks me. I look up at Miss Maxine, who's only looking at Dawn while rubbing all the sticky pink spit-up off the corners of her still-screaming mouth.

"There, there, sweetheart," Miss Maxine baby-talks her. "Mommy's here, darling."

Dawn giggles and passes gas. Now, I don't mean that she shoots out some cute baby toot. She lets one rip the size of an elephant. Like Timmy Velasco said once in school that got him a week's detention, Dawn plays a long note on a butt tuba. She doesn't just cut *the* cheese. She cut *all* the cheese. She dealt it and we all smelt it. Even worse than that, at the same time she breaks wind, Dawn belches and her tummy gurgles. All the pink in her face turns Casper-the-Ghost white and I know what's coming next.

"She's gonna blow!" I blurt out.

Miss Maxine holds her out as far as her arms can reach. I grab Dawn and race toward the kitchen sink. Dawn passes gas again, and well, there's no delicate way to put this, but her diaper springs a leak like an open fire hydrant all over the kitchen table.

You might think that this would be real upsetting to a baby. Not my sister. She sees all her pea-soup poo dripping down the family photo from Old Tucson and it's like the funniest thing she's seen her whole baby life. Miss Maxine and Robert holler, grabbing towels and opening windows, because while I might have joked that the candy cane would make her smell like Christmas, it does not. It does not *at all*. It smells more like someone decided to butcher all the reindeer. Even Rudolph.

Dawn laughs from deep in her belly. Then—from the same place as the laugh—she belches some more, then laughs some more. At least *she's* not upset.

"Bathroom, Charles! Aim for the toilet!" Miss Maxine sounds so freaked out that I'm thinkin' at first she wants me to put Dawn in the toilet. I'm not going to do that—even if it is what she means.

Just as fast as she started pooping, Dawn stops. Getting all that junk out of her musta felt real good. Now she's all giggly and happy. I hold her up to the mirror, since seeing herself always makes her laugh. Plus, Miss Maxine and Robert are squabbling while cleaning poop off everything. Dawn doesn't need to hear that. Heck, I probably shouldn't hear that.

"What in the Sam Hill have you been feeding her all day, Maxine?" Robert yells.

"Poison, Robert!" Miss Maxine snaps back. "Pure poison. Because that's clearly the sort of monster you think I am—"

"I think you've been giving her junk to keep her quiet—"

"Teething biscuits! They're made for babies!"

"Teething biscuits don't make a baby poop napalm!"

"Oh please, Robert, you think you know everything!"

"Really? Like what? Give me one example of me knowing anything when you're in the room?"

Miss Maxine needs a second to think about that. I don't like that they are getting noisy. The Walkers are right on the other side of this wall, and they don't seem like people who ever shout.

"You think you know more about raising children than I do." Miss Maxine's voice sounds all shaky.

"This whole pageant is the dumbest thing I've ever been talked into," Robert tells her. "And, mind you, I went to a Sadie Hawkins dance once." He dumps all of Miss Maxine's pooped-on table figurines into the kitchen sink. He turns the water on full blast, and Miss Maxine starts yelling over it.

"I'm not just doing this for myself, Robert! I'm doing this for you, for the tavern—"

"Oh bull, Maxine. You love this. All the photographs and constant attention. It's your world and we all live in it to serve you."

The water's off. They're still yelling. I've never seen anyone angry-dry a cowboy figurine before, but Miss Maxine is sure doing that. "So, this is about Douglas? For the last goddamned time, I didn't know he would be here!"

"You still put all of us at risk," Robert says, pointing a finger at Miss Maxine. He has to know she hates that.

I know you're not supposed to disrespect your elders, but this ain't good.

"Hey, guys?" I say, all polite and whatnot. I worry there's a judge zipping around outside on a golf cart, hearing every word of this.

They just keep going. Or at least Miss Maxine does.

"It's not as if that divorce certificate means—"

"Hey!" I say real loud.

They both look at me fast.

I think I'm . . . angry? Am I mad? I think I'm mad. I think I'm mad at my mom and dad, who aren't actually my mom and dad, so it's not so awful that I'm angry at them, right?

Next thing I know, *my* finger is pointing at Robert and Miss Maxine. "You two can't do that no more!" I tell them.

They stare at me and then each other and then me again. This makes me madder. "We got nice neighbors and judges everywhere and a mean ex-husband, and I'm working my tail feathers off!"

I figure the next thing they yell at isn't going to be each other. It's going to me.

Robert lets out a sigh and smiles at me. "You're right, Chuck. We're sorry. Aren't we, Maxine?"

Miss Maxine nods and has a smile on her face that's real, but also maybe trying not to laugh at me.

"Miss Maxine, you can't keep feedin' Dawn junk."

Miss Maxine stares down at her feet the way kids always do when the teacher calls them up in front of the class. I don't know what's coming over me. Maybe this is like Miss Maxine always talking about her "snapping." "I can't be the one always taking care of Dawn. There are contest people everywhere, and what are they gonna think if they see a kid like me doing all the baby work?"

Miss Maxine squeaks like a mouse, but a mouse who's also about to cry. "I'm no good at this mothering business," she cries. Big, sloppy tears drip off her face, and at first I think there's something super wrong with her eyes until I remember she puts black stuff on her eyelashes to make 'em bigger. "I only want Dawn to like me the way she likes both of you."

"She likes you just fine, Miss Maxine," I tell her. I pat her shoulder, but don't say the "there, there" that guys usually say to women when they get all weepy.

Robert brings Dawn over and puts her in Miss Maxine's arms. I'm holding my breath and trying to use my brain waves to send Dawn a message. Dawn squirms a little and makes some baby noises like *la-la-la-la-la-da*. But she seems okay with Miss Maxine cuddling her and all.

I back away and Dawn keeps staring at me. She reaches a hand out in my direction and for a second I think the screaming is gonna start again. Instead Robert puts out one of his fingers and Dawn latches on to it with her tiny baby fist and shoves it in her mouth, letting the bottle fall to the floor.

"Please tell me you've washed your hands," says Miss Maxine.

Robert nods. He squints. I know that look. That's the look someone makes when a baby's using their finger as a teether.

I don't say anything. Dawn seems all happy with Miss Maxine and Robert hovering around her, making baby noises. It's cute. If I didn't know better, I'd say Robert and Maxine look like her real mom and dad.

Dawn hiccups. Then another. And another. She giggles, but I know where this is going.

"I'm gonna go for a walk before bed," I tell them, opening the door.

"Oh, Charles," Miss Maxine says to me. "You're my eyes and ears, right?"

I nod, but I don't bring my knapsack with me. I don't want to spy on people. I got thinking to do.

I go for the longest walk of my life. I mean, maybe I've walked longer and farther before, but that was because I needed be somewhere. A walk is when you are just out wandering around with nothing to do and nowhere to go. If anything, I have somewhere I don't want to go—back to that cabin. Instead I walk behind the cabins, keeping low when I pass by a window with the lights still on. I know I shouldn't be sneaking around when there's light in any of the cabins. If I get caught, I'll look like a creeper. But if someone sees me alone on the paths, I look like a kid who wants to be far away from his family. I guess I don't know which one is worse: creeper or angry kid.

I don't know why—I guess it's on account of seeing all these moms in one place today—but I start thinking of my own mom. My real one—Sharla. I don't know where she is, which I've learned is something that's a weird thing for a kid to think. But I don't know. Up until a few days ago, I'd look in the paper every morning to see where the ball club she's working for is playing. Last I knew, she was in Kansas City.

One time, when I was a little kid—this was before Dawn was born—my mom and one of my uncles were living at a different apartment building than the one we're in now. I don't remember if it was morning or afternoon, but I wake up in my clothes in my bed. It's bright out and the house is hot, so maybe it's summer. I need to use the bathroom real bad, only I can't get my belt undone. I have a zipper on the front of my pants, but it's stuck shut on this pair, meaning if I don't get that belt done, I'm a goner. I'm gonna wet my pants. I can't find Ma, though. I remember walking all through the apartment calling her name, but nobody answers. I know I'm not supposed to leave the house, but the front door's unlocked, so I'm thinking maybe Ma is outside talking to a neighbor or something.

I go outside and right away wish I hadn't. First, the door closes behind me and that makes me scared. Then I feel how hot the cement is under my feet since I didn't think to put shoes on. Worse still is that I see this mean old lady coming up to me. I know it's not nice to call someone a "mean old lady," but I'm telling ya, that's what this lady is. She's super old and has a voice that sounds like that bad guy in the Popeye cartoons—Brutus. Mrs. Brutus sees me standing outside my apartment and stomps over to me.

"What are you doing? Where's your mother?" she yells.

I don't know what to say. I don't know where my mother is. I want to ask this mean old lady if she knows where my mother is, but I also know that's not something I should ask anyone.

"Didn't anyone teach you to answer when an adult speaks to you?"

I feel myself about to cry. I reach up for the handle but can't grab on to it cuz my hands are sweaty and small.

"Did you run off on your mother?" she shouts. "I bet you did, didn't you!"

I nod up and down and up and down to tell her yes. I push on the door as hard as I can and fall back into the apartment. I slam the door shut. The mean old lady knocks on it and then bangs on it. I run into the closet in my bedroom and stay there. I still need to use the bathroom so bad that it hurts, so I decide to rub my hands over and over on the thick carpet in the closet to get them dried off cuz I'm so sweaty. The banging on the door finally stops.

For some reason—I guess maybe cuz I was a dumb little kid—I crawl like a baby to the bathroom. My hands were finally working and I got my belt off. This is a crazy thing to say, but it felt good to use the bathroom. Like, it felt so good, I cried.

I went back to bed. I know I woke up back in my bed and it was dark out. I heard the TV was on and could hear my mom and my uncle making noise in the kitchen. The house smelled like someone was cooking hamburger and that made me awful hungry.

It's funny to think about how a little kid's brain works. I can remember the mean old lady and the busted belt, but I don't remember why my dad wasn't living with us. Maybe he was gone on business? It's like he was never there until one day he just was. Then he joined the army and was gone again.

It's after nine o'clock when I get back to the cabin. I'm kinda surprised no one's mad I was gone so long. Robert's singing some song about a boy named Danny to Dawn, who's nearly out in his arms.

"Did you have a good walk, dear?" Miss Maxine asks me. "I've laid your pajamas out on the bed for you."

I don't say anything. I just grab my new pajamas and take them with me to the bathroom. As I'm closing the door, I hear Miss Maxine grumbling about forgetting her favorite pillow.

"You'll just have to make do, Maxine."

"I'm simply cautioning you that I might be restless all night."

I on purpose don't turn the shower on so I can listen in on their conversation.

"Do you want to sleep against the wall or do you want the outside?" Robert asks.

"You can choose, dear."

There's a quiet, like both of them are trying to think of something to say.

"You did great tonight, Maxine," Robert finally says.

"I got tenth place."

"Yeah, but out of twenty. There's no way I could've done that."

"Was Charles proud of me?"

Robert laughs. "He was screaming for you the whole time."

"Really?" She sounds surprised and maybe a little happy.

"Absolutely, Maxine."

The next morning I'm the first one awake, thanks to the sun pouring through the window and hitting me right in the face. Or maybe it was also cuz Miss Maxine is snoring like a freight train. I don't know what happened last night, but I see that the couch is pushed up against Miss Maxine and Robert's bed. Just as I'm thinking how smart that is since it gives them a bigger bed, I realize that Dawn's crib is empty. I leap up, ready to start screaming, when I hear her making happy baby noises. She's sitting up in between Miss Maxine and Robert, looking cute as the dickens while waving her dolly at me.

Robert wakes up with a start, like he doesn't remember where he is until Dawn shoves her dolly in his face.

"What time is it?" he asks me.

"A little after six. Did you guys sleep like this all night?"

He nods. "She wouldn't settle in the crib, so we pushed the couch over to make more room. What time is the first event?"

I'm glad he knows I have the schedule memorized. "We have a group breakfast at eight thirty."

Robert gives Miss Maxine a little shake on her shoulder. She wakes up mid-snort and tears the pink sleeping mask off her face. It's always strange to see her with no makeup on.

"Did she sleep between us all night?" Miss Maxine asks. "How darling. How perfectly darling!" She pats down Dawn's messy blond curls and Dawn seems to like it. She holds out her dolly to Maxine and Maxine pretends to pat the dolly's curls, too. Robert and Maxine sit there in bed just smiling at each other, taking turns making baby noises at Dawn or petting her like she's an adorable puppy. Dawn makes this funny little face, squishing her eyes together real tight while her cheeks get all red, like she's holding her breath. She busts up giggling from a place deep in her belly.

Then the smell hits us.

All of us, all at once.

Our noses scrunch up and Miss Maxine throws back all the blankets on the bed, which only makes the smell stronger.

"Oh Christ!" Miss Maxine yelps as she leaps up. "She just shit the bed, Robert. Oh Christ!"

Robert picks up Dawn and holds her out at arm's length. Her diaper is gone.

"How can she have any poop left in her?" I ask.

"It's all over the bed," says Robert.

"And the divan!" Miss Maxine screeches, but in a quiet way.

"If it helps any, it's not *your* divan," I tell them.

"The boy has a point, Maxine."

Miss Maxine does the last thing I ever thought she'd do while sitting in a bed that's become a baby toilet. She laughs. She laughs and laughs and laughs until I start to think that she's about to do something crazy. But she doesn't. Instead she gets out of bed and walks right past me and Robert into the bathroom.

"Well, if this isn't becoming the Hogarth way. A perfect family, covered in shit," I hear her say.

Maxine Hogarth

Pageant Day Two

WHAT WITH ALL the Dawn shit-show antics, I'm awake a good hour before I remember that my previous day's points rankings are waiting for me on my front door. I tear them off and bring them inside to properly pore over every detail.

> MR. & MRS. ARIZONA PIE
> Home Decor: 4.6/5
> Neighborly BBQ: 4.6/5
> Family Presentation: 4.3/5
> Bathing Suit: 4.5/5
> Ironing Skills: 1.0/5
> Total daily ranking: Third Place, behind Mrs. Rhode Island Pie (Second Place) and Mrs. Illinois Pie (First Place).

"Fucking ironing," I say, forgetting that Dawn is in my arms. "I mean, sugar shoot ironing."

Robert looks at the list. "I don't remember any 'Family Presentation' competition?"

"That's the score they give for all the smiling and waving. Or having a family photo with Dick Goddamned Nixon."

"Third place isn't too bad," Robert tries telling me. "Especially considering your ex-husband is a judge." I was wondering when Robert was going to bring that up. "Do I want to know what you did to him last night, Maxine?"

"I didn't *do* anything," I explain. "I simply pointed out that his life will be infinitely more peaceful if he and I act like adults. Adults who don't know each other or hate each other."

"But he's scoring us," Robert unhelpfully reminds me.

"I'm more worried about the other judges," I half lie. "We need to step it up. Lots of endlessly adorable shit in public. No more screw-ups for me in solo competitions."

Charles takes the scorecard from me to study the itinerary on the other side.

SCHEDULE
8:30 a.m.–Breakfast at the Clubhouse
10:30 a.m.–Surprise Men's Outing (Casual Dress)
11:00 a.m.–Women's Grocery Trip
5:00 p.m.–Family Dinner: Theme "Father's Favorites"

We make it out the door at exactly 8:23 a.m., which is a good thing, since the walk to the clubhouse is six minutes provided we walk at a brisk pace, although not to such an extent that we draw negative attention to ourselves. I can't help but worry if we still smell like excrement. Charles had the brilliant idea to hide the soiled sheets in the water hazard on the third hole and Robert stashed the divan cushions in the shrubbery behind the cabin.

"Raccoons," Robert muses out loud to me, apropos of nothing.

"What?" I ask through a smile since, surely, someone somewhere is watching.

"We can tell the judges that some raccoons got into the cabin while we were at breakfast and you know, violated the couch."

I'll make a devious pageant husband out of him yet!

"I don't think they have raccoons around here," Charles whispers, handing a squirming Dawn over to Robert. "Maybe desert foxes or coyotes? Coyote and Road Runner cartoons are in a desert."

I choose to take it as a point of pride that my whole faux-mily is working together on this one. We might not have a photo with him, but I bet Tricky Dick would give us *his* vote.

"All right, Pies, I trust everyone had a good night's sleep?" Alice Depwelt announces as she takes to the podium. "Excellent. Day two of the competition is all about budgeting and shopping. Now, for you Lady Pies, this means you'll be given an allowance, a brief period of time to plan meals and a grocery list, and then taken to a grocery store for our shopping competition."

There are gentle murmurs and more smiling and nodding. It's the same competition every year when it comes to shopping.

"Gentlemen Pies!" Mrs. Depwelt commands. "You are not exempt from this competition." More murmurs, this time without the smiling. "Unlike in previous years, we've decided that since it's 1970 and you're all confident, modern men, it's high time you also participated in shopping. You will all be escorted to the Broadway department store, where you will be given a budget and . . ."

She drags it out for effect. I assume her next words will be "set loose to buy new golf clubs." I am dead wrong.

". . . and your wife's measurements!"

There's a nervous—or in the case of young Mr. South Carolina Pie, Roy Clarke, downright giddy—amount of laughter. Mr. Rhode Island Pie, Byron Biddle, even cuts loose with a vulgar wolf whistle and uses his hands to mime an exaggerated hourglass figure. I say "exaggerated" because his wife, Betsey Biddle, is built like a broomstick.

"You will need to buy your wife a suitable dress, which she will wear the following night and you will be judged on. Take this seriously, gentlemen," Depwelt begs.

I am worried. Openly so. Just last week I had to explain to Robert what a padded girdle was and how one uses it.

With a sharp clap of her hands, Depwelt tells us to clear out and get ready to shop. Once we're outside and beyond everyone's earshot, Robert whispers, "You think you look better in blue than pink, right? Nothing too bright?"

"*Think*, Robert, dear? I *know* I need a nice, clear, and strong azure for evening. Nothing paler or brighter than the sky in May."

A judge's golf cart comes up the path toward us. I instinctively move to grab Robert's hand before realizing I'm already holding it. When did that happen?

"Azure is blue, though, right?"

I snap my head toward him ready to stare daggers, and see he's smiling wickedly.

Robert Hogarth

Pageant Day Two

I KNOW I'M a somewhat fearful man, but some days you think more about death than others. Days like when your fake wife's very real ex-husband shows up looking for blood. Or when you're assigned a task at a beauty pageant that has you doing something completely outside of everything you know. Personally, if I see a brilliant flash of light from an atomic bomb, only to open my eyes and find myself in the ladies' dress shop at the Broadway department store, then I'll know I've died and gone straight to hell.

Missy makes good on her threat to dump us all at the store. We're now not so much men as strangers in a strange land, exploring terrain that is well traveled yet inhospitable to us. We don't have maps, but rather odd strings of numbers and letters scribbled down on a slip of paper. Our wives' "measurements" we're told, which I guess in a strange way *is* a sort of map, namely to a body that I do not own nor one that I've ever been remotely interested in traveling to.

Thankfully, the rest of this bunch is as dumb as I am. I don't know the difference between silk and a rayon blend, but I do know that one is roughly 30 percent more expensive, which I think also sums up my wife. I promise to save that joke for later when I can say it out loud and impress everyone with my ability to poke fun at my beloved like Johnny Carson! Women! They sure do buy a lot of expensive crap, don't they?

I get the attention of a haughty clerk. "Miss, do you have any dresses in azure?" I ask.

She stares at me blankly. Her huge blue eyes are heavy with makeup. "I don't know what *azure* means," she says. Her voice is much younger-sounding than I expected.

"Azure is a bright, clear blue," I tell her, trying to be quiet about it. "More like the color you have on your eyelids than the color of your eyes."

Someone behind me makes cat noises. I spin around and see Byron Biddle, Mr. Rhode Island, the husband of Betsey Biddle, who's currently in second place. "Sounds like the missus has you whipped!" he says in a voice that sounds like a more inebriated (believe it or not) Dean Martin.

Normally, when confronted by some puffed-up bonehead looking to out-manly me, I make a joke and change the subject. But as I'm realizing at this pageant, I don't need to do that anymore. I've got a wedding ring on and a wife at home who's taught me all sorts of things about how to out-bully someone. In a move Maxine would surely be proud of, I toss it right back in his face. "Happy wife, happy life," I quip to Byron with a smirk.

This comeback gets *ahhhh*s and a pat on the back from the other men, all of whom rack their brains trying to remember their wives' favorite color. Only Daniel seems to know what the hell he's doing, picking out a simple, flowy dress the color of ripe plums.

"Robert," he says, waving me over. "Is this too casual? The paper says they need to have a nighttime look?"

Maxine would immediately dismiss the dress as something one only wears because her mother-in-law gave it to her. *Women have shapes, Robert. And frump is not a shape!* "Maybe that color, but in something longer? And shinier? I think shiny equals formal?" I suggest. "Go for something you think is too expensive but still in our budget?"

"You're making a lot of sense to me right now, Robert."

I don't know how to take this. What about my ability to pick out a dress makes "sense" to anyone? "I really don't have a dang clue as to what I'm doing, Daniel. I'm mostly guessing based on what the mannequins wear. And stuff Maxine says."

While I was hoping there would be only one azure dress, the clerk finds four that I need to choose from. I cut the miniskirt one from the team immediately, knowing that Maxine would take one look at it and yell "whore!" Another one is the right length, but it also has these billowy sleeves that would "make even a ballerina's shoulders look like a linebacker's." Everything about the third dress screams, "I'm letting my dress have more personality than me!" what with its use of sequins, ruffles, and satin. Plus, Maxine likes her necklines simple so that all the attention is on her, um, chest. This leaves me with only one dress, and since Maxine doesn't magically pop up on my shoulder as either angel or devil, I figure we're fine.

Shoes and all that other stuff ("sparkly shit" as Roy Clarke helpfully puts it) are an easy choice. I find shoes and a bag the same "azure" as the dress and then buy everything else in silver. Some of the guys try to get creative with it and pick a complementary color, or if the dress is a print, they grab something that matches one of the colors. Byron Biddle went for the most expensive dress still in our budget. With its deep V neckline and feathers on cuffs and collar, Byron must be A-OK with Betsey looking like a trampy bird. Virgil Gail selected a black dress for Muffy and went with everything else in a leopard print. This makes sense to all of us, considering what we've seen of Muffy. Which is an awful lot.

And to think Chuck was disappointed he couldn't come with on this shopping trip.

Charles "Chuck" Bronski

Pageant Day Two

I AIN'T GONNA LIE, I was relieved to hear I didn't have to go shopping with Robert. First of all, it's boring. Secondly, it would be cheating, since I've done so much shopping with Miss Maxine back in Scottsdale. I know stuff a boy shouldn't know about his mom—even a fake one. I know her shoe size (seven and a half), what colors she thinks are frumpy (browns and grays), and that she'll never wear a skirt that is more than three inches above the top of her kneecap. Worse still is that I know what she means when she says she's a 32C.

"Why don't you do a little sleuthing on your own today?" Miss Maxine tells me while getting Dawn ready. They're in matching dresses, including hats. I want to make a joke about taking bets on how long it'll be before Dawn turns that hat into a Frisbee, but I keep my mouth shut. "Remember, if you get caught, tell them you're looking for the bathroom. It works every time."

I pack up my knapsack with my notebook, three sharpened pencils, compass, magnifying glass, and canteen, and head out the back door. Everybody's doing pageant stuff, so I figure that means maybe I can snoop around in the pageant offices. I hide in some bushes by the side door of the clubhouse, and when that Mrs. Depwelt lady leaves, I sneak into the building. Miss Maxine told me the pageant would need temporary offices and she was right. I find a door with a piece of paper on it that says: *Pageant Offices, Mrs. Alice Depwelt.* Her office is unlocked, which is good since I haven't learned how to pick a lock yet.

Mrs. Depwelt's office is tidy with nothing but a desk, a couple of chairs, and a couple of bookcases that have all sorts of golf awards on them. There's a closet, so I open the door on that to make sure there's no one hiding in there. Miss Maxine told me to look for stuff like interview questions or files on the contestants. When I asked if it was cheating, she told me how sneaking around is an "unwritten rule" of pageants, like throwing a knuckleball in baseball. I kinda think that isn't true, but then again, if this stuff were really a secret, Mrs. Depwelt would probably do a better job of hiding it. Sitting right here out in the open is a clipboard—like the kind Missy is always carrying around—with a bunch of papers with the word *Memorandum* at the top.

Now, I've seen a lot of TV shows with spies, detectives, and what have you in them, so I feel kinda dumb when I start reading the papers. Because whenever a fella does that on a TV show, it always means that someone is going to walk in on him. Sure enough, as soon as I read past *Dear Sponsors*, I hear someone in the hallway.

I hide in the closet. I'm good at hiding, since the Hardy Boys do it a lot and I learned from them. Through the crack in the closet door, I see that Missy's come looking for the clipboard. She hums to herself while looking under a few files on the desk and on the bookshelf. There's enough light coming in through the crack that I can read most of the memorandum. It's something Mrs. Depwelt wrote for the sponsors, telling them not to worry about what the judges are doing. Mrs. Depwelt says she is the one who tallies the final scores and can make "adjustments where fitting." I thought the scores were tallied with math. It feels like Missy's taking hours, and I almost want to jump out of the closet and yell, "I need a bathroom!" Finally she leaves. I count to thirty and get the heck out of there, taking the clipboard and the memorandums with me.

Mission complete.

Maxine Hogarth

Pageant Day Two

WITH ROBERT OFF buying me evening wear and Charles hope-fully digging up quality pageant dirt, I sip coffee in the cabin while finalizing which shopping list I want to bring with me. I prepared seven before we left Scottsdale, each with its own theme, since I didn't know what the pageant might spring on us. According to the itinerary, we're doing "Father's Favorites" this year, which is easy, since Robert's favorites will be whatever I put in front of him.

Grocery lists in hand, we Lady Pies are shipped via bus to the Safeway grocery store on Ramon Road. On the plus side, this is a store I've been in several times before, prior to me handing over shopping duties to Gina. On the downside, it's near my former neighborhood of Vista Las Palmas. We only have thirty minutes to shop, and the last thing I need is to be slowed down by haughty stares from the housekeeper of someone I once knew.

Aside from prepping my grocery list in advance, I also made sure to practice grocery shopping with Dawn in tow. Back in Scottsdale, Charles was usually present to keep her occupied, but I've learned a trick or two. For example, there's nothing I can do about Dawn greeting the good people of Safeway with her trademark banshee shriek. However, if I give her my sunglasses to inspect and chew on, she will stop squirming long enough for me to quickly cram her and her kicking legs into the seat at the front of the shopping cart.

"You be a good little angel and stay seated now, dear," I say, loudly enough for anyone standing within a few feet of me to hear. I pull her dolly and my grocery list out of my handbag. Mixed in with the grocery list is the rough draft of the essay I wrote for Robert to give about me tonight. It's quite a challenge to write about yourself, all the more so when you want to make yourself sound real, only of course also much better than real. Unburdened with children, Muffy Gail prances around the store in a blindingly pink skirt that's tighter than the casings on the sausages—and makes her look a good bit cheaper than the sausages (on sale for thirty-three cents for a half pound) too. Her ample breasts are lifted—but not separated—and appear as though they are trying to escape. As much as I'd like to think she's stuffed a bumper crop of Idaho spuds down there, I'm just about certain they are flesh and blood. As I said in my essay, I have a keen eye for detail. Thanks to the tight skirt constricting her movement, Muffy's unable to reach all but two shelves, meaning she has to buy the more expensive brand of toothpaste. Unlike her, I'm able to lift my arms three inches above my waist to grab the on-sale toothpaste (sixty-eight cents), the less-expensive-but-equally-fine razor blades (seventy-seven cents), because, as I wrote, "I'm frugal and don't ever like to waste all the wonderful things bestowed on me by the Almighty." I also grab a children's multivitamin ($1.78 for sixty chewable tablets), which ought to be enough to get Robert and Charles to stop giving me shit about what Dawn ate yesterday. I suppose this could also be an example of how I "think of others before myself."

Maisey smiles and nods as she rolls by with that darling Ruthie sitting like a good girl in the shopping cart. Unlike the rest of us, I don't see Maisey clutching a shopping list. She's got a giant turkey already in her cart, and how the hell she thinks she's going to get that bird defrosted, dressed, and roasted by dinnertime is beyond my comprehension. I suppress an evil cackle, and while I'm trying to do the math to decide between "tropical" mangoes (thirty-nine cents each) and a bag of "Hawaiian" papayas (three for $1.09), my thought process is interrupted.

"Mrs. Arizona!" I hear someone scream.

I turn to see that prissy and mysterious Mrs. Rhode Island Pie, Betsey Biddle, currently number-two Pie. She points accusingly at my cart, or rather at my child. While I've been engrossed in my bargain hunting, Dawn's monkeyed her way half out of the cart and is perilously close to dangling over the side of it. I swoop her up instantly and though she's no worse for wear, I fuss over her endlessly anyway.

"Oh, Dawnie! You are *such* a little athlete!" I gush, because as Robert will tell everyone tonight, I am quick to encourage my children. Then, to Betsey: "Her brother was the same way as a baby! So nimble! Why, he climbed out of his crib before he could even walk!"

Betsey is unimpressed. "How on earth do you know that, Maxine?" she asks, drier than the martini I am currently dreaming of.

"What?"

"You're not their real mother. You weren't around when the boy was little, so how do you know that?"

This unprovoked attack has drawn the attention of several other Pies. I feel them all staring at me, waiting to see if Betsey—the current Evelyn Rollins alpha-femme of this pack—has drawn my blood. If I show any weakness now, they'll dive in as team and rip me to pieces.

I think of waking up that morning after Thanksgiving—cue those waterworks, Maxine!

"No, I wasn't there," I say with a wobbly voice and a tiny sniffle. "But their dear late *former* mother kept the loveliest baby books for both children. She filled them with pictures and notes and stories, even." This is all straight from Robert's essay, but since none of these Pies are the judges, I don't mind giving them all a sneak peek.

Betsey's pack of jackals all exchange looks. Maisey and Mrs. Florida quickly push their carts away, while Betsey holds firm and unemotional. I go for the kill.

"Why," I say, pulling my lace-trimmed hankie from my purse, "it's almost as though the poor woman knew she wasn't going to be around forever. Robert says it's like she foresaw that someone else would need to step in to raise her children." I punctuate that last sentence with exactly three tears and a loving gaze at Dawn. It's a perfect, cinematic moment, if not for the fact that she's chewing on the box of razors.

"That's the m-m-m-most beautiful thing!" sobs that big-titted scene stealer Muffy Gail. I instantly lose my audience as they all rush to pat Muffy on the back for caring more than the rest of us combined. "My mother was an orphan, you know," she says through her blubbering.

Dawn throws her hat like a Frisbee into a bin of watermelon (five cents a pound), which I take as a sign that it's time for us to be moving on. I grab the hat and don't bother putting it back on her, ducking down an aisle with no one else in it. All I have left on my list is the meat, namely those Cornish game hens (an impressive sixty-eight cents each). They are going to be incredible with a spicy brown sugar and Tabasco glaze.

Dawn giggles and pulls the brim of her hat out of her mouth, holding it up for me, as if to say, *Would you like some?*

Triple shit in my handbag, there's no way this kid is going to eat that Cornish game hen. She's either going to send it into orbit or scream until she pukes, but, like most toddlers, Dawn doesn't give a hot goddamn about gourmet dining.

I look over my shoulder and see that no one is watching us. I give Dawn a big smile and lean down to the hat in her hand, pretending to gobble it up like it's an ear of corn. She squeals and kicks her feet while flapping her soft, chunky arms.

"It's supposed to be 'Father's Favorites' tonight," I say to my little coconspirator, "but why don't we sneak in a Dawnie Favorite?"

The clock is rapidly ticking down, so I fly over to the canned meats, grabbing exactly what we need for a meal Dawn will actually eat, then charge toward the checkout line.

"Fa-fa-fa-fa-fa!" Dawn tells me, flapping her arms to wave good-bye to the cashiers. She gives her hat a final triumphant toss at the bag boy as we glide out the door.

Robert and Charles are lying around the cabin like lazy cats when Dawn and I return from grocery shopping. I kick both of them out of the cabin, lest Robert get any crazy ideas about helping me.

"I found some pageant papers today," Charles whispers to me. "I hid them, but I'll show you when I get back."

I give him a thumbs-up and he runs out the door.

"Where am I supposed to go?" Robert asks.

"There's a bar at the clubhouse." I hand him a stack of note cards. "Park yourself and get familiar with the speech I wrote for you to give tomorrow night."

Robert gives the cards a glance. "Aren't the husbands supposed to write this themselves?"

I laugh and all but shove him out the door.

I have everything planned down to the minute. Robert and Charles have strict instructions to return home at 4:50 p.m.—ten minutes prior to dinner being ready. Ten minutes is, of course, the exact amount of time it should take a man to enter a room, announce his presence, kiss his wife and/or children, wash for dinner (with "wash" including doing something unmentionable in the bathroom), pour himself a drink, and sit at the table with his hot meal sitting before him.

Alas, my attempts at domestic bliss are mine and mine alone, thanks to this infernal judge, the ancient and emotionless Mr. Tipply, arriving five minutes early. Aside from having the slightly gray and wrinkled skin of an elephant, his ears are nearly as big and protruding as Dumbo's. I greet him with a hello and of course offer him a drink. He says nothing, instead choosing to point at his big blue judge ribbon. He positions himself near the beds. Standing slouched and rumpled in the corner, he looks like an old scarecrow.

JULIET McDANIEL

This truly chaps my ass, since it throws off the entire theme of the room.

Then Charles barrels through the door without stopping to wipe his feet. This technically isn't a problem, but since Old Man Tipply is watching, I'm peeved. Equally peeve-inducing is that Robert walks in and goes straight for Dawn. Now I understand that she's far more cute and cuddly than I am right now, but would it kill the goddamned man to give his wife a kiss? Instead I need to stop stirring the soup to be the one to kiss him. Honeymoon's over, I suppose.

"How was your day?" Robert asks me.

Somewhere around year three of our marriage, I took up the habit of saying to Douglas in a singsong voice he hated, "And how was *your* day, Maxine?" I did this every time he sat down at the table without a word to me, and he never once took the hint. Or he purposely ignored my hint.

"My day was great," I tell Robert. "Thank you so much for asking."

"What's that smell?" Charles demands, coming out of the "bathroom" from washing up.

All three of us instantly shoot our eyes to the divan, which is still missing a seat cushion, although that's not obvious thanks to my strategic placement of pillows and blankets over a suitcase.

"I mean, what's that *delicious* smell?" Charles self-corrects.

"We're having all your father's favorites tonight," I tell them both, sounding like a waitress at the classiest joint in town. Robert quickly takes leave for the "bathroom," and because sometimes shit goes my way, the kitchen timer dings right as he walks out, freshly washed.

The guys take their seats and I put Dawn in her high chair. No sooner am I back in the kitchen juggling three hot pans as there's a knock at the door. It's Alice Depwelt and a photographer. This pisses me off until I realize that Alice wouldn't waste her time and the photographer's expense on a Pie in the bottom five. Surely, we're contenders for the crown now. I perk up doubly when I see that the photographer doesn't have a photo camera, but a movie film camera.

"Arizona Pies!" Depwelt commands. "I know this is a bit of a surprise, but we thought we'd film your dinner for potential later broadcast. I trust that will be fine with all of you?"

Charles and Robert both sit up extra straight and I choose to ignore Robert's nervous glance my way. I head to the stove and, while walking past Robert, smooth his hair down in back. He doesn't flinch at my touch.

"There's sound," Depwelt announces. "So, if you could give a brief explanation of the meal, that would be appreciated."

Sure, Depwelt, I'll be your dancing monkey.

"As you all know," I tell my family, sounding like a lady in a commercial, "tonight's meal is titled 'Father's Favorites.'" I gracefully float my hand out toward Robert, as if I'm pointing out to my invisible audience a new car up for grabs on a game show. "We'll start the first course with a soup from the Betty Crocker Recipe Card Library."

I bring the soup pot over from the stove and move around the table, starting with Robert, ladling it into bowls. With the first ladle, I'm flooded with regret. The chunky soup contains every horrid color in the crayon box, from diarrhea brown to rotten meat puce to that off-off-white color spilled milk gets when left to harden on the countertop.

"This is Gold Coast soup, which reminds Robert of his birthplace in Chicago, where there's a beautiful neighborhood known as the Gold Coast," I say.

Robert and Charles, God bless them, dive right in and take hearty sips.

"Mmmmm," Charles says as his eyes begin to water.

Robert swallows hard. "You made it just how I like it, dear. With extra . . . peanut butter?"

"Yes, peanut butter," I turn to the camera and speak directly into it. "And also tomatoes, rice, nutmeg, and of course, that canned chicken you adore!"

"Say it to your family and not the camera," Depwelt orders.

I turn to Robert and Charles, "Yes, peanut butter—"

"Cut!" hollers Depwelt.

Stupid girl!

"We need to speed this up. Take the soup away and bring out the main course so we can get some footage of that," Depwelt tells me. "You can finish eating once we leave."

I clear the soup bowls and dump them in the sink, because let's face it, there's no way in hell anyone is going to eat that shit if they don't have to. My heart begins to race a little as I go to the oven to fetch the main course. This one I pulled out from the deepest depths of my own ass. Here goes nothing.

I place the dish in the center of the table with the lid still on.

"And our pièce de résistance is Robert's absolute, number-one with a bullet recipe. . . ." I remove the lid while imagining royal fanfare. "Spam 'n' Limas!"

I'm hoping for *ooh*s and *ahhh*s. I get something else entirely.

"What the heck—" says the cameraman, who then has the balls to choke back a gag.

I don't skip a beat. I keep that smile on my face, clench those ass cheeks, and think of Audrey Hepburn while spooning some dinner onto each person's plate.

"Robert's dear mother, um . . ."

"Lorraine," Robert whispers.

"Mrs. Lorraine Hogarth," I continue, needing to shake the serving spoon to force the dish onto Robert's plate. "My mother-in-law knew how to be frugal while still serving her family delicious, nearly exotic foods, like Spam 'n' Limas."

Depwelt motions for me to keep going, so I do, giving Charles a generous scoop. "This remarkable dish is easy to make. Simply make a tomato sauce, seasoned with onions, celery salt, sugar, and lard."

The sauce was not easy to make, requiring far more than the two to three minutes of whisking the recipe claimed it required. It was smooth when I set it on the burner to warm, but is now clumpy, like clotted cream, only bloodred. It's congealing faster than I can serve it.

"Mix the sauce with a bag of frozen lima beans, which are a great source of vitamins for growing children . . . and husbands," I say, chuckling gently at my own joke. The lima beans are mushed in with the sauce and not at all providing the contrast of colors shown in the recipe's picture. I'm going to write those Spam recipe people such a furious letter.

"Finally, tuck into the mixture slices of Spam—a whole can." *Dear Spam, I finally have a husband I don't want to murder and yet your recipe . . .* "Then sprinkle with pimento cheese crackers, place in a preheated oven at three hundred fifty degrees, and bake for thirty minutes." The Spam does look as pictured in the recipe, by which I mean it looks like slabs of brilliant pink flesh, slightly charred on the edges. I can't see any of the pimento crackers, but I know they're in there.

I put a small dollop on Dawn's plate. She gives a happy "fa-fa-fa-fa-!" and waves her spoon in the air. With everyone served, I take my seat next to Robert.

"Bon appétit!" I say with far too much joy.

My darling husband doesn't move. Although, to be fair, neither do I and neither does Charles. We sit there, staring at one another, our loaded forks suspended in the air, a mere inch from our mouths. Nervous glances are exchanged and, while we're all smiling, no one moves. It's like we're all playing a game of chicken, and given the stench rising up from our plates, it might be a deadly game of chicken. Which of us will dare to eat this murder scene of a meal first?

Charles, of course. My dear, sweet, angelic Charles. He shows the fortitude and bravery of a man three times his age. He closes his eyes and surely transports his mind and spirit to some other place. Knowing him, it's the McDonald's down on Central Avenue and Indian School Road back home. Rather than take just a taste, my Charles shoves an entire forkful into his innocent mouth, chewing it once, then twice, then swallowing it down with a laborious gulp.

"Wow, Mom," he says, breathing as though he just ran a mile. "That's some great Spam."

Robert and I look at each other as a bleak realization swoops over us like a funeral shroud: one of us needs to take the next bite. Who will make that sacrifice? She smiles back, only her grin is devious, like she's standing outside a gingerbread house. There's no way in hell she's calling "cut" until we eat this hot garbage.

I lock eyes with my dear husband. I give him a wee little nod, as if to say, *One.* He returns my nod. *Two.* On three, we each say good-bye to the rest of our lives and plunge into the Spam-y depths of hell.

The taste hits me first—the pungent lima beans, quickly followed by the too-sweet tomato sauce—and yes, there're those pimento cheese crackers. That's when the texture begins battering at my mouth. There's simply too much of it. Dry beans! Slippery tomatoes! Slimy—yes, somehow slimy—pimento cheese crackers! Right as I think the worst must surely be over, the Spam arrives: rubbery, almost metallic in taste, like when you accidentally bite the side of your cheek and taste your own blood. Swallowing is excruciating, since none of this was intended for human consumption. I'm like a snake slowly swallowing some field mouse whole. Thank Christ I'm wearing my stars 'n' stripes scarf so the massive Spam 'n' Limas bulge creeping down my throat isn't noticeable.

"And cut!" Depwelt finally yells.

The cameraman gags again and runs out the door.

"You'll have your score in the morning, Arizona Pies," Depwelt says while she and Mr. Tipply show themselves out. "Enjoy the rest of your meal."

She pulls the front door shut tight and the three of us are up from the table, plates in hand, a nanosecond later. I dump my plate in the trash. Robert spits his lone bite into the sink and turns the hot water on full blast.

"I'm sorry, Maxine. I couldn't swallow. I just couldn't!" He uses the wrong end of his fork to shove the bits of Spam, bean, tomato, and pimento down the drain.

"I love you so much for taking even a single bite." I'm sobbing, but I hope he knows that's true. "It's the worst thing I've ever swallowed," I cry. "And I've swallowed Douglas!"

Charles runs to the "bathroom," and I hear him scrape his plate into the toilet and flush, because as I keep telling everyone, my boy is a genius.

I grab the casserole dish, overflowing with steaming Spam 'n' Lima wretchedness. I'm about to dump it all in the trash when Robert stops me.

"We'll wait until dark and get the boy to bury it outside," he says. "Somewhere far from the cabin."

I nod in solemn agreement.

"Mom!" Charles whispers from behind us. "Dad!" he says more urgently.

We turn around and see him standing by the table, his arm stretched out, pointing to the night's biggest horror. Dawn's plate is empty.

"JesusMaryJoseph," I whisper as my knees wobble.

All three of us rush to her high chair, looking first on the ground, up to the ceiling, even down her diaper, hoping against hope that she didn't do the unthinkable and actually finish her dinner. But sweet holy fuck sticks, there isn't a trace of that genocidal casserole anywhere.

"She finally ate like a big girl," Charles murmurs as the shock settles in around us.

We sit at the table for what feels like hours, but it's only a minute or two, staring at that precious baby's face. Dawn giggles and smiles, making every happy-go-lucky baby noise in her repertoire, as if she didn't moments ago suckle at Satan's teat. Eventually, we move again. I take a cue from Charles and flush the rest of the Gold Coast soup down the toilet.

Robert makes himself and Charles peanut butter sandwiches while I give Dawn her bath. She splashes and squeals in the lavender-scented water, oblivious to the fact she's more courageous than all of us combined. Who's this tiny creature going to grow to be? If tonight's any indication, she'll be a girl ready to face whatever bullshit comes her way.

Night finally comes. True to his word, Charles puts the Spam 'n' Lima monstrosity in a garbage bag, which he then places inside three other garbage bags. I give him my Playtex Living gloves, and he says nothing about them being bright pink. He returns twenty minutes later—minus the gloves—looking suddenly less like a child and more like a teenager.

"It's done," he says in a firm, deep voice. "Let us never speak of it again."

We're all in bed with the lights out. Robert is pressed against the wall and I teeter on the edge of my side of the bed. Dawn is fast asleep and Charles is either asleep or once again practicing faking being asleep.

"I got the azure dress for you," Robert whispers.

I can't believe I'd forgotten about the dress. "All that's been on my mind all day is goddamned Spam, Robert," I tell him. I already know that per pageant rules, he had to surrender the dress to Missy at the end of the shopping trip. I won't see it until tomorrow.

"I think you'll like it," he assures me. "I hope it fits."

"I'll make it work. What about shoes? A bag?"

"I went with silver everything."

I know he can't see me, so I let myself grimace. "Like a Las Vegas silver or—"

"No, classy movie star. Like Ginger Rogers. But not in *The Barkleys of Broadway.*"

"She was too matronly in that," I tell him.

"I remember you saying that once. So I went more *Shall We Dance.*"

"That sounds perfect, dear-heart."

I roll from my back to my side to face his back.

"Robert?"

"Yes, Maxine?"

"I hope you know . . ." I pause for a second. I need these words to come out right. "I hope you know that I appreciate everything you're doing for me." I want to add that he's a million times over more kind and generous and, yes, loving than any man I've ever known.

"I know that, Maxine."

"You're a much better fake father and husband than either of the real ones I had," I tell him and mean it. "I don't even know my father's name," I whisper. I wanted it to sound nonchalant. It comes out sounding mournful.

Robert rolls over to face me, prompting me to roll to my back and stare up at the ceiling. He takes the hint and says nothing, although I feel his hand resting on mine.

I don't know how much time passes, but at some point, I open my eyes to find Charles at my bedside.

"Mom," he whispers, "I'm sorry, but I had an awful thought. If Dawn ate that stuff, don't that mean it's gotta eventually come out of her?"

Robert Hogarth

Pageant Day Three

THERE'S PLENTY OF STUFF about this pageant that can best be described as "weird," but walking outside in the morning to find a two-feet-by-two-feet gold star pinned to the door is maybe more "what in the heck?" than "weird." The Walkers have one on their door too, so I don't think much of it. I pull down the scorecard and bring it to Maxine as if it were as natural as bringing her the morning paper.

<u>MR. & MRS. ARIZONA PIE</u>
Men's Shopping: 4.8/5
Mother's Shopping Trip: 4.6/5
Father's Favorites Dinner: 4.8/5
Family Presentation: 4.8/5
Total daily ranking: Second Place, tied with Mrs.
Rhode Island Pie (Second Place), behind Mrs. Illinois
Pie (First Place).

"Holy fuck, we're tied now?" Maxine yips when she sees the scores.

"Our family is presenting five-tenths better," I say without a trace of sarcasm, surprising even myself.

"What sort of witchcraft did Maisey use on that turkey?" Maxine mutters.

I flip the card over to see what potential trouble this day will bring, assuming the pageant will save the most daunting for last.

SCHEDULE
8:00 a.m.–Breakfast at the Clubhouse
11:00 a.m.–Mother-Daughter Tea
11:00 a.m.–Father-Son Rocket Building
3:00 p.m.–Husbands' Essays/Wives' Interviews
7:00 p.m.–Televised Grande Finale

"You'll have time after the rocket thing to work more on your speech," Maxine gently chides me. "I trust you're memorizing it?

I nod, although the truth is, I'm terrible at memorization, and none of the words Maxine has written sound anything like me. It's crazy enough that I have one fake wife, but Maxine's also demanding I wax poetic about a dead one.

I get the rest of the family up and everyone just does what we're supposed to do. Maxine doesn't boss or badger anyone. Chuck and I put on the clothes she has laid out for us. Even Dawn entertains herself in her crib. Things are a little tense when it comes to her morning diaper change, but despite her eating what can only be described as the worst thing in the world wrapped in the second worst thing in the world and then dipped in sulfur, her little digestive tract is a real trooper. I know Chuck wants to join the CIA, but I think it's his baby sister who could withstand torture at the hands of the enemy.

We all know to expect that at some point early today the ten Pies will be cut to five. What surpasses "weird" and veers into "eerie" is that there's no announcement. The five who didn't make it are simply gone, not showing up for breakfast. Instead of finding gold stars on their doors, I picture the five losing families waking up to Mrs. Alice Depwelt in head-to-toe black, cracking a whip and demanding they vacate at once. Entire families, fleeing at night, dragging their children and party dresses and golf bags to their family sedans.

That the Walkers of Illinois and those obnoxious Rhode Island Pies are finalists is no surprise, since they've been in the top three the whole pageant. The Idaho Pies are also not that surprising—Muffy looks as though she were hand-built in some pageant-queen factory. Wanda and Roy Clarke of South Carolina round out the final five. They're good kids, but neither seems very polished, as Maxine would say. With all her big, fiery hair, Wanda looks like she's a better fit for the Grand Ole Opry. And Roy looks like he should be flipping burgers after school. I guess they start them young in South Carolina.

It is nice to see that the Walkers made it to this round. They are a genuinely nice family. I know that doesn't sound like a ringing endorsement, but they're Midwesterners like me, so being called "nice" is pretty much the highest compliment one can get. It's far more meaningful (though a lot less flashy) than a giant gold star.

"I told you the Walkers would make it to the finals," Maxine quietly says to me while in line for the breakfast buffet.

"I think they could win it," I tell her.

Maxine gives me one of her looks. I really should sit down and write them all out and then give them a number, probably based on how often they're used. What I'm expecting from her would be Look #1—the "I cannot f-ing believe you said that to me!" look. It is by far the most used look in her library. Yet when I suggest that the Walkers deserve the crown (oh goodness, I know the lingo!), Maxine gives me Look #203—the "If there were any justice in the world" look.

"She'll get third runner-up, and those judges will all pat themselves on the back for being so open-minded," Maxine tells me. Her eyes fall on the dining room's door.

Muffy Gail comes cooing into the room in a sky-blue dress so tight, it makes *my* ribs ache. "For some reason, I keep picturing her with a small dog under her arm. Like all those Hollywood starlets in your magazines," I tell Maxine, who stifles a laugh with a snort.

She takes my arm as we walk back to our table. "I love that I'm rubbing off on you."

Maxine Hogarth

Pageant Day Three

"ARE YOU READY for your first ladies' tea, Dawn?"

She stares back at me from her crib, saying and doing nothing, almost like she's studying me from a safe distance. I've noticed that she looks at me differently than the others. She's at her most animated with Charles, offering him a bite of her cookie or squealing at him when he does something that displeases her. With Robert, she'll hold out a toy, as if proudly saying, "Take a look at what I have!" When it comes to me, Dawn seems content to stand back and watch. I try telling myself it's because she's learning from me, but I get this nagging feeling it's because she's trying to figure me out. "You're more than just an adorable face, you know," I tell her. "If you decide to crank up the charm today, you could turn the tide for us in this contest."

I know she hears me and I know that while the meaning of my words might escape her, my tone will not. Her big blue eyes are wide and track me as I dash around the room grabbing everything we might need. "It would really mean the world to me if you could cooperate," I tell her, throwing a spare dress into the diaper bag along with a few pacifiers, a stuffed cat, and enough of those ingenious pre-moistened baby wipes to clean the filthy bottoms of all the Gerber Babies in the world. "I've been to these teas before, Dawn. We're walking into the lion's den, so you and I need to be a team, okay?"

I look up from the diaper bag and see that Dawn has her finger up her nose. There's no emotion on her little face, splotched red from the heat. Nothing about her suggests she's excited that her finger has found a new home. It occurs to me that Dawn probably thinks this is a perfectly reasonable place to keep one's finger. It's like the way an adult woman might slip her hand into her skirt pocket.

Well, when in Rome, I guess. I quickly shove my own finger up my nose, and thank heavens, it's dry up there. Dawn startles, her head pulling back quickly, and for a second I think she's about to cry. Instead she smiles at me. A wide, slightly drooly grin I've seen her share with her brother a thousand times, but never once with me.

So I shove another finger up my other nostril. Dawn's smile is a dam that breaks, giving way to an endless stream of giggles. Right as I'm debating whether it's worrisome that one nostril is dry and the other quite wet, Dawn bursts into a deep, uncontrollable belly laugh that knocks her off her feet.

"You have a juvenile sense of humor," I tell her before realizing that, well, of course she does. I pull my fingers out of my nose and decide it's best to not look at them. Dawn instantly turns off the laughter, but still beams a smile up at me from her crib. "I'm going to scrub myself clean and then do the same to you!"

I wash my hands in the kitchen sink, and when I return to the crib, Dawn reaches up to me with an eager "naa naa naan aa!" that I've come to learn is baby talk for "Pick me up!" Once in my arms, she cuddles up, her booger-streaked hands wrapping themselves around my neck so our faces are cheek to cheek. She gently fingers the pearl stud in my left ear, making curious humming sounds while rubbing a finger over its smooth surface.

"You like earrings? Not until your sixteenth birthday, young lady. Any younger is unseemly."

From my ear, Dawn's itty-bitty fingers walk across my face, skip-ping along my forehead, as if mapping some foreign land. She gets a little too pokey around my eye, causing me to flinch.

"Be gentle, sweetie," I whisper to her. "One smudge and my eyeliner goes from chic to whore."

She understands me and presses her nose-picking finger against my lips and baby mumbles, as if saying, "I really don't want to hear it, lady." I'm close enough to her to notice her blue eyes are flecked with gold and there's a tiny freckle (or maybe it's a leftover crumb from breakfast?) on her left cherub cheek.

Dawn babbles peacefully, her eyes looking deep into mine. I smile at her and she smiles back. With a boisterous giggle, she shoves her finger up my nose and throws her head back, hysterical with laughter. No sooner do I pull her finger out of my nose than she reaches over with the other hand to shove another finger up there.

"Oh dear," I tell her, laughing right back at her. "Looks like I've really started something here, haven't I?"

I pull her hand away from my face and hold it for a moment. Remembering that Dr. Spock business about confidence, I tell her firmly, "You can pick my nose later. Right now we need to make ourselves beautiful for a day out. Okay?"

Dawn smiles and gives me an exaggerated nod of agreement. I pretend I don't see that her finger goes back up her own nose the very second I put her down.

Here I am once more, sitting at the same table in the tearoom of the Thunderbird Country Club where I always sat with Evelyn Rollins and her pack of jackals. The chandeliers are every bit as bright; the table linens still a stark white. There's the same gleaming gold trays of cucumber-and-cream-cheese finger sandwiches, and I'm even in the same seat, pushed almost in the corner with a view of the ninth hole and the wide-open red desert beyond that. I reflexively dump way too much cream into my coffee—despite taking it black since moving to Scottsdale. I catch my reflection in the windows behind me and, for a moment, it's like I'm not really here. I'm watching a movie of myself from months ago.

Part of me can't help but wonder: What if all this is a setup? There's no question that Evelyn Rollins hates my guts, and despite the divorce and banishment eliminating me as a threat to her, she wasn't the one who defeated me. Douglas was. Worse still for her is that I was run out of town before the full brunt of her poison-tipped gossip arrow could affect me. In Evelyn's eyes, I surely haven't been punished enough. If anyone could engineer an entire housewives beauty pageant as a means to bring me to my knees, it's Evelyn Rollins.

I push that crazy thought out of my head because I have enough to juggle today. Plus, everyone knows Evelyn wouldn't dream of tea at 11 a.m., which is so obviously prime brunch hour.

At two-o'clock tea with Evelyn and company, there was a slick veneer of friendship that I always knew was pure bullshit. At least this time, with the pageant contestants, it's a given fact that we're in open competition. There are literal points being assigned to each of us by a panel of known judges. I can sit a little more confidently in my round-backed white dining chair knowing I have the experience needed to walk away from this tea unscathed by the verbal jabs and nasty glances.

Unlike the last time I was here, I can't gnaw off my bunny paw and flee the trap. I need both arms to hold the bundle of squirm and grabby hands sitting in my lap. This is far too upscale an establishment to have high chairs. Come to think of it, in the three times a week for four years that I lunched here, I don't think I once saw a child. Betsey Biddle is in Evelyn's usual seat, flanked by her creepy twins, Kitty and Katy. Call me crazy, but I swear those girls' hair got blonder overnight. The Katy one keeps scratching the back of her neck, a telltale sign of bleach irritation. Maisey's little Ruthie looks pleased as punch to be sitting with the grown ladies. Knock on wood the ugliness that's about to go down will fly right over dear Ruthie's head.

Not surprisingly, Betsey gets us off to a rollicking start. "Good heavens!" she says, gasping upon seeing Muffy Gail help herself to four bright pink macaroons off the pastry tray. "Please tell me, Muffy, that it isn't only Mrs. Wisconsin who's eating for two?"

Muffy plops three of the macaroons from her surprisingly meaty paw onto Ruthie's plate. "Of course not!" is all Muffy can come up with. And here I was thinking she might be more than a pair of triple Ds. Nope. This point goes to Betsey, who clearly understands that the food at tea is not for nibbling, but as fodder for conversations on whose diet is or isn't working.

Dawn reaches for Wanda Clarke's glass of water, which I push out of her reach. Thankfully, I remembered to put a sippy cup in my handbag and Dawn cooperates, sitting still in my lap while I fill the cup from my glass of orange juice. Muffy quietly points out that someone two tables over is wearing entirely the wrong shade of green. I turn to look, but I'm distracted by Dawn, who's loving the way the overhead lighting bounces off my cut-crystal water goblet. With a little help from me, she takes a sip out of the glass like a big girl.

"It's like the color of shower grout mold," says Wanda, oblivious that she's just stepped in a steaming pile of her own making.

"I wouldn't know," mutters Betsey. "My bathroom is scrubbed till it shines, twice a week."

"Fa-fa-fa-fa-fa!" Dawn tells the table.

"You're right, Dawn," Muffy says too loudly. "It *must* be nice to have help. The rest of us girls take care of our *own* houses. Don't we? Don't we?"

Dawn reaches for Muffy's sparkly, dangly earring, but I pull her arm down before any damage can be done.

Maisey gives Dawn a little wave, but the others keep right on talking about how no one wears gloves during the day anymore. Apparently, none of these bitches noticed that Maisey and Ruthie wore white gloves today, or that they sit in their chairs in the precise posture of a debutante. Am I really the only one who knows Maisey is a threat? I pull the cucumber out of a finger sandwich, handing it to Dawn. She holds it up close to her face before shoving it in her mouth, chewing slowly at first until she realizes she likes it.

"You girls will never believe what I learned about one of our judges," Betsey starts, practically clucking. "You know Douglas Simmons, the almost handsome, very tan man from Western Airlines?"

I jiggle my leg roughly, hoping Dawn will do something to distract from this line of gossip. No such luck. Dawn shoves her sippy cup out at me with a quiet grunt that sounds like a question. Maybe I should let her gently slide out of my arms to run screaming through the restaurant? How much of my day's grade is this tea? Instead I use the one free arm that isn't holding her back to pop off the top of the sippy cup, fill it with water, and push the top back on until I hear the all-important snap that lets me know the lid is firmly in place. I'm hoping like hell my remarkable one-handed sippy cup fill maneuver is enough to distract Betsey.

"Seems Mr. Simmons recently married some very young girl I hear is drop-dead gorgeous," Betsey continues.

Dawn decides that cucumber is not for her. Her little tongue evicts a half-chewed hunk from her mouth. Part of it sticks to her chin while the rest lands on my plate and right into my open-faced shrimp-salad sandwich. She reaches her pointy little hand down and helps herself to a deviled egg.

"The interesting thing," that goddamned Betsey goes on, "is that the new wife's not old enough to vote, and let's just say that as far as that new baby of theirs is concerned, the math doesn't quite add up."

Dawn lets out a squeak and I realize I'm holding her far too tightly in my arms. I smooth out her blond curls and since it's nearly her nap time, she rests her head against my chest, eager to fall asleep. She's warm and her hair smells like strawberry shampoo.

Betsey doesn't let up. "I also heard that his first wife lost her mind at Thanksgiving dinner. *This past* Thanksgiving dinner."

This is more than I can ignore. I stand up quickly enough to startle Wanda. "If you ladies will excuse us, Dawn needs the little girls' room."

I don't wait for a response. I whisk Dawn away, her head resting on one shoulder while the bulky diaper bag swings from my arm, bumping into chairs, tables, and at least one waiter. I charge right through the heavy wood door to the ladies' lounge and into a private stall, locking the door behind me. I'll say this for the Thunderbird Country Club: they have well-appointed facilities. Each bathroom stall comes complete with its own toilet, sink, and chair, which I gladly slump down in, Dawn still on my shoulder, squirming gently to find the most comfortable position for her head and legs.

"Maybe we can just stay in here all day." I rub her back and speak in the softest of whispers. "No more bitchy pageant queens."

She turns her head and faces me, her eyes opening just enough to see that I'm here, holding her. I kiss the top of her head and she drifts off to sleep. I can always tell when she's out cold because for some reason she weighs twice as much asleep as awake. I know none of this is real, but sometimes, it feels more possible than fake. I let my breathing fall in sync with hers and gradually slow the hand rubbing her back down to a full stop.

After all, what does *fake* mean anyway? Yes, I've borrowed this sweet little girl from her utterly absent mother and told everyone she's mine. But since I've never once claimed I birthed her or her brother, our family isn't entirely a lie. It's no lie that Dawn is sleeping soundly in my arms here in this upscale bathroom stall. It's not make-believe to say that I'm the one who feeds her, gets her dressed, rubs her back when she's fussy. And those diapers sure as shit aren't pretend. I'm not lying when I say that Dawn is mine. I'm merely walking a very fine line between reality and fiction. My family and I are a perfectly pleasant mix of the real and the fake, not unlike every family seen on television programs or in ads for hot cocoa.

"Don't worry, Dawnie," I tell her. "I'll take care of you always."

A gaggle of women enters the lounge, their click-clacking heels and singsongy voices startling Dawn. "We should be getting back to the tea, Dawnie," I whisper in her ear. "You need to eat a proper meal today. And no Spam."

I get everything packed back into the diaper bag and swipe the wrapped mints out of the vanity's candy dish. Dawn is fresh as a daisy and I'm back in pageant mode, prepped as hell for some competitive teatime. I open the stall door and walk right into a river of quicksand.

It's fucking Evelyn. Evelyn Rollins, the grande dame of Palm Springs society, lying in wait. My mind twists in a thousand circles.

"Maxine?" booms Evelyn. "Where the hell did you get a baby? "

I slam the stall door closed and say nothing. I go still and silent. Like those ninja people Charles told me about. Dawn has other ideas though. Her eyes open and her head cranes back, surprised and angry by the sudden disturbance to her nap. She rubs at her eyes and gives me a groany "na-na-na-na" that's almost always the sign of a tantrum bubbling toward the surface.

"We know it's you, Maxine," Evelyn snips at me.

Oh fuck it. Let's get this over with.

I unlock the door and let it swing gently open, revealing me with Dawn on my shoulder to Evelyn Rollins, Joyce Wittenburg Tully, and Mary Jones. They all seem adequately surprised to see me. Joyce looks as though she might cry.

"I just can't believe it," Joyce says with far too much enthusiasm. "Here we are out to brunch and we run into Maxine Simmons." Joyce puts her hand up to her mouth as if she understands she just made quite the faux pas—which she has.

"Since when do you three brunch?" I brusquely ask, hoisting Dawn farther up my shoulder. She's "na-na-na-na-ing," her cheeks blooming hot pink. Joyce and Mary exchange nervous glances like they're schoolgirls who got busted cheating on a test.

Evelyn folds her arms tight over her chest. "Since 1967, Maxine."

For three years they ate brunch without me? I hadn't made it as far up the social ladder as I thought I had, God damn it.

"I thought you weren't allowed back in town?" Evelyn helpfully asks.

"Whatever do you mean, Evelyn?" I muster, shifting Dawn so that she doesn't have to look at Dr. Evelyn Frankenstein or her two Igors.

There are any number of things Evelyn could do or say to me in this horrible moment that will turn my existence into ash. Her mere presence is leaving me with that sinking, snapping feeling all over again, like I'm falling into that pool. Only this time it's in slow motion and it's not a turkey in my arms.

"So you're a nanny now?" she asks loudly, simultaneously implying how far my social station has fallen while also seeming to accuse me of something sinister.

Startled by Evelyn's outdoor voice, Dawn bucks in my arms and lets out an annoyed yip. I pat her head, there, there. "This is my daughter, Dawn Lorraine Hogarth. Technically, stepdaughter, I suppose. Her mother is no longer with us."

"That's positively tragic," Joyce whimpers, tilting her head and smiling at Dawn.

Evelyn bares her fangs. "She's almost as cute as Douglas's baby. You know, the one he and his wife had together. They named her Jessica, isn't that right, Joyce? Mary?"

Jessica.

It's Dawn who saves me, letting out her banshee wail and tugging on her hair. Her white patent leather Mary Janes smack me in my thighs as she kicks. Dawn has a meltdown so I don't have to. She's saving me from giving Evelyn Rollins exactly what she wants from me.

"Will you broads excuse me?"

I don't want myself and little bunny Dawn anywhere near those vicious brunching jackals. Nor do I want to return to the Pies and their untouched desserts or the judges with their low scores for my antisocial teatime behavior. There are a few things I need to go see for myself.

"Let's get out of here, Dawnie."

The van that brought us here is sitting outside the tearoom, the driver nowhere to be found. As proof God doesn't completely hate me, the keys are in the ignition and there's an empty Dawn-sized box sitting right in the front seat. I need to go. I need to be anywhere but here. I need to go home.

It's not until I arrive on my former street that I remember none of this is mine anymore. I park one door down from the house that Douglas and I bought a lifetime ago in 1962. Marilyn Monroe was dead, but President John F. Kennedy was still alive. I was twenty-nine and I remember thinking how this house and this life were set for me. Surely a baby would come soon to make this house a home, or however that bullshit platitude goes.

I pick up Dawn and carry her to the house. We don't go to the front door, but rather cut around back, past the well-trimmed palms and behind the fuchsia bougainvillea vines that grow up the white trellis separating the pool from the patio. Dawn is content to look around and take it all in. I do what I have to do.

I look through the patio door into the dining room. There's music coming from the turntable in the living room—some tender, lilting Beatles song. The mirrored wall in the dining room is gone, replaced by crisp celery-green paint. My palm tree wallpaper on the opposite wall still hangs, though it looks a bit too busy now without the mirror stealing some attention from it. The French doors separating the dining room from the kitchen are either gone or opened all the way, giving me a clear view into the kitchen. There I see mother and child.

The Jennifer and the Jessica.

Neither seem particularly spectacular. There's no aura of unstoppable sex appeal oozing from the Jennifer. No halo of light coming off the Jessica. If anything, Jennifer looks older than twenty, probably thanks to the lack of sleep Jessica affords her. Jennifer paces barefoot across the terra-cotta tiles, humming the Beatles tune in a futile effort to get the baby down for a nap. They're boring and ordinary. Nothing to be afraid or feel ravenously envious of.

Jennifer looks up and her face contorts. Her eyes bulge and I see the veins constrict in her long neck. Her hand slowly rises, as if pointing out some monster who's emerged from some radioactive swamp. As she lets out a violent, desperate scream, I realize she's pointing at me.

This is not my home.

Holding Dawn tightly, I race back to the van.

Robert Hogarth

Pageant Day Three

THE FATHERS AND SONS all meet in front of the clubhouse, waiting to be taken away to our rocket-building site. Mr. Rhode Island, Byron Biddle, tries suggesting that as the father of only girls, he should be exempt from the father-son activity.

"Unlike the rest of these guys," Biddle argues to Missy's perpetually smiling face, "I'm the poor bastard who's gonna need to pay for two weddings at some point. I think the man Pies would have no problem with me sitting this one out, toots."

Mrs. Depwelt materializes behind Biddle, like some sort of angry apparition. "I'll not have you at the clubhouse bar all day. Off you go!"

We all pile into golf carts, with Biddle hopping in one with me and Chuck. Joke's on Mrs. Depwelt, since Biddle takes the bar with him, in the form of a flask. He doesn't offer me a swig. I am secretly hoping that these rockets don't take too long to build, since tonight is our big essay contest. I haven't put nearly the time I need into memorizing the speech about Maxine.

The golf carts drive in a line like white wheeled ducks, following Missy out past the fifteenth hole, which eventually gives way to the wide-open desert on the outskirts of Palm Springs.

"It's like how NASA tests rockets on the Salt Flats," Chuck tells me. "I saw it in a filmstrip at school."

It's the hottest day I can remember, but then again, this is my first summer as a southwesterner. Chuck seems unaffected by the fact that we're standing in the middle of an oven.

"You ever done this before?" I ask him, looking over the rather skimpy instructions that came with our Estes Industries model rocket kit.

Chuck takes a quick glance at the diagram of how to put this thing together and dives right in, popping one cardboard tube into another, then screwing on the bright red pointy rocket tip. Sometimes I think there's nothing this boy can't figure out. He's a lot like Maxine in that regard.

"It's the same construction as Saturn V," he tells me, not looking up from his work. "Except this rocket will all come back down to Earth. Saturn V had the Apollo 11 moon landing module and a command module," he adds wistfully.

I look over at the other fathers and sons. Roy Clarke's kid is way too young to give a darn about rockets, so Roy's taken to chasing him around. Virgil's twins stand slack-jawed in the shade of the golf cart while Virgil does the assembly himself. Daniel Walker sits right down on the hard desert floor next to Danny Jr. They laugh while fighting to hold the instructions in place against the wind. Danny Jr. says something hilarious that makes Daniel Sr. crack up.

Biddle mills around, kicking at the dirt, pouting like a child. When Danny Jr. puts a wing piece on wrong, Biddle is the first to point it out. As in, he literally points to the rocket and yells, "Wrong!"

"I sure hope NASA does an Apollo 14," Chuck tells me while putting what looks like a firecracker into the back end of the rocket. "I mean, they got all the astronauts from Apollo 13 back safe and sound. The Russians aren't going to stop going up."

The only judge with us today is that elderly Mr. Tipply, and he seems too focused on the rocket building to notice much else. He and his ever-present clipboard walk back and forth along the one-hundred-yard stretch of desert where the dads and sons prepare for outer space.

"You sure know a lot about space, Chuck."

He shrugs and stays focused on his rocket. "They teach us stuff in school, and I read about it in all the magazines and newspapers people leave around the pool back home. Did you know they launch spy satellites? To know what the Commies are doing."

I laugh a little to myself, because of course Chuck would know about spy satellites. "It's too bad we can't put a camera in this rocket, huh?" I tell him.

"Did you ever build a rocket with your dad?" Chuck asks while putting some sticky red, white, and blue decals on the cardboard tube. It's starting to look like a real rocket now.

I put my arm on Chuck's shoulder and while he looks at it, he doesn't pull away. "We built model trains sometimes," I answer. "But mostly he wanted me playing sports."

"Like what kind of sports?"

"Baseball, some basketball, but mainly golf. My dad thought golf was an important thing for a man to know."

Chuck looks up at me, his eyes crinkling nearly shut in the noon sun. "What's that mean?"

I shrug a little. "He was a businessman and he knew that businessmen use golf as a way to talk business with each other."

I'm hoping this is enough detail to keep Chuck happy. The truth of it is that my dad wanted me to be good at sports because he thought it would make a man out of me. Or at least, the sort of "man" whom no one would suspect of anything untoward.

"Are you like all the other man Pies and upset that we're on a golf course but ain't playing golf?"

I laugh and pat Chuck on the head. "Not even a little."

My first golf lesson came the day after the paper doll incident. Dad woke me up at 5:30 a.m. with a football in one hand and a golf club in the other. "Pick one," he told me, gruffly. I wasn't all the way awake, but I knew Dad loved to golf, so I pointed to the club. For all I know, my clubs are still sitting in my folks' garage, right where I left them.

Our rocket assembled, Chuck announces that it needs a name.

"You could call it the Apollo 14?" I suggest.

"Nah, I want NASA to have that one." He grins. He nods over in Mr. Tipply's general direction. "We should name it something the judge will like."

We both ponder this a minute, or I guess it's more fair to say that Chuck ponders it. I'm busy watching Biddle as he reaches the end of his flask while slumped over on a golf cart.

Chuck nudges me back to the task at hand. He's used a red pen from his knapsack to write *The Maxine Dawn I* in bold block letters down the side of the rocket.

"Nice choice, kiddo," I say to his beaming face.

Chuck plugs the rocket into the launchpad. I use the matches that came in the rocket kit to ignite the fuse, and since Chuck built it right, it sparks and fizzes, launching itself surprisingly fast up into the troposphere. Daniel and Danny Jr. cheer us on, and while Tipply doesn't make a sound, he smiles while craning his head back and squinting up into the sky. Chuck and I stand close, my hand resting on his shoulder as the rocket streams farther into the atmosphere.

"We came in peace for all mankind," Chuck says solemnly—but loudly enough for Tipply to notice. Like Chuck, Tipply places his hand over his heart as the rocket's orange engine glow slowly fades.

"Can you see it?" Chuck asks me, nervously scanning the sky. "How long you think until it comes down?"

"I don't know," I answer. I put my hand to my forehead to shield the sun from my eyes. "It's got a parachute, right?"

"A red one," Chuck says. "I need binoculars."

Biddle staggers off the golf cart and comes closer. Curious at what we're trying to see, he tips his head so far back to the sky that he loses his balance, tripping backward a few feet.

"There it is!" Chuck points to nothing I can see. Then he leans over and speaks quietly to me. "I've never done anything this cool in my whole dang life." Our rocket ebbs on the wind, carried down on its bright red parachute. "This pageant's been a lot of hard work, but it's worth it to do this."

It occurs to me that for all my grousing and worrying about the pageant, how I look, how I act, what I say, Chuck's had it worse. He's a twelve-year-old boy stuck watching a bunch of grown women parade around in evening wear and grown men bemoaning the cruelty of being on a golf course they aren't allowed to play.

"You're a great kid, Chuck," I tell him.

He smiles wide at me and runs after the rocket. It hits the desert floor softly, barely kicking up any dirt. Chuck picks it up and rushes it back to the launchpad while inspecting it for damage. As I open my mouth to tell him not to touch the engine, he drops the rocket with a yelp.

"Dang it!" Chuck moans.

Chuck's eyes well up with tears and he can't bring himself to look at his hand.

"I've touched lots of hot plates in my day, kiddo," I tell him. "Let me get a look at it."

He looks over his shoulder and throws a worried look in Tipply's direction.

"We're not going to lose any points over you being hurt, Chuck," I tell him in a way I hope is reassuring. "Let me see."

He holds out his hand with his three middle fingers bright pink on the tips, tender, but not badly burned.

"Ouch," I tell him. "They aren't going to blister, but pour some cool water on them."

Chuck nods intently and, with his non-singed fingers, opens the top of his canteen and lets the water flow. "That stings a little," he tells me.

"Come on, kid," Biddle grunts, slapping Chuck hard on the back. "Don't be such a damn baby."

What did he just say to my boy?

I take my hand off Chuck's shoulder and put an accusing finger in Biddle's face. My whole body burns hot, like I've surged into a high fever. I am no longer Robert Hogarth, friendly bartender who knows all forty versus of "Danny Boy." I'm now a guy who wants nothing more than to kick Mr. Rhode Island Pie in the shins and slam my fist into that square jaw of his. He needs to learn how to keep his crap, drunk opinions to himself. Putting his hands on Chuck? I'll rip him in half.

Now I understand Maxine's whole snapping thing.

"Don't you ever put your hands on my boy again," I growl.

Biddle puts his hands up in front of him, backing down instantly. Chuck also takes a step back, his eyes on me, then Tipply, then back to me.

"Sorry, kid," Biddle mumbles. Chuck nods, his eyes still on Tipply, who's busy with the Idaho Pies.

I don't know what to say to that so I fall back on my instincts. "Go easy on the sauce, Biddle."

Maxine Hogarth

Pageant Night Three

AFTER FLEEING THE Simmonses' residence, I pull up to the clubhouse just before 2 p.m. to find a frantic Missy pacing out front.

"You took the van?" she screeches. "I was about to call the police!" Even with the van's window rolled down, Missy's yelling is nowhere near as chilling as Jennifer's was just moments ago. Hers was a horrified howl that will surely bounce around my head for days, especially when coupled with that Janet Leigh look of pure terror.

"No need to alert the authorities, Missy," I assure her while getting a very fussy Dawn out of the van. "Dawn fell ill at tea and I didn't want to make a scene. I'm so sorry I didn't alert you immediately, but I'm sure you understand?"

Missy pats Dawn on her head and Dawn responds by jerking away like an ornery puppy. "Poor baby," Missy coos to Dawn, then terses up her voice for me. "The other contestants weren't happy about being brought back late." She looks to her watch pendant, which I now notice is in the shape of a crown. "You've only forty-five minutes until the next round, so chop-chop!"

As soon Missy is gone, I look to Dawn and smile. "That, my darling, is what you call a Peggy Fleming double axel on thin ice."

I race back to the cabin and hand Dawn off to Charles to feed. As expected, she doesn't give him any trouble. Robert, however, pounces on me.

"Where have you been?" he grills me.

"Dawn and I had a quick errand to run. Where's my mystery dress?"

It will never in a million years feel right to be wiggling into an evening gown at three in the afternoon. But I will say this, the azure dress Robert picked out for me is remarkable. I know he felt it was very Ginger Rogers, but considering how figure-flattering and formfitting it is—not to mention as sparkly as Las Vegas—I'm feeling far more Marilyn than Ginger. Douglas is going to positively shit himself when he sees me looking this pert.

Of course, my faux-mily is looking top-shelf as well. Dawn's in the sweetest ruffled dress, Charles is well scrubbed and bright-eyed, and that husband of mine . . . so broad-shouldered, with all that thick hair. We are going to win this tonight. I'm feeling like we're unstoppable. In fact, fuck all this faux-mily nonsense. We're the goddamn Hogarths. Of the Scottsdale Hogarths.

"You've got the speech down, right?" I ask Robert as we walk out of the cabin. I'm trying to speak in a way that assumes he's got this all wrapped up, but in truth, I have concerns. As a bartender, my Robert tends to be more of a listener than a talker.

"Yup," is all he gives me. "Yup."

At the clubhouse, Charles and Dawn are instructed to sit in the front row with the other children while Robert and I are brought backstage. Even though this isn't a portion of the pageant that will be telecast, there's still a good number of people in the auditorium, and of course the judges are assembling at their table. While all the other judges smile and say hello to one another, Douglas sits silent and still, staring off into space. I've seen him do this a million times before, usually when he's contemplating something important—and of course not telling me about it.

The five remaining Pie couples stand silently backstage. The music swells, the curtain rises, and one by one, our names are called. As I hear Dale Thunders announce Mr. and Mrs. Arizona Pie, I take Robert's hand and give him a gentle squeeze.

It will be fine. Just fine. Let's put on our smiles and get out there.

I see Robert squint a little under the lights, but it's nothing too drastic. He blinks twice and never drops that smile. Over all the clapping, I know no one can hear us, so I lean in and whisper, "You've gone past handsome and are well into sexy." His eyes widen, and he shakes his head a little. It's more of a "My darn wife!" sort of shake than a "Shut the hell up" shake, so I'll take it.

We stand onstage in a row with the other couples, and I don't let go of Robert's hand. Although I suppose another way of looking at it is that Robert doesn't let go of my hand. I give it another squeeze and he squeezes right back.

The women's interviews are up first. Calling it an "interview" is somewhat misleading, since each wife gets one question to answer. This is the most dreaded portion of any beauty contest. You can practice smiling and walking and cleaning and baking and blind-folded ironing and whatever talent you claim to have. Unlike those things, the interview question is a challenge to predict. Obviously, it's going to be about motherhood, wifehood, or being a good American, but beyond that it's anyone's guess.

"Mrs. Rhode Island Pie! Could you please step forward?"

Betsey walks in a straight line to the microphone stand about four feet in front of us and to the left of Thunders. She's not far behind me and Maisey in the scoring, so she needs to nail this.

"What's your favorite thing about being a mother?"

I cross my fingers and hope she cocks it up by saying "boarding school!"

Betsey looks out at the audience, smiling madly. "My favorite thing about being their mother is—"

She pauses and sniffles, because—dear audience—this is truly an emotional moment for her. Those babies she birthed are her reason for living! There are no tears on her face, but that doesn't stop her from dabbing at her eyes with her hankie.

"My favorite thing about being a mother is seeing my two daughters sitting next to their father in church," she says in a hushed, steady tone. Somehow there are tears now. Big, fat, wet tears running down her lightly rouged cheeks. "Knowing my girls are growing up to be good, pious Americans is my greatest joy." She blots the somehow-real tears away, and more quickly follow. "Never underestimate the moral influence of a mother!"

Betsey ends it all with a blown kiss to Kitty and Katy. As she waves to the audience and struts back in line to my left, she very delicately dabs at her still-wet eyes with one corner of the hankie. As it comes up to her face, I can smell VapoRub coming off the pink cotton square.

"Did she VapoRub her eyes?" Robert whispers to me. I nod. "Unbelievable . . . ," he mutters.

Wanda gets some light-as-a-feather question about how she keeps her husband happy ("Two words, Mr. Thunders: *pork* and *chops!*"). The audience laughs lightly, but it's too brief and jokey a comment to please the judges. Wanda gets back in line with the rest of us, looking less than pleased with herself.

Muffy positively kills her softball question about what she loves about America. She thrusts her shoulders back with such force, I'm frankly shocked she doesn't dislocate one. "The Fourth of July!" she blurts out with the chipperness of a thousand excited puppies. "I love the fireworks!" Muffy throws her hands up in the air, pulsating her fingers to pantomime sparks falling. "The rocket's red glare and bursting in air! *Boom! Boom!*"

That last boom is loud enough that Thunders ducks a little. The audience claps and Muffy blows them all kisses before turning on her heel and marching back to our line. Robert and I exchange quick eye rolls. The judges scratch down their scores on the pads of paper in front of them. Douglas catches me looking at him. I smile through the flub, hopefully covering up my errant stare by gazing up adoringly at Robert.

"Mrs. Illinois Pie!" Thunders cries out. "Get over here for your question!"

Maisey glides over to the microphone and doesn't even flinch when Thunders takes a step closer to her—so close that Maisey could probably count his nose hairs if need be.

"There's something that's been on all our minds, Maisey: Why do you want to be the next Mrs. American Pie?"

Jesus, they might as well be asking her, "What makes you think a black girl can win this thing?" The mother-daughter pageant queen judges lean forward, as if waiting excitedly to hang on Maisey's every word.

"That's a great question, Mr. Thunders," Maisey says with the poise of twenty Grace Kellys. "It's an easy one to answer too. Last year my family and I had the opportunity to meet President Nixon at our church in Chicago. He gave a very moving speech, talking about how the American Dream is for everyone who wants to work for it. I took those words to heart, Mr. Thunders. I decided right then and there that I wanted to be Mrs. American Pie because I think it's important to show the world that this country is a place where all women have the opportunity to be the best mothers, wives, and Americans they can possibly be. It's as simple as that, Mr. Thunders."

Now *that's* applause, folks. The audience eats it right up as Maisey gives them all a wave and walks back to our lineup.

All right, my turn. Robert flashes that hunky smile of his at me. I hope Douglas is watching. Because this is how a real husband does it.

"Mrs. Arizona Pie!" Thunders calls.

I wave to the audience while gliding over to Thunders. From here at the front of the stage, I can see Douglas staring intently at me. I smile and nod in his direction. He doesn't so much as blink.

"Your question, Maxine, is tell us your favorite remembrance of your mother."

Shit. I bet Douglas cooked this one up himself. Do I mention any of the minor misdeeds that earned me a slap across the face and a "You stupid little girl"? No, I do what I always do. I lie.

"I think my favorite memory of my mother was on my sixteenth birthday. My mother took me aside and told me that this birthday marked me being more a woman than a girl," I tell him. This part is all true, but I leave out that Mother also meant that I was on my own now. "She told me that I needed to remember everything she taught me and put it to good use. Sometimes the world isn't kind, she reminded me."

This part is completely true. Like Dawn and Charles's did to them, my mother dumped me. The day after my sweet sixteen, she hauled me from Los Angeles to San Bernardino and the home of two distant relatives I'd never met, Uncle Ken and Aunt Martha Wilson. I worked school nights and weekends at Wilson's Grocery to pay for my room and board. Doesn't take much to see why an abandoned teenager would latch on to the first man of means who offered her stability. Or I suppose why it would sting so badly when he abandoned her too.

I see Douglas sitting smugly with his hands resting behind his head.

I keep going. "So, when someone wants to pull you down or make you think less of yourself, you know what Mother always told me to do, Mr. Thunders?"

"What?" he says, sounding like he wants me to get this over with.

This was the point in my speech where I was going to will myself to cry. Turns out, the tears are coming naturally.

"She told me to stand tall. To set my goals. Let nothing stop me." Everyone is silent. Did I accidentally slip up and tell them how Mother would lop off my long blond hair every two years and sell it to the wig man in MacArthur Park? I sweeten up my voice and brighten up my smile.

"I'm the sort of girl who takes a basket of lemons and says, 'Thank you, God, for this opportunity to make some delicious lemonade!'"

The crowd applauds. I graciously smile and wave, returning to Robert's side and immediately putting his hand back in mine. He wipes the tears off my left cheek with a gentle swipe of his thumb and gives me a peck. When I pull away, I look over and see that Douglas is gone.

43

Robert Hogarth

Pageant Night Three

THE LEMONADE THING was clearly for Douglas's benefit, but I can't slow my racing mind down enough to work out what Maxine was trying to tell him. Were those tears real? They felt real to me, but then again, it's Maxine. It's too hot under these stage lights. A blinding, white-hot heat that sears right through my skin, bleaching my bones. It's not so much uncomfortable as it is numbing.

I can't remember the last time I had all eyes on me like this. I think it might have been my first Communion when I was seven. I had to stand in front of the congregation and say a prayer. I practiced for months, and yet when the day came and I was standing there in my Communion robe next to the imposing Father Dugan, all I could worry about was choking on the Communion wafer. There's no wafer tonight, but it definitely feels like I'm standing in judgment, if not of a higher power, then of the good people on the Mr. and Mrs. American Pie judging panel—and my new bride's mad-as-hell ex-husband.

The ex–Mr. Maxine Hortence Simmons glares at me from the judges' table. I saw an old late-night B movie once about a man with death-ray eyes. That's Douglas, only much more intimidating, since it's a fragile peace between him and Maxine that's keeping us in this contest. I tell myself that getting bounced out of a beauty pageant isn't the worst thing that could happen to us.

Biddle is called up and rushes through some over-rehearsed bit about Betsey being "a mom every man should have," which sounds all kinds of wrong to me. Roy Clarke brings up those pork chops that Wanda mentioned and gets about the same polite laugh. Virgil sounds like an old-time preacher, wailing on about his Muffy rubbing his sore feet at the end of a hard day. I blank out for Daniel's comments on Maisey, but from the applause in the audience and the slight slump in Maxine's posture, I can guess it was absolutely perfect. As with everything else this week, Daniel and Maisey are the ones to beat.

My name is called all too soon. Maxine leans over to give me a kiss on the cheek.

"Think of me and not them," she whispers.

Thunders puts the microphone in my hand and my mind goes blank. There are words somewhere in the back of my mind—words that Maxine wrote for me and that I stared at for hours on end—but I can't find them right now. Funny enough, all I can think of are the words to the Hail Mary.

"So, Robert . . . ," Thunders drones. I don't hear the rest of the question. The sound around me goes to thick fuzz.

I turn to my left and lock eyes with Maxine, hoping she'll see I'm in distress and maybe fake a heart attack or something. Instead she blows me a kiss.

The sound comes rushing back in time for me to hear Thunders once more. "I'll repeat the question, Robert. What do you want us all to know about your wife?"

"Good evening, everyone," I say, sounding off, but not completely terrible. I think. I try to picture the speech Maxine wrote, but there's nothing coming to mind. So I start talking, hoping my memory will kick in. "I want to tell you all about my beautiful wife, Maxine Hortence Hogarth."

At the judges' table, Douglas quickly picks up his pen and writes something down on his notepad. I'm guessing it's a big fat zero. If only Maxine had found that book on mind control.

"Some might think there's not a lot I can say about a woman I've only been married to for a few months." I pause, because while I can't remember what Maxine wrote for me to say, I do remember she wanted lots of dramatic pauses.

I think of Maxine strolling into my tavern like it was built for her, brightening my day with one hilarious tale after another of Palm Springs socialites politely destroying one another with mean words over catered dinners. That was her world, and yet she always spoke of it like she'd only been visiting.

"Maxine Hogarth is a woman who always knows what fork to use, always has a spare hankie in her handbag, and is never at a loss for words. She can take a napkin and fold it into a swan, which, while not a practical skill, is pretty gosh darn 'groovy,' as the kids say."

The audience politely laughs. Maxine gives me a tiny nod of encouragement.

I think about how effortlessly she took to those kids: feeding them, clothing them, listening to what they wanted and needed. Though maybe she goes overboard at times, she still encourages and supports Chuck in his love of all things super-spy. Then there's "Dawn will talk when she's ready," coming from a woman so controlling and exacting that she had her kitchen repainted three times until it was the "right" shade of avocado.

"Maxine does things with Spam that are . . . not of this earth."

That gets quite a laugh, although my stomach churns.

"More important, Maxine makes us all better. The kids and I—we were in rough shape when she found us. Maxine took us all in and in her own special way, she made us a family. We might not be a family like all the others you've met tonight, but I'd argue—" I have to pause here, not because I'm lying or want to build up drama.

There's Maxine in her wedding dress, threatening to publicly indict the entire Phoenix Police Department for sex crimes if they don't release me. "Maxine is simply undeniable," I tell the audience. "She loves like no one else. And that's exactly what Chuck, Dawn, and I especially need. Someone who loves us like crazy."

I hear nothing from the audience. I think I need to wrap this up. "Anyhoo, vote Maxine! Thanks! Good night!"

I turn and hightail it right back to Maxine. She hugs me tight.

"No one's ever said anything half as good about me," she whispers. "I love you, dear-heart."

Maxine needs to stick around backstage to get some instruction on the televised festivities, which start in a few hours. I get the kids outside where it's quiet and we're out of everyone's hair.

Mostly, I'm relieved that my part in all of this is done. We get a few hours to ourselves, and then everything else tonight is in Maxine's hands.

My solitude is short-lived.

"Hey!" I hear a voice say from behind me. I turn around and see it's Douglas. His hair is mussed, and he looks a little sweaty and out of breath, like he's been running. "We need to talk, Hogarth."

I don't like the way he says my name. It's an Old English word that means "lamb," and yet when Douglas says it, it sounds more like "dead meat." He motions for me to follow him behind the clubhouse, near where they keep the golf carts. I take comfort in him not wanting to attack right out in the open, and follow him.

"Stay here," I tell Chuck, pointing to the path. "Keep your sister close."

Chuck nods. His eyes are huge and don't budge from Douglas, who's pacing under a palm tree. "But isn't he . . . ?"

"It's no big deal," I tell him, knowing full well he doesn't believe me. "We're just going to talk.

I walk over to the golf carts and Douglas. I've dealt with plenty of worked-up guys at bars, but Douglas isn't drunk. His gait is frantically paced, but it's steady.

MR. & MRS. AMERICAN PIE   325

"What I want to know," Douglas sneers, "is if this is something you and Maxine cooked up together or if she has some dirt on you. Something bad enough to get you to go along with this cockamamie tale." He spits out "Maxine" like it's something rotten in his mouth.

"I don't know what you're talking about," I tell him, sounding as firm as I did to Biddle on the golf course. "And keep your voice down around the kids." Chuck has Dawn on his back while he runs around making airplane noises.

"Yeah, what about those kids?" Douglas waves some papers in my face before shoving them into my chest.

I unfold them and see it's a letter from Sharla—notarized, no less—giving Maxine permission to keep her children "indefinitely." The two smaller documents folded inside the letter are Chuck's and Dawn's birth certificates with my name clearly not listed under "*Father*." Dawn's dad is the missing Pete Bronski. Chuck doesn't have anyone listed under "*Father*" beyond a big black *X*.

"It's all her, isn't it?" Douglas seethes. "She told you they were her kids and you believed it. I can tell from your face how surprised you are. I've been there." He pauses, and I'm trying to think of what to say next, or if I should ask him where he got these or what else he knows.

"That bitch," he mutters, tearing the kids' paperwork away from my hands. He steps closer to me. "It's always something with that woman, isn't it? Bet she never told you why we got married." He stuffs Sharla's letter and the birth certificates back in his jacket pocket.

"I'm living in San Bernardino, running a few of my dad's gas stations. We sponsor the Miss San Bernardino pageant, and since I'm single, twenty-five, playing the field, I get to be a pageant judge. Maxine puts the moves on me one night and I think, *Okay, why not?* She was cute enough and it seemed like she was a real game girl." He says this to me with a wink, and I realize he no longer sees me as an adversary. He's talking to me like we're two guys in the locker room changing into our street shoes after a golf game.

I shake my head and give him a smirk because I want to see where he's going with this.

"I make sure she wins the pageant," Douglas continues. "I figured that would be it, but we end up dating. I'm thinking that we're having fun, right? Maxine is a real fun girl. I say, 'Let's drive to Los Angeles for the night,' and she drops everything to go with me. We slept on a beach in Malibu one night and she woke up with sand up in her hair and didn't bitch about it." He's downright wistful.

Dawn makes a loud noise and I snap my head away from Douglas toward the kids. Chuck's getting antsy and has managed to slowly work his way closer to me and Douglas, no doubt because he's hoping to listen in. I motion with one hand for him to move farther away and he obeys.

"About two months in, I tell Maxine I won't be around for the weekend since a buddy of mine is having a bachelor weekend in LA." Douglas doesn't sound so nostalgic now. He's getting tense again, his left hand balling up in a fist while the right hand nervously runs through his slightly graying hair. "Maxine's pissed. She doesn't want me to go, so I set her straight. We're just having a good time. She doesn't get to tell me what I can and cannot do. Hell, I probably don't have to tell you how *that* went over." He snickers loudly.

Douglas sits down on one of the golf carts. I step closer because I don't want him to raise his voice. "I get back to San Bernardino late Sunday night, and Maxine and my parents are waiting for me. Maxine looks like she's been crying for days. My mom also looks like shit and my dad . . . he looks like he wants to take me out back and whoop me."

He stops talking and stares off down the path toward the cabins. He stares for so long that I finally turn my head to see if he's looking at someone. There's no one there.

"While I was gone, Maxine took a bus all the way to Sacramento to my parents' house. She hadn't met them yet. I still don't know how she got their address. They were well known around town, so I don't know. But she showed up at their door, sobbing about being 'in the family way.' Jesus, I'll never forget that. 'In the family way.'

Took me a minute to understand what that meant. By the time the room stopped spinning for me and I figured it out, Maxine and my folks had everything set. We'd get married right away, before Maxine started to show and all of California would know that Douglas Simmons, heir to the Simmons Gas Stop Corporation, had knocked up some nineteen-year-old beauty queen." He kicks at the grass. "Who does that? Who tells a guy's parents that she's pregnant before even telling the guy?"

This isn't a rhetorical question. When people get this deep into telling their bartender their sad story, they always reach a point where they want a response, guidance, or another shot of whiskey. "Sounds like something a scared young woman does," I offer.

This was the wrong thing to say. Douglas hops up from the golf cart and gets back to pacing. "That's bullshit," he says. "She didn't even give me a chance to do the right thing. When Maxine decides that she wants something, she goes and takes it from whomever has it. She wanted to marry me, so she tricked me and beat me. It's how she operates.

"A couple weeks after we're married, she tells me she lost the kid. I'm thinking that's not the worst thing that could happen to me. About a year later I'm thinking it's time we start a family. It's good for business to be a family man."

It sounds harsh coming from Douglas, but it's true. After all, isn't the appearance of being a "family man" why I'm here?

"Baby never comes. We go to the doctor and find out Maxine can't make one. That's when I realize that whole baby thing—the whole reason we got married—all more of her lies." Douglas stops pacing. "Our whole marriage was like that. One manipulation after another. Christ, once I inherited all that money and we moved to Palm Springs, life went to shit. I'm thinking we have a nice house, I get to golf a couple times a week, that baby never came, so we're not tied down. Nope. Maxine won't let up on me. I'm not even for one day allowed to be my own man. I want a nice car, so I buy one. Week later, there's a credit card charge for a thirty-five-hundred-dollar mink coat. We live in the goddamn desert!"

Maxine needed kids and suddenly two were available. I've never spoken to Sharla. I only know her through Maxine.

"It gets to be this pattern," Douglas continues. "I tell her no and she does it anyway. I do something she doesn't like, she punishes me for it. My boss's wife is very attractive and maybe has eyes for me. Maxine tells everyone she's screwing the tennis pro at the club."

Douglas is all but panting now. His words flying out, crashing into one another. I can barely keep up. "Since there will be no babies and I got duped into marrying her, I start thinking divorce. She goes through my things, finds a lawyer's business card, and throws a surprise third-anniversary party and invites my parents and all their friends."

I'm not only suddenly married, but living in the same house as Maxine and the kids. I wasn't asked. It simply happened.

"She finds my stash of *Playboys*, cuts them up, and mails them in a package—to my office at Western Airlines!" He's yelling now. "Maxine knows my elderly secretary opens my mail. Poor Mrs. Klingschmidt sees a box full of cutout boobs and retires on the spot."

My stomach bottoms out and I feel like I've run a marathon. All the petty sniping, the backstabbing, the smiling in people's faces and then spitting on them behind their backs.

Douglas turns and screams in the direction of the clubhouse. "Joke's on you, Maxine! That's how I got my new secretary! The one I dumped your ass for!" He quiets down as quickly as he amped up. "You know that bitch came to my house today to scare the shit out of my wife and daughter?"

I shake my head. Why would Maxine do this? She promised me she'd stay clear of Douglas during the pageant. Mutually assured destruction.

"The whole reason she came to this damn pageant was to finish me off," he says. "Because I did the one thing no one's allowed to do. I beat Maxine. I won and she can't stand it."

I didn't want to do any of this. Fake family at a beauty pageant? Maxine convinced me it was for my own good. I had to do it to protect myself. What would she have done if I said no? What happens to my secret if I step out of line? There's sweat pouring down my temples now.

Chuck is at my side. I feel his hand tugging on my shirtsleeve. "Dad, I need to talk to you for a minute," he says quietly, his eyes drilled into Douglas.

"Take your sister back to the cabin," I tell him. "I'll be there in a minute."

Chuck does as he's told and I turn my attention back to Douglas.

"He seems like an okay kid," Douglas says.

I don't respond. I need this conversation to end now. I can't bear to stand here looking at this sad, wrecked, bitter man any longer. "What do you want?" I ask Douglas.

"Want?" he says, like it's the first time anyone has ever asked him this. "I want a decade and a half of my life back, which I won't get. So I guess I want Maxine wiped off the face of the earth. Barring that, I want her out of this pageant. I want her out of Palm Springs."

There's no question in my mind that he means this.

"These kids, Douglas," I say pleadingly, but firmly.

"Look," he tells me, "You don't seem like a bad guy. We've both been duped by that psychopath, right? I'm not some monster like her." He pauses for a moment to think it through. "Get the kids out of here ASAP. Because if you're still here for the finale, I'll call the cops and tell them the kids were kidnapped. You'll be in jail and they'll be in foster care by morning."

Maxine Hogarth

Pageant Night Three

ROBERT AND THE KIDS aren't waiting for me at the clubhouse, so I head back to the cabin. We've only got a few hours before the televised event, and I'm hoping like hell Charles has found some dirt for me.

As I reach the door, Robert comes walking out. Dawn's fast asleep on his shoulder and a glum Charles comes up behind him, carrying a suitcase in each hand.

"You scared the hell out of me," I chide Robert, putting my hand on Charles's forehead. He's not feverish and nothing looks broken. Charles looks up at me as though he might start crying. "Is he all right?" I ask Robert.

"Chuck, take your sister to the clubhouse," he tells the boy. "Wait for me by the valet stand."

"What the hell is going on, Robert?"

Charles looks up at me with wet eyes and throws himself around my waist for a hug.

"Chuck, please," Robert pleads.

Charles pulls away and takes Dawn in his arms. "I left you something," he says as he turns and starts quickly down the path.

"Robert, what are you doing? You're scaring me."

Robert doesn't care. "This is over. I'm taking the kids and getting—"

"The hell you are. We won big tonight. We're in the lead, Robert. The lead!"

"Douglas knows everything."

My throat tightens, and I feel the tips of my fingers and ears burn hot, as if stung by something venomous.

"What. No." My words tumble out too quickly for Robert to respond. "No one will believe anything about you—"

"The kids. He knows about the kids," Robert hisses at me. "He found your notarized letter from Sharla and the kids' birth certificates."

"None of this is going to matter after tonight. Once we win—"

"Have you gone a day in your life without a manipulation, Maxine?" he asks. "Did you enjoy duping a second man into marrying you the way you did the first?"

Oh God. He knows. Robert knows what I did all those years ago to Douglas. "I only married you because you needed my help," I insist.

Robert throws the valise in his hand clear across the front yard. It hits the path with a thud and skitters a few feet. I recoil, my back pressed against the cabin. "I'm getting these kids out of here before Douglas has them taken away."

"Let me fix this," I beg. I reach out for his arm, but he yanks it away.

"Fix what, Maxine? Fix that you're not their mother and I'm not their father?" he asks. "Fix that the whole reason we're in this mess is because you want a crown for your head?"

"That's not fair," I try telling him. "We all need this win, Robert."

His voice gets solemn and firm. "No, we all need to be away from you."

That one's a punch to my gut.

"How are you getting home?" I whimper. "Dawn didn't have her nap today."

Robert lets out an exhausted sigh. "I know how to take care of the kids, Maxine. We're taking the bus home to Scottsdale tonight."

He walks away, and I let him go, watching as he picks up the valise and vanishes down the path. I want to go after him, but Douglas has poisoned him. It's Robert speaking in Douglas's voice now and I can't bear it.

I walk in the cabin and barely make it to a dining room chair before my legs give out. My whole body aches and my head is pounding. The cabin looks strangely bigger now with the beds and other furniture back in their rightful spots. My suitcases are no longer under the couch, but rather stacked neatly next to the dresser, which now contains only my clothing. There are no colorful sippy cups drying in the rack by the sink. No aftershave sitting on the shelf in the "bathroom." The only evidence suggesting that anyone other than me existed in this place is the empty crib, a man's cowboy hat left lying on a bed, and a child's drawing pinned up to the fridge.

Right as I notice that Charles forgot his knapsack, the front door opens. I snap my head around expecting to see Robert or Charles and instead get the last person on earth I want to deal with right now.

"You are one dumb bitch, Maxine," my ex-husband says to me as he helps himself to a seat at my dining room table. I want to rip the mini-fridge from the wall and bash his brains in, but I barely have the strength to hold my own head up.

"We had an agreement, you lying prick," I growl at him.

"Yeah, one that started with you agreeing to not steal my car." He makes a show of slapping his feet up on the table, first the left and then the right. "I think we also agreed you would stay the hell out of Palm Springs. Then I find out you were snooping around my house? Scaring my wife?" He yells that last part.

"You threatened two children," I shoot back.

"Oh, look who's suddenly Maria von Trapp, clothing the orphans of the world in drapes. What bullshit did you weave into gold to get him to marry you? And to lie about those kids being his?"

I lift my end of the table up and slam it down hard, knocking Douglas's feet to the floor and sending my chair out from under me. I can't sit now anyway. I need to move, pacing the kitchen and trying to will myself into thinking of something to do next.

"Touched a nerve, have I?" He laughs.

It's Thanksgiving all over again, but this time he's taking so much more from me than my home, money, and friends who hate me.

"Those kids did nothing to you, Douglas. They're babies," I point out, trying to stay in control as the acid builds in my stomach. I rummage through my purse and find where I hid a couple of emergency cigarettes.

"Jesus, Maxine. I'm not a monster. I didn't call the police." He puts his goddamned feet back on my goddamned table. "I told poor Robert to get the hell out of Dodge."

"Why are you here?" I finally demand to know. He gets up from the table and glowers over me.

"I came to make sure you know that your little secret is out, Maxine. You're nothing more than a lying, manipulative, con artist bitch."

Douglas walks out, leaving the door wide open behind him.

It's somehow worse with Douglas gone. Everything in the cabin is silent. I'm standing in the bathroom taking my lashes off when I realize that I hear the Walker kids cheerfully running around their cabin before the final pageant event.

I let myself cry while I strip down to my slip. I want to curl up in a bathtub with a bottle of something brown and strong, but all I have is a grubby shower and maybe some of Charles's Hi-C Fruit Punch. Oh God, Charles. Does he know those awful things Douglas said about me? He'll know they're all true. He'll think back on everything we've done together and rather than see it as fun and exciting, he'll hate me for it all—the same way I eventually hated my mother.

I turn the shower on as hot as I can make it. I climb in—slip and all—and lie on the dingy shower floor, but the water barely singes me. I sob and kick at the walls, clawing at the grimy soot stuck in the grout between the tiles. Maybe Dawn won't remember me. That will be for the best. She'll be saved from my stink. Maybe her brother will tell her one day about the crazy broad who took them on a wild vacation once.

My stomach heaves. I haven't eaten anything since who knows when, so all that comes up is bile. The bitter stench of it fills the steamy room, so I shove it down the drain with my fingers. Will I even get to tell them I'm sorry? What if I never get to see them again? I can't remember the last thing I said to Charles. Was it asking if he had a fever? What did he say to me about leaving something behind for me?

I flop myself out of the shower like a fish onshore, leaving the water running. I stagger to my feet and slip and slide toward the dining room. The knapsack. Charles left it behind on purpose. My hands are too wet and shaky to open it, so I dry them on a tea towel. Fumbling, I pull out our framed family photo. Stuck in the frame is a note in Charles's handwriting:

Miss Maxine,

I'm sorry our cover was blown. Robert says we need to go where it's safe and that you'll find your own way home. I don't understand it. I found some evidence that might help you.

Yours truly,
Charles Hogarth (Bronski)

I flip the photo over to find a memorandum on Mrs. American Pie stationery.

Then I laugh until I think I'm going to throw up again.

I'm trying to figure out my next move when there's a soft knock at the door. I run to open it, hoping for a few seconds that it's Robert and the kids. It's Maisey Walker. More precisely Maisey Walker and a bottle of rye. I reach for the bottle and she pulls it away, pushing past me to walk in the cabin.

"What'd you hear?"

"Enough. A lot. Honestly, I just figured you could use someone to talk to."

"My usual bartender is not here at the moment, so I will take you up on that."

I bring over two glasses and Maisey uncorks the rye and pours a generous glass for each of us. She raises the glass as if to toast, but I slam mine down. Well, hello there, warm back-of-the-throat burn. I've missed you. Maisey smiles and refills my glass.

"Didn't peg you as a drinker, Maisey."

She laughs—not her usual charming Audrey Hepburn laugh. This one is deeper and throatier, like how Katharine Hepburn might laugh if she had a sense of humor. "My father-in-law swears by a single shot of rye each night before bed. Says it's for good luck and longevity. He must have snuck a bottle in one of our suitcases. Now what's going on here?"

I spill my guts all over her. She sits and listens, barely saying a word, even when I mention my Thanksgiving shit-show and how Douglas the Judge is also Douglas the Ex-Husband. I leave out everything about how Robert and I came to marry, but I'm honest about the kids being my wards rather than Robert's children. The whole time I'm talking, she sips her rye and gently nods. She doesn't interrupt or ask me anything beyond what I tell her. I imagine this is what it's like to go to a psychologist. I don't exactly feel good about my life, but it's a comfort, I guess, to share with someone else. *Unburdening?* Is that the word?

"Who pulled you out of the pool?" she asks.

"I really don't know."

"Well, I can see why you needed the pageant."

Finally.

I reach my hand across the table and take Maisey by the wrist. "*Need* is exactly it. Thank Christ someone understands this!" She laughs, with me more than at me. "Oh, Maisey, that feeling when you get a crown put on your head."

"There's nothing like it," she agrees, shaking her head gently. "You get the crowd cheering and all those warm, bright lights."

"Even when you look away," I remind her, "all you see for a few seconds is that fuzzy, bright glow. Too bad I'm fucked."

"That you are, my friend," Maisey says. "You know, my mama did pageants, back in Atlanta. I grew up always oohing and ahhing over her crowns and ribbons," Maisey tells me, her smile beaming. "There's this one photo of her when she was maybe eighteen years old and she's got on a fluffy white fur cape with red trim. Her hair's all done up with the crown tucked in it. She looked like a queen out of a storybook."

"That Ruthie of yours will make a stunning pageant girl one day," I tell her.

Maisey takes the last sip of her rye while shaking her head. "I want more for her."

She gets up from the table and goes to the sink, filling her empty rye glass with water. I help myself to her bottle for another snort. "I always hear the same things whenever I win a pageant," she says. "Somebody always tells me that I'm 'pretty for a black girl' or 'so articulate for a black girl.' Makes me crazy." Maisey sits back down at the table and puts the water glass in front of me. "So, when Mrs. Depwelt offered me this pageant, I knew it was a chance for me to show Ruthie that her mama can win against all these pretty white ladies. Ruthie needs to know that she and I can be pretty—and not with any of that 'for a black girl' nonsense attached. Can you understand that?"

I nod. There's a pit in my stomach, not from the rye, but from the memorandum.

Maisey must notice a look upon my face. "What, Maxine? You don't think I can win it? I've been in first place the whole damn time."

I take a step into the kitchen and grab Charles's knapsack off the counter. I sit back down and put it in my lap, feeling Maisey's eyes on me as I fish out the memo.

"Maisey, my dear: pour yourself another glass, because we're both fucked."

I slide the memorandum across the table to her. She picks it up and reads it. I watch her eyes move right to left, then down to the next line. Her perfectly groomed eyebrows raise in unison, but ever so slightly, before returning to their natural position.

I've read it so many times myself, I know it by heart.

FROM: Alice Depwelt, Director of Pageant Operations
TO: 1970 Mr. & Mrs. American Pie Sponsors
DATE: July 10, 1970
RE: Contestant "situation"

To summarize the meeting at my office earlier today, the pageant assures you all that your concerns over the potential win by Mrs. Illinois Pie have not fallen on deaf ears. The inclusion of the first Negro family was done entirely to bring glowing attention to the pageants' sponsors.

But as Director of Pageant Operations, I assure you that all final scoring is handled by me and me alone. Contestants never see final scores, meaning there is ample opportunity to correct any mistakes made by the judges before the final winner is crowned. I hope this soothes any frayed nerves. The Mr. & Mrs. American Pie Pageant will only allow the "cream" of the crop to wear the crown.

Once done reading it, Maisey sets the paper down on the table and folds her arms across her chest. She stares out the kitchen window, to where the late-afternoon sun is low in the sky. I expected tears, maybe, or even a small scream. She gives me silence.

"Depwelt isn't going to let either of us win this, Maisey. Can you believe the nerve?" I ask with genuine surprise at the gall of that bitch.

Maisey puts the back of her hand to her forehead as if swooning like Scarlett O'Hara. "My heavens!" she dramatically moans. "Racism! Oh me, oh my!" Laughing, Maisey takes my glass of rye and swigs it down.

"It's not funny," I insist.

"You think I don't know that?" she says. "I hate it. I'm just not surprised by it." She folds up the memorandum and hands it back to me.

I don't take it. She lets it drop on the table. "We could do something about this, Maisey. Force Depwelt into abiding by the judges. If the newspapers get this, we could burn the whole pageant down."

Maisey puts her hands out to tell me to stop. "I'm not lighting anything on fire."

"You're going to let them beat you?" I ask. "That what you want to teach your kids?"

"You think blackmailing some racist pageant biddy is going to teach my kids anything good?" Maisey says. "They're three and six. They've got a whole lifetime of Depwelts ahead of them. No reason for them to see that now."

She gets up from the table and goes to the door, stopping with her hand on the knob. "You do whatever it is you need to do, Maxine. I won't say or do anything to stop you. But I'm going out there tonight for my daughter with my head held high. She's gonna see her mama beat all those white ladies, and Depwelt can't do anything about that."

I nod in agreement.

"You can keep the rye," she says.

Before the door can close all the way, Maisey's head pops back in. "By the way, Maxine, my husband and I voted for Humphrey."

Charles "Chuck" Bronski

Last Night of Pageant

I KNOW ROBERT'S FEELING BAD about leaving Miss Maxine behind. I can tell because he's doing that thing grown-ups do when they try to act super happy about stuff that no one should be super happy about.

"How 'bout this bus station?" he says to me as we walk up to the ticket booth. "It doesn't smell too bad in here, now does it?"

I don't like being rude to my elders, so I nod. But on the inside, I'm hopping mad. Miss Maxine is never going to win that pageant without us.

Dawn and I sit down on the benches in the bus station waiting area. There's a TV! I've never been so happy to see a TV in my whole life.

"We can watch the pageant," I say while trying to remember what channel it's on.

Robert sits down and pulls Dawn onto his lap. "Chuck, she's not going to be at the pageant."

"But she is! I know it. I got evidence for her and everything."

"Chuck," he says, sounding sad but also bossy. "The bus will be here at seven thirty. We're going home. The pageant's over, kiddo."

I don't want to forget all this happened. I was having the best time ever, doing spy stuff for Miss Maxine, building rockets with Robert. I never had a summer vacation before, and this one was way better than what all the kids at school talk about. Then that Douglas fella had to come and ruin it. Now I'm going back to Scottsdale and a whole bunch of nothing. No more Miss Maxine. No more Robert. I don't even know where my mom is or if she's coming back.

46

Maxine Hogarth

Prelude to the Grand Finale

I POLISH OFF THE RYE in my cabin while pulling my look together. The rule book says we're all supposed to get ready for the pageant's big finish in the ladies' lounge at the clubhouse, but to hell with all that. Maisey's words about doing right by her kids are all I can think of as I cut seven inches off the bottom of my gown and tear off the black tulle overlay. What I'm left with is a hot pink sheath that clings to me like Saran wrap. My bra shows through, so I ditch it, but I need to put it back on again so I have a place to store the memorandum. I give my hair a quick hot rollering while practicing what I plan on saying to Depwelt. I pull the curlers from my hair and wrap it all tall and tight around my head like Cinderella on her way to the ball. I hope Robert knows to take the barrettes out of Dawn's hair before she falls asleep on the bus home. They poke into her delicate scalp if she lies down on them. The hairs on the back of my head keep falling and I don't have time to deal with them. So I Aqua Net my whole head until I can't see through the fumes. I'm sure Charles is glad he's not here with me making him hold up a mirror so I can inspect my finished do.

My black velvet pumps in one hand and my cigarettes in the other, I tromp toward the clubhouse. I'm nearly to the front door when Missy pops up from somewhere—maybe the valet stand?—and grabs my arm.

"Mrs. Depwelt needs a word with you immediately," she squeaks.

Missy all but drags me down the hall, then throws me into Depwelt's office and shoves me toward a chair. She might sound like a mouse, but with all that pushiness, I bet Missy was a helluva field hockey player in high school. Depwelt comes in right behind us and slams the door shut. Without so much as a glance at me, she takes a seat at her desk, Missy standing to her right like a good little henchman.

I light up a cigarette and think of jowly Allen Moore, Esquire.

"You have besmirched this pageant's good name," Depwelt starts in on me.

I flick my ash onto her floor. "Yeah, okay," I offer. "I'll give you that one."

"You're out, girlie," Depwelt announces. "Go quickly and quietly and we won't sue you for fraud."

"I'm not leaving," I tell her. I take a long drag, then let it out. "We still have the final round, and I have always wanted to be on TV."

"The Mr. and Mrs. American Pie pageant is well within our rights to bring you up on a slew of charges, both in civil court for fraud and in criminal court," she fumes. "Mr. Simmons informs us the children—"

"The children were here with their mother's permission," I say loudly and firmly. "They are my concern—not yours."

"We can still sue the pants off you, girlie!" Depwelt yelps.

"Not a chance," I tell her. "Because you"—this dress is tight as hell and the memo rips a little as I pull it from my bra—"you are a racist asshole who's rigged the pageant." I wave the memo in front of her. "This bullshit right here is fraud."

Depwelt grapples for it and I let her have it.

"You can keep that one. There were three others on Missy's clipboard."

Missy swallows hard. I wish I had time to tell her how she was bested by a brilliant twelve-year-old. But I would never give Charles's secret identity away.

Depwelt scowls at me over the top of her pearl-rimmed glasses. "What do you want?"

I wanted two and a half million and the pied-à-terre in Los Angeles. I got a condo in Scottsdale and a family. I'll be goddamned if this pageant takes that away from me.

"The crown," I tell her. "Wave your magical wand of racism over the scores and make me the winner."

"And what is there to keep you from double-crossing me and this pageant if we do that?" she asks, folding up the memo.

I put my cigarette out on the surface of her desk. "You ever hear of mutually assured destruction?"

Maxine Hogarth

The Grande Finale

I STRUT FROM Depwelt's office and join the other Pies backstage as Missy shuffles us all into position. She hands out bright yellow rain slickers and I for a fleeting second wish I had made rehearsal earlier in the day so I'd at least have some idea of what's coming next.

"Remember, girls," she announces, "this is live television. There are three cameras—left, right, and center of stage. When the light on the camera is green, that means we're live. Red means we're on commercial."

The music blares as we parade out onto the stage. As expected, I can't make out anyone in the audience, or at the judges' table, but I do see a pair of big green lights blaring from atop two television cameras. I'm sandwiched between Muffy and Maisey, so I follow their lead as we all link arms and form a dance line. The yellow slickers suddenly make sense when Thunders appears from stage right singing "Raindrops Keep Falling on My Head." He's nearly in tune as the Pies all begin to kick like Rockettes—provided the Rockettes had precious little grace or balance. While I completely miss the first right kick, left kick, I quickly bring myself in sync. From the corner of my eye, I catch Maisey giving me a look of concern, but I don't respond. It's all smile, kick, kick, smile, kick, kick.

I get an extra kick in when I don't realize that us Pies are supposed to sway back and forth for the last verse. Oh well! I'm sure no one noticed, not that it matters if they did. In fact, nothing matters anymore. I simply need to get through the next twenty minutes and all will be right as rain. And I'm not talking about this fake silver confetti "rain" that is dumped on us all as Thunders misses the long high note at the end of the song.

The green lights go out on the cameras, and I let Maisey and Muffy lead me offstage. We throw aside our slickers as Missy comes dashing over to realign us.

"That was great," she bleats, clapping her hands. "Nobody fell!"

She lines us all up in the right order for talent, and when the green lights come back on, Thunders takes the stage once more, calling for Mrs. Rhode Island Pie to come delight the audience.

The talent competition was the one thing I feared most walking into this pageant, which in hindsight is hilarious. While all these women are certainly beautiful and cunning, and know how to pretend to be perfect, we're a goddamned untalented lot of performers. Thank Christ we only need to fill up ninety seconds of time apiece. For Betsey, this means giving a cheerless presentation on how to properly assemble a lattice-top pie.

"So, it's like weaving a basket?" Thunders asks her, his voice dripping with marvel.

"No, Dale. It's a pie. Made out of dough."

Wanda is next and she goes the circus route, Hula-Hooping while whistling "Dixie." The hoop falls twice, but to Wanda's credit, she can whistle like a goddamned train.

Muffy does a one-woman cha-cha that basically serves as a chance for her to wiggle her tits and ass. The 3M Company deserves a special award for all the hard work its double-sided ultra-sticky tape is doing at keeping Muffy's double Ds wrangled inside that dress.

It's phenomenal how at peace I am as I take the stage. As I walk out under those bright lights, the only thing I'm certain of is a guaranteed win. There's no pressure now. I only need to tread water until the crown is on my head.

I put my right hand over my heart and aim myself facing the far left corner of the auditorium.

"I pledge allegiance to the flag!" I holler, letting each word ring out with equal importance and gravity.

The audience instantly snaps to its feet and all eyes turn to the back far left corner. Of course, there's no flag, which flusters everyone a bit.

"Of the United States of Ahhhh-merica!" I bellow.

By now everyone in the audience is pledging to an invisible flag.

"And to the Republic—for which it stands!"

There's no flag because there's no Charles here to hoist one up for me.

"One nation, under GOD!"

There's no Charles. I feel myself start to cry but fight it. Crying can come later.

"Indivisible. With li-li-liberty . . ." I tremble toward the finish line.

I push my hand hard against my chest, as if it's the only thing holding my heart in.

". . . and justice for all."

I scurry offstage as the crowd claps. I get a good eyeful of the judges' table, where surprisingly, Douglas isn't glaring at me. He's instead got his furious eyes aimed at Depwelt, who refuses to look at him.

The microphone is reset to the center of the stage. Maisey is cool and collected as she walks up to it, like she's meeting an old friend. She smiles and gives a little wave, and then blows the roof off the dump with that voice of hers. It's Dionne Warwick's version of "Didn't We," which would cut me deep even on a good day. No one can take their eyes off her as Maisey floats up and down and over and under each and every note with heart and soul poured into her voice.

The last line she holds for eternity and a day. *"Didn't we almost make it this time?"* Maisey asks the world.

God damn it, I have almost made it. Just a few more minutes and I will set this right.

Robert Hogarth

The Big Finale

LEAVE IT TO CHUCK to remember which TV station the pageant is playing on.

The bus to Scottsdale is due in three minutes as the pageant goes to a commercial for Mr. Tipply's electronics store. Chuck doesn't budge. He's been glued to that damn pageant since the opening song-and-dance number, and even the tedium of Mrs. Rhode Island's pie crust demonstration wasn't enough to turn him away. Something about Maxine looked different as she did her dramatic recitation of the Pledge. The act of performing was pure Maxine, but her heart wasn't in it. I remind myself that she should feel bad.

"Chuck, we gotta go now, kiddo," I tell him for the third time.

"They're about to announce the winner," he insists, sounding as close to defying me as I've ever heard him. "The bus can wait."

I don't argue. Neither of us has said anything about what happens when that bus drops us off in Scottsdale. The truth is, I don't know what's coming next for either of us. All I know is that Chuck and Dawn haven't asked for any of this mess, and yet here they are, neck-deep in it.

The pageant returns. The five Pies all stand, arms linked, in a line next to Dale Thunders. There's a drumroll and at least three too many dramatic pauses as Thunders opens the first envelope, reads it, rereads it, and says, "Well, this sure is a historic night!"

All the Pies look to Maisey, who keeps on smiling as if none of this has anything to do with her.

"For the first time in the history of the Mrs. American Pie Pageant, we have . . ." Another dramatic pause. "A three-way tie for fourth—no, make that second runner-up."

"Wow, those ladies really know how to smile big," Charles mutters to himself.

Another drumroll and Thunders finally spits it out. "Mrs. Rhode Island Pie! Mrs. South Carolina Pie! Mrs. Idaho Pie!"

The three women burst into tears and, still clinging to each other, as if huddled for safety while lost at sea, they move forward as a clump to Thunders. He awkwardly hands the microphone to Mrs. Rhode Island Pie while he tries to figure out what to do with one second runner-up sash to share among the three women. After much fumbling, Muffy, Wanda, and Betsey settle for each placing a hand on the sash and walking offstage with it.

"Maxine can still win this!" Chuck tells me.

Outside, the bus honks its horn and revs its engine. I stand up and grab the suitcase, ready to shove us all out the door the second the winner is revealed. On TV, Thunders is handed an envelope and does his open, read, pause, read, pause routine again. This time, it works. I'm feeling sufficiently tense and eager for the outcome. It doesn't matter anymore who wins. We all just need this to end.

"First runner-up is—"

A drumroll.

A cymbal crash.

"Mrs. Illinois Pie!"

As the camera cuts to a politely smiling Maisey, it gives Chuck a long second to register who actually won. Once it hits him, he erupts. He snatches little Dawn up in a hug and holds her as he jumps up and down. "We won! We won! Holy cow, we did it!"

He looks to me and I muster up a smile and nod. How in the hell did Maxine do this? Here she is, getting a crown put on her head while she smiles and cries her makeup off, for all the greater Palm Springs area to see.

The spotlight centers on Maxine as Thunders puts a micro-phone in her face for her to blubber out some grateful acceptance speech. Maxine shoves her bouquet of roses into Thunders's arms and takes the microphone from him. This is her show now.

"Thank you all so much for this," she whimpers, wiping away her tears. "I need to thank the pageant, my fellow Pies, and of course, my loving husband, Robert, and our children, Charles and Dawn."

"She remembered us," Chuck gushes.

What the hell are you doing, Maxine?

"You know, this pageant is all about finding the ideal mother. That's why we had all these competitions the last few days. To see which of us was best at living and breathing for her family, her home, her country. Let me tell you, it was a challenge. Was it worth it, Pies?"

None of the other Pies answer since Maxine is the only one onstage.

"No, no, it wasn't. Because all this—" Maxine waves her hands around the stage and then up and down her body. Jeez Louise, her skirt is short. "All this is a steaming pile of lies."

"What?" I blurt out, partially because I can't believe she's saying this and partially because I can't believe they haven't cut to commer-cial. Instead the camera jerks suddenly and goes in for a close-up.

Maxine's smeary eyes are brimming with tears. "I'm going to share a little truth with you all. My gorgeous, sweet husband, Robert Hogarth, is my second husband."

The crowd gasps and I suddenly can't remember how to breathe. "It's true. My first husband divorced me after impregnating his nineteen-year-old secretary."

The crowd has moved from gasping to loud murmurs. The camera suddenly cuts out, but the picture quickly reappears from another angle of the stage.

"And our two darling children, not mine, or at least not from birth. Their mother asked me to care for them, so that's what I've done. I love them both."

Chuck smiles wide. "That's us she's talking about, Dawnie."

"There we all were, out in Scottsdale. The perfect husband. Two perfect kids. A perfect little condo on a perfect patch of desert." Her voice begins to crack. "Sure, we had to scrape it together with what we could find lying in the ruins around us. But damn if we didn't make it happen."

Depwelt pops up next to Maxine and tries to wrestle the microphone from her hands. The camera jerks around more, as if trying to follow the frantic onstage action, before Depwelt drops out of sight as if her legs were kicked out from under her.

Maxine rebounds and gathers her strength. "This pageant decided my family—my loving, beautiful family—wasn't good enough to win. To hell with that." Maxine tears the crown off her head and lets it drop. "I want my family and not this cheap, fake crown."

A clueless Thunders picks up the crown and tries putting it back on Maxine's head, as if she dropped it by accident. She swipes him away, keeping her eyes front and center to the camera. He holds the crown out to someone offstage and shrugs.

"I disqualify myself!" she yells into the microphone. "Robert, Charles, Dawn, I love you. I'd never do anything to hurt you. The rest of you, go fu—"

The screen cuts to black. Then a "technical difficulties" image and cheery music takes the pageant's place.

Chuck is on his feet and in my face, pleading his case. "When you were in jail, she didn't think about it at all. She just ran out and rescued you. Cuz that's what families do. Now can we please just go get her?"

Maxine Hogarth

Aftermath

I KNEW THE MOMENT I let that *fuck* drop that I needed to hurry my ass offstage. I kick my heels into the audience and run barefoot up the auditorium aisle. Onstage, Maisey doesn't wait for anyone to prompt her. She puts the crown on her head and by the time I reach the back of the auditorium, Thunders is serenading her with "She's a Lady."

I burst out the clubhouse doors, but where next? A golf cart seems a fitting getaway vehicle, although I have no idea where the bus station is or whether my family will be there when I find it. Do golf carts take gas? If I need to drive one all the way to Scottsdale, I will. It might give me time enough to figure out the right thing to say to Robert to convince him and those babies to stay with me.

I get my getaway cart all of ten feet before Douglas throws himself in front of it.

"I'm going to kill you!" he screams.

I panic and hit the gas, sending the cart right into his crotch. He falls over with a loud groan that fades into screaming. Oh Christ, what if I've killed him? I hop out of the cart and race to his side as he rolls around on the path like a dying fish.

"You had this coming!" I scream at him.

He can't form words to scream back at me. I don't see any blood pouring out of him, but I do see a lump in his pants pocket. His keys. I manage to rip them from his pocket, but Douglas isn't hurt badly enough. He grabs at me, leaving me no choice but to kick him in the side and take off running.

Crossing the parking lot blacktop is like walking on hot coals, so I keep moving. As I spot the E-Type, there's a honk behind me. It's a yellow cab with Charles hanging out the window, clearly ignoring everything I've told him about wearing seat belts. The cab screeches to a halt and Charles rushes to my side, throwing his arms around me in a hug.

"You won and then you lost because you love us!" he says, and I think he might be crying.

Robert stands with Dawn in his arms and all the luggage and her car seat spilled in front of him. I run to him and give him a hug, which he accepts.

I feel Dawn's fingers poking through my hair. She squeals as I pull away. I wipe my eyes, leaving a long black smudge on the back of my hand. Dawn laughs in delight at what's surely my clown-like appearance. "I ran over Douglas with a golf cart," I tell Robert, while holding the E-Type keys out to him.

He smiles and takes the keys. "Chuck! Grab these bags and get in the car. We're going home."

Charles "Chuck" Hogarth (Bronski)

Aftermath

WE DON'T GO straight home. We instead go to . . . DISNEYLAND!

I know this makes me sound un-American, but I was really worried at first that Disneyland was going to be as boring as Old Tucson. I was dead wrong. It's the funnest thing ever. Maxine doesn't like scary rides, but Robert takes me on all of them. We see pirates and haunted houses and real horses that I get to ride on. My favorite thing is the Swiss Family Treehouse. It's not a ride, but I've always wanted to live in a tree house, so it's cool.

Dawn just about loses her baby mind when Minnie Mouse walks up to her. It's too much for Dawn to handle. She screams and clings to Maxine.

"It's Minnie, sweetie. You don't have to be afraid," Robert says, patting Dawn's back.

"It's a giant rodent in a dress, Robert," Maxine tells him. "She has every right to be terrified."

Then Maxine whispers something in Dawn's ear and, before you know it, Dawn's smiling next to Minnie and getting her picture taken.

At the end of the day, we watch them shoot fireworks off over Cinderella's castle. Every one of us enjoys that. Robert thinks we should stay in a hotel overnight, but Maxine wants to get us home. So we pile back in the E-Type and drive off.

It's late and dark out and no one in the car is talking, so I keep dozing off. I wake up and see a sign telling us we're fifty miles from Scottsdale. Maxine starts whispering to Robert. I don't mean to spy, but she turns down the car radio and I hear everything.

"I don't want to pretend anymore, Robert."

"I don't either," he says.

"Robert?"

"Yes."

"Stop gripping the wheel like you're choking it to death."

Dawn Hogarth

West Hollywood, California

August 9, 1982

IT NEVER FAILS how every year on my birthday—for some damn reason—the Hogarths have to go through family photos. It's like tradition or something. Right after they sing "Happy Birthday" and I blow out the candles, Mom cuts the cake while Dad grabs the photo albums from the shelf in the den. He always starts with the photos from this crazy-lady beauty pageant Mom entered us all in right before I turned three. In the photo that everyone in my family loves the most because they're nuts, Mom is posing with me next to a palm tree on some golf course. I'm wearing this insane frilly pink dress and have my hair pulled up in a high pony right on top of my head. Worse yet is that my finger is up my nose. It's beyond grody. I'm glad I don't remember any of it.

I also don't remember that Mom used to dress us both in identical outfits. But the pictures don't lie. It totally happened. Let's just say that from 1970 to 1974, my sense of fashion was butt-ugly.

"Why would you commit an act of abuse like that on an innocent child?" I ask her, pointing to a photo of us both in matching lime-green Hawaiian-print sundresses with huge pink flowers pinned in our hair. Dad says I have Mom's "theatrical streak," but whatever. I'd sooner shave my head and become a nun than dress like her.

Mom looks over my shoulder at the photo. "I will agree that the flowers in our hair might have been a bit too 'on theme,'" she says, putting a slice of birthday cake in front of me. "But I make no apologies for dressing alike. I love you and wanted to show the whole world that you were finally all mine."

It's weird how sometimes I forget I'm adopted. That's why the photos always start at the beauty pageant. We weren't a family before then. If you want to get all technical about it, we weren't a family until 1971, when we all went to the courthouse and got adopted. We have photos of that too. This was after Mom and Dad paid a bunch of money to private detectives who went looking for my so-called real mom. They never found her. I don't think about her a lot, but Mom made me promise that if Sharla ever came back, I'd give her a chance to explain herself.

"She knew she couldn't raise you and she trusted me to do it. That's not an easy thing for a mother to do, Dawn." That's what Mom always tells me. It makes sense, I guess.

Dad points to one of his favorite photos, where I'm in the pool of the duplex we live in now, here in West Hollywood.

"Our mermaid. We just couldn't keep you out of the pool," Dad tells me.

"Or lawn sprinklers," Mom adds.

"Or that fountain at the mall," Chuck piles on. He's in law school now in Chicago, but he came home for my fifteenth birthday because I'm his only baby sister and he worships me.

"The mall thing only happened once," I insist.

"Three times!" Mom and Dad say at the same time.

My parents do that all the time—the whole mind-meld thing. It's totally freaky, like they are sharing the same brain. I know that's not possible, but how else do you explain it? They order for each other in restaurants. Mom will be in the bathroom, fixing her face, and the waiter will come over and Dad will know exactly what she wants and how she wants it prepared. It's like they're psychic for each other. Chuck says it's because they are best friends and have been since forever.

"This one's my favorite!" says Chuck. He holds up a photo of me and him standing outside La Dulcinea, the tavern my parents own, and for some reason gave the same name as the one they owned years ago in Arizona. Chuck's holding up his high school diploma and I'm wearing his graduation cap. His graduation gown is open and he's wearing the dress pants our parentals insisted on, but also his favorite Queen concert T-shirt. He left that shirt behind for me when he went off to college, and I lived in it. Chuck flips the page in the photo book and there's my fourth-grade school picture. Sure enough, I'm in the Queen T-shirt.

"I can't believe I let you wear that horrendous shirt on picture day," Mom mutters. "But you were missing your big brother." Mom musses up Chuck's hair and he lets her.

Dad and I look at each other and try not to laugh, because it's hysterical she'd accuse me of being sentimental. Right after Chuck left for Chicago, Mom built what Dad and I called "the Altar of St. Chuck" on the dresser in his room. It was this way-crazy collection of photos, stuff he was into: these old spy novels, his Boy Scout badges, report cards (all As). Oh yeah, and candles she would actually light. I'd have friends over and show them the St. Chuck Altar and be like, "Dudes, my mom is a total spaz for my brother!" Chuck came home for Thanksgiving and never said a word about the altar. It was, like, too weird for him to form words for.

"Sure, Maxine. You cry every time the boy comes home for a visit, but Dawn's the sentimental one," teases Winston. Mom laughs and sticks her finger in Winston's scoop of vanilla ice cream, teasing him right back. These two are hilarious together. Last year they won the West Hollywood Talent Show doing this routine where they were these old singers called Sonny & Cher, except that Mom was Sonny and Winston was Cher. Mom can't go to the grocery story anymore without someone screaming, "I got you, babe!" at her. It's beyond embarrassing.

Winston is a newspaper reporter who got me the best tickets ever to see the Go-Go's at the Roxy, even though I'm underage. He's also Dad's boyfriend of five years and we all love him.

Go ahead. Hit me with all the usual boring questions. I've heard them all and, like, I really don't give a shit.

Yeah, so Dad is totally gay and not in the way those dumb jocks at school say stuff is "gay." My dad's not "gay" because of the color of his shirt or how he does his hair or because he listens to A Flock of Seagulls. (He doesn't, by the way. He's into Barry Manilow.) My dad's totally gay because that's how he was born. It's 1982 and this is West Hollywood so how about we all get over it?

This is also why we live in a duplex, which my parents always call "the Arrangement." There are four bedrooms on one side and two on the other side. When we first moved to West Hollywood, we all lived in the same side together, each of us with our own room. Then Dad met Winston, and now they live in the two-bedroom side, although they are both over here with me and Mom all the time. Sometimes Mom's "special friend" Greg will be here too (he doesn't live here because Mom's a women's libber and says she's tied down enough).

Pretty much it's like no matter where I turn, there's some adult looking at me and questioning my every move. *Who's that boy you walked home from school with, Dawn? Promise us you're not smoking, Dawn. Why are you wearing leg warmers if you're not going to a dance class, Dawn?* It's, like, totally the same thing all my friends with divorced and remarried parents have to deal with. Except everyone in my family loves each other and there isn't a lot of screaming and fighting.

"You ready for this?" Chuck asks me the morning after my birthday. He tosses me the car keys and I catch them with one hand because, like, I was born ready for this.

It's a Sunday morning and our street is dead. No one will be awake for at least an hour, so it's the perfect time for me get some on-road practice. Legally, I can't get my learner's permit for another four months, but I totally want Chuck to be the one to give me driving lessons. Dad is a little too jumpy, Winston's from New York and only learned to drive a few years ago, and Mom is Mom. She's forever telling Dad which route to take or to not drive like an old broad on her way to her own funeral. She also can't parallel park to save her goddamned life.

"I'm a little nervous," I admit to him while checking all my mirrors.

"At least you can see over the steering wheel," he tells me. "When Mom taught me how to drive, I had to sit on a stack of porno mags."

I laugh in his face. Chuck is always trying to trick me with stuff and then calling me a dumb blonde. No way in hell I'm falling for it this time.

He leans in close and says quietly, "I drove her to the liquor store for vodka and cigarettes."

Mom doesn't smoke anymore, but I am totally the only fifteen-year-old who knows exactly how many dashes of Tabasco per ounce of vodka go in a Bloody Mary (it's three, by the way).

"It's the truth. We kept you in a box in the backseat."

Well, now I know my big brother is completely full of shit. Mom's totally paranoid about me. Whenever I leave the house, she makes me show her the dime I have in the bottom of my shoe in case I need to make an emergency call.

Even though he's full of shit, Chuck's a good driving instructor. I go up and down Norma Place, from the curve at Lloyd, turning around in the parking lot of the apartments right before Doheny. We do this for forty minutes, and I always check my mirrors and use my turn signal like I promised Dad I would do. He's never had so much as a parking ticket. We make it home safely and nobody dies! Sucks the E-Type doesn't have a tape deck, though.

As I pull into our driveway, Mom and Dad wave in unison from the front steps. They have a tennis lesson in a half hour, which explains why they're dressed in matching outfits, right down to their too-white shoes.

I roll the window down. The car is ancient, so it only goes down partway. "You two look like the twins from *The Shining*!" I call out, knowing only Chuck will get the joke.

"Since when are you allowed to watch R-rated movies?" Dad asks.

"Oh, Robert, don't be so old-fashioned. That movie is a hoot," Mom tells him. "Dawn, I thought I was going to give you your first lesson?"

"I went with St. Chuck," I tell her. "You make me nervous."

"Didn't your brother tell you that I taught him how to drive?"

"She didn't believe me, Mom," Chuck says, as if it breaks his heart to say.

"That's probably for the best," Dad adds, taking the car keys from me.

"Wait. That's all true?" I ask Dad, knowing he's totally incapable of lying to me. "And the thing about Chuck sitting on pornos?"

Dad nods. "I had nothing to do with it," he tells me. "It was all your mother."

"Mom, you won't let me stand too close to the microwave because of radiation, but you let Chuck drive around with me in a box?"

Mom shrugs. "You lived, didn't you? Besides, it was 1970. We were all a little crazy."

ACKNOWLEDGMENTS

The first big thank-you goes out to all the people at my awesome publisher, Inkshares, who saw potential in my way-beyond-rough rough draft. There's the organized and patient Avalon Radys, who assures the book looks phenomenal and physically gets into readers' hands. Publicity goddess Angela Melamud gently and firmly pushed me out into the world. Editor (and awesome writer) Matt Harry helped shape my stream-of-consciousness into a real storyline. Thanks go also to my copy editors, who didn't once chide me for my crap spelling, Kaitlin Severini and Jessica Gardner, as well as artists/magicians Lauren Harms, who made this book gorgeous on the outside, and Kevin G. Summers, who made it gorgeous on the inside. I also need to thank the good folks at the Launch Pad Manuscript competition.

Then there's Adam Gomolin—publisher/editor/life coach/hype man/force of nature/all-around stand-up dude. This guy is relentlessly passionate about his work, and I was lucky enough for our paths to cross. The book wouldn't exist without you, Adam, and I adore you for all you've done for me and the Hogarths. You're the best.

Huge props to the lovely folks who took time out of their lives to read the book and give me loads of insightful feedback: Emma Mann-Meginniss, Jacqui Standel, and Alex Rosen. And non-weird hugs to the wonderful people who read it prior to publication and let me splatter their kind words all over the cover: sweetheart Sarah Nivala of Book Soup, librarians/book superheroes Magan Szwarek and Becky Spratford, Andy Lewis of *The Hollywood Reporter*, and all-around badass Cat Marnell. Photographer Dianna Gonzalez of Red Baryl Portraits taught me how to turtle and showed me that author photos are nothing to be terrified of.

I also need to thank every English teacher whose classroom I've sat in, especially those who saw me not only as a weirdo, but a weirdo who can write. A few highlights are Mr. Perry Montoya (Pomeroy Elementary), Mr. Steve Heck (Dobson High School), Mr. Mike McClellan (Dobson High School), and Prof. Darcie Bowden (DePaul University). Extra special shout-outs to Prof. Ted Schaefer and Prof. Ben Goluboff of Lake Forest College, who made it very clear to me that law school was the dumbest idea I've ever had. I love and appreciate you all. So sorry for those petulant teen years, Mr. McClellan and Mr. Heck!

Like the Hogarths, I'm someone lucky enough to have found my own people. My dad and baby sis, Rachel, have always been there and always loved me. My dear friends, Heather and George Green and David Wheeland, took me under their protective wing when I needed them and their wine the most. My platonic life partner, Alexandria Frenkel, is a bottomless fountain of love and support and huge laughs. (Plus, she hooked me up on the best blind date in the history of the universe.) All those wonderful Schaefers—Carol (best mom-in-law EVER), David, Amy, Madison, Jackson, little E and J, and all the aunts, uncles, and cousins! I was a stranger for all of five seconds before you all made me family. I love you.

Finally, to my tight little circle of awesomeness. I wouldn't be here without any of you. My fur babies, Ginsberg and Toki, the best gently used cats ever. My brilliant, beautiful, unabashedly himself son, Dylan—Mommy loves you, kiddo. You are the bones down my back. Lastly, Jonathan Schaefer—my Forever Person. I have not the words, baby. And thankfully you're cool with that.

INKSHARES

INKSHARES is a reader-driven publisher and producer based in Oakland, California. Our books are selected not by a group of editors, but by readers worldwide.

While we've published books by established writers like *Big Fish* author Daniel Wallace and *Star Wars: Rogue One* scribe Gary Whitta, our aim remains surfacing and developing the new author voices of tomorrow.

Previously unknown Inkshares authors have received starred reviews and been featured in the *New York Times*. Their books are on the front tables of Barnes & Noble and hundreds of independents nationwide, and many have been licensed by publishers in other major markets. They are also being adapted by Oscar-winning screenwriters at the biggest studios and networks.

Interested in making your own story a reality? Visit Inkshares.com to start your own project or find other great books.